Could I Have This Dance?

Could I Have This Dance?

HARRY KRAUS, M.D.

ZONDERVAN™

GRAND RAPIDS, MICHIGAN 49530

We want to hear from you. Please send your comments about this book to us in care of the address below. Thank you.

GRAND RAPIDS, MICHIGAN 49530

WWW.ZONDERVAN.COM

ZONDERVAN™

Could I Have This Dance?

Requests for information should be addressed to:

Zondervan, *Grand Rapids, Michigan 49530*

Library of Congress Cataloging-in-Publication Data

Kraus, Harry Lee, 1960–.
Could I have this dance? / by Harry Lee Kraus.
p. cm.
Includes bibliographical references and index.
ISBN 0-310-24089-1 (Softcover)
1. Women physicians—Fiction. 2. Interns (Medicine)—Fiction. 3. Huntington's chorea–Fiction. 4. Fathers and daughters–Fiction. 5. Virginia–Fiction. I. Title.
PS3561.R2875 C68 2001
813'.54–dc21 2001006891

Interior design by Nancy Wilson

Printed in the United States of America

02 03 04 05 06 07 08 09 /❖ DC/ 10 9 8 7

Dedicated with compassion and admiration
for all those at risk for
inheriting Huntington's Disease.

Acknowledgments

Special thanks to Roy W. Ferguson Jr., a friend and attorney, for his advice on legal matters pertaining to the story.

Prologue

Summer 1973

My patient's scream penetrates the delivery room.

"Slow deep breaths, honey," the nurse coaches. "Slow deep breaths."

I sense that she is going to scream again and turn my head toward the door, so I do not see her eyes.

Her voice is high-pitched and shrill, nothing like the softness I've heard in it before. Now, each cry is a dagger, finding its mark in my chest.

The room is hot, thanks to a faulty thermostat that I've had maintenance look at three times this week. But fixing the temperature won't make this one any more pleasant for me. My discomfort arises from a whole different level, a dread from the bottom of my gut that doesn't seem to be responding to the antacid I still taste in my mouth. I roll my tongue, scraping more of the metallic medicine toward the back of my throat. It's not working. My hands are trembling, and I can't bear to look into my patient's eyes.

I've never treated a more beautiful woman. I gaze on her writhing form for a moment, studying her in this vulnerable position as if for the first time.

But it is not the first time I've seen her like this, exposed and unprotected. Her forehead is beaded with sweat, her lips full and pursed, her breathing quick and shallow. In her face I see pain, and fear, and yet even in this moment of agony, I see her loveliness. I watch her, careful to avoid her eyes. Her eyes, wonderful, innocent blue. Deep pools I wish now I'd never looked into. I cannot bear to see her eyes now. If she catches my gaze, she'll see my fear—and then she'll know that I know.

I turn away, desperately trying to recapture the confidence that has carried me through the rigors of a country family practice. I've prided myself in being able to handle anything. From earaches to hernia repairs, from colicky babies to depressed, out-of-work farmers, I've seen it all. I've done it. And while other professionals in the city are specializing, here in

Stoney Creek I've stood proud like the docs of the old frontier: I can handle anything, including this routine vaginal delivery. I steal a glance at my patient again. Nothing different about this one. Except—

I interrupt my own thought. I can't let myself finish it. I cannot let myself think that it might be possible. Certainly the odds are against it. We were always so careful.

Clandestine encounters are supposed to remain a private matter, right? Nothing helpful can be gained by exposure now. I cough nervously and look at the clock on the wall. It's eleven P.M. and I haven't eaten since early this morning when I heard the first rumor that she was in labor.

The nurses are moving faster now, as the patient is close to delivery. The contractions come in a slow rhythm separated by only a minute, each one punctuated by a low groan. The patient is mumbling under her breath between contractions. I can only imagine her cursing, as her words are too quiet for me to hear above the room's clinical noise. Her husband, to my relief, is stationed in a waiting room. I hear that in big-city hospitals up north, they are letting the husbands into the delivery rooms. Well, just try that foolishness down here and we'll see how long I stay in this business. Thank God saner heads have prevailed in the South.

Since her husband is not here, I am the object of her scorn. I do not hear it in clear words, but I feel it in her moaning. She curses me as if she knows. It is not possible that she should know, but somehow, at a level deeper than mere reasoning, she knows. I am a scientist, not prone to such intuition. Still, I will not look in her eyes.

"How much Demerol has she had?" I can't stand to see her like this.

A nurse, a veteran named Mollie, wrinkles her nose at me. "A hundred milligrams. It doesn't seem to have touched her."

"Give her another twenty-five," I say, heading for the swinging door. "I'll be right outside."

Mollie knows I need to smoke. I always do when I'm nervous. I see her shaking her head in disapproval before I turn away. I let the door swing shut, leaving the commotion behind. In another minute, I'm standing in a small doctor's quarters inhaling a cigarette in long, deep breaths.

I pace the little room, wondering what would happen if anyone knew the truth about me, the truth about my patient. In the silence, with the smoke curling toward the ceiling, I think about breaches in professional ethics, standing before a state review board, and losing my license. My career could be over if anyone knew. And I vow that no one ever will.

The door pops open, and Ben Jasper, a general surgeon, heaves a sigh. "Hey, Jim. You're here late."

I nod. "Labor knows no respect for time. What's up?"

"I've got an appy to do."

An appy. Not a real person with a real problem. Not even a patient with appendicitis or an appendectomy to perform, but an appy. Dr. Jasper, like most surgeons, abbreviates everything. I find myself wondering if he asks his wife for sup or if he calls his car a caddy.

"One of my patients?" I ask, feigning interest.

He laughed. "Everyone in Stoney Creek goes to you." He held up a note card. "His name is Billy Burgess."

I've treated Billy for ear infections a few times. His mother works in the McCall shoe factory with everyone else and had a huge melanoma removed from her back three years ago. I'm amazed she's still alive.

I push my cigarette into an ashtray overflowing from the doctors' tobacco addictions, an irony that doesn't escape me. I reach for the doorknob and notice my hands are trembling. "I've got to get back to L and D."

Once there, I slip on a pair of sterile exam gloves. I address my patient in a professional tone that feels forced and inappropriate. "I need to check your progress."

The nurse coaxes the patient into position. "Come on, honey. Doc needs to see." Mollie refers to me informally. It's a rural thing, a small example of a more relaxed way of providing medical care. I wouldn't want it any other way. Homey. Personal. Part of a one-stop country practice. But nothing seems homey about this. This delivery carries a big-city foreboding. I'm out of my element here. This one seems dark in a way that I can't articulate.

Mollie sprays an iodine wash onto the patient's perineum and I insert my glove. The cervix is wide open, completely effaced. I report the findings to Mollie. "Okay," I add to the patient. "Let's have this baby."

The patient's voice is urgent. "No! Nooo!"

I'm already putting on a sterile gown and a new pair of gloves. "Let's get her in the stirrups."

"I need something. It hurts!" she gasps. "Jimmy!"

I wince as the patient yells my name. I'm sure the nurses will think this is odd, but I glance at Mollie's face, and it doesn't seem to have fazed her. Labor makes women crazy. They say crazy things. Hopefully Mollie will think this, even if I don't.

"Get me the pudendal tray."

A second nurse, a young one who loves to flirt with me, is washing the patient again, this time applying the iodine paint in broad strokes to the thighs, perineum, and buttocks. Mollie opens the pudendal tray and places it on the sterile field, before gowning and gloving herself. She always stands to my left. I never have to tell her what I need; she always hands me what I want before I ask. Sometimes, I suspect that she is in control and I am assisting her. She directs me in her silence, allowing me to be the leader. I let her, because although I've been here hundreds of times, Mollie's been here thousands.

Quietly, efficiently, we cover my patient's legs with sterile drapes. I pick up the lidocaine anesthetic that Mollie has prepared, keeping the needle concealed from my patient's view. It is over six inches in length, enough to frighten a linebacker. I insert the index and long fingers of my left hand into the vagina and palpate the ischial spine. I then slide in an Iowa trumpet which will serve as a needle guide to protect the birth canal from accidental injury. I slip the needle through the trumpet, and puncture the sacrospinous ligament. Slowly, I inject ten cc's of the clear liquid anesthetic just inside and below the spine I am still touching. All the while, I keep repeating, "Okay, okay, this will make it easier. I'm giving you some medicine to dull the pain."

"Jimmy, I—can't—take—this!" My patient's voice is halted by distress.

"Okay, it's okay," I reassure her. "Here's more medicine." I change hands and repeat the pudendal nerve block on the other side.

My patient relaxes for a moment between contractions. I cannot. I have to see the baby.

With the next contraction, I see the baby's head and shudder. The hair is blond and thick. Just like mine.

Two more contractions pass. The patient has shifted into a cooperative mode and follows the nurse's pushing instructions. She's determined to get this over with.

I massage my patient for a moment, encouraging the skin to stretch even more. "Bee sting," I say, before I infiltrate more local anesthetic for an episiotomy. I make the cut in the midline posteriorly.

"One more push . . . *now!*"

I deliver the head and suction the nose and mouth with a bulb syringe. The shoulders come next, and soon, I am holding the screaming infant, a boy, cradling him against my body. For a moment, I am frozen in thought. There is a special energy I feel, holding this infant, an unseen bond as real as anything I've seen with my eyes. I cannot describe it beyond that. I am warmed. And frightened. But I cannot reveal it.

I look at my patient, no longer able or willing to avoid her searching eyes. I see her and I am speechless. We communicate without words, the way we did at our first meeting. She knows. I know. But there is no one else who will ever know the truth about this baby.

I break away and see Mollie's hand, holding up a clamp to cut the cord. How long have I been standing here?

"I–It's a boy," I stutter.

Mollie catches my eye, but not my attention. "The baby is too small."

Following Mollie's lead, I clamp and cut the cord. I hand the child to the young nurse who wraps him in a soft blanket and lays him upon his mother's breast.

The mother is restless, still writhing, not enjoying this infant as I think she should. I deliver the placenta with my mind in another room. I am working with my hands following a practiced pattern, but my mind is spinning with a dark memory of secret pleasures and secret lies.

Reality dawns and slaps me to attention as I finally comprehend the nurse's words. *The baby is too small.* I'm frozen, staring at my patient's still swollen abdomen. From the way my patient had been carrying this pregnancy, I knew this would be a large baby. I slip my hand onto the patient's abdomen to feel the fundal height and my heart skips a beat. I clear my throat. "You're going to have twins," I say with plastic enthusiasm.

My patient is not amused.

I want to leave, to smoke a cigarette, to be anywhere but here. *How could I have missed this? Twins?* I look at the clock, then back down. Another scalp is presenting. There will be time later for regrets.

I numbly deliver a second baby, this one a bit bigger than the first. It's a girl, and she screams with vigor. Mollie places her in a bassinet and I deliver the placenta and repair the episiotomy, barely aware of the nurse's communication about the lovely new babies.

Only two people on earth know the truth. And that's the way we agreed this will stay. Forever. This secret, this sin, is buried.

My patient is weeping.

And on the inside, so am I.

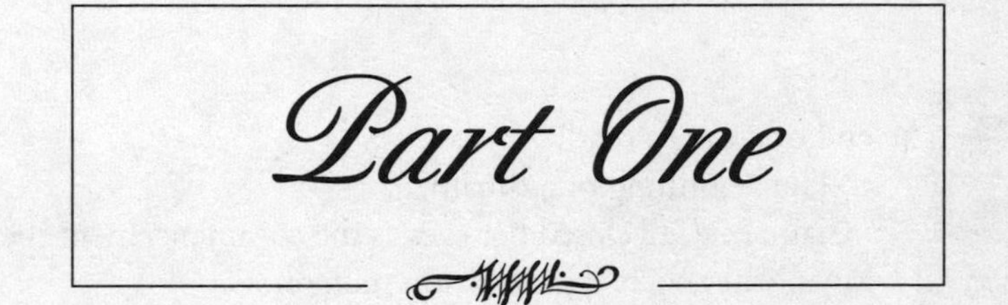

Part One

Chapter One

May 2000

he end of a tough road.

"The beginning of a dream."

Claire McCall closed her eyes as the commencement speaker droned on with another clichéd graduation metaphor.

She was about to do what everyone in Stoney Creek had said would never happen. In a few minutes, with diploma in hand, she would join the ranks of the medical profession as Elizabeth Claire McCall, MD. She wanted to savor the moment, to not think about the future, the years of training yet ahead. But she'd heard too many of the horror stories about internship to relax for very long. Stormy water was dead ahead. She only hoped she'd be ready when the wind picked up.

Claire kept her eyes closed and smiled. She'd shown 'em. The people in Stoney Creek, that is. *God bless 'em,* she thought. *They're simple people, with simple dreams.* Her smile faded. *Too simple. And narrow, too. People need vision to stay alive.*

Thankfully, she hadn't listened to the town gossip, though she knew exactly what they thought. Little girls shouldn't grow up to be surgeons. Especially girls with fathers like Wally McCall.

Around her, the portraits of past medical school deans lined the mahogany-paneled walls. They were near-idols at Brighton University, those who had risen to lofty heights by hard work and academic excellence. They seemed to be watching her today, welcoming her with their long white coats and studious expressions.

"A new dawn. An open door."

Claire yawned. The speaker had over a hundred book chapters to his name, but couldn't seem to find an original phrase to captivate his nodding audience.

She turned and squinted to see her family. Della, her mom, sat motionless in the back. Looking at her was like looking into a magical mirror, capable of revealing the future. Della was gorgeous and youthful and enjoyed every stranger's confused insistence that she must be Claire's sister. Strawberry blond without a hint of gray, high cheekbones, a figure that could turn a man's head, and a smile that could melt his heart. Fortunately for Claire, she looked just like her mother. "I know I'm pretty," Della would tell her, "but you're pretty *and* smart."

Next to her, Claire's grandmother, Elizabeth McCall, cast a worried glance toward the rear exit. Clay, Claire's twin brother, sat next to Grandma, leaning against the bench back with his eyes closed and his mouth open. Oh, well—she couldn't expect Clay to stay awake if she was having trouble paying attention herself. Next to Clay, John Cerelli, Claire's fiancé, was hidden by a woman with a large hat. If Claire leaned to the left, she could just catch a glimpse of his wonderful dark hair.

But where's Daddy?

Claire looked at the clock hanging on the back wall and checked it against her watch. Her father must have gone out to the bathroom. Or to smoke. Or worse.

Wally, her father, was the one person in Stoney Creek that she'd been glad to leave behind. Their relationship, close during her early school years, had been on a roller coaster since Claire entered high school—up when he was dry, and down and dangerous when he was drinking. Their communication had been on a continuous slide since she'd left for Brighton for undergraduate studies eight years ago. Now, she barely visited, and when she did, his erratic behavior and mood swings transformed every family gathering into a shouting match. When she'd last talked to her mother, Della had hinted that he'd given up on AA again, and hadn't been able to find work.

He's probably out for "a little drink."

Claire touched her throat and tried to refocus on the speaker, who sidetracked into a story of his own triumph in the discovery of some obscure gene responsible for a rare form of kidney disease. Genetics didn't interest Claire. She liked real, hands-on medicine, not futuristic theories of gene alteration. It went without question that she would be a surgeon. She was captivated by the prospect of making quick decisions on her feet, of seeing the gratifying results of her hand's work without delay. Yes, she'd known it since the first day of her surgery rotation. Surgery was for her. For Claire, it was more than a practical match. Her decision ran much deeper. It seemed a destiny, a calling. And in a few short weeks, she would start one of the most grueling years of her life as a surgical intern.

The smile returned to her face. *Claire McCall, surgeon. Send that through the gossip mill in backwards little Stoney Creek!*

Movement in the back of the auditorium interrupted Claire's dream. She watched as her father moved slowly down the aisle in search of his row. Her hand covered her open mouth as her father stumbled forward. Each step was practiced once or twice, then executed in a slow, deliberate slap. Della lifted her hand quickly, then lowered it as a murmur escaped the crowd.

Wally seemed lost, wobbling past his bench and down the carpeted aisle. Midway to the front, he turned and began a labored journey back, his face twitching in constant rhythmic motion. His right arm flailed forward, then returned, a swing propelled by an erratic, unseen wind.

How long had it been since she'd really seen him, studied him like this? Months? Years? It was close to a decade that Claire had avoided her father in the name of her educational pursuits. Now she gasped and felt a flush burn her cheeks. Drunk again.

Claire turned her head away, clenching her jaw, silently grateful that her classmates didn't know the identity of the strange man. She stared forward, oblivious to the speaker's monologue. *How could he do this to me?*

Long minutes later, she stole a glance behind her. Mercifully, her father had found his seat, and the disturbance seemed over.

For the time remaining, Claire fixed her eyes on the podium, not even looking back when the dean returned to the stage and asked the parents of the graduates to stand. The ceremony passed in a blur. She stood to be recognized with the Alpha Omega Alpha honor society graduates, and then, a few minutes later, walked the stage to receive her diploma, not risking a glance toward her family.

After the benediction, happy graduates spilled onto the sunny lawn outside Brighton University's Memorial Hall. Claire followed, staying safely in the middle of the pack, but vigilant to observe the doors as the proud parents exited to find the new MDs.

She struck a cheerful pose for a picture with a classmate.

There were hugs, tearful good-byes, and more photos. Claire was mobbed by her fellow MDs, filled with triumphant revelry like that of a high school football team after winning the state championship.

Ten minutes later, she retreated into a white gazebo at the center of the vast lawn, her eyes still watchful of the crowd emerging onto Memorial Hall's columned front portico. John Cerelli found her first and kissed her cheek. "You did it."

She feigned a smile and lowered her voice. "Let's get out of here."

John looked over his shoulder. Claire followed his eyes. Della McCall was marching across the grass, ignoring the sloping sidewalk that led to the gazebo.

"Claire. There you are. I've been looking everywhere!" Her arms were open.

Claire surrendered to her mother's embrace.

"Come on. The family wants a photograph."

Claire stiffened against the pressure of her mother's arm as she attempted to nudge Claire toward the building.

Della knitted her forehead. "Claire?"

"Take my picture with John. Right here."

Della backed up a few steps and obeyed.

"Now," her mother enjoined. "Your father wants to see you."

Claire shook her head and tried to keep her voice steady. "No."

John reached for her elbow. "Come on, Claire, it's—"

"I said no!" She shook free, watchful of the crowd of celebrant graduates and their families. Her mother's confused face prompted her explanation. "Mom, I saw him! Stumbling like a common drunk."

"Claire, it's not—"

"Wake up, Mom," Claire protested, then softened her voice. "How could he do this to me today?"

Della stared at her daughter. "Your father's a sick man, Claire. Come talk to him."

"Take him to a doctor."

"He won't go."

"Take him to Dr. Jenkins. He'll tell him to straighten up."

"Believe me, he won't see a doctor." She lowered her eyes to the floor of the gazebo. "Especially not Dr. Jenkins."

"Then bring him up here to Brighton. Take him to AA. The man needs help."

"He's been through AA. He won't go back. He doesn't drink that much anymore anyway."

"You're in denial. You're codependent."

"He doesn't need your fancy analysis, Doctor. He needs to see his daughter." Della retreated back onto the lawn. "Will you come to Stoney Creek?"

"I'm leaving for New England tomorrow. I've got to prepare for my internship."

"Surgery isn't everything, Claire."

"Don't start with me, Mom. You know this is important to me."

Della nodded without speaking.

Claire could feel her mother's judgment. "Mom, this is what I was made to do. Don't you get it?"

Grandma Elizabeth McCall appeared through the crowd, approaching Claire with her hands raised. "Congratulations, Claire. I knew you'd make us proud." She hugged her granddaughter warmly, oblivious to the tension.

"Thanks, Grandma."

"Let's find your father." Elizabeth raised a spotted hand toward the portico. "He's in there with Clay."

"I—I've got to run, Grandma. Some of my classmates are . . . well, I need to finish packing. My apartment's a wreck."

Della placed her hand on Elizabeth's shoulder. "She won't go near her father today."

"Grandma," Claire pleaded. "He's drunk."

Elizabeth's shoulders pitched forward. She sighed slowly before responding with a quiver in her voice. "He's not drunk, Claire."

"Grandma, I saw him." She reached for John's hand. "Let's go." The duo stepped away but couldn't escape Elizabeth's reach.

"Hold on," she insisted, latching onto Claire's wrist. "You don't know everything yet, young doctor." She paused, her voice low, and her gaze locked upon Claire's. "I've seen this before. And I've been around Stoney Creek all my life. This is a curse, pure and simple—the Stoney Creek curse."

Claire was too polite to pull away. "Grandma, I know you believe that. I suspect just about everyone in Stoney Creek would too." She paused. "But if those rumors have some basis in fact, then it's related to alcohol, not the supernatural."

"Don't ignore this. It's darker than you realize, child. I fear your father is a marked man."

"Your *son* is the town drunk!" She hated hurting her grandmother, but the words were out before she could stop them.

Elizabeth blanched.

Claire felt John's hand tighten around hers. "Claire, let's just go."

Elizabeth released her grip. "One day you'll understand," she said softly. "I just hope your generation is spared."

Claire looked at her mother and grandmother. Elizabeth knotted the end of a white shawl in her hand.

"I'm sorry, Grandma."

The old woman nodded.

Claire dropped John's hand and slipped her arm around his waist. They walked across the lush lawn toward John's red Mustang.

After a hundred yards, John chuckled. "The Stoney Creek curse." He shook his head. "Your grandmother's a hoot."

"Don't laugh. To her, this stuff is very real. Stoney Creek has never laughed about the curse."

John opened the passenger door to his Mustang, and Claire climbed in and nestled into the leather seat, wanting to disappear. John started the car and headed down the road. With the convertible top down, her long blond hair swirled in the wind and her eyes watered, both from the gusts and from the emotions she vainly tried to cap.

John slid his hand from the gearshift to her thigh. "Well, Dr. McCall, shall we join the others at the Oasis?"

She grabbed his hand and stared away.

He tried again. "Come on. We should celebrate. Would you rather drive over to Henley? Pringle's Café? We could sit on the deck and watch the ducks."

She shook her head. "Just take me home, John."

"Claire, this is what you've been working for." He tapped his left hand on the steering wheel. "*Doctor* McCall," he added, raising his voice above the whine of the engine.

She didn't see it that way. This was just the beginning. She wasn't even halfway to her goal. The MD degree was just the entrance ticket to another level of training. From where she stood, she couldn't even see the light at the end of a dark tunnel. A dark tunnel called surgery residency.

Sure, Claire was glad to have the degree behind her. But with her father's behavior at the graduation, and with her sharp words with her family still fresh in her mind, she didn't feel like celebrating a milestone.

John prompted again, "Oh, Doctor," he continued, pinching her leg, "paging Dr. McCall . . ."

She flinched and squeezed his hand. "I just want to finish packing. I want to be ready for an early start in the morning."

She watched him shrug. He waited until he pulled to a stop at the next light before he turned and lowered his voice. "Just forget about your father, okay?" He paused. "That's what this is about, isn't it?"

That and everything else, Claire thought. She couldn't articulate the rising restlessness she'd been feeling. It was deeper than a desire to get her surgery training under way. It was more than wanting to put the stigma of being a student doctor behind her. John was right. She wanted to erase from her memory the feeling of being the town drunk's daughter. She had wanted her graduation to feel like a victory. Instead, it felt like an old scab, picked open and oozing fresh pain.

She nodded slowly. "It feels smaller than I thought it would. For years, I wanted to show everyone in Stoney Creek that I could do what they thought was impossible."

"You did, Claire. You're a doctor!"

How could she tell him what she felt? She bit her lower lip and twisted her hopelessly tangled hair.

Here, on the pinnacle of her medical school education, she felt curiously defeated. The air rushed from the balloon, just as children come to realize that all those foot races with Father were won because he *let* them win, not because they were so fast after all. Here she was, a child again, with a medical diploma in her hand, feeling cheated of the elation she thought she'd earned. The degree meant a lot when it was obtained by others. For Claire, she couldn't suppress the nagging feeling that they'd let her win. Someone somehow had turned the tables on her emotions. Instead of celebration, she felt mired again by the inescapable anchor of her small-town identity as the daughter of Wally McCall.

She forced a smile, hoping her emotions would obey and follow.

John pulled to a stop in front of her apartment. "Want some help?"

"I just have a few things to pack yet." She lifted the neck of her graduation gown. "It *would* have to be ninety degrees today."

John nodded and leaned forward. Claire accepted his kiss as a perfunctory good-bye.

"Why don't you bring some Chinese takeout later?" she offered. "I've packed away all my kitchen stuff."

He smiled. "Sure. Our regular?"

General Tso's chicken. Extra spicy. Small side of shrimp lo mein. Two egg rolls with hot mustard. "You know me."

She watched him go, the Mustang convertible disappearing behind the corner Exxon.

She turned alone, diploma in hand, and trudged up the cracked sidewalk to her front door.

An hour later, Claire sat in the middle of the small living room struggling to fit her blow-dryer into an already full box. She pulled out the last three items, a small jewelry box, an anatomy textbook, and a photo album, and restacked them for the fourth time, creating an opening just large enough for . . . a hairbrush, but not the blow-dryer. "Ugh," she gasped, lifting the blow-dryer by the cord. She stomped across the room and dangled the appliance over the open trash bag, which overflowed with the last few items she hadn't been able to fit into the box. *I'm going to cut these curls soon anyway. Surgery residents don't have time for this sort of vanity.* With the blow-dryer hanging precariously by its cord, Claire touched her thick blond hair and sighed. She paused, then grabbed a pillow that leaned against a box of dishes. She shoved the blow-dryer into the pillowcase against the soft foam. *There. Never know. I might chicken out about the haircut.*

The front door opened after a quick knock. John appeared, arms laden with Chinese takeout and a small bouquet of cut spring flowers. He smiled. "Congratulations, Doctor."

Claire smiled and planted a kiss on John's mouth.

"Hey, let me put these down first," he responded, putting the large white paper bag onto the kitchen counter. Then he gathered her into his arms.

There, for the first time in days, she felt herself begin to relax. He kissed her slowly, luxuriously, before pulling back. He met her eyes before asking, "Hungry?"

"Starved." She felt him edging away, and she tightened her grip around his waist. "Just give me a minute, Cerelli. I haven't felt this good in weeks."

He smiled, and lowered his lips to hers. She kissed him again, then buried her face in his shirt, inhaling his cologne. *I'm going to miss this man.*

After a minute, she released him and opened the bag of food. As she lifted out the containers, the wonderful aroma made her mouth water.

"Where'd you get all this stuff?" John asked, looking at the boxes. "You had all this hidden in here?"

"Four years of medical school accumulation." She shrugged. "You should have seen the stuff I threw out."

He pointed at a poster leaning against the kitchen trash can. "What's that?"

"Old undergrad genetics project on blood types and inheritance. I did all the blood-typing myself in the biochemistry lab." She picked up the poster. "See? Here's my father," she added, pointing at the upper left. "He's blood type B negative. Here's my mom. She's O negative." She moved her arm down to the next line. "My sister Margo—B negative, just like Dad." She looked at John. "What type are you?"

"Beats me. I've never been checked."

"Come on. Haven't you ever donated? They give you a card with your blood type."

"Not me. I hate needles. You know that."

She nodded. "Well, let's just say you're type A. That means you have either two A genes or an A gene and a second gene that doesn't code for any blood type. If you have type A and I have type O, our kids could be—"

"Kids? Did you say 'our kids'?"

"Stop interrupting. I'm trying to teach you something."

"Our kid? You mean John Jr.? Or how about Clyde? I've always wanted a Clyde."

"Ugh! Okay, Clyde. Little Clyde, could be Type A or Type O."

John studied the poster. "What about Clay? I don't see his name anywhere."

"He was too chicken. He wouldn't let me draw his blood."

"Can't say I blame him."

"You're chicken too."

John yawned. "Okay, Doctor. Am I going to have to listen to you talk about medicine all my life?"

She picked up a fortune cookie. "Yes."

"Let's eat," he whined. "And no talking about blood or guts while we eat."

"Get used to it." She giggled. "Blood and guts are my life."

John laughed and busied himself with setting out two paper plates and serving portions of General Tso's chicken and shrimp lo mein. They ate, talking about anything, everything.

Anything except their upcoming separation. But the subject remained, unspoken, a smoldering threat, like thunderclouds on the horizon.

John Cerelli had whisked her into happiness during her first year of medical school. She was introduced to him by a friend at the Baptist Student Union. He was from a stable family in Charlottesville. The oldest of three boys, he was an athlete, a warm communicator, and a Christian. He worked for a small software company that sold patient record-keeping software to physician's offices. She was driven, glad to be free from her family, but without an anchor in the high seas of graduate medical education. Soon, perhaps too soon, she found the stability she craved, the security that was lacking in her own family, in John.

Now, Claire found herself on the brink of an adventure that would carry her to her goal: a career in surgery. Why did she need to move so far away to pursue that career? That question had dominated many of their conversations. Claire was aiming high. The program at Lafayette offered prestige, cutting-edge research, and an opportunity to train with authorities recognized worldwide. It was a program that, if she survived it, would open any door in any surgical field she wanted.

John accused her of running from home.

Claire blamed it on the match—a computer program that places medical students in the proper internships based on program rankings chosen by the students and student rankings chosen by the programs. The computer matched her in Boston—which sounded to Claire as if it must be the Lord's will.

John insisted that she should have listed only programs closer to home. He argued that she could find good surgical training outside the academic ivory tower she had chosen.

But to Claire, this was a once-in-a-lifetime chance.

John wanted to be near her all the time.

That's what hurt the most.

Finally, after they had talked all around it for an hour, John broached the subject. Leave it to John to try to change her mind one last time. "Couldn't you stay a few extra weeks? You don't have to be on the job until July first. We could spend a few days on the shore."

Claire rubbed the back of her neck, unwilling to simply articulate the same arguments again. Instead, with her eyes boring in on his, she began to hum. Softly at first, then louder, as John pushed back from the table, she hummed the theme from *Chariots of Fire,* drowning out John's sigh.

"Come on, Claire, answer the question. I'm serious. I could take a few days off next week."

She stopped humming long enough to ask, "Remember Eric Liddell?"

He rolled his eyes. Of course he remembered Eric Liddell. Claire knew that John's favorite movie of all time was *Chariots of Fire.* Over the course of their relationship, they'd watched it no less than six times together.

"Remember his passion, his motivation?" Claire stood and resumed the theme song, directing a symphony with her arms and pacing around the boxes in her small apartment.

"What's this got to do with us? With you leaving for Massachusetts?"

She shook her head, refusing to answer directly. "Liddell left his sister and the mission they had started. Why? Just to train for the Olympics? For glory?"

"Come on, Claire. Liddell *needed* to run. It was personal. Spiritual."

Claire tried to imitate Liddell's accent. "When I run I, feel his pleasure." She studied her fiancé. His lips were pursed, his brow wrinkled. He wasn't getting it.

She went on. "That's how it is with me and surgery. Whenever the residents let me participate in a case, throw a stitch, use the scissors or the knife—that's when I feel God's pleasure in me . . . when I'm operating."

John's expression was blank. Perhaps he had never felt something so deep. Maybe he would never get it. For Claire, it *was* personal. It *was* spiritual. Surgery felt more like a calling than anything else she'd known.

John sighed.

"I just want to be ready," Claire said. "I feel like I'm moving to a new level. I've been called up to the big leagues, and I'm up to bat, John. I'm facing Greg Maddux and he's about to throw me his best stuff. I don't want to strike out."

"You *are* ready, Claire. You've done nothing but study for four years."

"John, I can't lounge at the beach right now. I want to get settled in and find my way around." She started clearing the paper plates. "You could come and visit me. Spend a few days checking out the history around Lafayette."

He nodded slowly. "So that's it. End of discussion. Straight to Lafayette. Do not pass go. Do not collect two hundred dollars."

"Right."

He lowered his voice. "What about Stoney Creek? Your mother wanted you to come home."

Claire clenched her teeth. Not after today. Not after how her father had been at graduation. When she hesitated, John spoke again.

"Your father looks like a sick man, Claire. He was so restless during the ceremony today that I thought he might fall off the bench."

"He was drunk, John. He embarrassed me."

"No one knew he was your father."

"Good thing, too."

John put his foot into the overflowing trash can, smashing the contents together. "What if your mother's right? What if it's more than alcohol?"

"My mom's in denial. My father's an alcoholic."

"What about your grandmother? You should apologize. And what about Margo? You should see her."

Claire paused, leaned over the kitchen sink, and stared out the window into the gathering darkness. "What is it, John? Why the sudden interest in me going back home?"

John put his hands on her shoulders and placed his lips against the back of her neck. "I don't want to lose you, Claire. I want you to stay connected to Virginia, to Brighton, to Stoney Creek. Don't forget your home, Claire."

She let her shoulders sag. John always did this to her. He knew just how to probe the recesses of her heart, to pierce the protective shield she wanted so desperately to keep intact. She thought about her home, her family, and the events of the afternoon. She knew John was right. But after today's fiasco, she didn't want to see her father regardless. "I spoke too harshly to my grandma. I'll write an apology."

"Go back and talk to her in person. It's not that much of a detour. I can go with you. I'd like to get to know your family better. Your grandmother seems like a character."

A smile escaped her lips. "She is. She's a bright spot in Stoney Creek, that's for sure." She felt John's hands withdraw, and she turned to see him opening up another fortune cookie, his third.

"What was she talking about—the Stoney Creek curse?"

Claire smirked. "Grandma takes old legends too seriously."

"Well, she believes what she was telling you—she had fire in her eyes." He pointed at Claire and raised his voice to a high-pitched screech. "'I just hope your generation is spared!'" He chuckled. "What'd she call your father? A marked man?"

Claire waved her hand dismissively. "Who knows? Grandma's been in Stoney Creek all her life. I think it's finally getting to her."

"Tell me the legend."

Claire sighed, then reluctantly began. "It's about a Pentecostal evangelist who got riled up and led a group of men up to an old moonshine hideout and smashed a still owned by two brothers. One brother, Gregory Morris, had come to the Pentecostal camp meeting and got religion—or at least, he got Eleazor Potts' version of it. Mr. Morris confessed his sins with a multitude of tears and told the preacher about the secret still." She sat down opposite John, who was quietly stroking his chin.

"The story goes," Claire continued, "Gregory's brother Harold knew nothing of Gregory's new religion, or his betrayal of the still's location. The next night, after the revival meeting, the self-proclaimed prophet Eleazor Potts led a band of fervent followers up the hollow and into the mountains, where they smashed the devil's still and righteously pronounced a curse on anyone drinking from the still should it ever be built again."

"What happened?"

"Eleazor Potts kept up his fire and brimstone preaching for an entire summer. Practically all of Stoney Creek came and heard him. My grandmother says she first heard the gospel message the night Gregory Morris cried and told the preacher about his still. She was just a little girl at the time."

"What about the curse?"

"Well, sure as the night is dark, Harold rebuilt the still. Soon, he started stumbling all over town, slurring his speech and losing his mind."

"Sounds drunk to me."

"Exactly. But that's not what the folks who remembered Potts' curse thought. When Potts returned the next summer, Harold lost it completely and ended up hanging from the end of a rope in his own apple orchard."

"Suicide?"

"Yep. Left a note saying he hadn't had a drink in six months, but couldn't escape the misery of his body or his mind, which he could no longer control." She shrugged. "I don't think anyone with brains believed him, but there are a few, my grandmother included, who took Harold's note as definite proof of the curse's power."

"I don't get it."

"If his symptoms weren't due to the alcohol, then they had to be the result of Potts' curse, right?"

John nodded. "For someone who doesn't pay attention to old legends, you sure seem to know the details."

"You can't grow up in Stoney Creek and not hear about the curse."

"Anyone else suffer from it?"

"A few over the years have kept the rumors alive. Most of this happened a long, long time ago. Harold Morris must have been thirty or forty years older than my grandmother, and she's eighty-one. Since Harold Morris, I would guess just about anyone who stumbles out of the tavern with a good drunk has revived the legend to one degree or another."

John twisted his mouth. "So what about your father? What if your mother is right about him not drinking that much?" He lifted the left side of his mouth into a scowl. "Did your father drink moonshine from the still?"

"Probably. Everyone in Stoney Creek who loves alcohol seems to know how to get the stuff." She hesitated. "John, my father lies about how much he drinks. Maybe Mom believes him. Maybe she's just covering for him. Families do that."

"What if something else is wrong with him?"

"I know my family, okay?"

He shrugged. "So can we go? Will you take me to Stoney Creek?"

"I'm going to Lafayette tomorrow. As soon as I get the rest of these boxes into the U-Haul trailer, I'm out of here."

John got to his feet, then paced around the living room and into the bedroom. He called back, "Where are you going to sleep? You've packed away the bed."

"I've got my sleeping bag."

John reentered and appeared to be studying the floor, shaking his head. "You can't get a good night's sleep like that. You need to be rested for your trip."

"I'm so exhausted, I think I could sleep anywhere." Claire turned back to the sink, looking for a cloth to wipe the table.

John slipped up behind her and wrapped his arms around her waist. "I don't want you to go away. That's no secret."

She turned toward him. "John, we've—"

"Let me finish," he spoke softly. "I know you're leaving. I know it's right for you. It doesn't mean I have to like it."

They kissed, and Claire felt her throat knotting. She didn't want to cry.

John brushed back a tear from her cheek. "Come stay with me tonight. Mike left for the weekend. It will be our last night for a long time."

Claire lay her head on his chest, her vision blurring.

After they had fallen in love, Claire had held out for so long, not giving herself completely to John, wanting to be sure he was the one, wanting to keep her Christian commitment to wait until marriage. But after the engagement, the compromises had begun. She prolonged the kisses. His hands were never still. *He's going to be my husband anyway,* she thought, *and all of my friends think I've been a fool to wait.*

The night they'd clumsily lost their virginity, John had prayed so fervently, gripping her hands, asking God to marry them in his sight.

She felt her body begin to relax against his. His arms felt so right around her. She knew what he'd say if she resisted. *The license is only a piece of paper, honey. In God's sight, we're one already.*

John kissed her ear, her neck. She wanted him so badly. *Just one more time, okay, God? I'm leaving tomorrow anyway. I can sort all of this out when John's not around.* His hand pressed the small of her back. His kisses were hungry, searching.

She pushed her hand against his chest. "Help me get the rest of this stuff in the trailer. I'll just leave from your place in the morning."

Chapter Two

laire glanced at the glowing red numbers on the clock radio. Five-thirty. She held perfectly still, listening to the night sounds around her. John snored softly; a neighbor's dog barked, his raspy voice crisp and sharp against the night. The ceiling fan above John's bed emitted a low rhythmic hum, something Claire had never noticed during the day. Now it seemed obnoxious, impossible to ignore.

She had slept for only five hours, a restless slumber punctuated by images of her home. She had awakened moments before, struggling to remember the dream that seemed to leave her with such longing, an emptiness she couldn't describe beyond the vague feeling that she had missed something of importance, something just beyond her grasp that retreated before her into oblivion. She'd had the feeling before, a haunting that gripped her in the early hours of the morning when she found herself in sleeplessness. *You were made for something more.*

She shook off the feeling and concentrated on the events of her graduation. This time her anger softened into sadness, and soon tears flooded her eyes, blurring the red numbers on the clock. For the first time, Claire thought of her reactions the day before and winced. She had been so wounded by her father's behavior that she hadn't been able to respond to her mother's or her grandmother's requests. She had returned hurt for hurt, and she'd compounded the problem by speaking so harshly to her grandmother. Maybe John was right. Maybe she should go back to Stoney Creek. She could at least see her father sober. And maybe she could leave her grandmother on a more pleasant note. She needed to tidy up this graduation weekend, so it wouldn't be forever etched in her memory as a total failure. She wanted to move on, start a new chapter in her life, pursue her dream in surgery, and put her past in Stoney Creek in proper perspective. What was everyone calling it these days? Claire stared at the ceiling, listening to the fan noise and searching her mind for the psychological buzzword: *Closure.* She nodded in silent resolution. *That's what I need. I'll bring an end to the "country girl from Stoney Creek" chapter and write a new story.*

A bigger story. What will it be called? "Dr. Claire McCall, skillful hands, compassionate healer"? She smiled and wiped her eyes, trying vainly not to sniff too loudly. The new title was too corny, but she couldn't think of anything better offhand. She could name it later. Anything had to be better than the story of her dysfunctional upbringing.

If she left now, she could watch the sunrise over North Mountain, eat breakfast at the little café in Fisher's Retreat, then drive over to Stoney Creek to say good-bye. She smiled. *I'm a doctor now. I'm on to bigger and better things. Nothing, not even my family, or a backwards little town like Stoney Creek, can hold me back.*

She glanced at John's sleeping form, then slipped silently from his bed. The moonlight through the window lit his thick brown hair, and, in spite of the dim light, Claire could easily appreciate his well-muscled chest and arms. But instead of desire, the image invoked a return of regret, a memory of promises made to herself and broken. The haunting resurfaced, this time with a hint of remorse. Each time, the morning after she slept with John, she had the same feeling: loss, not joy. Guilt, not satisfaction. And each time, she promised herself that she'd do better. She'd stick to her guns for a while—then, in a moment of passion, she'd let down her guard again. Each time it seemed easier to fall, and easier to shove aside the feeling that she'd lost something she'd never regain. But the conviction would remain: She was made for something more.

She dressed silently and quickly, wanting desperately to be rid of the chill, and of the memory of another night of compromise.

She tiptoed into the bathroom and shut the door, finishing her preparations alone. Five minutes later, she emerged, careful to shut off the bathroom light before opening the door. Then, without looking back into John's bedroom, she silently fled the apartment into the cool morning.

Outside, she whispered, "Good-bye, John," and opened the door to her aging Toyota.

Highway 2 between Brighton and the first small town in the Apple Valley, Fisher's Retreat, carried a reputation all its own. With only a single lane in both directions, and with a grade demanding low gear, the white-knuckled passage over North Mountain had both awed and frustrated almost every sane driver in western Virginia.

Claire gripped the steering wheel tighter, depressed the accelerator to the floor, and wondered aloud why she had decided to pull a trailer over a curvy mountain road before sunrise.

"Lord, have mercy," she muttered, offered more as an offhand comment than a heartfelt prayer. Actually, heartfelt prayer was something of a rarity anymore for Claire, reserved for crises or for nudging the Atlanta Braves closer to a pennant.

The car lurched forward, straining at the incline, as Claire squinted at the highway, wishing the clouds hadn't gathered so thickly, blocking out the moonlight. Her headlights illuminated the guardrail and the pines arising from the steep mountainside. The trees' eerie shadows waved wildly as she downshifted her Toyota again around the hairpin turn.

As she neared the top of the mountain, the rain began—large, menacing drops, testing Claire's resolve. She flipped on the windshield wipers and ducked her head closer to the steering wheel, peering beneath a large water streak left by her car's aging wipers. *Wonderful! I think I'm doing the right thing to say good-bye to my family, and now I have to face the rain!*

Thankfully, as she crested the top of North Mountain, the rain lessened and Claire relaxed her death grip on the steering wheel. She maneuvered through three more S-turns and then started a slow descent, her foot resting on the brake.

Halfway to the valley below, Claire pulled off into the small paved overlook from which she'd hoped to see the sunrise. She checked her watch and sighed. The sun, even if it was up by now, was hidden by a dense bank of clouds. She opened the car door, stepped into the light drizzle, and squinted back toward the east. There wouldn't be any promising sunrise this morning.

Even so, Claire spent a few minutes stretching her legs, glad to be away from the driver's seat for a moment, even if it meant getting wet. The rain felt cool and invigorating, and she made no attempt to keep it off her face. The only thing that would have felt better was coffee. Claire yawned, missing her morning caffeine jolt. Starting the day with strong coffee flavored with a generous dollop of French vanilla creamer was a delight that bordered on addiction.

She glanced at her watch again. The café in Fisher's Retreat would be open for the Monday morning breakfast crowd. She would stop for breakfast and celebrate a safe passage over North Mountain after towing a trailer in the rain. She might even see a familiar face or two from Stoney Creek—many of the locals stopped there to eat, since they didn't have a restaurant of their own.

After a minute longer in the rain, Claire slid back behind the wheel and shifted into low gear to descend North Mountain into the Apple Valley.

Fifty minutes later, she pulled into a small parking lot behind Fisher's Café, a watering hole in Fisher's Retreat. There, she spotted her brother's pickup, a red Chevy that Clay had rebuilt and coddled since high school.

Inside, she scanned the early breakfast crowd, inhaling the wonderful aroma of fresh coffee and frying bacon. The regulars were there: Tom Shifflett, the mayor of Stoney Creek, sat with old Dr. Jenkins, a general practitioner who had cared for the people of the Apple Valley for over thirty years. Mike and Larry Martin, brothers who had grown up on the hill adjacent to the McCall's, were there, probably fueling up before heading into Carlisle to work at their father's sawmill. There were others that Claire didn't know—some reading the local paper, others chatting above the noise of breakfast dishes, seemingly content with small-town life and a simple cup of coffee. Mr. Knitter, the owner, was working the grill behind a counter, his grease-spotted white apron inadequate coverage for his ample stomach. She saw Clay at the end of the counter, slumped over a tall mug, his back to her, but his strong arms and shoulders and his blond curls recognizable to his twin in an instant.

She had hoped to slip in quietly, unrecognized, and surprise Clay, but knew there was little chance of that. The second best thing would be to find her brother, say a few quiet hellos to the regulars, and eat breakfast in peace, without anyone making a big deal out of her visit. Mike Martin spoiled that. He was on his feet as soon as he saw her.

"Well, ain't you a sight for sore eyes." His grin was wide, his voice loud, and his arms open.

"Hi, Mike," she said quietly, wincing as she accepted his hug.

Mike passed her to his brother, who seemed embarrassed to make such a display. Larry gripped her hand and mumbled, "Heard you were up in Brighton at school. You a nurse now, or what?"

"What," she responded with a wink.

Dr. Jimmy Jenkins, one of Claire's biggest fans, joined in before Larry released her. "Dr. McCall, I believe? Is it really you?" He chuckled. "You should hear your mother brag."

"Hi, Doc." She dropped Larry's hand and threw her arms around Dr. Jenkins, noting the faint, familiar scent of iodine antiseptic. Claire had worked as a receptionist at Dr. Jenkins' clinic before attending Brighton University, and she'd kept in touch with him—less often since starting medical school, but she knew she could count on his encouragement. In fact, he was the only voice in Stoney Creek, outside of her own mother, that had encouraged her to pursue a medical career.

For as long as she'd known him, he'd smelled the same. She inhaled purposefully, enjoying the memories his clinical fragrance invoked: watching Dr. Jenkins sew up a lacerated child; filing away thick patient folders; studying physical exams, lab values, and X-ray reports for the stories of illness they provided.

"You've made us all so proud." He pushed her back to arm's length and smiled.

She knew that was an exaggeration. Most of Stoney Creek, if they knew she was off studying medicine at all, were like Larry, who thought she was in nursing.

She glanced over Dr. Jenkins' shoulder to her brother, who sat motionless, still slumped over his coffee. "Thanks, Doc." She shrugged. "I just came by to say good-bye. I'm leaving for Lafayette this morning."

He shook his head. "Always aiming for the top."

"I guess." She began to edge away, wanting to talk to Clay.

Doc Jenkins patted her hand gently. "Be careful, Claire. And watch out for Dr. Rogers."

"You *know* him? Tom Rogers?" She referred to the renowned chairman of the surgery department at Lafayette General Hospital—and director of the American Health Institute. Under Dr. Rogers' iron tutelage, the department had scavenged more grant money for medical research than the Rochester Mayo Clinic and Harvard combined.

He lowered his already soft voice. "I didn't spend my whole life in Stoney Creek, Claire. I went to med school with Tom." He smiled. "Johns Hopkins, class of sixty-five."

"I never imagined that you—"

"He never liked women, Claire, at least not women doctors."

"Times have changed, Doc. You can't believe that, in this day and age, he thinks that—"

He interrupted her with a squeeze of her hand. "Maybe you're right. That was a long time ago." He looked over his shoulder at Clay and motioned his head. "I'll let you go." He paused. "Nice to see you again."

Claire nodded without speaking, then watched as he laid a five-dollar bill on his table and turned to leave. She waved at the mayor, smiled again at the Martin brothers, and walked to the counter.

Mr. Knitter set a steaming mug of coffee in front of her and smiled without speaking. His eyes were on Clay, who was drawing a line through the pancake syrup on his plate.

Claire sat and lifted the coffee to her lips. She knew better than to ask for French vanilla creamer here. "Morning, Bro."

Clay kept his eye on his plate, continuing to stir the syrup with his fork. "Mom said you weren't coming."

"Surprise."

He stayed silent, leaving Claire to sip her coffee and swivel back and forth on the bar stool.

"I wanted to say good-bye." She hesitated. "I wish I'd seen you yesterday, after the grad. I—I just couldn't bring myself to face Dad." She huffed. "Not like he looked yesterday."

Clay squared off and looked at his twin. "He looked *good* yesterday. At least until you refused to see him."

"Clay, I *saw* him. He couldn't even walk a straight line to find his seat."

Clay sighed, massaging his temples. He looked hung over, with dark circles beneath his eyes and his chin unshaven. "You've been away too long." He shook his head. "That was the best he's looked in weeks. He hasn't been out of the house since Uncle Leon's wedding."

"What was that, four months ago?"

"Six." He paused. "Since Grandpa died, I don't think he's even spoken to Grandma. I was kind of hoping that this graduation thing of yours would be an excuse for them to mend some fences."

The thought of her father staying in their little house, week after week, seemed beyond depressing. She waited, hoping Clay would admit that it was an exaggeration. He didn't.

She swiveled the bar stool toward her brother. "You've been drinking."

"I was toasting your success, Sis." He looked away. "Somebody had to celebrate, since you didn't care to."

Before she could reply, he changed the subject. "You hurt him, you know."

She was incredulous. "Dad?"

He nodded.

"*He* hurt *me!*"

"He wanted to see you. All the way to Brighton he couldn't shut up about how great you've been. Claire this, Claire that. Wonderful Claire. Claire, the honors medical graduate." He smirked. "Until you snubbed him."

"He shouldn't have been drinking!"

"You made him drink. He didn't have anything until after the graduation. Then your snotty departure and Grandma's talk about the town curse were enough to send him on a binge."

"Don't even start that town curse stuff with me. I'm a scientist. Medical doctors don't believe in—"

"I'm not saying I believe it," he huffed. "But Grandma sure is nutty about it." He shook his head. "If she'd seen him over the past year, his appearance wouldn't have come as such a surprise. As it was, she couldn't seem to stop talking about that stupid curse."

The duo looked up as Mr. Knitter approached and refilled their mugs with coffee.

Claire slid the mug back toward her. "Thanks."

"Any breakfast this morning?"

She had lost her appetite. "Um, no thanks, Mr. Knitter." She forced a smile. "Coffee's fine."

She watched him retreat to the grill before lowering her voice. "I wasn't born yesterday, Clay. Dad looked ripped at the ceremony."

"He always looks like that anymore, even when he's not drinking." He shrugged. "To tell you the truth, alcohol doesn't seem to have that much effect on him."

"All alcoholics build up a tolerance."

"Whatever."

"If he wasn't drunk, how do you explain his behavior?"

"Maybe he's just fried his brains with the stuff." Clay took a sip of coffee, then rubbed his head again, squinting at his watch. He chuckled and added sarcastically, "Or maybe it's the Stoney Creek curse." He yawned. "You should have heard Grandma. She railed about the curse halfway up North Mountain, until Dad exploded and made her be quiet." He stood up. "I gotta go. I'm on first shift at the cabinet shop."

Claire sighed. This wasn't exactly how she wanted to say good-bye. "I guess I'll see you around." She paused. "I'm going up to see Dad. Maybe apologize."

Clay shook his head. "Not a good idea. You had your chance to say good-bye yesterday."

"I'll just stop in and—"

He took her arm and squeezed. "Trust me. Mornings are not Dad's time. He won't want to be surprised. If you want to apologize, write a letter."

"But I want to see—"

"I've got to go," Clay interrupted. "Do not drop in on Dad unannounced. It won't be a pretty sight." With that, he dropped her arm and pivoted on the heels of his cowboy boots. "Bye, Sis." He walked a few steps away before turning. "Oh, and congratulations."

She watched him disappear through the café's front door and wondered how twins could turn out so different. He seemed content with small-town life and the work of a small cabinet shop. She wanted so much more. She was *called* to do more, and she cared enough to do something about it.

She turned to see Ralph Knitter setting down a plate of steaming blueberry pancakes.

"Mr. Knitter, I—"

He cut off her protest. "You've got to eat. It's on the house." He smiled. "Say, Doc, do you mind looking at this mole?" He started to roll up his sleeve, then laughed when she leaned forward to take a better look. He pulled his arm away. "Just kidding, Claire. But get used to it. Now that you're a doctor, everyone will want advice."

She smiled, then looked at the pancakes. "Thanks, Mr. Knitter."

He held out his hand. "Go ahead. It's what you used to order, back when you worked for Doc Jenkins."

"You remember everything."

He winked. "It's my business to remember." He was right. If there was information to be had about Stoney Creek, Mr. Knitter knew it. "Say, Claire, I don't mean to be butting into your family business, but I couldn't help overhearing." He gestured toward the door where Clay had just disappeared. "Not everything in life can be explained by science. I've seen enough around here to believe in the curse."

She shook her head. "Not you too."

Mr. Knitter glanced toward the grill where another order of pancakes bubbled. To Claire's relief, he had to excuse himself.

Claire sighed and wished she had an appetite. She stabbed at the pancakes and questioned her resolve to visit Stoney Creek. She wanted to return to say good-bye, to leave on peaceful terms with her family, to create a happy ending for her graduation weekend. She cringed. As if peaceful terms were possible with her dysfunctional relatives.

Early this morning, this had seemed like such a good idea. Last night, John had seemed to think so too. But now, she'd not even gotten home and she was already facing a myriad of stupid, small-town rumors. Each time she visited, the town seemed to shrink a little more—at least in Claire's opinion, in how she valued it as her hometown. The further Claire progressed in her education, the further behind Stoney Creek seemed to fall. Maybe it was time to just move along. Fix her eyes upon her goal of becoming a surgeon and forget the past.

She drained her mug and checked her watch. Her father should be up by now. She'd come this far. She might as well see her plan through.

She paid for the coffee and walked to her car, trying to push her brother's warning from her mind. *Do not drop in on Dad unannounced. It won't be a pretty sight.*

By the time Claire pulled into the gravel lane leading to her parents' home, she had changed her mind about visiting six more times. She had traveled from Fisher's Retreat past Ashby High School and on into Stoney Creek, bombarded with images from her childhood. Playing in the river. Fishing with her father. High school track and volleyball, her mother never missing a game.

With each good memory, she was sure she was doing the right thing. But then, when more recent memories collided with the past, she questioned her decision again. She remembered her father's drunken abuses, his explosive outbursts, and the quiet way they tiptoed around when he was sleeping off a binge. She recalled a fight during Thanksgiving break in her sophomore year at Brighton and how her father had stormed out, not to return until she was gone, two days later. She thought of the broken promises, her father's job failures, the loss of his driver's license.

She thought about the years when he was dry, faithfully attending AA, even attending church, and how he couldn't praise Della enough for her patience in seeing him through.

As she headed up the lane, she remembered the frantic way she had raced the old go-cart her father had made, up and down the gravel driveway, always competing with Clay to get the fastest time and to make her father smile. Oh, what she wouldn't do to make him smile again.

She pulled to a stop in the circular driveway, wondering at first whether she'd find anyone awake. Her father liked to sleep late if he didn't have a job to go to. She slipped from the car and skipped up the cracked concrete sidewalk. At the top of the third step there was a small stoop, and she turned and stared down the long gravel lane toward the road. Rhododendron and dogwoods bloomed along the side of the hill, and the morning cloud cover was beginning to lift. She looked back toward North Mountain, whose peak was just breaking out of the clouds. *Yes,* she thought, *coming home was a real good idea.*

Claire listened for noise inside. Satisfied that the clatter and bump she heard must be breakfast under way, she knocked rapidly.

A moment later, the door opened slowly just a few inches and halted, before swinging wide to reveal her mother. Della stepped quickly onto the small stoop and closed the door behind her. "What on earth . . . ," she said haltingly, staring at her daughter.

Claire smiled and shrugged. "Morning, Momma."

Della clasped her daughter's shoulders. "What are you doing here?"

Claire stepped back. "You asked me to come."

Her mother gasped, "Oh, I know that, but—well—you said you couldn't make it. I just wasn't expecting you is all." She cleared her throat. "Perhaps you'd like to see the spring flowers." Della stepped down onto the sidewalk and pointed around the side of the house.

"They're beautiful, Momma. But I came to see you. You and Dad. I really think I acted pretty snobbish yesterday and I wanted to say good-bye, and . . ."

Her mother's knitted brow caused Claire to stop. "Perhaps you should have given us a little warning. Your father is not a man to like surprises anymore."

Claire studied her mother for a moment. Her silky housecoat partially covered what appeared to be a revealing nightgown. Claire thought of her own sleeping arrangements last night, another item on a growing list of regrets from graduation weekend.

Why was her mother wearing such a seductive outfit? Why did she seem so reluctant to invite Claire in? The way her father had been acting, who would blame her mother if she was entertaining another man? Maybe her father didn't even live there anymore. Maybe her parents' graduation trip together had been nothing but a charade.

Claire went straight for the heart. "What are you hiding, Mom? Is there someone in there you don't want me to see?"

Della looked down at her sleepwear, then put her hands on her hips and squared off in front of her daughter. "Yes," she said, glaring at Claire, "your father!"

Claire felt her face flush. She shouldn't allow herself to jump to conclusions. How could she think that her mother could be hiding anyone else? Not her mom, who seemed to be the perfect picture of a submissive wife. Claire must have been projecting her own guilt about John onto her mother. Or at least she imagined that's what her professors in psychiatry would have thought. She squeezed her eyes shut and shook her head. "Can I come in?"

"I'm not sure that's such a good idea."

"You thought it was yesterday."

"Yesterday, I would have had a chance to prepare. Today's a surprise. Your father may not be so presentable." Della fumbled with the silky belt of her robe.

"Mom, that's who I came to see. I felt bad for running off yesterday."

Della lowered her eyes and blew her breath out noisily. "Yesterday, what a day that was." She shook her head. "It was the first time in months I've been able to coax him out of the house."

"Mom, we need to get him some help." Claire took her mother's hand. "If he isn't getting out at all, how is he getting the alcohol? Are you buying it for him?"

She shook her head. "Mostly Uncle Leon and a few friends, but honestly, Claire, it almost makes him bearable. It seems to take the edge off his irritability."

"It probably just keeps him out of DTs, Mom."

"He's not interested in help. I can't talk to him about it anymore."

"Can I see him?"

Della sighed. "I don't guess I can talk you into giving me an hour?"

"Mom, I'm family."

Her mother walked back up the steps. "Come on. You're as stubborn as he is, you know." She pushed open the door. "Wally?" she called, lifting her voice. "Claire's here." She disappeared down the front hallway toward her bedroom.

Claire glanced around the dimly lit den and kitchen. An empty bottle of Jim Beam was on the kitchen counter, and the trash can overflowed with aluminum cans. Thankfully, most of them appeared to be Mountain Dew. The refrigerator had a picture of Margo, Claire's sister, standing next to a pony. On the pony's back sat her two nieces, Kelly and Casey. Claire touched the picture and looked closely at her sister's obviously pregnant abdomen. She was expecting her third girl, Kristin, any day. It was her pregnancy that had kept Margo away from Claire's graduation. *Lucky Margo. Maybe I should have stayed away from graduation, too.*

She strained to hear her parents' conversation. Her mother's voice was muffled, her father's loud but garbled. Bumping noises punctuated their speech, and it sounded as if a large object hit the floor.

She looked at the coffeemaker. The brew smelled old, the pot half-empty. Yesterday's newspaper was open on the table, and a box of Rice Krispies was on its side, next to an empty bowl.

Claire took a seat at the table and scanned the paper, intermittently watching the hallway and the bedroom doorway beyond. The door swung open, and her father, in boxer shorts only, appeared momentarily in the hall. Della ushered him forcefully back into the bedroom again. More bumping, crashing noises followed, and her father's protests seemed muffled. Claire imagined a shirt being forced over his head.

What is going on around this house? Can't he dress himself?

Eventually, he appeared in the hallway again, slowly moving toward her, his gait wide-based and insecure, his hands reaching for first one wall and then the other. That's when Claire noticed the bare walls. Once, dozens of family pictures had lined the hallway. It had been a constant joy for Della to show off the family to her friends. No longer. The pictures were gone, apparently to keep Wally from knocking them down during his clumsy passage through the hall.

To Claire, just the fact that her mother had taken down the pictures reeked of codependency. Why was her mother facilitating his self-destructive behavior?

Her heart was in her throat. She watched his lips twitch, as if he wanted to speak but didn't know how to begin. She stood to greet him. "Hi, Daddy."

"Hi, Claire." His speech was thick.

Her hand was against her mouth. "Oh, Daddy."

He stumbled forward and on into the den. There, he collapsed onto the couch and stared at the floor. His arm lurched outward, then slowly descended to a resting place behind his head. He appeared to be chewing gum, his mouth in constant motion. His cheeks were sunken and his shirt hung on him limply, failing to conceal his wasting frame.

"Con–con–congratulations." His head swayed gently.

"Dad, are you okay?" It was a dumb question. Claire regretted it instantly, but she didn't know what else to say.

"I'm fine." He looked up from the floor. "I thought you were heading off to be a surgeon. No time for your family anymore, is that right?"

"I want to be a surgeon. But not everyone makes it, Dad." She paused, trying vainly to hold his gaze for more than a second. "But I did want to come and say good-bye. I wanted to see you before I left."

"I—" He halted as his head jerked forward. "Hope you're happy now." His voice was flat, his face expressionless. It was as if his brain hadn't notified his face of the emotions he should feel.

Claire looked at her mother. Della shrugged and pursed her lips, not speaking. She didn't have to. Her look said it for her: "I told you this wouldn't be a good idea."

"Daddy, how long have you—uh—" Claire stuttered and looked at her mother. "How long's he been this way?"

"Going downhill for months. Years, really," Della responded.

"I'm fine. I need a little drink is all."

Claire shook her head. "Let me take you back to Brighton. They have a detox unit there. You can dry out. They can take care of you." She attempted a smile. "Maybe fatten you up a bit."

"I got all I need right here. Leave me be."

"Daddy, you need help."

He waved his fingers in the air, pointing first at Claire and then the floor. "Stop playing doctor, Claire. It's okay for you to play that in the hospital, but you leave it at the door when you see me. I'm fine!"

"But Daddy—"

Della stood up. "Leave it alone, Claire."

"Is that what you want? For me to leave him like this?"

"Shut up, Claire! Shut up!" he screamed. "First my mother, and now my daughter. And neither of you can leave me in peace." His hands were flying around him again, this time one coming to rest on the couch, and the other onto an empty beer bottle on a side table.

"Just look at yourself, Daddy," she cried, her voice breaking. "You used to be so much more."

His fist closed around the bottle. "I said—said—said—" He lurched forward to the edge of the couch and threw the bottle over Claire's head. It shattered loudly against the wall behind her. *"Get out!"*

She shrieked, ducked, and watched her father tumble into a heap on the carpet in front of the couch.

Immediately Della was at his side.

"I want her out!" he cried.

Her mother looked up. "You'd better go. I'll take care of this."

"But—"

Wally mumbled something unintelligible.

"Go," her mother urged. "I'll take care of him. We'll be okay." She nodded. "Really, it would be best if you'd leave." Della turned her attention to Wally, leaving Claire standing by the front door, her mouth open in disbelief. "There, there," Della said softly. "Just a little fall. Let me help you up, dear."

Claire wanted to scream. *What about me? He could have killed me with that bottle! And you just get down and comfort him?*

She reached for the door and moved numbly to the car. In a minute, with gravel spraying behind her, she turned onto Route 319 to take her back to the interstate.

Five minutes later, she slowed at the paved lane leading up to her grandmother McCall's mansion. She thought momentarily about stopping, then stepped on the gas. She couldn't stand any more heavy conversation. Her short visit to Stoney Creek had already exhausted her, and it wasn't even nine A.M. She could handle her grandmother with a letter. At least that way she wouldn't have to listen to more foolishness about the town curse.

It was time for Claire to move on. She needed to be far away. Far away from the distractions of this crazy family and from the small-town atmosphere that fostered it. And, as much as she loved him, she wanted time away from John Cerelli, time to sort out her feelings and gain some objectivity.

She purposefully loosened her death grip on the steering wheel. "Just calm down, girl," she said softly to herself. "Just calm down."

Some things you can't change. But you can take charge of your own future.

She thought about her father's outburst, then brushed back tears so she could drive. She had wanted so much more from her visit.

So much for closure!

Part Two

Chapter Three

June 30, 2000

here is a deceptive softness to the mountains viewed from my bedroom window at my father's house. When I was just a little girl, I used to imagine the tree-covered peaks as a colorful blanket cradling my body as I nestled into the wrinkled terrain. The illusion is only appreciated from a distance, however. Like life, my fantasy of pampered comfort dissipates with closer inspection. Thick prickly pinecones and briars appear. Jagged rocks come into view. Huge ones, the kind Easterners call boulders, with outcroppings the size of Uncle Leon's Cadillac.

Tomorrow, I think I'll miss those mountains. Tomorrow, July first, the day that strikes terror into the hearts of sick and dying patients in teaching hospitals everywhere. At least terror for those who are lucky enough to know. You see, July first is the day new doctors begin their training, unleashing their fresh degrees and arrogance, their clumsiness and naïveté, their aspirations for diagnostic greatness, all upon the innocent patients, none of whom volunteered for illness on the first of July.

Terror grips not only the hearts of the patients, but claws the soul of the intern as well. I know because I will be one: Dr. Claire McCall, intern, department of surgery.

I feel sick. I bet I've forgotten everything. Tomorrow. Everything changes tomorrow, the day when I'll be expected to know what to do when the nurses call.

Yep, I'm gonna miss those Blue Ridge Mountains tomorrow. Tomorrow? Who am I foolin'? I miss 'em now. Today.

Claire closed her diary and slid it beneath the residency handbook in her lap and sighed. If surgery internship was anything like she'd been told, there wouldn't be any more time for this. Recording her thoughts would be a thing of the past.

Her thoughts evaporated as the conference room erupted in laughter. Dr. Dan Overby, the administrative chief resident in surgery, smiled broadly before chuckling at his own joke, the last in a string of one-liners about those physicians who had chosen the field of internal medicine. "Fleas," he called them: the last ones to leave a dying dog.

Claire smiled nervously and wondered what she'd missed. She focused on the overweight man at the podium. He had short brown hair, moist either from grease or hair gel, and little round wire-rimmed glasses that sat halfway down his pudgy nose. Along with his enormous size, rumors about Dr. Overby's feats within the university hospital made him legendary among the house staff. All the new interns had heard of his operative speed, his finesse under the attending's glare, and his memorization of the current surgical literature. "Dr. O," the patients called him. To the house staff, he was just "Dan," or "O," or "Dan-the-man," or "the O-man."

"Welcome to the medical Mecca," Dan chuckled again, straightening his tie and pulling his white coat lapels forward in a futile attempt to cover his expansive abdomen. "Your mother may think that the Cleveland Clinic or the Mayo Clinic represent the pinnacle in medicine, but I'm here to inform you otherwise." He made eye contact with Claire. "Being a surgical intern in this university places you among the elite." He paused, taking time to look at each of the twelve new recruits seated in front of him.

The chief resident continued. "Dr. McGrath has already explained the division of services. Now I'm here to tell you how to survive."

There was more nervous laughter from the twelve interns. Claire watched the others from the corner of her eyes and fought the urge to pull out a legal pad to take notes. *The last thing I want is to look like a medical student again.*

"Rule number one. Eat when you can." He looked around the room before pulling a pack of crackers from his pocket. "Here," he added, tossing it to the closest intern. "There will be many days and nights with too much to do, when you think that you can't make time for a meal." He smiled. "But don't believe it. If you don't eat, you can't work to your potential.

"Rule number two. Everyone teaches a tern."

Claire nodded. It was apparent that this was a term of endearment to the chief resident. It was his slang for "intern."

"You can and will learn from everyone around you. Your patients are your teachers. Their families are your teachers. The *nurses*, as irritating as they can be, are your teachers. Even the medical students, as exasperating as they will be, have more time to read than you do. Treat them right, let them help you with a procedure, and they might be willing to find an article that will help you on rounds.

"Conversely, come in here with a God complex . . ." He paused and turned his nose in the air and imitated the attitude he discouraged, "*I'm* a surgical intern in the Mecca." He shook his head. "Come in here with that attitude, and you won't be around long enough to see what it looks like from the top of the pyramid."

The *pyramid.* It wasn't a word Claire wanted to be reminded of. Half of the interns audibly groaned. It referred to the structure of the surgical residency. There were twelve spots for interns, eight spots for second-year residents, five for third-year residents, and four spots each for the fourth year and the fifth, or chief residency, year. There were also a variable number of research lab spots when grant money was available for residents who had academic or research aspirations. The lab also served as a holding tank, a place for residents to study to improve their in-service test scores in the hopes that they could propel themselves back into a coveted third-, fourth-, or fifth-year clinical position. Almost everyone spent time in the lab, making the residency a six-year program for many, and a seven- or eight-year marathon for some. The pyramid fostered competition. The pyramid prompted long hours, desperate commitment, and ruthless back-stabbing. You needed to shine, to perform, above the level of your peers, or you might not be promoted to the next year.

"Rule number three. If you don't know, ask. We won't tolerate lone rangers. Anyone acting like a cowboy or a loose cannon is sure to sit before the residency review board before next May when we select the second-year residents. It's better to ask than guess. You're not taking a test on paper anymore. Tomorrow, you will have real patients, God help them, and *what you don't know will hurt them!*"

Claire ran her fingers through her newly cut hair. Even though it had been a week, the absence of her long blond hair still surprised her. She had traded her flowing locks for a more efficient style, just off the collar. Feminine, for sure, but without the time hassle that long hair required. She looked at her fingers, long and spindly, adept at the craft she pursued. Her styled nails were the last thing she'd given up. She'd cut them last night and removed the last traces of the chartreuse polish she loved so much. She clicked her fingernails on the resident handbook in her lap and winced at their appearance. *Oh well,* she thought, *surgery isn't the place for attractive nails. And internship isn't about fashion; it's about survival.*

Claire quietly studied the faces of her fellow interns, vaguely aware of Dan's voice saying something about "chain of command." The other terns seemed relaxed, laughing at the O-man's expressions. She forced herself to smile, belying her anxieties. *There are twelve of us. Only eight next year. A third of us will be cut! And there are only two women here . . . Beatrice Hayes and me! Have they ever had two female chief residents in one year before?*

Beatrice was well-moneyed. Her father was an academic dermatologist across town, a fact Claire learned in the first two-minute conversation with "Bea." *"And what does your father do?"* Beatrice's eyes had seemed to focus on a spot two inches above Claire's forehead.

"He's retired Navy."

Claire's gut churned with the memory. *Why did I say that? It's technically the truth, I suppose. My father was in the Navy once.*

Bea was composed, reeking of self-confidence. Here, at an informal gathering of the new house staff, she was dressed in a sharp gray business suit. *We're in the minority here, Bea. And they won't likely finish us both. So it's you or me. One of us is going to get the axe . . . and it's not going to be me!* Claire pulled her eyes from her competition, abruptly aware that she had been clenching her jaw.

Dan's wild gesticulations prompted her to refocus. "There are no guarantees that you will make it. But you wouldn't be here if you weren't the best. All of you represent the cream of your medical schools, the pride of your hometowns."

He obviously hasn't visited Stoney Creek. Claire looked at the interns again. *We're the cream?*

Dan seemed to be wrapping things up. "Let me conclude with a quote from Dr. Jonas Salk, the man responsible for the polio vaccine. 'The reward for work well done is the opportunity to do more.'" He pounded the podium with a meaty fist, jerking his small audience to attention. "And remember what Arthur Rubinstein replied when questioned by a passerby, 'How do you get to Carnegie Hall?' 'PRACTICE, PRACTICE, PRACTICE!'" Dan's voice was near stadium volume. "And so it is here," he preached, towering forward over his underlings. Then, abruptly, he lowered his voice and glared at the terns, who were all pressed back into their seats. "Practice," he whispered. "Practice."

The chief resident paused for a moment, as if waiting for applause.

There was none. In fact, the terns were so silent, apparently shocked by Dan-the-man's theatrical conclusion, that they just sat, unsure of their next move.

After the awkward pause, Dan cleared his throat and pointed to a side table, where a dark-haired man in a three-piece suit offered a nod. "Bill Joiner, our Ethicon suture rep, has brought each of you a knot-tying board. I would strongly suggest that you take one home and don't waste any time before you become proficient at one- and two-handed ties. The surest way to be tossed from a case is to show a deficiency at the basics." He held up his hands. "That's it. Make sure you know where you are supposed to report in the morning. And the tern reception tonight at the Bay Club is not optional." He paused for a moment, as if caught in a memory of his own. "Take it from me. Stay away from the punch. Getting drunk is no way to make a first impression on Dr. Rogers."

The crowd started dispersing as Dan added, "Let me see Doctors McCall, Hayes, Button, and Neal."

Claire gathered her things and joined the other named physicians in front of the small podium. She held her hand up to Dan. "I'm Claire McCall."

"I'm Dr. Hayes," Bea responded, following Claire's lead.

The two other interns nodded. "Wayne Neal."

"I'm Howard Button."

The large resident beamed. "My new terns. You four have been assigned to the trauma team. And for the next three months, it's *my* trauma team, and you're *my* terns. We'll rotate every other night with two terns on each night. We only have one call room for the terns on this team, so I'd suggest keeping McCall and Hayes on the same night. Not that you'll ever see the inside of a call room," he added with a tense smile.

"I don't mind sharing call quarters with a guy," Bea interjected quickly. "I don't want any special treatment."

Claire stayed quiet. *I'm not sharing my call room with a man.*

Dan raised his eyebrows. "Uh. Okay. I'll decide how to divide the duties in the morning. We need to meet by six A.M. in the SICU."

"The SICU?" Howard scratched his forehead.

"As in Surgical Intensive Care Unit. Second floor, directly across from the MICU, the Medical Intensive Care Unit. Come early and wear scrubs. This isn't a street clothes type of rotation."

The four nodded. Bea leaned toward Dan. "See you tonight?"

"Wouldn't miss it. The Bay Club has great food. And this reception is your first chance to meet the house staff outside the confines of this place."

Claire made her way to the Ethicon display to receive a knot-tying board. She already had one, but another would be nice. Besides, maybe she'd send it back home to her cousin who was showing an interest in medicine. The board had several tall thin cylinders mounted on a plastic base. At the bottom of the transparent cylinders, a small hook had been mounted. The object was to tie a knot around the small hook, simulating the placement of a knot within a small body cavity or through a small incision. Claire had been tying practice knots since the first week of medical school. Surgery was the whole reason for her medical training. She'd never considered anything else.

She greeted Bill, the sales rep, who immediately turned his attention away from the other interns to the only women in the group.

"I'm glad to see a few women in the ranks this year," Bill began. "I was beginning to think I'd never see another in this program. The one they matched last year didn't last six months."

"They only take the best," Bea snipped. "And not many females are cut out for this."

Claire eyed her pensively. *I'm surprised to hear that chauvinistic junk from you.* She changed the subject. "Thanks for the knot board."

"Where'd you go to med school?"

He was clearly focused on Claire, but Bea interjected. "Yale."

Bill seemed to be appreciating Claire's blouse. She cleared her throat, hoping to lift his eyes to her face. "I attended Brighton University." Then she backed away and turned for the door.

Bill called out, "See you ladies tonight."

Claire walked out with Bea, Howard, and Wayne. "*He's* going to be at the Bay Club?"

Wayne chuckled. "Ethicon picks up the whole tab for the intern reception every year. I suppose they think it will make us buy their products."

At the end of the hall, Bea made a right turn. "I think I'll go to the SICU and review some patient charts."

Wayne shook his head. "Not me. They don't own me till tomorrow."

Howard kept plugging toward the front entrance. He looked at his watch. "I've got sixteen hours of freedom left. Just sixteen hours."

Claire waved weakly in Bea's direction, who was either suddenly interested in getting to know her new patients, or competitive enough to want to shine on the first day. Claire thought momentarily of following her, then skipped to catch up with the others. She knew her life would change drastically soon enough. Why rush the torture?

For most of her life, others had told her it couldn't be done. Little girls from Stoney Creek just don't grow up to be surgeons. Little girls should grow up to be mothers, housewives, help out on the family farm. Maybe a few could be teachers at the elementary school. Or maybe become nurses to help make ends meet when income at the shoe factory proved inadequate. But little girls don't become surgeons, especially not girls with a father like Claire McCall's.

For most of her life, she had refused to listen. Now, as she mingled with the other new interns, residents, and surgery-attending physicians at the exclusive Bay Club, she imagined any number of circumstances that could again block her goal. She surveyed the scene, feeling suddenly misplaced, a country girl at a sophisticated city gala. Music from a live string quartet drifted around the tuxedoed men and their wives wearing sequined dresses. A Volkswagen-sized glass chandelier hung in a massive foyer over a fountain containing enough coins to keep Claire in groceries for a month.

She analyzed each of the other eleven interns with a critical eye, imagining their strengths and weaknesses and wondering which eight would make it to the next year. Six were married; two had children. Two were already MD, PhDs, with multiple publications in the surgical literature. Three were Harvard grads. One was from Southern California, two were from University of Michigan, one from Yale, one from Duke, two from Johns Hopkins, one from Georgetown, and one from Brighton University: Claire.

Each intern seemed so much more capable than she. Everyone was so articulate and proper. How had she traveled so far out of her league? Maybe it was all some huge computer mistake. Claire politely declined a third offer of punch, held up by a young man with a white shirt accentuated by a black bow tie, and mulled over the possibility that the computer matching program had gone awry, placing her in this elite program by mistake.

This is ridiculous, Claire mused. *I ranked this program number one, and they obviously ranked me high on their list, too. There's no mistake here. I'm just as capable as these Harvard grads.* She sighed, listening to a fellow intern make a reference to an article he'd read in *The New England Journal of Medicine.* She drifted away from the small crowd to sample the hors d'oeuvres. *Didn't that guy know we were supposed to be on vacation since med school graduation? It sounds like he spent the last two months in the library.* She smiled at the thought of the long hours she'd spent studying in the two months since her stormy graduation. *The others are just like me.*

"You must be Elizabeth." A tall man with gray hair and a relaxed smile held out his hand. Claire knew who he was immediately: the general surgery residency director, Dr. Tom Rogers.

She shook his hand firmly. "Yes, but I prefer to be called Claire. It's what I've been called all my life."

"E. Claire." His grin widened.

"Yes, sir." She shrugged, reading his thoughts. "I've lived with a name that sounds more like a French pastry than a surgeon. And I grew up in a town so backwards that you couldn't even buy French pastry there."

"Yes. Oh," he chortled. "Eclair." He took a sip from a tall glass and dropped his smile. "You'll be starting on one of the busiest rotations, our trauma service."

"So I hear. But at least I get to work with Dr. Overby."

"Dan-the-man," Dr. Rogers responded reflectively, a hint of a smile returning to his face. "You'll be glad for your sense of humor, E. Claire. Bring it with you tomorrow. You're going to need it."

Claire parked her aging Toyota in the driveway and fumbled with the keys to her rented brownstone house. She'd left the party early, but not until the program director preceded her, just in case he was watching.

She opened the door, adjusted the thermostat up, and opened a window in her second-floor bedroom for ventilation. She'd chosen the house after a marathon weekend search. The apartments close to the university were less expensive, but run-down, and appeared unsafe, a haven for drug pushers or worse. The houses further out were expensive, and the commute would be too long. Here, three miles from the hospital, seemed just about right. The rent was more than Claire wanted to pay, absorbing half her intern salary, but safety and peace of mind were worth the extra cost. She didn't have anything else to spend money on anyway. She was single, at least for now, and had no children, and her surgical residency would put a damper on any expensive social activity. Being too busy to spend money did have its advantages.

She looked at the answering machine. No messages. *At least he could call me for once.* She chewed her lower lip. *He's still sore about how I left him after grad.*

She changed into a cotton football jersey, her normal sleeping attire. It was John's, of course, and the comfort she received from it had little to do with its warmth. It was nine o'clock, too early for bed, but getting too dark for a jog.

Claire adjusted a small picture on her desk, one of her and John at U-Hall at a basketball game a few years earlier. John's dark skin tone contrasted with hers, and her long blond hair cascaded onto his shoulders as the couple put their heads together for the snapshot. *I miss my hair. I miss John. I miss his arms around me, the way he smells, the way he makes me feel.*

She sighed and picked up Sabiston's *Textbook of Surgery.* It was a massive book, almost eight pounds. She had wanted the more manageable two-volume set, but couldn't afford it. So she settled for the single volume and the added benefit of a biceps workout. She turned to a chapter entitled "Trauma: Management of the Acutely Injured Patient" and quickly lost herself in a discussion of airways, fluid resuscitation, and shock, paying close attention to the yellow highlighted areas from her previous reading.

At ten, the phone jarred her eyes from a gruesome photograph of a man with a crossbow injury to the neck. She welcomed the diversion. "Be John. Be John," she whispered. "Hello."

"I was hoping you'd still be up." The voice was John Cerelli's, deep, calm, and confident. As usual, Claire smiled.

"I'm up. Doubt I'll get to sleep very early. I'm too keyed up."

"I wish I was there." He paused. "As long as you're not sleeping."

"John." Instinctively, she looked at herself in the full-length mirror next to her bed. She pressed her hand against the front of the jersey, bringing it against her stomach. She was pleased with what she saw. She hoped her long hours as a surgical intern wouldn't be too detrimental to her figure.

"What are you wearing?"

"John! Why do you want to know?" She giggled.

"I'm just trying to imagine . . . the football jersey, right?"

"Let's talk about something else. How'd your sales presentation go?"

"You're wearing my jersey again. Admit it."

"So what?"

"I knew it."

"It's comfortable. That's all."

"Right." His voice was laced with playful sarcasm.

After a moment's silence, Claire's voice thickened. "There was a reception tonight for all the new interns."

"Great. Was it fun?"

"Not exactly fun. It was typical superficial cocktail communication. I just went to scope out the attendings." She cleared her throat. "I, uh, didn't wear the wedding band . . ."

"Claire, I thought we'd agreed."

"It—it just didn't seem right. I know what we—"

"Claire, do what you want," he interrupted. "I just thought it would make your life easier if you didn't have to fend off hordes of men. We're almost married anyway. A ring, or a piece of paper, won't make us any more married, you know." She had heard this tone of voice from John before. The hurt, the sarcasm, rolled too easily off his tongue.

"I know, John. And I am committed, you know that. And I'm not fending off hordes of men."

"You should be," he sulked. "Fending them off, I mean."

"I don't know anyone up here to fend off. Even if I did, I'd be too busy. Why don't you just move up here now? Then we wouldn't be having this conversation."

"You're asking me to move up? Now?" He paused. "I seem to remember that you're the one who insisted on this separation, time for you to get your head together after graduation."

"The separation *was* my idea. But it was a head decision, not a heart one."

"What's that supposed to mean?"

"It means I think we need to be apart, at least for a while. But it doesn't mean that I thought I'd enjoy it. With my head, I think it's right. With my heart, well, I get mixed up."

She heard him sigh into the phone. "I wish you'd get your organs together up there. Your heart and your head, I mean."

She looked in the mirror again and edged the hem of John's jersey higher on her thigh. "I just need to know that you're as interested in our relationship as you are in how I look in this jersey."

"And how can I prove that if you won't let me visit?"

I shouldn't have to spell it out. "Call me. Write to me. Pray for me. Be there when I cry. This is going to be the toughest year of my life, John. I need to know you're supporting me."

He sighed again. "Okay, baby. I'm going to try."

"I know." She softened and changed the subject. "Everyone keeps asking about my father. It's like the second or third question in every conversation. 'So, what does your father do?' It's like they think a woman couldn't make it in surgery without her father's coattails."

"They're just making conversation. Probably don't know what else to ask. What do you tell them?"

"Uh. Well. I ignore the question half the time. Sometimes I make a joke about him being the dean of some medical school." She yawned. "I told a few that he's retired military."

John laughed. "Oh, that's rich."

"It's not exactly lying. He was in the military once."

"Whatever."

"It's really none of their business," she huffed. "And it certainly wouldn't help me through this pyramid if they knew the truth."

Ugh. The pyramid again. She didn't know why she'd brought it up. She didn't want to think about it.

"I miss you."

"Ditto, girl. I'm going nuts here alone."

"John, I'm scared. You should see the rest of the new interns. They act like walking textbooks."

"You're not intimidated by that stuff. You're better than most of them. I can tell you that without even meeting 'em. You know why you're there. And you wouldn't be there if it wasn't right." He paused. "This is your calling, remember?"

"I don't know. Maybe this wasn't such a good idea. I'm not sure I can do this. I could come back to Virginia . . . take that family medicine spot they offered. . . ."

"You wouldn't be happy. You were born to do this. You can't tell me you don't believe that. I must have heard you say it a thousand times."

Claire sighed. She knew it was true. But hearing him repeat it back sure sounded nice. "You really believe it?"

"Every word."

"I love you, John."

"You too," he said. "Tomorrow's your big day. Get some sleep."

"I'll try."

"Night."

"Good night."

Click.

Claire ran her finger over the small picture frame on the desk, staring for a moment at the image. She dabbed her eyes with the sleeve of the jersey and plodded to the bathroom to brush her teeth.

She set the alarm for five and collapsed into the comfort of her double bed. She lay still for a moment, thinking of John, lonely for his touch. *I shouldn't be missing him this much. Not yet. It's gonna be a long internship without him.*

She closed her eyes in a forced attempt to silence her longing and to quiet her anxieties about the start of her surgical training. Tomorrow would come too soon.

Tomorrow, for the first time, she would put her medical degree to the test.

Chapter Four

July 1, 2000

The next morning, Claire's eyes were open at four-thirty. So much for needing her alarm. She showered, applied her makeup, and put on a pair of scrubs she'd obtained during her orientation. As she passed the mirror, she smiled. *I'll probably not have this much time to get ready in the future. The boys on the trauma service better not expect me to look this good every day.*

After a breakfast of generic bran flakes, she readied her on-call supplies and began a systematic nurturing of her houseplants, all twenty-three of them. She had scaled back her obsession with plants since her college days, having given most of them away before she moved. But in the last two months, she'd started over a dozen African violets, most of which she kept under a special UV light in her small apartment kitchen. She meticulously watered each one, proud of the care she'd been able to provide. The last one, a thirty-inch-high jade plant, was her favorite, the only one she'd kept since high school.

She made it to the university hospital before dawn but still arrived after Beatrice Hayes and Howard Button, who were chatting nervously outside the double automatic doors to the SICU. A few minutes later, they were joined by Wayne Neal. It was obvious to Claire that Wayne and Howard were as nervous as she felt. Beatrice, however, was the picture of calm. Her hair and makeup were perfect. With an air of confidence, she displayed her patient data cards.

"I have a card for every patient on the service." She held up the three-by-five cards for everyone to see. "I have a problem list, the record numbers, and their current meds."

Claire looked at the small, immaculate printing on the cards and resisted the urge to roll her eyes.

Wayne feigned disinterest, but Howard stumbled forward for a closer look. "Wow." He patted his empty lab coat pocket. "Do you have any extra cards?"

Beatrice apparently didn't feel his question worthy of a response, and quickly turned her attention to another group of four who had gathered a few feet away in the hall: medical students. In contrast to the new interns, the students appeared battle-weary, with stained scrubs, wrinkled lab coats, and unwashed hair. There were three males and one female, and all were holding steaming cups of coffee. The tallest of the four held two cups. In a moment, Claire understood why.

Silence fell over the group when they saw Dr. Dan and his entourage approach. He seemed like a proud mother mallard, with his ducklings following obediently behind. In order, Claire recognized the house staff from her orientation: Jeff Parrish, fourth-year resident, Elaine Kirklin, third-year resident, and Basil Roberts, second-year resident.

The tall medical student held up the coffee to Dr. Overby. "Dan-the-man! I survived the night."

The chief resident beamed. "I knew you would, Rick. Did you remember to eat?"

"Eat when you can," the student responded, quoting Dan's first rule of survival.

The female medical student coughed. "If you consider crackers and coffee in the CT scanner a meal, we ate."

"Crackers are good," Basil responded. "But"—he raised his index finger as if making a serious point—"never use the vending machine in the basement of the nursing dorm." He shook his head in apparent disgust. "I lost seventy-five cents there last week."

Elaine scoffed. "In your dreams, pal. You've never been to the nursing dorm."

Dan held up his hand. "Enough. We've got a lot of ground to cover this morning. It's July first, which means new terns."

The other surgical residents made groaning noises until Dan silenced them with a single glance. He paused for a moment and looked at the interns who remained in a clump near the SICU doors. "And none of them went to school here, so you guys need to show 'em the ropes," he said, addressing the medical students. "Rick, Sally, Josef, and Glen, meet Howard, Wayne, Beatrice, and Claire."

The two groups eyed each other pensively.

"Terns, these are the best medical students you'll see for a while. They are at the end of their third year, and they know the ropes. Don't underestimate the value of an initiated student. They know where everything is, and they know how to get things done." He nodded with appreciation at the ragged group who threw their shoulders back in mock appreciation to their chief. "It won't be like this next month, when we get a green group of third-year students without an ounce of practical experience.

"The team is divided into two halves, covering every other night in house." He smiled at the terns. "That means you don't leave the hospital when you're on. The first half is led by me, and consists of myself, Basil, Beatrice, and Claire, as well as two students, Josef and Glen. The second half is led by Jeff, and consists of him, Elaine, Howard, Wayne, and the two students, Rick and Sally. Since Jeff's team was on last night, he will lead rounds this morning. Every service works a little different, depending on what chief resident is running the show. I like to make discovery rounds in the morning, which means the terns don't have to pre-round to find out how the patients are doing. We'll discover that as a group when we go around. As much as we can, we'll let the interns write their daily notes while on rounds, because, as soon as the ER starts paging, we'll have limited time to get the daily grunt work done." He looked at Bea and Claire. "As for you two, I'd suggest splitting the daily scut list until we get the first hit in the ER. Then one of you will be responsible for writing up the new admissions, and one of you should man the floor work until it's all done."

Jeff Parrish tapped his shoe impatiently. "In the morning, we have resident rounds. In the evening, usually right before supper, we have attending rounds. During attending rounds, the interns will present the new patients, and the students will give the daily progress reports on the patients already on the service. Any questions?"

The interns responded with blank stares.

Dan shrugged his massive round shoulders. "You'll get the hang of it soon enough. Don't worry."

Claire forced herself to nod. *Now there's a novel idea: don't worry. I wish I had some Pepcid AC.*

"We've got to get moving," Jeff prodded. "We got five new players last night to tell you about."

With that, the team moved en masse through the automatic double doors into the ordered world of the Surgical Intensive Care Unit.

Four hours later, Claire smoothed the lapels of her white lab coat and looked down at her picture ID pinned to the jacket pocket. "E. Claire McCall, MD," she whispered, reading the name tag. *This is what I've been waiting for, training for, all these years.* She touched the pager clipped to the waistband of her scrubs and walked forward down the broad hallway leading to the med-surg nursing station, conscious that she was pulling her shoulders back in a confident pose. She slipped behind the counter and gathered the patients' charts to review. To her right, her assigned medical student, Josef Cohen, diligently transferred the morning lab values onto a clipboard so he could memorize them before attending rounds. He was compulsive to a fault and seemed knowledgeable, but appeared quiet on rounds, only speaking when asked a question and then only quietly. Perhaps he was only shy, but his inability to speak up would certainly bias his attendings against giving him an excellent evaluation.

"Josef, what field do you want to go into?"

He looked up and responded with the first hint of excitement Claire had seen in him. "Surgery."

She smiled, wanting to give him some pointers on his form, but quelled the urge. Maybe he was only having an off day.

Just then, a nurse appeared at Claire's elbow. "Dr. McCall?" The nurse, many years senior to Claire, held up a patient chart and opened it to the physician's order page. "Mr. Jones in 518 is complaining of a headache. Can I give him some Tylenol?"

Claire took the chart from the nurse, refreshing her memory of just who Mr. Jones was. *Hmmm. Fifty-eight-year-old male with a right chest tube to treat a punctured lung sustained in a fall from a ladder two days ago. His only other medical history is significant for hypertension. Interestingly, he was on treatment for pneumonia at the time of his injury.*

Claire felt her palms dampen. It would be her first official doctor's order. She looked at the nurse, who towered above her. "Any mental status changes?"

The nurse shook her head and took a deep, audible breath.

"Any change in blood pressure or heart rate?"

"No."

Claire looked at Josef to explain, hoping to make a teaching point. "Mr. Jones was in a fall. Perhaps his headache is due to an intracranial bleed. It could cause hypertension and bradycardia."

Josef shifted in his seat. "Oh."

Claire continued. "How does he describe the headache? The worst he's ever had?" Without waiting for the nurse's response, she turned again to Josef. "Intracranial berry aneurysms are associated with hypertension, which Mr. Jones has. A rupture of the aneurysm is often described by the patient as 'the worst headache I've ever had.'"

The nurse checked her watch. "No, it's not the worst headache he's ever had. It's just a tension headache." She flipped the chart back to the physician's order page.

"How about fever? Or a stiff neck? He could have developed a meningitis. Meningitis is associated with headache."

"Dr. McCall, he isn't febrile."

"Any visual disturbance? A migraine headache can be associated with visual changes, and migraines don't usually respond to Tylenol."

"It's only a tension headache. He gets them all the time at work."

Claire stared at the order sheet. *The headache could be some rare reaction to a medication that he's on.* She flipped to the medication list. *Hmmm. He's only on Tylox for pain, and Unasyn for his pneumonia. I don't think they cause headache.* "I suppose giving some Tylenol would be okay," she responded with more confidence than she felt. She couldn't quite dispel her worry that Mr. Jones might be suffering from some intracranial tragedy related to his accident. "Josef, could you look at Mr. Jones for me? Look in his eyes. Make sure there isn't any papilledema . . . you know, signs of brain swelling."

Now Josef audibly sighed, but stood obediently to find an ophthalmoscope to look into Mr. Jones's eyes.

Claire continued her careful inspection of Mr. Jones's chart. "Let me just make sure that Tylenol won't interact with his other medications." *Is there any known reaction between Tylenol and his antibiotic? Not that I know of, but I've never been asked before.* She looked up to see Dan Overby coming up the hall. She remembered Dan's rule number three*: If you don't know, ask.* She caught his eye. "Dan?"

Before she could ask about the drug interaction, the exasperated nurse turned to the chief resident. She lifted the chart from Claire's hands and addressed Dr. Overby. "Mr. Jones in 518 has a headache. May I give some Tylenol?"

"Sure. Six-hundred-fifty milligrams every four hours as needed," he responded as he wrote the order. "He's also on Tylox, as I recall, so be careful not to give the Tylenol within a few hours of the Tylox. They both have acetaminophen, you know."

The nurse tossed a quick sanctimonious smirk at Claire before marching off.

Dan inhaled deeply. "Aah. The first day of surgical training. A new beginning. A new dawn." He looked down at Claire. "What was it you wanted?"

She winced. "Nothing."

Dan shrugged and walked off toward the elevators. "By the way, a drug rep brought some donuts to the surgical residents' lounge. Better get some calories while you can."

Claire felt her face redden and was glad to see her jolly chief resident disappear behind an elevator door. *My first doctor's order was for an over-the-*

counter drug that mothers all over the world give to their children every day . . . and I was too scared to order it!

Josef returned from Mr. Jones's room. "No papilledema. No signs of any intracranial problem. Mental status, vital signs all check out okay."

She looked up but didn't meet his eyes. "Thanks for looking."

The medical student leaned forward and spoke softly. "You know, you can trust Lucille," he said, referring to the nurse. "She's been here a long time."

Claire nodded, and thought of Dan's second rule: *Everyone teaches a tern.*

Josef continued, "If you put yourself through that every time a nurse asks you for Tylenol, you'll be insane in a week." He paused and put his hand on her shoulder.

She resisted the impulse to shake it free.

"You wouldn't be here if you weren't smart, Dr. McCall," he said, "but don't let your brains get in the way of making a no-brainer clinical decision."

Trying not to show her embarrassment at being corrected by a med student, she attempted to salvage her image. "A missed intracranial hemorrhage would have had disastrous consequences for the patient." *Not to mention providing a quick exit for me . . . right off the pyramid.*

She looked straight ahead and grabbed for the next chart on her list. *Now please leave so I can find a hole to crawl into!*

After supper, the trauma team logged three hits—or three new players, as Dan called them. A motorcycle crash during evening rush hour provided the first business. Then, just after midnight, a two-vehicle head-on prompted the team back into action, consuming Beatrice and Claire with write-ups, IVs, and tracking down and recording numerous X rays and lab tests.

Because Dan was a firm believer in the "see one, do one, teach one" philosophy, he carefully instructed Claire while inserting a chest tube on the motorcycle victim, then walked her through the same procedure for another patient later that night, with Claire using the scalpel.

Proudly, she entered the patient's name and medical record number in her procedure logbook. In one twenty-four-hour time period, her emotions had ranged from humiliation to pumped. She had attempted four IVs, started three, and changed one arterial line on a patient in the SICU. From what she'd seen of Beatrice's skill in sewing up a scalp laceration, Claire, at least in her own mind, held a clear advantage in the area of technical skills. Later, when she saw Beatrice blow an IV that a student eventually started, she recognized the same distasteful pride resurfacing. *This is ridiculous,* she chided herself. *I've got enough to worry about without constantly comparing myself to the other interns . . . and it's just our first day!*

Claire survived attending rounds with Dr. McGrath, head of the trauma surgery service, and avoided any first-day snafus. She was intimidated by but warming to Dr. Dan's rough exterior, and tried to keep an open mind about his peculiarities. By the next morning's rounds, she teetered on a precarious emotional edge, thrust there by her own anxiety, sleep deprivation, and excitement over her first minor procedures. With her med students' help, she had survived her first night of trauma call, and had the haggard appearance to prove it.

Only one more patient, and she could revive herself with a shower. There was light at the end of the tunnel. At the end of morning rounds, she would hand the pager to another intern and be free. She had held her own. She could do this. One day down. Only 1,825 to go.

Josef began the presentation, while Claire became a quick scribe to write the daily progress note. "Mr. Adams is a forty-four-year-old white male admitted with closed head injury and a sternal fracture. He is hospital day two on observation for myocardial contusion." The medical student paused and fumbled through the bedside nursing data before continuing. "His blood pressure has been stable. His ins total 2800 cc's and his outs were 2100 cc's."

"Wait a minute." Dan Overby held up his hand. "Go to the nurse's recording of the heart rate." His eyes were riveted to the patient's overhead cardiac monitor. "How long's his heart rate been this high?" The monitor registered 162.

"Looks like two hours."

"Who was told about this?"

"I was," Claire offered, ready to take credit for her management. "I had the nurses get a twelve-lead EKG, but I couldn't tell whether he was in sinus tach, paroxysmal atrial tachycardia, or atrial flutter."

She sensed Dan's eyes boring in on her face. "So?" he asked. There was tension in his voice.

"If you don't know, ask," Claire responded by quoting Dan's third rule of survival. "I consulted cardiology to sort it out." When she saw Dan's clenched jaw, she fumbled forward. "Basil was tied up in the SICU, and I knew you'd just gotten to bed, so . . ."

Dan turned to the patient and laid his stethoscope on his chest. After a few moments of quiet conversation with the patient, Dan placed his right hand over the patient's neck and began to massage the area beside his voice box. In a few moments, the rhythm abruptly reverted to a slower, regular rate of eighty-two.

Satisfied, Dan looked at the group. "This man was in P.A.T. Carotid sinus massage helps distinguish the rhythms. Just make sure you've got resuscitation equipment handy before you try it," he added as he strode from the room.

The group followed. Once in the hallway, Dan's collectedness dissolved. He gave curt instructions to Jeff Parrish to cancel the consult, before turning on Claire. "Never, never call a medicine consult on my patients without talking to me! Especially not the first week of July! You'd probably get an intern who knows even less than you do!" He turned and walked away a few steps before pivoting. "Rule number four: *Keep the fleas away from my patients!*"

Speechless, Claire winced, stifling the urge to cry. She wanted to dissolve into the floor.

Josef watched the big man disappear down the hall. "I think he likes you."

Basil shrugged and slapped Claire's shoulder in a good-ole-boy gesture. "Hey, that's the way we learn."

"Tomorrow, six A.M.," Jeff snapped, dismissing the team. "My squad will take it from here."

Claire stood numbly observing the medical students heading toward the cafeteria. *Tomorrow? If I decide to return. Right now I'd rather die than face that man again.*

Chapter Five

Claire stared at the red light and tapped the steering wheel, whispering the phrase of an old song. She did it almost by rote. It was a phrase she'd whispered many times before, hoping for comfort when there was none to be found. "Everything's gonna be all right. Just you wait and see. Everything's gonna be all right."

The phrase peeled off a scabbed-over memory, and immediately, she was transported to a time of earlier humiliation. She'd relived this one dozens of times before. A smell could bring it back. Burning popcorn. The sour smell of old beer. Or humiliation, like her experience with Dr. Dan.

Sixteen-year-old Claire had heard her father before she'd seen him, his irregular footfalls landing on the wooden back porch without rhythm, the erratic stumbling of a man in love with rum. He entered, his body swaying, never still even when he attempted to sit. He moved like a man swimming through the air, hands and legs in constant motion, his feet feeling and testing before actually coming to rest for any given step. It appeared as if each movement were practiced three or four times before he could follow through and get it right, or almost right. Claire winced when she saw him, conscious of the anxiety he provoked. In the previous year, since he'd lost his job at the mill, a change, a cloud had enveloped him, slowly overtaking anything she'd loved in him. He grew dark, moody, flying off into irrationality, screaming at the least problem.

Clay, her twin brother, was making popcorn. He was practiced in trying to appease his old man.

Claire helped her father to a chair in the den, inhaling the odor of his sweat and alcohol. Clay brought him a bowl. Popcorn with salt, no butter, just the way he liked it.

In a minute, the bowl was on the floor, their father cursing loudly about the burnt taste.

When Clay disagreed, their father exploded, throwing first the bowl and then a kitchen chair through the front window.

Claire followed Clay out onto the front lawn, where he retreated from the conflict. Broken glass and popcorn littered the sidewalk. Methodically, she cleaned up the mess and stapled plastic over the front window.

She found Clay hiding in the old tree house that overlooked the mountains. There, she stroked his head and whispered, "Everything's gonna be all right. Just you wait and see. Everything's gonna be all right."

And even then, Claire had known it was a lie.

She stiffened, shook her head in disgust, and tried to concentrate on the traffic signal in front of her. She was over this. There was little to be gained by obsessing over the past. Use it as a stepping-stone. The past, even our worst humiliations, can be used to strengthen us for future greatness. At least that's what her counselor back in Brighton had said. "You're over this, Claire. Don't let the memories of your father's abuse paralyze you. Put it behind you. Put *him* behind you. Use your wounds to realize your potential. You can do anything."

She turned left onto Devonshire Boulevard and counted the traffic lights. At the fifth, she turned right, then immediately turned right again, up the alley, and skirted behind the Safeway until she reached Thompson Street. She'd stumbled onto this shortcut by accident, during her house hunt. From there, she crossed the street at a diagonal and entered her driveway.

She plodded into the house and took inventory of her first day as a real medical doctor. She hadn't been able to bring herself to give a Tylenol order for a man with a headache. She'd been guided by a shy medical student whom she was supposed to be helping, and had been ripped apart by her chief resident for calling a medicine consultation without asking. She hadn't slept, hadn't even seen a call room; her makeup was long gone, her stomach empty, and her life lonely in a big city far from anyone she cared about. She looked in the bathroom mirror and started to cry.

She was still crying when she checked her phone messages ten minutes later. She had one call. It was her mother. "Your father's back in AA. Finally." There was a pause with a clicking sound. Claire could see her mother's polished nails tapping against the kitchen counter, something she'd done as long as Claire could remember. "I think he's serious this time." She paused again. "But he's still so jerky. He's having more and more trouble with his walking. But don't suggest taking him to a doctor. Lord knows he won't accept that. He keeps saying how sorry he was about your last visit. He really would like to see you again." A pause, with more fingernail clicking. "Call when you get in. Bye."

"Like I believe that." Claire spoke loudly, with sarcasm. *He doesn't care about me.*

Claire hadn't lived with her father since the summer he threw the kitchen chair through the front window. Three days later, after an argument with Clay, he'd discharged a shotgun through the same window, still covered by black plastic. Clay was on the front stoop at the time, and took a shotgun pellet through his left calf. Wally, her father, spent a night in the county jail to sober up, but was released because it all looked like an accident. Claire hadn't been home when it happened, but doubted her father's ability to comprehend the real truth. Claire found herself in the middle of a constant battleground with a man with little patience and explosive anger. Her older sister, Margo, eloped at eighteen—anything to get out of the house. Della, afraid of her husband's temper and his apparent return to the bottle, urged Clay to move in with a cousin out of dread that the next accident wouldn't be so minor.

Fear and embarrassment over her father's irrational public behavior pushed Claire to withdraw from her family. Finally, with her tolerance at its limit, she jumped at the opportunity to move in with her mother's mother, Sarah Newby. She dropped out of high school when her grandmother became ill, giving most of her attention to the daily care of her grandmother's medical problems. Claire watched her grandmother's diet, gave her insulin shots for her diabetes, and carefully dressed her leg ulcers. It was during her time with Grandma Newby that Claire had felt the first stirring of desire for a career in medicine.

After her grandmother's death, Claire had worked first as a waitress, then in Dr. Jenkins' office—then, after taking night EMT classes, volunteered on the Stoney Creek rescue squad. She studied for her GED, then went to Brighton for college and medical school. She had proven everyone in Stoney Creek wrong. She was the first female from her community to get an MD. She was in debt to her earlobes, with over 120,000 dollars in outstanding school loans. But she'd done it—after everyone had said Wallace McCall's kids would never amount to anything.

But right now, her goal of becoming the first woman surgeon from Stoney Creek seemed impossibly far-fetched. She'd failed at ordering a Tylenol tablet! How could she possibly feel comfortable cutting someone open?

She ignored her mother's phone message and collapsed in a heap on the bed she'd left unmade the morning before. Exhaustion drove her to sleep.

At noon she pried herself from the sheets, knowing she wouldn't sleep tonight if she didn't get up.

She changed into shorts and a tank top and picked up her pepper spray. She would go for a long jog—and decide whether to return to the Mecca in the morning.

Della McCall pulled into the parking lot outside the administrative offices of the shoe factory bearing her name. It was her husband's name, actually, and if the truth be known, his name was the only similarity between Wally and his father, John McCall, founder of the McCall Shoe Company. Wally had been expected to join in the family business, but that had never worked. Leon, Wally's younger brother, had toed the line, and had inherited the helm of the operation when Robert retired a decade ago. Wally, on the other hand, had played the rebel, partying his way through life, in and out of work, and in and out of his father's favor. That Della worked here was due to a minor family miracle and the grace of brother Leon, who admired her stamina and hired her as an administrative assistant, knowing his brother would not, or apparently could not, provide for his own.

She hated the idea that she worked for the McCalls out of sympathy, but other work near Stoney Creek was tough to find, and practicality won out.

What she hated even more were the rumors that circulated through the factory—rumors about her husband, and why she stayed with him. Exaggerated rumors about his drinking and abuse. Last week, she'd overheard one of the janitors talking at the water cooler. He'd laughed and said that Della only stayed with Wally in hopes of getting the McCall money. She'd almost come around the corner and confronted the gossip head-on. Instead, she had bit her tongue and stayed quiet, less afraid of the rumor than she was of telling the truth.

She saw the same janitor as she closed her car door. "Morning, Fred," she said.

"Morning, Mrs. McCall." He waved and grinned.

At least he shows respect to my face. She remembered his comments at the water cooler. *If he only really knew. What's really amazing is not that I stay with Wally, but that he stuck with me.*

She entered the building and took the stairs to the third floor. She always took the stairs. Her continual avoidance of the elevator was just one more skirmish in her successful battle of the bulge.

On the third floor, she walked to the end of the hall and entered the upscale suite that included Leon McCall's office and those of two vice presidents. Here, plush carpeting replaced the linoleum or concrete seen in the rest of the building. The smell of fresh coffee greeted her. Charlene Benson was typing rapidly at a computer terminal. She looked up. "Mr. McCall was asking for you."

"Thanks, Charlene. Did you finish the payroll?"

"Almost. The checks should be coming off the laser printer in Mr. McCall's office."

"Good."

Della walked past Charlene and knocked on a heavy oak door. She pushed it open slowly. Leon was on the phone. He motioned her in. He was the picture of a polished gentleman, the spitting image of his father, who had pushed the shoe factory to its present position as the most successful manufacturing business in the Apple Valley. Behind his desk hung a heavy, ornamented oil portrait of John McCall, the company's founder and Leon's father, adding to the starchy feel of the wood-paneled room.

After a minute, he put the phone in its cradle. "Thanks for stopping in. I'm worried about Mom." He watched her for a moment, then gestured to a padded chair. "Have you seen her lately?"

She glanced at the image in the painting, an image that could easily be mistaken for the man in front of her. She shook her head. "Not for a few weeks." She sighed. "Ever since Claire's graduation, she's been very difficult around Wally. All she wants to do is talk about getting him free from the curse. It's very upsetting to him. He doesn't want to see her anymore."

Leon nodded. "She's talked to me about it, too. She wants me to intervene, to talk him into seeing a priest or someone. I don't really understand. I was hoping you could shed some light on it for me." His tone was stiff, which was not unusual for him. He treated everyone, even his wife, with the same objective formality.

"Oh, come on, Leon. You've heard this stuff before. She believes in the old town curse, just like all the rest of her generation around here." She tapped her nails on his walnut desk.

"She feels guilty. Responsible."

"Mothers of alcoholics often feel guilt."

"But this is unlike her." He shook his head. "Maybe it's been there all along but it's just now showing itself, without Dad to keep her in check."

"He overshadowed everyone, Leon. Elizabeth found her identity in Robert for a long, long time. Give her some time, maybe things will even out." Passivity was a life philosophy for Della, the way she treated every problem. Just wait it out long enough. It's bound to get better sooner or later.

Leon rolled an unlit cigar between his palms. "Maybe so." He shifted in his seat and leaned forward. "How's Wally?"

"Not good. He may not be drinking, but his problems haven't gone away."

"Look, Della, I don't want to pry, but you've got to get the man some help. He's going downhill. It doesn't take a rocket scientist to—"

"Leon, I've talked to him till I'm blue in the face. He won't see a doctor. He's afraid of what they'll say."

Leon paused, studying her. "Tell me the truth. It's not that he won't see any doctor. He just doesn't trust Dr. Jenkins. Am I right?"

Della felt a chill. *How much does Leon know?* She was caught. How should she answer? "He's never liked Dr. Jenkins."

Leon's eyes bore in on hers. "That's pretty understandable after what the doctor did, don't you think?"

She uncrossed her legs. "What are you getting at? What do you know about this?"

"Only that faced with similar hurtful circumstances, I think I'd make the same choice as Wally."

"Wally *told* you?" Until this moment, she had never thought her confession would travel outside their marriage. Wally had always been far too proud to admit to something like that. She'd been sure he would take her secret to the grave.

Leon nodded slowly. "Of course. I'm his brother. He was merely trying to sort through his feelings."

"That was a long time ago. Past history."

"Wally has a good memory."

"He's also very forgiving."

"But forgiving someone and regaining trust may be two different things." He held the cigar under his nose and inhaled. "Get Wally to a doctor. If he won't see Dr. Jenkins, take him to a specialist."

"I've tried that, Leon. But the health plan that *your* company signed us up for will only allow us to see a specialist if they are referred by a participating family doctor."

Leon nodded, apparently beginning to grasp Della's dilemma. "And the only one on the list for Stoney Creek is Dr. Jenkins."

"And even if I get around that, I'm still not sure Wally would agree to see another doctor. He thinks they'll just tell him what he already knows: he drinks too much."

"Which seems to be the essence of the Stoney Creek curse."

"Perhaps," she said, standing up. "But I'm sure Elizabeth could enlighten us on that one." She retreated to the printer in the corner of the room and picked up the payroll checks from the tray. She didn't like the tone of this conversation. She felt exposed, as if Leon were implying that she was responsible for Wally's not getting help.

She fumbled with the papers, tapping them gently on top of the printer to straighten them again. She wanted to get back to her desk and forget this conversation.

"I'll come by, talk to Wally. Maybe he'll listen to me." He gently touched the edges of his silver hair. Apparently satisfied that every hair was in place, he smoothed his silk tie against his chest.

"It's never helped before."

"Maybe this time will be different."

She cleared her throat. "Leon," she asked, her eyes on the floor in front of his desk, "does Elizabeth know why Wally won't see Dr. Jenkins?"

"Not from me."

Della felt her stomach knotting. *Good answer, Leon. Vague. Gets you off the hook, but leaves me wondering. You should have been an attorney.* "That's not exactly what I asked." She lifted her eyes, imploring. "Does she know?"

He shrugged. "Wally may have told her."

That possibility had never occurred to Della, but neither had the thought that Wally would share their deepest marital secrets with Leon. She nodded her head slowly.

"Look, Della," he said. "I'm sorry if this conversation has made you uncomfortable, but present circumstances being what they are, I thought it was time to get everything out into the open."

Everything? Not in my lifetime. Not if I have any say in the matter. She lifted the corners of her mouth. It was a polite smile, not a genuine one. "Sure, Leon. You're interested in helping Wally, I'm sure." *Or is it that you'd like to be sure that all the McCall family money is sifted only through your hands?*

She pulled open the large oak door. "I'll be working on the payroll."

Claire checked her watch and slowed her pace. She'd covered the last mile in 7:28, fifteen seconds faster than the one before. It was time for a more leisurely stride. There certainly wasn't any reason to race back to her place just to spend more time alone.

She had chosen a route traversing Foster Park, a wonderful sprawling acreage along the east side of Lafayette, bordering the Danberry River. An asphalt jogging trail meandered for three miles along the river, providing a welcome refuge for Claire and other urban dwellers wanting to escape the sterile city blocks of concrete downtown.

The river here was only a few hundred yards wide, but two or three miles to the east it widened into Oyster Bay which, in turn, emptied into the Atlantic Ocean beyond. Birds were abundant. Claire had counted two great blue herons and a score of Canada geese, and as she rounded the bend, she smiled at a group of children who threw bread to a growing number of seagulls.

It was outside, close to creation, where Claire had always done her soul-searching. Her memories of important decisions seemed inseparably linked with the locations where she'd made them. A decision to return to school to seek a medical education was made at Painter's Lake, just at sunrise, with the sun a brilliant orange ball pushing from the surface of the water. The image of Chimney Rocks, shiny after a surprise rain shower, would forever remind her of her decision to pursue a career in surgery. Her decision to marry John Cerelli was made on a hike to Smith's Mill during peak autumn color. She could point out the exact boulder where she had made up her mind. And her decision to follow Christ was made during a youth retreat at a campfire rally next to Bear Creek Falls.

Running had also become a time of reflection for Claire. Whenever she seemed to be in mental overload, it always seemed to lessen her stress to pound it out on the pavement for a few miles.

Today, like so many times before, she sought an inner reserve, some strength to prod her to continue to her goal. Claire was proud of her self-sufficiency. She reminded herself of the sense of calling that had motivated her toward surgery, and of the hurdles she had already overcome. Slowing to a walk, she picked up a flat stone and threw it out onto the river's surface. It skipped a dozen times before sinking. She stood, watching the spot where it had disappeared from view.

She thought of the pyramid, and of her inadequacies on her first day as a surgical intern. She thought of her relationship with John and how she'd broken the promises she'd made to God to remain pure. She thought about her father and the royal mess he'd made of their family. Here, far from home, she felt isolated and incompetent.

"Oh, God," she whispered, "I haven't slowed down enough to talk to you for a long time. I'm not doing so well on my own."

Chapter Six

Claire arrived at the entrance to the SICU with five minutes to spare. The medical students, Rick Gentry and Sally Barringer, were already there, coffee in hand.

"Hi, guys."

Sally yawned and Rick grunted. "Morning, Dr. McCall."

"Call me Claire."

Sally protested. "Dr. Hayes said we should use professional titles when we're in the hospital."

Rick imitated Beatrice's soft voice. "It fosters professional conduct and establishes the proper authority of the house staff over the medical students."

Claire rolled her eyes. "Believe me, we'll get along fine, even if you call me Claire. I know I'm a doctor. You will be too, soon enough."

"Not unless I survive this rotation," Sally responded, pushing a rebellious strand of blond hair behind her ear.

"You'll survive," Claire said. "I made it. You'll make it."

"Sure," Sally responded. "I'll survive long enough to make it to my internship. And then I'll be eaten alive."

Just like me. Claire nodded numbly and stayed quiet. She couldn't seem to formulate an encouraging response.

Beatrice arrived and curled her lip at Rick. "What happened to you?"

He looked down at his blood-splattered scrub pants. "I spent most of the night holding a retractor so Jeff—er, Dr. Parrish—could do a liver resection."

The remaining members of the team arrived together, and Rick held up a large cup of coffee for the chief resident.

The O-man smiled. "Ah, vitamin C," he said, inhaling the steam rising from the top of the cup. He looked at Jeff Parrish, the fourth-year resident. "Heard you did a liver last night."

Jeff beamed.

"You dog. I baby-sit the largest trauma service in Massachusetts, night after night, and what reward do I get? I'll tell you. Forty-four blunt trauma cases, and only two major abdominal operations in a whole month. You've been here two nights, and you get a liver resection." He huffed. "This stinks."

"It was pretty awesome. We auto-transfused twenty units." He held up his thumb and index finger nearly touching at the tips. "We came this close to cracking the chest."

Dan Overby raised his eyebrows. "Was this case a RANDO?"

"Yep," Jeff said. "My first liver resection."

Sally wrinkled her nose. "Rando?"

Parrish smiled. "Trauma-ese for Resident Ain't Never Done One."

"In terms of patient mortality, it's one up from a RANSO," Basil Roberts, the second-year resident, explained. "Resident Ain't Never Seen One."

"But the highest mortality is from the riskiest patient group of all," Overby added with a ghoulish laugh. "The dreaded ASANSO. Attending Surgeon Ain't Never Seen One."

The students laughed.

Beatrice smiled and sorted her patient data cards.

Howard Button seemed to be writing the initials down.

Dr. Overby held up a patient census. "So he lived?"

"She." Jeff pointed to a name on the census. "ICU bed four."

The chief resident smiled and muttered, "A RANDO, and she still pulled through. That's what it's all about, folks."

"Come on," Jeff added. "We've got rounds to make."

"Not so fast," Overby responded, gesturing for his team to move closer. "First, class, we need to review." His tone was condescending and overdone. "Shall we all recite Overby's rules for survival?" He held up his index finger. "Rule number one," he prompted.

Basil lifted a pack of crackers from his white coat pocket. "Eat when you can."

Overby lifted a second finger.

Claire joined with the group in a jumbled unison, "Everyone teaches a tern."

The chief resident held up three fingers.

"If you don't know, ask."

Overby grinned. "And four?"

Claire felt the color rising in her cheeks. She waited for the response. No one volunteered. Rick laughed. Sally shuffled her notes for rounds.

Dan made a clicking noise with his cheek. "Come now, class. You remember." His eyes rested on Claire. "Keep the fleas . . . ," he prompted, his grin widening.

"Away from my patients!" The group's response was enthusiastic, but hardly in unison, as they stumbled over the exact wording.

Claire tried to focus on her patient cards. She forced a chuckle. "Ha, ha," she mumbled. "Ha, ha." *I can be a good sport, guys, but excuse me if I don't laugh all day.*

Claire forged her way through the day's work with renewed determination. She was a tern. She was there to learn. She would accept criticism and use it to get better. She wouldn't make the same mistake twice.

And, as she worked, she mulled over her own situation as a lonely intern in a powerful surgery program. The way to survive, she convinced herself, was to become a team player. Support the residents above her, teach the students below, and link arms with the interns around her. She wouldn't be the one to back-stab the other interns. If she couldn't be a compassionate friend to the other terns, the year was destined for pure torture. Isolate yourself and die. Forge friendships with the other interns, and you'll have a chance.

She'd decided yesterday, during her soul-searching at Foster Park, to reach out to Bea Hayes. It was a no-brainer. The only two women in the intern group should be friends. Claire would lay aside her first impressions and make an honest attempt to see things through Bea's eyes. She could rise above her own competitive impulses and help Bea to make it, too.

After morning rounds, there were X-ray and lab reports to gather, two chest tubes to pull, and six discharge summaries to dictate. Claire and Beatrice split the work and finished just before rounds with the attending on call, Dr. Stan Fowler. Pulling together, the two women seemed to make an efficient team.

Dr. Fowler was forty, nearly bald, and enjoyed his reputation as a pit bull. The interns had all been warned: *He never lets go except to get a bigger bite.*

The team walked into the ICU in pecking order. Dr. Fowler led the way, with the chief resident, Dan Overby, on his heels. The second-year resident, Basil Roberts, was next, followed by the interns, Beatrice Hayes and Claire. The students, Josef Cohen and Glen Mattingly, brought up the rear.

They approached the first bed, occupied by Sid Johnson, a twenty-two-year-old male, five days out from a gunshot wound to the abdomen. He was Josef's patient, so he started the presentation. "Mr. Johnson is five days status post small bowel resection, splenectomy, left nephrectomy, and colostomy for injuries sustained in a gunshot wound to the abdomen. Over the last twenty-four hours, his T-max has been 101.6 Fahrenheit. His other vital signs have been stable. He has been—"

Dr. Fowler interrupted. "What are the most common causes for post-operative fever?" His eyes darted around the group. The chief resident was calm. This was clearly not a chief level question, at least not yet. Typically, the attending starts at the bottom of the pecking order. He squinted at the name tag of the blond student at his right. "Dr. Mattingly?" All were aware that he was according the students a special honor to address them as *doctor.*

"Infection."

Fowler nodded. "What type?"

The student shrugged and offered, "Infection in the surgical wound."

"I'll accept that, but what's the most common postoperative infection?"

Glenn stayed quiet. The attending looked at Josef. "What would you say, Dr. Cohen?"

"Pneumonia."

"Wrong. That's another possibility, but not the most common." He looked at Beatrice. "Enlighten the students, Dr. Hayes."

"Urinary tract infection."

"Correct."

Beatrice smiled.

"Why don't you explain the most common causes of fever in the surgical patient, starting with the first day post-op?"

As Beatrice answered the question, Claire reviewed all the possible causes of post-op fever. Eventually, the question would be bumped to her, if the other intern failed. After a few moments, Beatrice paused.

The attending surgeon prompted, "Any other causes?"

Beatrice hesitated, looking at the floor.

Claire jumped in to assist. "I can think of two more, both possibilities caused by our interventions. One is line sepsis. The other is drug fever."

Fowler nodded. "Very good."

Claire relaxed a notch—until she caught the expression on Bea's face. Her teeth were clenched and her eyes bore in on Claire's. After Josef was allowed to continue his presentation, the attending examined the patient and gave instructions for the team. As they moved to the next bed, Claire felt a tug on the back of her lab coat. She turned to see Bea's reddened face.

Bea motioned her to move away a few steps, then spoke with quiet tension. "Try not to interrupt, Claire. That was my question."

Claire shrugged and returned a whisper. "I was only trying to help. I thought you were done."

Bea rolled her eyes. "Don't try to be so helpful. Try keeping your mouth shut."

Claire watched as the team moved on toward the next patient. She stood by herself momentarily, stunned by the reproach. She choked back an uncivil response and shook her head.

So much for camaraderie in the trenches.

In general, Claire learned, the chief residents were classified as either "walls" or "sieves." A "wall" is a resident who refuses patient admissions. Patients have to be critically sick or dying to deserve an inpatient spot on a wall's service. The patients, if they are admitted at all, will be "turfed" to another service. A "sieve" is a resident who admits all comers, regardless of the nature of the patient complaints.

For an intern, having a wall above them means a certain amount of protection from being overworked. A sieve above you almost guaranteed countless hours of scut work and sleep deprivation.

Dan Overby was a classic sieve. His extreme level of competence in internal medicine made him a ready target for patient transfers from other medical services. His pride in his own ability prevented him from ever saying no to a patient admission, even one that seemed nonsurgical. Every area of medicine seemed to fall under the umbrella of the O-man's expertise.

The attending physicians loved him.

The interns endured him. On the nights when the trauma service had a moment to breathe, Dan would surf the ER, looking for general surgery cases.

By eleven P.M., after eighteen hours of call, Claire was beginning to think she might see the inside of a call room. She was just leaving the ER when she heard his voice.

"Hey, Claire."

She turned to see the chief resident with his finger pointing to a name on a large washable marker board. He picked up a chart from the rack. "I smell a case." He smiled. "An intern case."

She walked toward him and held out her hand. She was tired, but never too tired for a chance to operate. "What've you got?"

"Thirteen-year-old boy with right lower quadrant pain."

She brightened. "Appendicitis?"

"You decide. You're the doctor." He lowered his voice. "If you wait for the new intern on ER call, you may have to wait another two hours before they figure this out. If you help them out by seeing a patient before they ask, they'll look out for you."

Claire accepted the chart and walked to the ninth cubicle. She knocked on the door and entered. Inside, a young man reclined on a stretcher, surrounded by what Claire assumed was his family. She counted three adults and two more children in the cramped examining room. She made eye contact with a woman sitting on a stool beside the patient. "Hi. I'm Dr. McCall, with the department of surgery." She held out her hand.

The woman, wearing a Boston College sweatshirt and blue jeans, took Claire's hand. "Surgery? Does Jeremy need surgery?"

"That's what I'm here to find out." She looked at the boy on the stretcher. His eyes were wide and his hands were resting over his lower abdomen.

"When did you get sick, Jeremy?"

He looked at his mother before answering. "Yesterday."

"Does your stomach hurt?"

He nodded without speaking.

Claire could feel every eye in the room watching. She tried a more open-ended question, attempting to get more than a word out of the boy.

"Tell me in your own words what has been going on."

He looked at his mother again.

"Go ahead, Jeremy. The doctor needs to know," his mother coached.

"I got sick at school, after lunch. I think it was the pizza."

Claire studied him for a moment. Open-ended questions obviously weren't designed for this thirteen-year-old boy. "Where did the pain start? Can you show me?" She lifted his shirt to expose his abdomen.

"Here." He pointed to his navel.

"Has it moved? Point with one finger to the spot it hurts the most."

He moved his finger down, pressing and wincing as he looked for the worst location. He stopped in his right lower abdomen and pointed. "Here."

Claire recognized the spot as "McBurney's point," from the classic description of appendicitis. She pressed gently on the spot and watched his face. She quickly lifted her hand.

Jeremy grabbed her hand. "Ow!"

"What's your favorite food, Jeremy?"

"Ice cream."

"If I could get you a bowl of ice cream right now, would you want it?"

He shook his head. "I'm not hungry."

Claire suppressed the urge to smile. So far this boy was textbook. She was about to reel in her first abdominal surgery case.

She completed the interview and the exam and ordered a complete blood count and a urinalysis. If his white blood count was high, she would call the O-man and lay claim to her first appendix.

She felt her heart quicken as she slipped a small book from her lab-coat pocket. She opened *The Surgical Resident's Companion* to a section on appendicitis and reviewed the operative procedure.

Thirty minutes later, armed with the lab work to confirm her suspicions of the need for surgery, she presented the case to Dan. He, in turn, examined the patient, and called the attending on call, Stan Fowler.

Dan hung up the phone and looked at Claire. "Dr. Fowler will be in to help do the case. He always scrubs in with the interns. And he likes to ask questions."

She thought about rounds. "So I've seen."

"I was just at the OR a few minutes ago. You'll probably get to do the case right after the neuro boys finish up with their crainy." Dan squinted to the back corner of the emergency room.

Claire followed his eyes. A man wearing a large bandage around his head stumbled forward toward a stretcher following Beatrice Hayes. The student, Glen Mattingly, appeared to be wrestling with the man, coaxing him forward.

She immediately recognized the wide-based walk, so characteristic of her father. The man's arms seemed to flail randomly into the sky. Glen ducked and put his arm around the patient's waist.

Dan tilted his head toward the action. "Why don't you give 'em a hand. Looks like they got themselves a winner."

The last thing Claire felt like doing was lending a helping hand to Bea. She clenched her jaw. "Sure," she responded, choking back her feelings. "On my way."

As she approached, Bea pointed at the stretcher and raised her voice. "Okay, Mr. Davis. Get on the stretcher and lie down."

The man appeared to be shaking his head. His left arm flung forward as he fell onto the stretcher. His hand struck Bea's buttocks.

Bea's eyes flared. "Watch it, buster!"

The patient's speech was slurred. "Sh sorry."

Claire stepped forward. "Can I help?"

Bea looked up and groaned. "Just another of Lafayette's finest."

Claire put on a pair of gloves and began to unwrap the bloody bandage from the patient's forehead.

Bea began opening up a sterile suture tray. "The ER resident said he has a long scalp laceration." She looked at the medical student. "Draw his blood. I want to send off a blood alcohol level."

The patient's head continued to bob. His words were slurred, but understandable. "I–I don't drink."

Bea rolled her eyes. "And I'm Oprah Winfrey." She pointed to Glen. "Draw the alcohol level."

Glen nodded. "Did you see the size of his chart? Looks like this isn't his first visit."

"A repeat offender."

Claire finished taking off the bandage. The deep laceration ran from the middle of his forehead back into his hair.

Glen put a tourniquet around the patient's upper arm and jabbed a needle into his vein. He deftly drew the blood and put it into a vacuum tube. "The way he looked when he stumbled in here, I'll bet his alcohol level is way over the legal limit."

Claire frowned. "Was he driving?"

"No. He slipped and hit his head on the edge of the coffee table." Bea pursed her lips. "At least that's his story." She pushed the patient's cheek to the left. "Hold still so I can get a better look."

Mr. Davis's head continued to weave. He appeared to be keeping time to an unheard song.

Bea shoved his head down onto the stretcher. "Hold still!" She looked at the med student. "Hold him down. I'll never get this sewn up with him jerking all over the place!"

Glen attempted to hold Mr. Davis's head. While Bea was prepping the scalp with some iodine solution, the patient's arm swung wide and knocked the edge of the sterile tray, sending the instruments to the floor with a clatter.

Bea cursed and looked at Claire. "Hold his arms!" She looked at her sterile field, now contaminated by the patient's arm, and shook her head. "No, better yet," Bea added, looking at the medical student, "just wrap this guy's head up like it is. If he won't cooperate, he can just live with a big ugly scar for all I care."

Claire watched Bea stomp off in disgust, then turned back toward the patient. There, instead of Mr. Davis, she saw her father. She sighed. "Glen, we can't just wrap this up. It's gaping so widely, it'll take weeks to heal without sutures."

Glen nodded.

"Go get Josef. I'll set up another sterile suture tray. Between the three of us, we can get this fixed up."

Forty-five minutes later, Claire looked up from her work and smiled. The laceration, once jagged edged and oozing, was now closed with a neat row of nylon sutures. Josef and Glen were happier than she was to have the job completed.

Josef rotated his shoulders and groaned. "Man, he may be small, but he's strong. I could barely keep his hands from jerking free."

"I couldn't have done it without you." She looked at her watch. "I need to check with the OR to see if my appendectomy patient is ready."

Glen looked at Mr. Davis. "Nice job, Dr. McCall."

"Could you make sure he's up-to-date on tetanus? And don't let him leave without being sure someone else is behind the wheel."

Claire walked away, a knot tightening in her stomach when she passed the ninth cubicle where her appendicitis patient had been. The space, once occupied by her patient and his family, was now empty. Could he have already been taken to surgery?

She jogged toward the elevator. She couldn't afford to be late to the OR for her first opportunity to do a real case. First impressions with the attendings were too important. Dr. Overby had mentioned that her case would likely follow the craniotomy. Certainly they wouldn't have finished with that by now.

She took the elevator to the fourth floor and strode through the OR door. Donna Pritchard, an OR nurse, sat behind the main desk alone, intent on the computer screen in front of her. "Have they completed the crainy yet?"

"Oh goodness, yes. They've been finished for at least thirty minutes."

"Have they brought the appendectomy patient up?"

Donna tucked a strand of hair beneath her OR cap. "Check room three. They should be about done by now."

"Done? That was *my* case."

Donna shook her head. "You can't keep Dr. Fowler waiting. He'll go right ahead if the resident isn't present."

Claire grabbed a mask and OR cap and hurried down the hall. There, looking over the scrub sink through the window into room four, she saw Dr. Fowler operating, standing opposite another assistant, who stood with her back to Claire.

Claire squinted in disbelief. It was Bea! She was operating on Claire's patient!

Slowly, while clenching her teeth behind her mask, Claire pushed the door open. Dr. Fowler looked up. His tone was as sharp as a surgical scalpel. "Dr. McCall, nice of you to join us. If you work up a case in the future, I expect you to be on time. Fortunately for you, Dr. Hayes was kind enough to step in. Yessiree, and she did a bang-up job of it, too. Her first hot appendix." He stepped back from the table and pulled off his gown. He looked at Bea. "Put in a subcuticular stitch to close. Do you know how to do that?"

"Sure thing, Dr. Fowler."

She was kind enough to step in? She stole my first case while I sewed up her patient in the ER! Claire cleared her throat. "Dr. Fowler," she began timidly, "I was repairing a scalp laceration in the ER. I didn't know they'd brought my patient to the OR."

The attending nodded. "Scalp lacerations can be handled by the med students."

"Not this one, sir. It took two students just to hold the man down."

Dr. Fowler grunted. "Nonetheless, Dr. McCall, your primary responsibility was to your appendicitis patient." He paused. "If you want to be a surgeon, you have to do cases. It's the only way to learn." With that, he balled up his disposable gown and slam-dunked it into a large red garbage bag.

Claire felt her cheeks burn. She was thankful for the surgical mask. "Yes, sir," she responded quietly.

She turned on her heels and stepped back into the main OR hallway, trying not to lose her cool in front of the attending. She slowly unfolded her clenched fists, pulled off her mask, and trudged back to the front desk, shaking her head.

Donna looked up. "He did the case without you, eh?"

"Not exactly," Claire huffed. "The other intern on the service scrubbed in and did the case that I worked up."

"Oh." Donna raised her eyebrows.

Claire sighed. It was one A.M. She had been up since five. She was tired. She was angry. "I'm gonna try and get some sleep."

"There will be other appendectomies, Dr. McCall. You won't remember this long."

"It was going to be my first one." Claire felt her eyes begin to sting. She couldn't let herself cry over a lousy missed appendectomy. Not in front of an OR nurse.

Donna pushed her chair back from the desk and locked eyes with Claire. "I've been here for fourteen years, and I've seen a lot of females in surgery, fighting for a chance to operate in a male-dominated world." She paused. "And I've only seen a few make it through this program."

"I can make it."

"But you won't make it if you pout over every missed appendectomy."

"I'm not p—" Claire's denial caught in her throat. She pressed her hand to her upper lip. What could this nurse know about the pressures

Claire felt as a surgical resident? What did she know about being a doctor? "Okay," she responded. "I'm sure you have an opinion."

"There are two ways for a woman to make it in surgery residency." She held up a finger. "Sleep your way to the top."

Claire's head snapped back.

"Don't look at me like you haven't heard the stories. There are a few powerful men in this program who would love to lay a hand on you. And you have the goods to make it that way."

"I have no intentions of making it to chief resident by sleeping around." She turned to leave.

"You haven't heard the second way."

"I'm listening."

"Be a man."

Claire leaned forward, not speaking.

"There are ten men in your intern group. Beat them by being more of a man than they are."

Claire sighed.

"Not every woman is cut out for this. I'm sure you heard about Lisa Dunn."

Claire shook her head. "No."

Donna raised her eyebrows in surprise. "She was an intern last year. I thought she had what it took. She was brilliant, but after six months, she snapped."

"She quit?"

"Yes. She got gun-shy, didn't trust her instincts."

"Hmm."

"She was frightened."

"Frightened? Why?"

"She claimed she was being threatened, but the word around the hospital was that the girl just got paranoid. She worked way too hard, stayed here even on her nights off."

"As if every other night isn't enough torture."

"You'll do okay, girl. Just be a man." Donna broke her gaze and pulled her chair back up to the OR desk, signaling the end to the conversation.

Claire nodded and walked away. She didn't feel like a man.

And, at this moment, she didn't want to fight like a man.

She plodded numbly toward the emergency room, hoping to find that the med students had taken care of getting Mr. Davis safely home.

Once there, she was greeted by Glen Mattingly, studying a patient record. He shook his head. "I'd never have believed it."

Claire didn't feel like guessing. "What?"

Glen handed her a computer printout of Mr. Davis's labs.

She looked at the alcohol level: "None detected." Her eyes widened. "Are you sure you didn't get his blood sample mixed up with someone else?"

"I don't think so. I gave the blood to the ward clerk myself."

Cliff, a ward clerk with a large dragon tattoo on his forearm, leaned over the counter. He'd obviously been listening. "And I labeled it with his name sticker and tubed it up to the lab."

Glen scoffed. "The guy couldn't even walk straight. He had to be drunk."

Cliff shook his head. "You guys would learn a thing or two if you just talk to the patient. Paul Davis isn't a drunk. I've seen him in here a hundred times in the past decade that I've manned this desk." He lifted a stack of charts, volumes one through four, all belonging to Paul Davis. "It's customary for the doctors to review the patient record."

The med student scoffed. "What's to review? He fell and hit his head."

The ward clerk frowned. "Mr. Davis has HD."

Glen wrinkled his brow. "HD?"

Claire was relieved that he had asked the question, so she wouldn't have to.

"Huntington's disease. His old man had it. So did his brother."

Glen smiled and poked a finger toward Claire. "Everyone teaches a tern."

Huntington's disease. Claire remembered hearing about a patient with HD back during her medical school neurology rotation. It was some kind of movement disorder, but she remembered little else. All she knew was that it was rare and that you couldn't cure it with a scalpel, so she had little interest. "Oh sure," Claire responded, "HD."

"His brother Rufus died last year," Cliff added. "He was in a nursing home, only forty-five. Rufus was always comin' in here all bruised up or cut from falling down. Huntington's robbed him of his life." Cliff pointed at the stack of Mr. Davis's records. "And now it's doing the same thing to Paul."

Claire nodded and made a mental note to look the disease up later. She turned away and surveyed the ER for signs of the O-man. A child was screaming in the first cubicle. A respiratory technician held an oxygen mask over the face of an elderly man in the second cubicle. The patient's chest was exposed and so thin it reminded Claire of an old birdcage. Another man, apparently asleep, slumped awkwardly on a stretcher in the hall. He snored gently as Claire passed. An ER resident was sewing up a hand laceration in the trauma bay, and an ortho resident was applying a splint in the cast room. Claire yawned. Then, satisfied that there didn't seem to be any current action for the trauma intern, she retreated to a call room with an empty bed and collapsed.

Fifteen minutes later, she awakened to the sound of the door. Beatrice stumbled into the dark room and turned on the light.

Claire resisted the urge to scream and feigned sleep. She didn't want to talk to Beatrice in her present state of mind.

Bea mumbled something about Claire sleeping while she worked, then noisily climbed onto the top bunk and promptly fell asleep, her breathing coming in rhythmic faint whistles, just loud enough to keep Claire from slumber.

In five minutes, Bea's beeper sounded. Instead of touching the top of the beeper to silence it after one or two shrill tones, she allowed the obnoxious beeping to continue until it stopped on its own. She reached for the phone, a wall-mounted model beside the bed. Claire listened to the one-sided conversation. Bea had obviously forgotten to leave orders for pain medication for the appendectomy patient.

Claire pulled the pillow over her head. *Come on, Beatrice, everyone knows you have to write complete post-op orders or you're gonna get tortured by the nursing staff.*

In a few minutes the whistling noises resumed above her. Claire tossed in frustration for the next hour before exhaustion led her from her anxiety again, and brought a temporary respite with sleep.

Chapter Seven

In the morning, Claire crawled from the call-room bed thirty minutes before rounds, only to find Bea already locked in the adjoining bathroom. Claire waited a few minutes before rapping on the door. "Bea?"

She listened for a reply. When she heard none, she spoke again, "Bea? I need to use the sink."

There was no answer, only the sounds of running water.

Claire sighed and waited. And waited. When the water stopped, Claire knocked again. "Bea, can you let me in?"

The sound of a blow-dryer was the only response.

Claire opened a small compact mirror and resorted to applying her mascara with the small mirror propped on the top bunk. She pulled a brush through her blond bangs and listened to the noise in the bathroom. Finally, with only five minutes left until rounds, Bea appeared, looking like she was ready for a fashion magazine. She brushed past Claire and glanced pointedly at her watch. "Don't be late again," she tossed over her shoulder. "You never know what you'll miss the next time."

Claire clasped her hand on Bea's shoulder. Bea spun around. "Don't touch me."

Claire lifted her hand. "I was late because I was taking care of your ER patient, Bea. You wouldn't have gotten to do my OR case if you'd been doing what was right for Mr. Davis."

"I did what was right."

"He had a gaping wound. It would have taken forever for that wound to heal without sutures."

"That drunk wasn't worth my time." She backed to the door of the small call room. "I made a disposition. You shouldn't have been involved."

"He wasn't drunk," Claire countered. "Your patient had Huntington's disease, a fact you'd have known if you'd read his chart like you should have!"

"It doesn't take a chart review to diagnose his problem." Bea turned and slipped through the doorway.

Claire watched Bea's back disappear down the hall. She gritted her teeth and hurried to the ICU.

Outside the SICU, the trauma team gathered around Dr. Dan, who stood grinning, with a Nike shoe box in one hand. He extended his free hand to Rick, who surrendered a large Styrofoam cup. "Aah, Rick, how thoughtful." He held the cup into the air. "There is a tradition here at Lafayette. Every time an intern manages to nab his or her first major case, we offer a toast." He looked at Beatrice Hayes. "For your appendectomy."

Jeff, Elaine, and Basil lifted their coffee cups. "First blood!"

Dan smiled and echoed the phrase, "First blood." He held up the shoe box and handed his coffee back to Rick. "And for the first intern in a new year to draw first blood," he said, lifting a tarnished trophy from the shoe box, "this prestigious award." He held up a trophy that appeared to be a crude modification of an old sports award. At the top, where you might expect to find a little baseball player or perhaps a bowler, stood a large scalpel dripping with red plastic. On the base, "FIRST BLOOD" was printed in red letters. "This year's recipient is our very own trauma tern, Dr. Beatrice Hayes." He held out the award to Bea.

She gripped the award and laughed, while the other members clapped.

Everyone except Claire.

Dan explained. "This award is to be kept on display in the surgery resident's lounge." He turned the trophy around to reveal a series of smaller engraved nameplates listing the names of interns from prior years. "As you can see, you are joining a highly select group of individuals." He pointed his index finger to his own name.

Beatrice read off the names.

"We'll see to it that your name gets added to the list," he added.

Beatrice clutched the front of her scrub top. "I'm honored."

Claire forced a smile and clenched her jaw. *Stupid award. What do I care?*

Dan put the trophy back in the shoe box. "Okay, team, let's get this show on the road." He punched the small panel on the wall to activate the door to the ICU. "Who's presenting the first patient?"

By midday, Claire was relieved to be officially off duty. Before heading home, she stopped at the medical school library to see what she could find out about Huntington's disease, the mysterious illness that had afflicted her ER patient, making him look for all the world like a common drunk. She was troubled by the encounter, and hoping to dispel her anxiety with knowledge, she opened a neurology textbook and began to read.

Unfortunately, the written descriptions about the disease only tightened the growing knot in her stomach. Huntington's disease, or simply HD, had been first described by Dr. George Huntington in 1872. It was a degenerative disorder with catastrophic, progressive effects on movement, emotions, and the intellect. Originally known as Huntington's chorea, it was named for a Greek word for "dance," because of the repetitive, dance-like movements of the arms and legs which characterized the disease.

Claire read on about the early signs of the disease, which often included subtle changes in emotional stability, with patients showing irritability and angry outbursts. *Just like Daddy.* As the disease progressed, patients experienced more and more involuntary movement until they were no longer able to walk, dress themselves, or even sit in a chair without support or restraints. With each new paragraph she read, she saw her father. Every symptom seemed to fit. Patients with HD often appeared inebriated, and in the alcohol user, symptoms were confused with signs of intoxication.

The problems usually surfaced in midlife, she learned, and progressed to death in ten to twenty-five years. The disease was inherited. Children of patients with HD had a fifty-fifty chance of inheriting the disease. The worst part was that there was no cure, and most people who came down with the illness had already had children, who would be at risk for inheriting it.

Claire sat back in relief. The descriptions had sounded so much like her father. But since her grandparents didn't have HD, it would be impossible for her father to have it.

She yawned and closed the reference book. *Poor Mr. Davis. He has an incurable progressive disease that will certainly kill him. And while he's on the downhill slide, everyone who doesn't know him thinks he's a common drunk . . . like my dad.*

Claire stepped out the large glass doors at the entrance of Lafayette University Hospital and held her hand up to cover her eyes. It was sunny and hot, the kind of a day made for sand castles and cool surf. She paused and lifted her face to the wind. There was salt in the air, a light scent of the ocean. Yes, this day, Claire resolved, would be about relaxing. She'd spent the last eight weeks holed up in her brownstone cramming for her internship. Maybe she should grab a towel and some sunscreen rather than a textbook for a change.

Some good all that studying did, she mused. *Internship survival seems to have little to do with how much you know. It's more about following the O-man's stupid rules.* She smiled. *Eat when you can. Everyone teaches a tern. If you don't know, ask.* Her smile left as she thought of the latest rule. *Keep the fleas away from my patients.*

Maybe I should add my own. Never turn your back on Beatrice Hayes.

She trudged to her car alone, longing for a few hours away from Beatrice, uncooperative ER patients, and the medical Mecca.

She drove home in a daze, her little car finding its way through the city streets with minimal input from Claire. She had turned her thoughts to John Cerelli. Their summer separation had been helpful, in a way. At least she knew that her love for John would outlast a physical separation. But, she was discovering, long-distance communication did not seem to be his strong suit. She e-mailed and called, expressing her feelings about everything she experienced. He returned e-mail with short reports of his activities or calendar. *He tells me what he does. Not what he feels.* And a nagging anxiety remained: John seemed better able and more willing to communicate with his clothes off.

She thought back to her last night with John and frowned. *How come all my friends think sex is so great, when all I seem to get out of it is guilt?* She thought through the virtues her mother had instilled in her: Good Christian girls don't smoke. They don't drink. And they wait until marriage to surrender their virginity. *Is two out of three really so bad?* She tapped the steering wheel, hoping the traffic light would turn green, and promised herself that she would do better. But she knew the true test was yet to come, when John would come to Lafayette for a visit.

Claire arrived home and pulled a single letter from the mailbox. Her excitement disappeared when she saw the address label for "occupant." She checked her answering machine and e-mail with similar deflating results.

She walked through the house telling her plants she didn't care that John hadn't called. "I'm sure he just didn't want to leave a message. He wants to hear me in person," she said. "I'll just go on to the beach like I planned."

She selected a revealing two-piece suit, something she used only for tanning, not social events. She held it up to the mirror. *I'll find a quiet spot to myself.*

Claire changed and put John's football jersey over her swimsuit. She grabbed her sunscreen and a pair of sunglasses and looked at her desk. An old Bible, her Sabiston's surgery textbook, and a *National Geographic* seemed to be the only options for beach reading. She paused a moment, heaved a sigh, and hoisted the large textbook. "Let's go, Sabiston," she whined. "You knew I wouldn't be able to spend a few free hours without you."

She drove to a sandy cove ten miles southeast of Lafayette and parked at a public beach access. The lot was crowded with cars from Pennsylvania, New York, and Massachusetts. She'd forgotten that school was out for everyone else, and her hopes for a secluded getaway diminished. She exited her car and glanced at the sun before picking up her beach bag and her surgery textbook.

At the end of the parking lot, she noticed a man about her age waxing an old orange pickup. As she passed, he smiled, and she quickly diverted her eyes. He was blond, shirtless, and well-tanned, and would have looked at home on a lifeguard stand. Claire moved on, not wanting to initiate a conversation with the handsome stranger.

She picked her way through beach towels and sunbathers, the scent of suntan lotion and surf urging her forward, the sand quickly getting between her feet and her flip-flops. She slipped them off and dug her toes into the sand, feeling herself beginning to relax for the first time since leaving the hospital. She trudged slowly to the end of the beach, where she spread out her towel and slipped off John's jersey. She applied her sunscreen and lay down on the towel.

In a few minutes, she gave in to her fatigue, shut her surgery text, and closed her eyes.

She startled moments later to the sound of a man's voice. Claire sat up, unsure whether the man was speaking to her. She squinted and recognized him as the young man who'd been waxing his truck. "Excuse me?"

He smiled and lifted his hand in an open gesture. "I said, it's easier to study surgery with your eyes and the book open."

Claire smiled self-consciously. "Do I know you?"

"Brett Daniels. We met at the Bay Club, during the welcome reception for the interns."

She searched her memory. Yes, she did recall a resident by that name, but he sure looked different out here. She couldn't help noticing his muscled chest and shoulders, and when her eyes met his, she quickly looked away, suddenly aware that she was wearing her skimpiest swimsuit, the one she only wore when she was alone. She contemplated pulling on her shirt, but thought that might seem too awkward. "You're a resident?" Her voice was incredulous. "Then what are you doing here?"

"I might ask you the same question," he responded, sitting on the sand by her towel. "Is it okay if I sit down for a minute?"

She shrugged. "Sure."

"I'm a second-year resident, but I'm out of the clinical rotations working in Dr. Rogers' GI lab. The best part about a year in the lab is the flexible hours. There's a ton of reading to do, and a lot of it I can do from home."

She held out her hand. "I'm Claire McCall."

"I know. E. Claire. Dr. Rogers told me what you said about your name."

"I wasn't sure the chairman would remember me. There's so many interns."

Brett shook his head. "He remembers everyone."

This all seemed so crazy to Claire. Here she was making an attempt to escape the hospital for a few hours, and the first guy she meets is yet another person with aspirations to be a surgeon. She didn't know what to say.

She looked out at the ocean. "So you came to the beach to wax your truck?"

He laughed. "Not exactly. I live here," he said, pointing to a row of town houses across from the parking lot.

"I thought residents had to live within Lafayette limits."

"Only if you're on hospital rotations. The lab guys are exempt. Besides, it doesn't really take me that long to get in. We're usually in long before morning rush hour."

"Really."

"What about you? How does an intern swing a day at the beach?"

"It's not a day, just a few hours." She held up her hands. "I'm on the trauma service, so I'm up every other night, and off every other afternoon."

He nodded. "The intern group looks pretty strong. At least, that's what I hear from Dr. Rogers' secretary."

"Thanks . . . I guess."

"I'm sure you'll do fine. Just do your job. Don't worry about the competition."

"I think I'm starting to get the rules." She smiled and quoted the O-man. "'Everyone teaches a tern.'"

Brett's face broke into a wide grin again. His blue eyes seemed to twinkle in the sunlight. "I can tell who your chief resident is."

She paused and dug her feet into the warm sand. "So if you've completed your intern year, and you're in the lab, what's next?"

"Hopefully, I can win my way back into a clinical spot. If I work hard, get Dr. Rogers' name on a few papers, I suspect he'll smile on me and put me into your year next July."

"Hmmm. Just how many guys are working in the lab, hoping for a spot in the second year?"

"Just two. Sam Kowalski and I opted into the lab when it became obvious we weren't in the top eight." He shrugged. "It was better than being cut."

Claire sighed and turned her eyes to the surf, contemplating the impact of this new information. "So there are really fourteen people vying for eight second-year resident spots. Twelve interns plus two in the lab."

"Right." He paused, looking down at the sand, drawing a circle with his hand. "But it's not as bad as it sounds. Some will quit on their own, realizing they just don't have what it takes. A few will decide to go into orthopedics, maybe one or two into urology after the intern year. So that will cut down the numbers a bit."

That was little consolation. It was common knowledge that you couldn't reveal your plans to give up a general surgery spot until you had assurance that your future was secure with another position elsewhere. She shook her head. "I hate the competition," she confided. "I've only been here a few days and I find myself comparing myself to every other intern I meet, trying to convince myself that I have what it takes. Instead of making clinical decisions based on what's right for the patient, I see residents concerned about how they'll look to the attendings."

Brett dug his hand into the sand and let it sift slowly through his fingers onto the beach. "That pretty much sums up resident life at the Mecca."

She felt her eyes beginning to mist, as if the emotions she'd been holding back were about to come flooding out at this first opportunity to talk with someone who actually knew what she was going through. She reached for her sunglasses, thankful that the bright sun provided a reason for her to cover her eyes. She kept her face pointed toward the ocean, but diverted her eyes behind the dark shades to examine Brett's torso.

His voice was gentle, steady, full of confidence. "Are you open for advice from someone who's been there?"

This was new. A resident who asked permission to give advice. "Sure."

"Just do your job. Don't get caught up in competing. The residents who get promoted are the ones who just get the work done and aren't as concerned about looking better than everyone else." He paused, his eyes resting on Claire. "Listen to what the O-man tells you. He's rough around the edges, but he's got the attendings all figured out, and he knows how to survive."

"He doesn't like me. He treats me like a child."

"He treats every intern that way." He made an exaggerated attempt to stick out his gut and patted his stomach. "Come now, terns, let me show you the way," he mimicked.

Claire laughed. "Maybe so." She paused, aware that Brett had easily soothed her anxiety.

She watched a young mother chasing down a toddler who was making a beeline toward the water. The little boy squealed with delight as his mother swept him up in her arms. For a moment, Claire contemplated how comfortable it would be to escape the rat race of her career pursuits and be a mother. She could return home, marry John, live a comfortable middle-class life as a soccer mom.

Brett interrupted her thoughts. "Just get into the mind-set that you're there to learn. You can't expect to know everything the first day."

"I called a cardiology consult on July first without asking Dr. Overby."

She watched Brett's face. He winced but recovered quickly. "Wow," he responded, shaking his head. "But it happens every year. Don't worry about your first day."

"Did *you* do it?"

He seemed to hesitate. "No."

"He made up a new rule just for the occasion." Now Claire tried an imitation. Striking her hand against her slender abdomen, she added, "'Keep the fleas away from my patients!'"

He chuckled. "Oh, baby. A new Overby rule."

"Just for me."

He chuckled some more.

"Don't rub it in, okay? I told you he didn't like me."

"Give yourself a break. It's all part of maintaining his image in front of the house staff. Just be glad you did it on the first day, rather than right before they select the second-year residents."

Claire responded with sarcasm. "That's consoling."

"Claire, believe me, every intern does stupid things. It's all part of learning. Hey, if I survived, you can survive."

She studied him for a moment, listened to his voice, watched his expressions. He knew what she was going through. He had been there. She couldn't help but be warmed by his encouraging smile.

"I guess so," she said.

He paused and leaned forward. "You're not from the northeast. Your accent is . . ." He hesitated.

"Is what?" Claire put her hands on her hips. "What's wrong with a little Southern drawl?"

"Nothing! Er, I think it's . . ."

"What?"

"Endearing." Color highlighted his cheeks.

"That's not what you were going to say."

The corner of his mouth lifted, hinting at a smile. "You've only just met me, and now you know what I'm thinking?"

She diverted her gaze toward the surf. "I'm sorry. It just seems that some Bostonians think that everyone with a Southern accent drives around in an old pickup truck with a Confederate flag in the back window."

Now Brett put his hands on his hips to imitate her. "And what's wrong with old pickups?"

Her hand went to her mouth as a laugh escaped. She looked back toward the parking lot and the bright orange pickup. "Ooops." She attempted a sober expression. "Nothing's wrong with pickups. Where I'm from, everyone drives 'em."

"So the Bostonians are right?"

Claire sighed. "Only partly. We don't all have Confederate flags hanging in the rear window."

"That's a relief. By the way, I'm from Baltimore. My father is the chief of vascular surgery at Hopkins."

She lifted her sunglasses. She was impressed. "Oooh, I suppose you've always wanted to be a surgeon."

"Something like that." He paused and picked up another handful of sand. "At least my father has always hoped so."

She studied his face for a moment. It seemed like a sore subject, so Claire backed away. "So how is it that a surgeon's boy ends up driving an old orange pickup?"

He shrugged. "My mom's brother owns a body shop. I worked there every summer since high school. I must have painted every vehicle I own a dozen times."

"There are others?"

"I drive an old Mercedes most of the time." His eyes flashed. "I have an image to preserve, you know." He paused. "But my Chevy truck is my favorite."

Claire thought about her own car. She'd never even given a thought to maintenance of an image. She was concerned with survival.

A comfortable silence fell between them as they looked out at the blue ocean. Claire dug her feet deeper into the sand, enjoying the cooler sensation a few inches beneath the surface.

Brett asked her about her first few days as a new intern, questioning her first impressions about attendings, residents, and the other interns.

It felt good to talk to someone who knew what she was going through. And he seemed to actually care about her opinions. Claire relaxed and told him all about her tumultuous experience with Beatrice Hayes, including the story of the man with HD and how he reminded her of her own father.

Brett's expression turned serious. "Your father? He has Huntington's disease?"

"No," Claire responded. "I just said it was eerie how much my patient reminded me of my father."

Brett leaned forward. "I think I'd keep this quiet around the hospital, Claire. You certainly don't want anyone getting the idea that you might be at risk for Huntington's disease."

"I'm not sure I'm following you."

"Claire, it would be a sure ticket off the pyramid. No one with HD would be a safe surgeon, and certainly couldn't practice beyond midlife." He paused. "And if you haven't noticed, most of us are approaching that by the time we finish this marathon of training." He shook his head. "I'm sure Dr. Rogers would find a good reason to keep someone like that out of training."

"That's ridiculous. You can't keep someone out of training just because they're at risk for an inherited disease. That's discrimination."

"Maybe so. But just the same, I wouldn't let the rumor circulate. It couldn't help your chances for Dr. Rogers to think that someone he's put years into training might only carry his legacy into the future a few short years beyond residency."

Claire felt her gut tighten. "Well, I haven't told this to anyone else, Brett. And, just for your information, my dad doesn't have HD. It's nowhere in my family tree. My father ... is an alcoholic." She looked away and fought a sensation of rising dread. Maybe she shouldn't have been so open with Brett so quickly. But he seemed so friendly and understanding.

Apparently, he sensed her discomfort. "Hey, it's okay," he said, touching her arm. "My family has similar demons. My brother's been in and out of alcohol rehab so many times, I've lost count." His hand lingered for a moment, gently squeezing her forearm.

For the second time since meeting Brett, she found herself blinking back tears. Thankful for her sunglasses, she forced a smile. "Hey, I'm all right. I've accepted the hand I've been dealt. I don't let my father's choices get me down."

As he withdrew his hand, Claire was acutely aware of the adolescent goose bumps his touch had stimulated. *Good grief,* she chided herself. *I'm just upset thinking about my father.*

She avoided his gaze as he stood, fumbling with a small towel he had been using to buff his truck. "I'd better let you get back to your reading."

Claire smiled. "Right. But I'm afraid I was using my text as a pillow."

He retreated a step. "Come back, Claire." He shrugged with feigned awkwardness. "I could show you my truck."

"Is that a pickup line?" She laughed at her own pun.

Brett waved and walked away, laughing at her response.

She watched him as he picked his way through the sunbathers, not taking her eyes from him until he had made it to the parking lot at the far side of the beach.

Chapter Eight

Della McCall bowed her head over an open book on her kitchen table. The quietness of the morning offered little comfort as she took inventory of the McCall family. The months since Claire's graduation from medical school had taken their toll. Wally was picking up speed in his long journey downhill. Della, under pressure from Leon, Wally's brother, and from Elizabeth, felt a growing urgency to intervene. Somewhere, someone could help.

Her husband became insufferable. When drunk, he was belligerent. When sober, his jerky movements reminded Della of watching someone illuminated by a strobe light, catching only brief intervals of movement separated by blackness.

She'd promised herself years ago that she would stay. She owed him. Wally had stayed with her through tough times, when normal men would have left without another thought. Now, it was her turn. She would stay with Wally and accept her just desserts. Now, in the silence of the morning, before her husband would rise with a noisy clatter, Della sought strength to follow through. "Oh, Father," she prayed. "Help us to make it through." She rotated the ring on her left hand, a reminder of her promise.

Guilt is a powerful motivator. Love is even stronger.

She drank coffee and read quietly from the passages open in front of her. When she finished, she nodded her resolve. Claire wasn't here to help her anymore. Clay wasn't about to help. Margo was too busy with her own young family. Uncle Leon was too absorbed in the family business, way above the fray of helping out his brother. And Elizabeth, while concerned, was too caught up in her own theories of Wally's problems. That left Della alone to get Wally to someone to help. She'd tie him up if she had to. She'd sign him into the new rehab program in Carlisle with the help of a judge if she had to. She couldn't face another day of watching her husband grow more and more helpless. If alcohol had irreparably damaged Wally's brain, there had to be some test, some X ray that could show it. She had to know what was wrong. She had to know if something, or someone, could help.

She heard Wally stirring in the bedroom. Quietly, she whispered a prayer that Wally would be receptive to her plea. She helped him dress, shave, and fix breakfast. She waited for just the right opportunity to, once again, suggest that he see a doctor.

The chance came when Wally knocked his coffee mug onto the linoleum floor. He stared at his hands and shook his head. He looked up, his eyes meeting Della's. "I just can't stop," he said, his arm jerking wildly again. "I just can't hold still."

She grasped his face and caught his gaze for a moment before his head jerked away. "Let's go to a doctor in Carlisle. We have to find out what's wrong."

Maybe it was the desperation in her voice. Maybe it was her prayer, but Wally seemed to sense the futility of resisting. He was giving up. His head bobbed up and down.

She studied him for a second. Was this a positive response? Or just another example of his nervous twitching?

"I'll go," he slurred.

Her relief escaped in a clumsy hug. "Oh, Wally," she gasped, as their heads collided. "I'll clean up breakfast. Then we can go."

After a thirty-minute drive up the Apple Valley, they endured an hour's wait in a crowded waiting room outside the hospital's emergency ward. Then, after another twenty minutes in a cool hospital gown, Della was sure Wally would give up and leave. She could sense his reluctance returning, and his patience, if he'd ever had any, growing thin.

Finally, a young doctor appeared and began a barrage of questions.

Della fumbled with her scarf beneath her chin and winced at the doctor's tone as he questioned Wally repeatedly about his drinking. She'd been afraid of this. It had taken forever to convince Wally to seek treatment, and now this doctor was badgering him. An explosion was inevitable. Della regretted even mentioning to the triage nurse that her husband was a dry alcoholic. That was probably why the physician seemed so intent on getting a confession of alcohol consumption.

She tried to catch the doctor's eye. She cleared her throat and shook her head. But it did no good. Apparently frustrated by Wally's denials, the physician, who looked no older than her own children, turned to Della. "Has he been hallucinating? Seeing insects on the wall? Maybe picking at his skin, complaining of ants or insects bothering him?"

She shook her head. "No."

The doctor lowered his voice and leaned toward her. "Could he be getting alcohol without your knowledge?"

"I'm not deaf. And I ain't been drinking!" Wally stood. "Let's go!" He stumbled to his feet from the edge of the stretcher.

"I can vouch for him, Doctor. He's been dry for weeks."

The young man shook his head. "I wasn't born yesterday, ma'am. Look at his eyes. Listen to his speech."

Wally pulled back the curtain and started across the emergency room.

"Wally, put some clothes on. You can't leave like that!"

"Watch me!" He jerked his arms and legs forward in a motion that reminded Della of a marionette.

"Wally, stop!"

The doctor took Della's arm. "Listen, ma'am, if he's not drinking, this could be early alcohol withdrawal, delirium tremens. That can be quite serious, even fatal. He should be in the hospital."

Her husband continued his labored trek toward the exit. Two nurses approached with their arms in the air, looking like bank tellers in a holdup. They backed toward the exit in front of him, speaking in soft, childlike voices. "There now, Mr. McCall, calm down. I'm sure we can find you some help."

Wally's hand flipped forward, striking the pudgy nurse in the nose.

The nurse screamed. The doctor yelled for security, and Della grabbed her husband's clothes before running out the automatic doors behind Wally.

Della began to sob as she hurried across the lot to help her husband into the car.

As she passed the entrance to the ER, the young physician was standing beside a uniformed security guard, who had arrived two minutes too late. The doctor raised his hand and yelled, "That man ought to be committed! He could be in DTs!"

The voice behind her faded as she accelerated away from the hospital, turning right and heading back toward Stoney Creek. As she did, she cried. Cried because Wally wouldn't get help. Cried because the doctor had been such a jerk. And cried because there wasn't a thing she could do about it.

Claire stopped for supper, a salad at Wendy's, and sat in her car to eat. As she did, she couldn't suppress the idea that her father might really have Huntington's disease. The idea wasn't rational, she told herself. You couldn't have Huntington's disease unless one of your parents had it. She thought about what Brett had said about her own situation, should it be true that she was at risk for HD. But that idea was preposterous! *I can't be at risk for HD if it's not in my family.* But the implications in her own life were so serious that she couldn't seem to quiet the remote anxiety.

What if my father was adopted?

That's ridiculous. Why would Grandma keep that a secret?

What if Grandpa McCall really wasn't my father's biological father?

A bite of lettuce stopped in midflight, on the way to Claire's lips. *This is crazy. I'm allowing my thoughts to spin out of control.*

She became conscious of the lettuce hovering frozen in front of her face. She glanced each way, thankful no one seemed to be watching, before depositing the food in her mouth. Slowly she chewed, determined to manage her runaway thoughts. *But what if?*

She shook her head and sighed, finishing her salad with only limited success at keeping her mind from wondering over unlikely family secrets. She had modest victory at that when she turned her attention to her memories of Brett Daniels, his handsome appearance, and the emotions he aroused when he gently touched her arm. But she felt guilty and unfaithful dreaming about someone other than John, so she let her mind drift back to her father's symptoms. Finally, in an effort to subdue her worries, she promised that she would call her mother. Surely she would know the information she needed to dispel the outlandish notion of family secrets.

Claire closed the plastic lid and took a long swig of the diet drink she'd ordered. Then, in a quick trip home, she saw the light flashing on her answering machine. John, perhaps? Her heart quickened, but only momentarily, as she recognized her mother's recorded voice.

"Hi, Claire." Her mother paused, the tension recognizable in her brief greeting. "I'm calling about your father."

What else is new?

"I took him up to the hospital in Carlisle today. It was a disaster. The doctor thought he should stay. Accused him of being drunk, then thought he might be in alcohol withdrawal—DTs or something or other, he called it. Your father got offended and barged out of there wearing his hospital gown and everything. I ..." Her voice caught. "I don't know what to do. I have to work. But it's getting so I'm afraid to leave him." There was silence for a moment. "After today, I don't think he'll ever go to a doctor again. But he can't go on like this. He can't even get himself dressed without help." Della sighed heavily. "Listen, I know you've got your own worries. I just didn't know who else to call. Your sister is busy with her family, and Clay stays out of your father's way. Not that I blame him." Her voice trailed off. "Call me if you have any ideas. I'm running out of my own."

Claire stared at the answering machine and shook her head. "The man is beyond help, Mom," she muttered. She picked up the phone and dialed.

After three rings, her mother picked up. "Hello."

"Hi, Mom."

"Claire. It's so good to hear you again."

"I got your message."

Claire heard the screen door slam. She envisioned her mother retreating into the backyard so she could talk in private. "I don't know what to do with him, Claire. I'm beginning to think I'm the crazy one around here. He says he's not drinking. But he still looks drunk. I keep my eyes on him all I can. But I can't watch him every second, and I can't watch him while I'm at work."

"Do you believe him, Ma?"

She heard Della exhale sharply into the phone. "Yes. Your father has been a lot of things, but he's not a liar. He knows I wouldn't tolerate that."

"You took him to the doctor, Ma. The doctor thought he was drunk, too. Did he draw any labs? An alcohol level would be good evidence that he's not being truthful."

"They didn't draw his blood. He didn't stay that long. After waiting for two and a half hours to talk to the doctor, your father was mad enough. Then the doctor focused on his drinking history like there were no other possibilities. That went over real well with Wally."

"So you've said."

"Claire, if he's not drinking, why can't he walk straight? His arms and legs jerk around like he's out of control."

"Ma, you've hit on the crux of the issue. *If* he's not drinking. Could it be you're in denial? Maybe you're too close to be objective."

Claire could hear her mother tapping her fingernails on the phone. She didn't reply right away. "Maybe. Maybe I am. How would I know? By definition, if I *am* too close, then I wouldn't know." She paused again. More clicking. "No. No, I think there is something else going on. Maybe the liquor has just pickled his brain beyond repair, but I don't think he's still drinking. Something else is going on. Something mysterious."

"It's the curse, right?" Claire responded with sarcasm. "Don't tell me you've started listening to Grandma."

"Claire!"

She softened. "I'm sorry." She picked up a watering can and began watering her African violets while she talked. "There is another unlikely possibility I wanted to ask you about. In fact, even before I got your message, I intended to call you."

"Okay. I'm listening. What?"

Claire gave an abbreviated version of her encounter with the patient with Huntington's disease.

"I don't see how that could apply to Wally. You said yourself that the only way to get the disease is if one of your parents had it."

"Right." Claire hesitated. "But what if Grandpa McCall wasn't Daddy's biological father? Could Daddy have been adopted? Or . . ."

"Or what?" More clicking.

"Figure it out, Mom. I'm asking if someone else could have been Daddy's biological father. Someone with Huntington's disease."

Della gasped. "Listen here, Claire. I've known your father's mother all my life. She's as close to sainthood as they come, always quoting the Bible, always attending church. She puts me to shame, I'd be the first to admit. And what you're suggesting here is that Elizabeth had an affair?"

"I'm not suggesting anything. I just—"

"Well, put that notion out of your head. Someday, you stand to inherit a substantial amount of money from that dear old woman, and the surest way for you to screw up that possibility is to suggest something like that."

"Could he have been adopted?"

"No."

"So the only way that—"

"Claire! Don't persist in this. I can vouch for her character. Nothing like what you're proposing could possibly be true."

Claire shrugged. "Okay, okay, I hear you. I didn't think it was possible either, but I just thought I'd make sure. The idea that Daddy could have such a horrible disease has serious implications for me, too. So I obsessed over it, and I had to ask."

"So that's it!" Della snapped. "All along you deny the possibility that something else could be wrong with your father. You never believed it could be anything but alcohol. But now suddenly when you think your future might be at stake, you start to worry."

"Mom, I never said it couldn't be anything else, I just denied the possibility of Grandma's crazy theory about a town curse."

"Well, I think you should forget *your* theory. Your grandmother has always been a good Christian woman." Della sighed. "Why don't you try supporting your family, instead of coming up with these accusations?"

"I was only asking a question. And how can I be more supportive? I can only do so much from up here."

"Do what your grandmother would do, okay? Pray for us, Claire. Pray that your father's brain will be restored, that whatever this crazy thing is, call it a curse or addiction, will pass and give us a little peace."

Claire nodded. "Sure, Ma. I'll pray." She didn't know what else to say. She hadn't heard such desperation from her mother before. Della had always seemed so strong.

"Keep in touch, honey. I'd better go check on your father."

"Bye." Claire looked at her phone. The line had already gone dead.

Her mother's reaction to Claire's question had been a surprise. Claire hadn't even considered the possibility that her question might be considered offensive—mainly because Claire hadn't questioned her grandmother's faithfulness. Instead, she had been thinking of something like a secret adoption. But Grandma having an affair? Her mother was right. Nothing should be further from her mind.

She continued watering her houseplants, encouraging each one and complimenting them on how strong they looked. Eventually, she tired of that and started telling them about the nagging similarities between her HD patient and her father. It felt silly to talk out her problems to her plants—but then, no one else would listen as long without interrupting.

What harm could it do to just explain the dilemma to Grandma? I'll make it clear to her that I'm not suggesting that she had an affair, just that maybe Daddy was adopted or something. I know the idea may be far-fetched, but I just have to know so I can put it out of my mind forever.

Grandma would never write me out of the will just for asking a stupid question.

She picked up the phone and dialed.

Her grandmother's voice was strong, and always a little loud because of her hearing loss. "McCall's residence."

"Grandma? It's Claire."

"Claire! So nice of you to call."

"I'm calling about Daddy. I'm concerned about him."

"We all are, Claire. He's going to be the ruin of your mother."

Claire launched into her story, stepping as lightly as she could into the question about Huntington's disease in the family, and whether it was possible that her father could have been adopted.

Elizabeth McCall laughed—another response Claire hadn't expected. "Adopted?" She chuckled again. "I wish he was—then I wouldn't feel so responsible for the way he's turned out." She laughed again. "It took twenty-four hours of labor for me to have that child. I think an adoption would have been more fun."

"Well, I feel silly for asking, but adoption is the only way I could see Daddy having a parent with Huntington's disease." She paused. "It's funny, Grandma. I just accused my mother of being in denial. Maybe I'm the one who's looking for another explanation for my father's behavior. It's not easy knowing your father is the town drunk."

"He's not the town drunk, Claire. We've all had our problems. Your father's has just been a bit more visible than some."

"I guess."

There was an uncomfortable silence for a few moments before her grandmother spoke again. "Say, Claire—is it possible for Huntington's disease to skip a generation?"

"No. Everyone with the gene for Huntington's gets it from an affected parent."

"Hmm." There was a pause. "Well, Claire, I'll let you go. I know you've got a lot of studying to do. Nice of you to call. Bye."

Click. "Yes, well—" Claire looked at her phone, realizing her grandmother had already gone. *Boy, what is it with everyone today? Finished talking? Just hang up on me, Grandma.*

Claire set the phone in its cradle and mumbled, "At least she didn't talk to me about the curse."

She walked to the bathroom and pulled off John's jersey, then frowned as she pulled down her bikini top to check her tan line. *I think my surgical training is definitely going to affect my tan. Oh, well, a healthy tan is really a misnomer anyway.*

She showered, her mind drifting lazily as she washed away the suntan oils. She thought of Brett, and how easy she found it to talk to him. *It's strange, I've only just met him, but I felt so open to share my thoughts. There's something to be said for shared experiences. Like soldiers in the trenches together, I guess. There's nothing like another surgical resident to understand your stresses.*

And what a build. He doesn't seem arrogant like most surgeons. He's probably got the nurses eating out of his hand. I'll bet they'd do just about anything for a chance to be with—

Thump thump thump.

Claire stuck her head out from behind the shower curtain and listened. Someone was pounding on her front door. Alarm rushed through her as the pounding continued, accompanied now by the doorbell. She wasn't expecting guests, and no one, as far as she knew, knew where to find her. Who could be knocking?

She shut off the water and grabbed a towel. She yelled at the front door, "Be right there!" She hurried into her bedroom, pulled on a pair of jeans, and threw on the jersey she'd just removed. She crept to the door and peered through the peephole.

She gasped with relief and joy. John Cerelli had come to Lafayette!

Chapter Nine

laire yanked open the door and launched herself into John's arms like a reckless child. "John!" she squealed, loud enough to alert the neighborhood of his arrival.

John pulled free of her grasp and planted a kiss on her lips. "Surprise."

"What are you doing here?"

He smiled sheepishly. "I knew you had to be under a ton of stress starting your internship. I just wanted to be around for support."

She led him into her brownstone. "How did you find me?"

"I had your address. I can read a map."

"How did you know I'd be home? I could have been at the hospital."

"I called the paging operator. She told me you weren't on call." He shrugged. "So I just thought I'd try here."

She hugged him tightly before remembering how quickly she'd dressed to come to the door. The only thing between her and John's thin shirt was the jersey. She enjoyed the sensation for a moment before pushing him away. "I'll be right back." She took a step back, before feeling the restraint of his grip on her wrist.

"Wait a minute." He stared at her and smiled.

"What are you staring at?" She lifted her hand to her uncombed wet hair. "You interrupted my shower."

"You cut your hair."

"You knew that. I told you about it."

"But I hadn't seen it." He paused. "You look great."

She wasn't convinced. "I look like a wet poodle. Just give me a minute, Cerelli." She retreated to the bathroom.

There, she started to blow-dry her hair, stopping long enough to call out to John to make himself at home and help himself to whatever he could find in the kitchen.

After fixing her hair, she put on some clothes and lipstick. She found John in the kitchen, frowning at the refrigerator. "What do you live on? Campbell's soup? Cheerios?"

"Hey, I wasn't exactly expecting guests." She looked at the clock. Seven-thirty. "Have you eaten? We could go out."

John stretched his back with his hands extended high above his head. "I've been driving for ten hours. I stopped once—at a McDonald's for lunch. Other than that, I had a bag of Combos and some malt balls."

Claire wrinkled her nose. "I'll take you out for some vegetables."

"Okay, Mom."

He moved past her toward the bathroom, stealing a kiss as he squeezed between Claire and the kitchen sink.

Her heart soared. She had told John to stay away, but it was so romantic that he hadn't obeyed.

She took him to a seafood restaurant overlooking the Danberry River. As they feasted on shrimp, fresh fish, and scallops, she unloaded the stories of her first days as a surgical intern. She told him about Dan-the-man and his silly rules, about Beatrice and her cutthroat antics, Claire's struggle with giving her first orders, the thrill of putting in a chest tube, the first-blood award, and about the unfortunate man with Huntington's disease who reminded her of her father.

John yawned and pushed a lonely lemon wedge across the large plate. Claire looked at her own food and wondered if John was listening.

"You need to eat," he coaxed. "Those shrimp are wonderful."

She pushed her plate toward him. "I had a salad at Wendy's before you showed up."

He helped himself to his favorites and seemed content for the time being, allowing Claire to add one more bit of news—that there were not only twelve interns in her year, but two additional residents who had opted for a lab year, all of whom were competing for eight spots as second-year surgical residents in the program. What she didn't tell John was where she was when she learned that, and about the shirtless Brett Daniels who had told her.

She studied John as he ate, unable to stop the comparisons between his listening skills and Brett's, who had made eye contact and seemed to hang on her every word. John reached over and skewered another scallop, sliding it through a trough of butter-herb sauce on the way to his lips.

"This is great stuff," he grunted.

She nodded and lifted a shrimp from her plate, which now rested closer to John than to her. She chewed, silently mulling over his reaction to her stories. At least he could have acted as if he cared that she was under such pressure.

"I've been selfish. All I've talked about is me." She paused. "How long can you stay?"

"Two days. I need to do a sales presentation in Boston. I talked Tom into letting me have the days if I'd save the company some travel dollars for a flight. I need to leave Thursday morning so I can be in Boston by noon." He sighed and pushed back from the table. "That only gives us two nights together."

She shook her head. Obviously John hadn't caught on to her schedule. "Not really. I've got to spend tomorrow night at the hospital. I won't be home until noon on Thursday, if I'm lucky."

John leaned forward and squinted. "So we can spend the day together, visit the historic sites."

"John, I've got to be in the ICU by six A.M. It isn't a day *or* night job. It's a day *and* night job."

"That's crazy. They can't work you like that."

"Actually, this schedule is the best I'll have all year. On most rotations, they expect you to be in house every day, in addition to every other night, and you can't expect to get out by noon on your days off."

His jaw slackened. Apparently, he was beginning to understand reality. "Can't you trade call or something?"

She shook her head. "It's not that easy."

"I drove ten hours to be with you. I didn't come to tour Lafayette by myself."

She didn't know what to say. She held up her hands. "I'm sorry."

John looked out the window. He didn't appear to be enjoying the sunset over the river.

"Maybe things will be slack at the hospital tomorrow evening. If you want, you could come into the hospital and eat with me."

John sighed. "Unless you're working."

She winced and nodded. "I think you're getting it."

He mumbled a curse word under his breath. Claire could hear it and widened her eyes in response, but decided it was best to let it pass. It definitely wasn't part of his normal vocabulary, and she was disappointed. It wasn't the right time to start critiquing his less-than-Christian response. Especially when it summed up how she felt, too.

She reached over and took his hand. "There will be other times for us, John. This is just the beginning."

He nodded resolutely. "I know." He continued looking at the river. "So I guess it was okay that I broke our little separation?"

She smiled. "I'm glad that you did." She squeezed his hand. "I've missed you something awful."

"Has it accomplished what you wanted? Has being away from me proven anything useful?"

"I know my feelings for you have lasted in spite of the miles."

He looked back into her eyes. "Mine too. So you still want to be my wife?"

She paused. Why did she hesitate to verbalize her commitment? Her throat seemed suddenly dry. "Yes."

John pulled his hand from hers and put his hand in his pants pocket, retrieving a small felt box. "I was going to wait until tomorrow night. But it looks like this may be my only chance." He pressed it into her palm and whispered, "Marry me, Claire. I want you to be my wife."

Claire gripped the small box, her head spinning. Instead of the thrill she was supposed to feel, the memory of Brett Daniels' hand on her arm popped into her mind. Why did she have to think of him now? She shut her eyes and pulled the box toward her. "Oh, John," she gasped, opening the lid. A solitary diamond reflected the light from their table's lantern. "It's beautiful."

She'd known this moment was coming. They'd made their commitment to each other months ago. She'd been introducing John as her fiancé for almost a year. So why did the physical evidence of a ring make her stomach churn?

She slipped the ring on her finger. "It's perfect." She felt tears welling in her eyes. The ring was beautiful. She loved John. She also felt confused and a little dishonest at proclaiming her unreserved feelings of lifetime commitment to a man more interested in her shrimp dinner than her trials as a new intern.

Oh, maybe she was being unfair. He'd driven for ten hours and he was hungry. She lifted her napkin to her cheek. Fortunately, tears of joy and tears of emotional turmoil were indistinguishable to men.

John apparently accepted the tears as a sign he'd done the right thing. She could almost see his lungs swell with pride. She leaned forward. *You're supposed to kiss when you get a diamond, aren't you?* She kissed him lustily, tasting her own tears, and sobbing through her attempts at making the right response. His mouth was warm, and open for more.

She pulled away and looked at the others in the room. Fortunately, the other patrons seemed to be paying little attention to the young lovers. John's hand urged her face forward again.

She broke the kiss and pressed her napkin under her nose. "I'm a mess," she said, standing. "I'll be right back." She escaped to the rest room and sat, fully clothed, on the white commode in the first stall. She pulled off a yard of toilet paper and blew her nose noisily before pressing her face into her open hands.

What's wrong with me? I thought this was what I wanted.

Oh, God, she sobbed the beginning of a prayer. *Help me.*

Claire stared out the window of John's red Mustang in silence. It was ten P.M., and in spite of the exciting events of the evening, exhaustion was gaining the upper hand. She yawned and closed her eyes, already dreading the sound of her alarm clock.

When they arrived at her apartment, John dragged his suitcase toward the front door and Claire braced herself for the inevitable discussion about the sleeping arrangements. It was already apparent that John felt he was welcome to stay for the night.

Once inside, Claire turned and kissed him luxuriously, but resisted when he nudged her toward the couch. She feared her resolve would weaken if she fell into an old pattern. "John, it's late. I've got to be up at five, and I hardly slept at all last night."

"It's our only night together." He kissed her again.

Claire pushed him back. "I can't, John." She took a deep breath. "This is what our time away from each other was all about. I told you I thought we needed to cool it. I wanted to make sure our relationship could handle not having sex."

His face fell. "I thought the persistence of our feelings for each other in spite of our separation proved that."

"But it's not right. It's not that I didn't enjoy it. But I felt so guilty. I wanted to save myself until I got married."

"We've been over this, Claire. We're committed. A marriage license is basically a formality. In God's sight, we're already one." His voice was gentle, and although he had backed off in response to her reaction, his hands remained on her shoulders, slowly massaging her tension away.

"But we're not married, John. And a prayer didn't change that. There will be a lifetime for us to get to know each other in that way."

He didn't speak but pulled her head to his chest. She sighed and hoped he was getting the message. She spoke quietly into his shirt, enjoying his arms around her, but not lifting her face to his. "When I was a teenager, I made a commitment to follow Christ. I decided then and there to do, as best as I could determine, what he wanted in every circumstance." She tilted her neck, allowing John's lips to brush her forehead. "I've not always obeyed, and somehow I fell into justifying our physical relationship, but I never felt any kind of peace about it."

She felt his breath, a deep sigh of frustration, as she continued. "So I needed to be away from you. Not necessarily emotionally, but physically. I couldn't handle being in your arms without wanting more."

John moved his hands to her lower back, then lower still. He wasn't hearing.

"I'm not sure I can handle this," he whispered.

"Yes, you can. You've handled it since graduation."

"That's different. We weren't together."

"And that's what I needed to test my resolve. A physical separation. And, even if we're seeing each other face-to-face, we still need to maintain a relationship without sex." With that, she backed away, holding him at arm's length.

"This is our only night together."

"And I want to remember this night without feeling guilty."

"I drove ten hours to be with you."

"John, begging doesn't become you."

He sighed and sat down on the couch, testing the seat cushions with a pat of his hand. "So this is my bed."

"I'll get you a blanket." She walked to the hall closet and retrieved a well-worn comforter. "Here," she said, tossing it onto the couch beside him. "You can use the bathroom down here." She tussled his hair and kissed his forehead. "Thanks for surprising me."

His response was less than enthusiastic. "Sure." He waited a moment and kept his eyes on the faded rug in front of the couch. "For the record, I know you're right about this." He paused. "I don't like it, and I don't like admitting it, but I know you're right."

Her reply was soft, barely above a whisper. "Thanks."

She left him sitting on the couch and retreated up the stairs to the bathroom to prepare for bed. A few minutes later, she went to her bedroom and slipped off her clothes, donning John's jersey as a nightshirt. She flipped off the light and stood by her open door listening to John's preparations downstairs. He'd obviously left the bathroom door open. She listened as he undressed, his belt buckle striking the old hardwood floor. Water ran for a moment, and then she heard vigorous sounds of a thorough toothbrushing.

Claire pushed the door partially shut, enjoying the sounds of having a man in the house, comforted by the familiarity of the noises he made, the knowledge that she wasn't alone. She pushed the door shut but didn't lock it, then collapsed into bed. There, in the darkness, she listened as John prepared to sleep. She imagined his well-muscled chest and arms, and more, as she nestled her head into her pillow. She turned on her side and reached out toward the empty space beside her. Oh, how she longed for him to be near her, holding her, bathing her with kisses, massaging her with searching hands.

Her heart beat faster. This seemed like torture. He was so close, and she knew he wanted her fiercely. It would be so easy to invite him up.

She stared at the ceiling before whispering a prayer, wanting to be strong but feeling so very weak. *This is crazy, God. I just made such a strong stand with my lips, but now everything in me wishes he would ignore my plea and come to my bed.*

One moment I'm strong. The next minute I desperately want to fall.

Help me. I'm so confused about my feelings. She twisted the ring around her finger. *I know I love him, but now I find myself afraid. Where is the thrill I'm supposed to feel?*

She drifted into a restless, intermittent sleep, as if stepping across a pond of slumber by jumping from stone to stone. She looked at the clock at midnight, one-thirty, and three. At three, she heard John rise to use the bathroom, and found herself again longing for his arms, her heart quickening as she listened intently for the footfalls on the stairs that never came.

She must have fallen asleep sometime before her alarm at five, as she startled at the sound of music blaring from her clock radio.

"Ugh," she groaned, as her feet hit the floor. "The Mecca beckons."

Chapter Ten

Elizabeth Bunker McCall hadn't slept a complete night since her husband's death the previous summer. Not that sleeping with her husband, John McCall, had been particularly peaceful. He snored like a child with heavy tonsils, snorting and gasping his way through the night, drowning out any other noise that could possibly disturb her. But now with him gone, she found herself alert and alone, conscious of every creak of the old mansion, and even with her hearing aid on the bedside table, imagined noises nudged her from slumber every few hours.

Often, she replayed memories from her youth, mostly happy with the emotions they invoked.

Tonight, she tossed with restlessness, replaying a memory a half-century old, a remembrance of pain, a secret, stimulated by her thoughts of her son's deterioration. Each time she remembered, her heart quickened, the emotions of the moment experienced anew. With each recollection, a guilt long buried grew fresh, almost palpable, threatening to engulf her again.

It was supposed to have been one of the happiest events of her life. She'd left the rehearsal dinner only thirty minutes before, planting a kiss on the cheek of her fiancé, John McCall. It was a kiss that capped an exhaustive evening of rehearsal, getting everything in proper order. A McCall wedding, she'd come to understand, would be done properly, a wedding everyone would admire. It was a dinner rich with delicacies most of Stoney Creek would never taste again, and wine in abundance.

Tomorrow, she would marry up, join the one family in the Apple Valley that seemed to thrive in spite of economic hardship around them. For this moment, in spite of her need for sleep, she found herself invigorated, entranced in the magical thoughts of her wedding night, in anticipation of sex for the first time. She pinched her eyelids shut and nestled beneath a worn quilt.

It was then, in the middle of a restless night, that *he* came. She heard the rhythmic *peck . . . peck . . . peck* of a creek pebble tossed against her window. The sound had been his signature during their tumultuous courtship.

It was not an announcement befitting the arrival of John McCall—this was the clandestine frivolity of a country boy, a moonshiner's grandson whose heart had never recovered from the loss of his sweetheart.

Steve Hudson had been scorned, rejected by a family who had set their sights on higher social standing. In her heart, Elizabeth, Steve's Lizzy, had cherished him. But under pressure from her mother, and with a fear of the insanity rumored to plague Steve's family, she had pulled free, at least from the visible ties that linked them. But sometimes, the unseen bonds drew her.

She jumped from the bed and struggled with the old window, yanking it half open. Peering out, she knew where she'd find him. Beneath the maple tree, he stood gazing up, his face reflecting the moonlight, his body straight and strong. His shirt was open, as he often wore it in the summer months, a social faux pas that John McCall's mother would have pointed out in disgust.

His voice was pleading, almost a whisper. "Lizzy! We have to talk."

"Go away. Don't do this."

He didn't budge. She saw his hand close into a fist over his bare chest. "Lizzy!"

She shook her head, her mind telling her to push the window down and ignore him. *Just go back to bed, pull the covers over your head, and he'll go away!*

But her heart wouldn't let her obey.

"Give me a minute," she whispered. She cast a worried glance over her shoulder into the darkness of the room. "Meet me at the barn."

She pulled an old coat over her nightgown and studied her reflection in the mirror. She primped for a moment, then sighed and tiptoed to the door.

Walking barefooted across the stepping-stones leading away from the back porch, she whispered her resolve. "There is nothing to talk about. Our relationship is over." She skipped ahead, jumping a small puddle. "It's over. It's over," she whispered again. And again.

He was pacing like a caged animal, under the window of the hayloft. How long had he practiced this encounter? Dozens of times? Hundreds?

She decided to begin. It was best to take control, to not let him get started. "There is nothing to discuss. Go back home, Steve."

"Lizzy," he whispered.

Why did he use that name? Only he called her that. It had been her playful name, one that he'd used to break the ice when they'd first met.

"You can't go through with this."

"Steve, it's too late for us. We've been through this before."

"I love you more than life." His words were slow and practiced. "Lizzy, I need you."

His voice quivered, and she felt her heart in her throat. "Stop." She shook her head. "I shouldn't have come." She turned away and stepped toward the house.

She felt his hand grip her arm. His strength both frightened and allured her. She pulled away, her jacket slipping from around her. She clutched at her nightgown and turned forcefully toward him again.

"This isn't what's in your heart," he said. "I know you want me too."

She grabbed the jacket from his hands.

"This is about my family, isn't it?" he asked. "You're afraid of the curse, aren't you?"

"I never believed it, Steve. You're the one living under your grandfather's shadow."

She studied him a moment in the soft light of the moon. He was a lost puppy, eyes wide with unimaginable hurt. She lifted her hand to his cheek, her heart touched by a tear just released. It struck her in a tender way. *John would never cry for me.*

"Good-bye," she said, attempting a firmness she didn't feel.

He nodded slowly, his jaw clenched. "Good night, Lizzy."

She leaned toward him, then halted in indecision, then forward again as he lowered his face to hers.

A good-bye kiss was all she'd intended. Quick. Then pull away, and walk—no, run—back to the house and her plans for her life and her future with John McCall.

The jacket in her hand was lowered for a second, and the thin nightgown offered little barrier between them.

She broke away once, then surrendered again, her emotions on edge, her resolve and her jacket falling to the ground.

She pushed him away, her hand on his chest, but he held her tightly behind the small of her back.

His eyes were locked with hers, intense and full of fire. "You always promised that I would be the one. That I would be your first." His eyes were scaring her, his countenance changing. He was no longer pleading, but demanding, his face no longer filled with love, but revenge.

The transformation caught her off guard, and in a moment, he was pulling her into the barn. She stumbled up the steps to the loft, his grip a vise around her. Suddenly, he was on her, moaning and ripping her gown.

Why didn't she cry out? Why didn't she yell for her parents for help?

She remembered resisting, but never calling out.

She remembered the hour she spent crying in the hayloft alone.

But mostly she remembered her kiss that had initiated it all. That alluring kiss, the one she'd willingly given, the one that sparked his desire ... and hers.

Elizabeth McCall sat up, clutching her flannel nightgown with one hand and rubbing her thinning white hair with the other. She slipped from bed, troubled by the memory, and driven by the thought of her own guilt. She moved slowly to the library and pulled a dusty book from the shelf, agonizing over a partially remembered phrase, one she'd heard a hundred times before, preached from the pulpit of a legalistic country church. *What was it? The sins of the fathers are visited upon the children unto the third generation?*

She opened the King James Version of the Bible. It was the only one her mother would allow. In the back, she ran her finger through the concordance, then turned to the verse for which she searched.

"Thou shalt not bow down thyself to them, nor serve them: for I the LORD thy God am a jealous God, visiting the iniquity of the fathers upon the children unto the third and fourth generation."

Her hand began to tremble as she counted the generations from Harold Morris, a man who bore the Lord's curse declared by Eleazor Potts for rebuilding the devil's still. Beginning with Harold, and ending with her own son Wallace, she whispered, "One, two, three ... four."

Her hand went to her throat. "Maybe this will be the end. Wally's the fourth generation. Margo, Claire, and Clay are the fifth." *Hopefully, they will be spared.*

She thought again of Steve Hudson. *It was a rape, pure and simple.*

Wasn't it?

But why did I kiss him like that? I must have wanted him, just like he said.

"Oh, God, can you ever forgive me?"

She thought of her son Wally and his shocking behavior at the graduation. And before the graduation, it had been months since she'd seen him. He had become a hermit, hiding away in his little house, making it clear that he would see her only when he cared to. That he'd agreed to have her along in the car seemed a minor miracle.

He'd gone into such a decline. How long had it been since she'd really looked at him with open eyes? She had suppressed the fear of the curse, never wanting to believe it to be a reality. For years, her secret had been successfully hidden. No one needed to know. No one seemed affected. But seeing Wally at the graduation had unearthed the buried fears.

Wally looks so much like Steve Hudson did shortly before his death.

The reality of the thought struck her again. *Could it be? I thought my secret would affect only me.*

"Oh, Wally, could you ever forgive me if you really knew?"

Della McCall awoke early to a jabbing pain in her side. "Come on, Wally, stay on your side."

She looked at her husband's face. He was snoring, sound asleep, yet still his arms were as busy as during the day. This was ridiculous, Della thought. Wally had always been the nervous type, always tapping, frequently pacing, never standing still, but this was new, even for him. He couldn't seem to stop moving even when he was sleeping.

And his temper! Sure, he'd blown up at the kids before, but to strike a nurse the way he did at the hospital? That was definitely out of character.

The evening before, she'd confronted him about it. He'd broken down and cried like a baby, saying he didn't mean to do it, that it was all an accident, something he couldn't control. She wanted to believe him, but she'd seen it with her own eyes. He'd landed a square punch right on the bridge of the nurse's nose.

All evening, she'd fretted about a possible police investigation, watching the driveway through the window, expecting a police cruiser to show up at any moment. And after her conversation with Claire, she'd worried even more, contemplating the possibility that her husband suffered from some rare disease.

Now, in the faint light of morning, her anxieties returned full force. Something was robbing her husband of life. He was losing control, sinking without a life vest, and Della felt like she was going down with him.

What options did she have?

The doctor in Carlisle had been no help.

If she listened to Grandma, she'd have to cart her husband off to an exorcist or someone like that. And if Wally wouldn't see a doctor, he certainly wouldn't agree to an exorcist! Besides, she knew what the clergy would say: *He's brought it on himself with the lifestyle he's chosen. You reap what you sow.*

She'd have to figure out something. And if it got any worse, she'd just have to call Clay to help her force Wally into a hospital.

She slipped from the bed and plodded to the kitchen to make coffee, adding an extra scoop of fresh grounds to make up for the interruption of her sleep.

She added sugar and milk until the coffee sloshed onto the side of the mug. She lowered her mouth to the rim and slurped noisily, pulling the warm liquid into her mouth. She'd started her day the same way for years, rising before Wally, quietly preparing her coffee and opening her Bible in the solitude of the kitchen before the troubles of the day could assault her.

Could it be that you've abandoned me, Father? Have you set things in motion, then withdrawn your hand when I need you the most?

Does everything in life have a root cause? Or is it all random?

Is Wally reaping what he sowed?

Or am I reaping what I sowed?

"Dear God," she whispered, "am I the reason? Is this all just payback for the way I treated him? Is it fair to make Wally suffer if it's only to teach *me* a lesson?"

Elizabeth McCall rose from her rocking chair after concluding her prayer with a heartfelt *amen*. Getting up took some effort due to her arthritis, and she wondered whether the creaking she heard was her knees or the antique rocker she loved so much. She had been troubled by her conversation with her granddaughter the evening before. And she was bothered by the response she'd given Claire, motivated by the secret fear she had held for so many years. What troubled her the most was that Steve Hudson, whom she secretly suspected was Wally's biological father, seemed to have the same affliction that Wally did. But it was all alcohol, right? Both of them were cursed by a love of the still—and the curse that was proclaimed by Eleazor Potts was still valid.

Could she be wrong? Could Wally be suffering from a mysterious inherited disease? She shook her head. No, Steve's mother, Mary, had lived to a ripe old age, hand in hand with her husband, Benjamin Hudson. Neither had shown signs of the illness Claire had described. Only Steve had any symptoms of erratic behavior or problems with controlling his movements. And Claire had assured her that Huntington's disease does not skip generations. So if Benjamin and Mary were free of the disease, then certainly so was Steve. So even if he was Wally's biological father, the point was moot. Wally couldn't have Huntington's disease regardless of whether Steve Hudson or John McCall had fathered him.

She busied herself making a cup of tea, but sipping the liquid did little to ease her mind. Why did she feel so uncomfortable? She knew the answer. While she hadn't actually lied to her granddaughter, she'd let Claire believe that John McCall was Wally's biological father. She shook her head. So what? What good would telling her suspicions do now? And the story of what had happened between Elizabeth and Steve Hudson, if it got out, could upset Wally, Della, and the whole family.

A secret this old should remain buried. She'd kept up the charade for so many years, there didn't seem to be any point in bringing the truth to light now. She really didn't know for sure, she justified. She'd never had blood proof that Wally didn't belong to her husband. And without that confirmation, she'd been able to suppress her secret.

Why hadn't she told her husband? At first, she'd felt guilty enough that she had doubted her own heart. And then, once Wally was born, she was afraid that her husband would resent the child. So she had tucked it away, with layers of denial, never allowing herself to believe that one fateful night with Steve Hudson could possibly have been responsible for her pregnancy.

But it was seeing her son during her daughter's graduation that had brought it all rushing back. Wally was acting just like Steve had shortly before Steve's death.

So what did that prove? Only that Wally was infatuated with the same liquid that had infected so many others from the hollers in and around Stoney Creek. And only that the proclamation brought forth by Eleazor Potts after he smashed the still was true. A curse rested on anyone who drank from the still should it ever be rebuilt.

Harold Morris had rebuilt the still, then gone crazy. Steve Hudson, Harold's grandson, had loved the liquor, and he'd gone crazy, too. Wally seemed to be walking the same path. Wasn't that evidence that Wally had come under the same curse? Maybe it was a generational curse, an example of the sins of the father being visited to the third and fourth generation. And if that was true, then it only proved to Elizabeth that her worst fear was true: that Wally was the result of her infidelity. Oh, how she wished she could have that moment back.

Elizabeth swirled the tea in her cup, feeling nauseated at the whirlwind of her own thoughts. She went to the medicine cabinet and took a long gulp of a pink antacid, then wiped her mouth with the back of her hand. "Aggh," she gagged. Anything that tasted that bad was certain to help.

She walked to the library room and pulled out an old photograph album. She turned the yellowed pages until she came to the period she sought. There, she carefully studied the images of her son Wally, including his wedding with Della. She ran her index finger over his face. He showed no resemblance to her husband at all. She left the album open and returned to the shelf, this time retrieving a much older volume. Slowly paging through her own teen years, she came upon her graduation picture. *He should be around here somewhere.* She ran her finger from picture to picture, freezing on the image of a young man holding a bouquet of flowers. *Steve Hudson.* She hadn't seen this picture for years. And she had never dared to compare it to Wally's. She slipped the photograph out from the old four-corner fasteners and carried it to the other open album. There, she laid the pictures side by side, Wally McCall by Steve Hudson. The similarities made Elizabeth gasp.

She shook her head in amazement, then looked over at another photograph that sat on the bookshelf. It was a picture of Claire and her boyfriend, John Cerelli, taken just a few months ago, at Claire's graduation.

"Okay, Claire," she whispered to the photograph, "I know believing in a curse isn't very scientific. And maybe I wonder a little bit about it myself. So, since it seemed so important to you, I guess the least I can do is be sure about a few things. But I'm not about to tell the world my secrets unless it's really going to make a positive difference."

She knew just who to talk to about this. If anyone would know the truth about Steve Hudson's medical history, it would be his brother, Dale. She decided to make a visit to the Pleasant View nursing home.

Chapter Eleven

Elizabeth McCall swore she'd turn ninety before she stopped driving, and it was summer mornings like this one, with the windows of her old Buick rolled down, her left arm out in the breeze, that made her renew her vow never to lose her independence. She honked at Red Smithford as she passed his gas station, and waved at Wilda Huggins as she unlocked the hair salon beside Raymond's paint store.

She wound around the road leading up to Pleasant View nursing home, wondering aloud why on earth someone would plan to house a bunch of medically needy old folks at the top of such a steep hill. Lord knew, if it snowed, getting one of the residents to the hospital in Carlisle would be a feat tantamount to catching a greased pig at the county fair. But what did the architects care? She'd argued with them herself, after donating a cool million to the project. But no, they had a site to design, and the hilltop provided the perfect panorama for a nursing facility named Pleasant View.

She parked in the visitors' lot, proud to park at the far end and then strut past all the handicapped parking places. She knew she was older than many of the residents inside, and she smiled at the thought that she could still come and go as she pleased.

She entered the front door, giving a cursory nod to Harvey Georges, a maintenance man who was installing a new handrail along the lobby wall. She took the elevator to the second floor. Although she was fine on level ground, she wasn't about to put her knees to the test by taking the stairs.

She found Dale Hudson's door at the end of the hall. A ragged note taped to the door appeared to have seen better days. The edges were curling and a corner was torn. In large, shaky letters, the note warned visitors to use the doorbell.

He's more deaf than I am. Elizabeth shook her head and punched the button. A loud buzzer sounded from behind the door.

As she waited, she recalled their conversation earlier in the morning. Dale was glad to receive visitors, but surprised to hear from her. She had been intentionally vague about the reasons for her visit. She had always believed that serious matters deserved a face-to-face encounter.

Dale opened the door and invited her in, pointing with his cane to a chair by a window. "Have a seat, Liz. Can I have 'em bring us a beverage?"

"Don't go to any trouble for me."

"Hey, it's no trouble. The staff here is available twenty-four hours a day. It's what I pay the big bucks for," he added with a snort.

He settled into an easy chair equipped with a mechanical lift, something Elizabeth thought looked a bit scary, kind of like a catapult or some such medieval device. For a moment, she imagined Dale flying across the sculptured lawn, screaming like a circus performer shot from a cannon, launched into the air by the rehab chair gone mad. *Good grief,* she thought, dispelling the picture. *I've got to stop taking that Tylenol PM.*

Dale's loud voice interrupted her thoughts. "What's on your mind, Liz? I got the feeling you were upset about something."

"Upset?" She lifted her hand. "Not me. Not really." She paused, looking around the apartment, spartan but neat. She supposed the paucity of furniture must make it less likely that he'd stumble over things while using his cane. "I wanted to ask you about your brother."

He put his hand to his chin, which was covered by white stubble. He rubbed it contemplatively. "I forgot to shave." The revelation seemed to derail his thinking for a moment. After a few seconds, he replied, "Tommy?"

She shook her head. "Steve. I wanted to talk to you about Steve."

"Steve." He nodded. "You were sweet on him."

"A long time ago."

"I remember."

"What do you remember about Steve's last weeks? Why did he die?"

Dale leaned forward on his cane and steadied his gaze on Elizabeth. "It was suicide, Liz. Of course you remember that, don't you?"

"Of course. But a man doesn't just kill himself without reason."

"You think he killed himself over you? Are you feeling bad after all these years?"

"No, Dale, it's not that." She hesitated before launching into her rehearsed answer. She couldn't just outright tell him that she thought Steve had fathered her oldest son, could she? "I'm concerned about the Stoney Creek curse. Certainly you've heard of it. My son looks like he's the latest victim. And to me, he looks a whole lot like Steve did before he died. Glassy-eyed. Twitching. Stumbling about. Slurring his speech." She cleared her throat and continued. "He was poisoned with alcohol from the still, wasn't he? Poisoned by that wretched curse that haunts everyone who drinks in Stoney Creek."

"You're worried about Wally?"

She nodded.

"You think he's under a curse?"

"It sounds so silly, I know, but—"

"It *is* silly, Liz," he interrupted. "You won't find me supporting that idea. If Wally looks like Steve, it's not because they both have a curse, it's because they both are fighting the same demon of alcohol."

"But I remember the rumors, the stories about a curse affecting your family. Steve accused me of being afraid of it, accused me of leaving him for fear of how it would affect my children. I know your grandfather built the still that the reverend cursed. I thought if anyone would be an expert on the curse, it would be someone from your family."

"Wait a minute," he responded slowly, his voice undulating with a hint of Parkinson's disease. "I have never believed that family curse hocus-pocus. And even if I did, it's not my family under the curse. It's Steve's bloodline, not mine. It was his grandfather who built that still, not mine."

"What do you mean?" she asked, her eyes widening with alarm. "He was your brother, wasn't he?"

"Half-brother, Liz. Our father, Benjamin Hudson, was married to Evangeline Morris, Harold's daughter, first. Evangeline was Steve's mother. My father married my mother, Mary Templeton, after his first wife died."

"But all during the time we grew up together, Mary was the only mother I'd seen around Steve."

"Of course. She's the only mother Steve ever knew."

"How did Steve's mother die?" Elizabeth's hand went to her throat. "Could she have carried the curse, and forwarded it to Steve? Did she have a bizarre illness like her son?" *Or like her grandson, Wally?*

"She died in childbirth," he said resolutely. "Bled to death after Steve was born." He shrugged. "She didn't have any illness, Liz. She was healthy as far as I was told. She just died from complications at delivery."

She must have looked pale, since Dale leaned forward again and asked if he could order them some tea. "Are you okay?"

She nodded without speaking.

He rose with the assistance of the lift device, Elizabeth noting how smoothly it buoyed him from the chair, and how silly her thoughts about the catapult had been.

"You really shouldn't be worried about an old curse," he said, pressing an intercom button. He waited a moment before hearing a voice.

"What is it, Mr. Hudson?"

"My guest and I would like some hot tea."

"Right away, Mr. Hudson. I'll have it brought up."

Elizabeth waved her hand. "I'm okay, Dale. I just hadn't understood that Mary wasn't Steve's birth mother. The information just shocked me a little, I guess."

He looked at her and deepened the wrinkles in his forehead. "I don't see why that should bother you. What does all of this have to do with Wally?"

She didn't know how to answer. "Oh, don't bother with the confused ramblings of an old woman," she responded, thankful she had her age as an excuse. She stood and walked toward the door, hoping to escape before the tea arrived, and before he asked her to explain her worries. "I really must be going. I'll let myself out." She quickened her pace to the door and hurried out, knowing she could get out before her host could hobble across the room.

She lifted her hand in a wave, and tossed a smile over her shoulder. The last thing she saw as the door closed was Dale rubbing the stubble on his chin.

Claire pulled the latex examining glove over her left hand and watched it tear as her diamond sliced the thin material. She sighed and twisted the ring around, diamond down, before pulling on another glove. But that felt awkward, so she pulled the glove off, removed the ring, and tied it into the waist of her scrub pants with the drawstring. The day's business had been fast, the evening's frantic. Lafayette trauma cases were bursting the hospital's seams, and the team was in the trenches.

"Come on, Claire! I need you in here!" yelled Basil Roberts.

Although Basil was just one year senior to Claire, the militaristic chain of command followed in the residency program demanded prompt attention to anything asked by a more senior resident. She responded by pulling on another left glove and coming to his side in an ER trauma bay containing a twenty-two-year-old Hispanic male with a gunshot wound sustained during an attempted robbery. Apparently, he was the perpetrator, but looked as if he'd encountered a store owner who'd taken the law into his own hands.

She looked around. The O-man was in the next bay with another victim, the store owner, who had taken a shotgun blast to the abdomen. Beatrice was assisting the O-man. There were med students and nurses galore, but no trauma surgery attendings were to be seen.

Basil called to a nurse, "What's his pressure?"

"Eighty by doppler."

"More lactated ringers." He looked at Josef, the medical student. "Tell blood bank I need four units of O-neg stat!"

Josef ran.

A respiratory tech placed an oxygen mask over the patient's mouth.

The patient screamed something in Spanish. In spite of the language barrier, Claire could understand the expression of pain.

Claire checked the IVs. The patient had two, both started in the field by the Lafayette paramedics. She looked up to see Basil cutting off the patient's clothing. When the man grabbed Basil's hand, the resident got right in his face and rapidly spoke to him in Spanish. The man nodded and allowed him to continue.

With his shirt off, Claire could see an innocuous entrance wound over the patient's chest, just medial to the patient's left nipple.

She heard Basil curse. His eyes were on the monitor. The regular EKG rhythm had deteriorated into an undulating, irregular line. "V-FIB!" He cursed again, and checked the carotid pulse of the now lifeless body on the stretcher. "Claire, get an airway!" He grabbed a med student by the white coat. "Glen, start CPR!"

She obeyed while Basil called to the O-man. "Dan! We've got to crack a chest over here!" He looked at a nurse. "Call and get us an OR ready. We'll need a place to put him if he makes it." He raised his voice. "Get me a thoracotomy tray!"

Claire opened a laryngoscope blade and slid it into the back of the patient's throat. A respiratory therapist was breathing down her neck. "Can you see the cords? Can you see the cords?"

"Let me have a tube." She held out her hand, taking the tube and straining to see the patient's vocal cords, to mark the entrance into the trachea, where the tube belonged. The patient was coughing up too much blood for her to see anything. "Suction, I need suction," she yelled. The therapist complied and handed her a stiff plastic tube, which she used to clear away the secretions. "Okay, I can see better . . . Glen, hold CPR for a few seconds . . . there! I should be in."

They hooked the endotracheal tube to an ambu bag and squeezed. The chest began to rise. Basil looked on. "Good work, Claire."

By that time, the O-man was on the scene to help Basil open the chest. The medical student stepped back as Dan coached the second-year resident through the procedure. "This shouldn't take but a few seconds. There," he said, pointing to a spot on the front of the patient's chest. "Start here and with one slash bring your incision all the way through the skin, subcutaneous tissue, and between the ribs."

Basil complied. Once he was in the chest, he cranked open a rib-spreader to visualize the heart.

Blood. Massive amounts of jellylike red clot spilled onto the stretcher and onto the floor.

Claire and two nurses began squeezing bags of blood, infusing them as rapidly as the IVs would tolerate.

Dr. Overby's voice was slow and steady, giving Basil enough time to follow each instruction. "There's a hole in the aorta. Put a clamp above it. Open the pericardium. Do it longitudinally so you won't cut the phrenic nerves. Now, put your hands around the heart, one behind and one in front. Massage it like this." The O-man demonstrated by making a slow clapping motion with his hands. "Good, good." He looked at Claire. "Get in here. I want you to do the cardiac massage while we get a stitch in this aorta."

Claire put on a gown and a pair of sterile gloves. She placed her hands into the patient's chest. The heart felt warm in her hands. She held it without flinching and began the rhythmic pumping motion to mimic the way Basil had done it only a few seconds before. She diverted her eyes to the patient's face. It was a surreal moment for Claire. *Your heart is in my hands.*

"All right, Claire, make yourself small, and continue to squeeze that heart. We need some room to work." The O-man stepped in front of her, edging her to the side. "Give me a sidebiting aortic clamp."

With a few swift movements, he isolated a small hole in the jaws of the clamp to stop the bleeding. "It looks like you've got a little volume in the heart now. Let's have the internal paddles."

Basil lifted the paddles. To Claire they looked like long flat spoons, the kind her grandmother had hanging on the wall of the dining room to toss salad. He placed the paddles around the heart. "Charge to twenty."

"Paddles charged to twenty," the nurse echoed.

"All clear."

She pulled her hands away, dripping blood across her gown and shoes.

Basil shocked the heart. Claire watched in amazement as the heart began to squeeze.

"He's got a carotid pulse."

The O-man slipped his hand into the chest. "There's pressure in the aortic root. Let's get him upstairs where we can get this clamp back off and repair the aorta." He looked at Basil. "You go with this one. Tell them to get a second room ready for the store owner. I'll stay here with Beatrice. You take Claire with you. And don't close the chest until Dr. McGrath shows up to check your aortic repair."

Basil nodded. "Okay, team, let's roll."

A nurse covered the open chest with a sterile towel while Claire, Basil, and Josef maneuvered the stretcher, a heart monitor, and two IV poles toward the open elevator.

In the OR, in the absence of the attending surgeon, Claire took the first assistant spot. Twenty minutes later, after Basil had closed the hole in the aorta and released the aortic cross-clamp, Dr. McGrath bounded into the room.

"Sorry to leave you stranded, Basil. My daughter was at a violin lesson and my wife had the twins at soccer practice. I got here as quickly as I could."

"Things have chilled here considerably," Basil reported with a relative calm. "Claire and I have this under control if you want to go help Dan."

"Sure," he said, stepping up on a stool behind Claire. "Just show me what you've done there, so I'll know how to bill him."

"You won't get a dime from this one, boss. He was holding up a convenience store when the owner tried to take him out."

"Seriously?"

"Right here in quiet Lafayette."

"How's the store owner?"

"Dan's with him now. Evidently our patient's buddy here blasted him at close range with a twelve gauge." He shook his head. "The ER looks like a battle scene." He chuckled. "Quite a bloody immersion into the trauma service for the new terns, eh, Claire?"

"Hey, this is what it's all about," Claire said. "This guy was dead. You saved him."

"You helped. It's a team effort."

"All right, all right, we're all cozy and sentimental here," moaned McGrath. "I'm gonna leave the syrup to you two and go help the chief resident."

As the attending surgeon disappeared, Patricia, the evening OR desk clerk, came strutting in. "Dr. McCall?"

She looked up. "Yes."

"There's a young man out at the desk looking for you. Called himself your fiancé."

Claire rapidly looked for a wall clock. "What time is it?"

"Almost ten."

"Oh, great. My fiancé comes to town, and I was supposed to call him to drop by for supper. But that's when all the fun began. I forgot all about him."

Patricia groaned. "You're in trouble, girl."

"He'll get over it."

"You mind if I tell him I'm available in case he doesn't? He's cute."

Claire rolled her eyes. "Just tell him I'll be out in a few minutes. After Basil finishes closing the chest."

"After I close the chest, *and* you write the post-op orders, *and* you see that this patient arrives in the ICU alive," Basil corrected.

"Yes, sir, Dr. Roberts," Claire responded, smiling beneath her mask.

She didn't care what he said. He could have told her she needed to clean up the floor. She would have gladly done it. She was pumped. A first assist on a chest trauma case was the ultimate carrot on a stick for a new intern. She was too excited to worry about John. She was sure he'd understand once he heard about her day.

Patricia opened the door to the hall and called out loudly enough for John and Claire to hear, "Dr. McCall's too busy operating to pay you any mind. But I'll give you my phone number, so . . ." She let the door swing shut to drown out the rest of her conversation.

"That woman," Claire muttered. "My boyfriend will understand."

Basil cleared his throat.

At least I hope he does.

Claire sat at the counter in the recovery room and began to write the postoperative orders. In spite of the late hour and her interrupted sleep the night before, adrenaline had prevented her from feeling fatigue. She would never forget the feeling of holding a human heart in her hand.

She finished the orders and chatted with the nurses, asking them to call if the patient changed in any way and to report the chest X ray that she'd ordered.

Meg Thompson, a nurse, looked at Claire and winced. "You'd better change those scrubs before you talk to the family."

Claire looked down. Blood spotted the front of her scrubs. "I look like a red Dalmatian."

"More like a holstein," Meg offered, smiling.

When Claire scoffed at the idea of being compared to a cow, Meg held up her hands. "Hey, it's the only animal with huge spots I could think of."

Claire ran her hand over the front of her scrubs, her hand catching on the ring she'd tied to the cord. *John! John's been waiting at the OR desk!*

She dashed from the recovery room and down the hall, jogging past the operating rooms and the multiple rows of scrub sinks. At the front desk, behind the counter, John leaned back with his head against a computer screen. His eyes were closed, his breathing deep and regular. Claire sighed. At least Patricia wasn't flirting with him, filling him in on all the down-and-dirty shenanigans that characterized the university surgery department. In fact, she was nowhere to be seen. John was asleep and alone.

"John," she said softly. "John." She nudged his shoulder.

He aroused and opened his eyes. He blinked once and shook his head, studying Claire for a moment as a look of alarm spread across his face. "What happened? Are you okay?"

"I'm okay, John," she assured him, looking down at her spotted scrubs. "It's not my blood."

He twisted his face into a disturbed scowl. "Oooh, yuck. How can you stand it?"

"You get used to it. I was on my way to change. It's not like we walk around the hospital like this."

He rubbed the sleep from his eyes. "Where's the ring?"

"Here." She untied the waistband of her scrubs to release the ring. "Oh man, the setting is bloody. I need to wash it."

He sighed. She could tell he didn't approve of the way she'd treated the ring, but what else was she to do? If she was going to wear it at work, this was going to happen.

"You were supposed to call."

"John, this has been an unbelievable day. I've seen more in the last twelve hours—" She stopped short when she saw the dejected look on his face. It obviously wasn't the time to tell him how excited she'd been to be in the center of managing trauma, of inserting her first emergency airway, and of holding a human heart. "I'm sorry, honey. I meant to call."

John stood up and held open his arms, then, after a careful inspection, he placed his hands on the tops of her shoulders, the only place without obvious bloodstains. He leaned and planted a kiss on her lips, careful not to let his shirt brush hers.

She giggled.

"And what's so funny?"

"I think you've just invented a new kissing style. What shall we call it?"

"I don't get it."

"I know," she said, offering him a quick kiss, touching only his lips, her body perched awkwardly away to avoid leaning against him. "We'll call it porcupine kisses."

"Porcupine kisses?" He lifted his hands from her shoulders, straight up and away into the air. "You're losing it."

"Come on, John. How would you kiss a porcupine?" She held up her hands. "Very carefully."

He laughed. "You're sleep deprived."

"I'm a surgery resident. I'm supposed to be sleep deprived."

"When do you get off? You've been here all day."

"I'm on until tomorrow. I told you that."

His smile faded. "I had hoped you could trade. I didn't drive all this way just to see you for a few hours."

"Welcome to life at the medical Mecca."

"This is insane."

"This is reality."

"No, Claire. This is what they want you to think is reality. No one should have to work this hard. How can you stay awake all night?"

"Adrenaline, John. When life is on the line, you don't sense fatigue."

"Come back to the house. You can carry the beeper."

"John, I'd get fired."

"How would they find out?"

She shook her head. This was an argument she wasn't going to have. "No."

"Will I see you tomorrow? I'm leaving for Boston at nine."

"I can never be home by nine. I've got to do rounds, write notes, make sure that— "

"Then this is good-bye, I guess." He paused. "It was nice seeing you, Claire."

She bit her lower lip. "I hope you understand."

"I understand."

He was hurt. Whenever he acted so formal and polite, he was hurt. But right now, as much as she hated to leave John dejected, she found herself yearning to return to the ER to help resuscitate the next gunshot victim. It wasn't worth the time it would take her to explain the feeling of exhilaration she'd had at successfully placing an endotracheal tube in the right spot, or helping with the emergency repair of the patient's aorta. Right now, she just needed to leave well enough alone. She didn't have time to explain.

He opened his arms wide, placing his hands on her shoulders again, and jutting his butt out away from hers. "Porcupine kiss?"

She smiled and nodded. "Porcupine kiss," she echoed.

Their lips met and lingered for a moment before Claire's beeper sounded. She pulled away and looked at the number. "Uh, oh. ER's calling."

He nodded. "You go ahead. I know my way out."

She frowned. "Bye."

He tipped his head forward without speaking.

She turned and walked away, leaving John at the desk, glancing back only once as she closed the door to the women's changing area. There, she placed her ring in her locker, stripped off the bloody scrubs, and grabbed a new pair.

In a moment, she emerged again and hustled toward the emergency room, wondering what more excitement the night would hold.

Della nestled the phone against her ear and sat on a lawn chair in the backyard. The night seemed alive with an orchestra of crickets and cicadas, and the stars over the Blue Ridge were spectacular. They dotted the cloudless sky on a broad canvas behind the flicker of a thousand lightning bugs. Yes, summer nights like this were made for sipping lemonade and watching barefoot children gleefully capturing the illuminated creatures in jars with nail-punctured lids.

But there were no such gleeful voices left for Della McCall. Her children were grown, all away from the house, leaving her with a deteriorating man and a heart of remorse.

One ring. Two. Three rings. She sighed. *Maybe Jimmy's on a house call.*

His phone greeting was professional, as always. "Dr. Jenkins."

"Jimmy. It's Della. I need your advice."

"Hold on," he grunted.

She could hear a TV in the background. A sporting event perhaps. Suddenly the sound increased, then disappeared altogether.

"There," he said. "Blasted mute button is too small." His chair squeaked. "What do you need?"

"It's about Wally. And about Claire. Something she told me has been bugging me all day." She hesitated.

"I'm listening."

"Claire has come up with this idea that perhaps there is something wrong with Wally. Something other than his drinking, I mean. I've been worried for months that he's got something worse, but I'm no doctor. And of course Wally's mother is no help. She just thinks he's fallen under the mysterious town curse."

She heard the TV again, this time at a lower volume.

"Jimmy? Are you listening?"

"I'm listening, Della. Claire has concerns."

"Right. Like I was saying, I've long thought something else might be going on with Wally, but I don't have the medical degree like Claire does. She graduated with honors from Brighton, you know."

"I know, Della. The town's very proud."

"I just wanted to ask you about a genetic disease, something she called Huntington's disease. She told me that she saw a patient who had it, and that he looked just like Wally. I think it worried her. She called me kind of upset. She wanted to be sure that there wasn't any history of the disease in the family."

"She's worried about Wally? Or worried about whether she could develop the disease?"

"Both."

"Tell her not to worry. There's no one in Wally's family with this. You know the family history as well as I."

"Well, I started thinking." She cleared her throat.

"Thinking . . ." he prompted.

"Well, I just guess I started wondering if you knew of anyone in this valley with Huntington's. I knew if anyone around here had something so strange, you'd be the one who would have seen it."

"Della, if no one in Wally's family had the disease, Claire doesn't need to worry about it."

"Jimmy, I don't need to remind you how mixed up things can be. There are some people around here who have no idea who their real fathers are."

She heard his breath, exhaling in a snort. "What is this conversation about, Della? We've dealt with our problems long ago."

"This conversation is not about us. It's about Wally. I just want to be absolutely sure you've never seen this rare disease Claire was thinking about."

"Well, I've read about Huntington's disease, but I can assure you that no one in the Apple Valley has ever had it. Besides, I'd be the last one on earth to question the matriarch of the McCall shoe family. She isn't the type of woman to not know who fathered her own—"

"And I am?"

"I said nothing of the sort, Della. You said this conversation is not about us, remember?" His tone was biting, laced with sarcasm.

"Okay, okay," she responded, slapping a hungry mosquito. "I shouldn't have reacted like that. I had the same initial reaction, and told Claire as much. Elizabeth's moral character is beyond reproach." She twisted in the old lawn chair. "But still . . ."

"Still what."

"I just started wondering why Wally always seemed different from the rest of the family. He's nothing like his brother, Leon, and he never got along with his father."

"Della, stop. Look at your own twins. They're as different as night and day."

She nodded and cast a glance toward the back screen door. Wally would be missing her soon.

"Okay, I'm listening. So you've never seen a case of Huntington's disease in the valley."

"Not in my career."

"Good. I'm going to pass that along to Claire. She's under enough pressure without adding unjustified concerns about her father."

"Della," he added, his voice turning serious, "I do think you should talk to Claire. Urge her to forget about genetic diseases in Wally's family. If this continues, next she'll be worried about her personal genetic risks. And I don't think we want her digging in that closet, do we?"

Her reply caught in her throat. "N–no," she stammered. "Some things are best left undisturbed."

Chapter Twelve

The next day, Claire left the hospital with the satisfaction that grew from knowing she had done a great job and made a difference. She smiled knowing that Dr. Overby was proud of her too, telling the whole team that morning about the performance of his star tern.

She walked in the house and collapsed on the couch, ignoring the red blinking light indicating she had a phone message. She slept soundly for two hours, awaking to the rumbling sound of a school bus at three. She yawned and stretched, knowing she'd better get up or risk a fitful night of staring at the ceiling if she stayed on her couch.

In the kitchen, she found a solitary pink rose in a vase, with a note that simply said, "Love, John." She smiled and lifted the rose to her face, inhaling the fragrance with a long breath.

She punched a button on her answering machine and began to listen, the rose still tickling her cheek.

The first message was her grandmother McCall. Her voice was tremulous, and not as strong as usual for the matriarch. She wanted to discuss some matters with Claire directly, not talk to some ridiculous machine.

The second message was her mother. Claire was not to worry about Huntington's disease anymore. Her father certainly didn't have it, and Dr. Jenkins had never seen a case in the Apple Valley since he'd been in practice. "Have a nice day," her mother concluded.

Have a nice day? Come on, Mom, you sound like a grocery checker at Kroger.

Claire contemplated returning her grandmother's call, then looked at the summer sun.

I've still got a few hours of late afternoon sun left. I'll bet the beach would be less crowded now. I could get some reading done and maybe talk to Brett.

She felt a twinge of guilt for her last thought when she looked at the rose in her hand. She put down the flower and headed to her bedroom to change.

In twenty-five minutes, she was walking across the sand lugging her surgery text and a water bottle. She glanced back at the far end of the parking lot. An orange pickup occupied its usual place. She squinted toward the town houses across the street from the beach. *I wonder if Brett's around. He said he doesn't often drive the truck.*

Her thumb instinctively ran over her ring finger. She slipped the ring off and dropped it into the pocket of the shorts she wore over her swimsuit. *John certainly wouldn't want me to wear this at the beach. Sand couldn't be good for it, I'm sure.*

She looked at the town houses again, then turned her attention to finding a secluded spot for her towel. She had just found a spot, settled in, and closed her eyes for a short nap when a voice spoke above her head. "Hi, stranger."

Claire looked up at Brett Daniels and smiled. "Hi. I saw your truck. I wondered if you were around."

"My truck's always here. I don't usually drive it. Say, would you like to walk with me? I want to walk down to the fishing pier and see if anything's biting."

"Sounds like fun."

She stood and followed him down to the firmer, wet sand near the water's edge. There, they turned south and headed for the pier, just visible in the distance.

"How far is it?"

"A mile and a half." He squinted. "Is that too far?"

"No." She laughed. "I think I walked ten miles in the hospital yesterday."

"The life of an intern."

She nodded. As they walked, she told him about her remarkable day, about the ER thoracotomy and the excitement at saving a man's life. She told him about the O-man's calm demeanor explaining to Basil how to open the chest, and about the sensation of seeing the heart shocked back to life. He listened, really listened, and asked questions about how she was getting along with the attendings.

But she didn't tell him about her new diamond ring, the news that every girl is supposed to be too exhilarated to silence.

Instead, she questioned him about his research, and laughed at his description of the fat rats they had genetically engineered to help figure out the chemical neurotransmitters responsible for our desire to eat.

"It must have been thrilling to grow up with a surgeon as a father."

"I wouldn't exactly describe it that way."

She raised her eyebrows and kept silent.

They jogged to the left to keep from getting hit by a wave.

"How would you describe it?"

"Like boot camp."

She studied his face. He looked serious. "Boot camp?"

"Up studying during high school at five every morning. And during the summer I went to private camps for gifted students to swim, hike, and learn Latin."

"Latin?"

"I'm serious. And A's weren't good enough. I had to be the best." He stretched. "Fortunately, I was."

"Right."

"I'm not bragging, Claire. Anyone who spent as much time as I did studying would have been number one."

"Wow. All I did at summer camp was make an acorn necklace."

Brett laughed. When he did, his blue eyes sparkled and dimples appeared at the corners of his mouth.

"How's the rest of the family? As brilliant as you and your father?"

"Smarter. My sister was a straight-A student at Prescot High." He looked down and slowed his pace.

"And?"

"She developed anorexia nervosa. Went down to eighty pounds. She hated my father and hated herself. It got so bad that my parents had her committed, forced her to eat. But she became bulimic and wouldn't keep anything down. Eventually, they tube fed her, so she ate just so they'd discharge her." He shook his head. "She died a week later in a single-car accident."

"Suicide?"

"My father would never say so. The official police version was accidental death. They said she fell asleep at the wheel, but I knew her best, and I say different."

"Brett, I'm so sorry."

"My brother Lawrence's story isn't much better. He's alive, lives in California, but my father has disowned him. Tough love, he calls it. My brother's life is art, alcohol, and cocaine. He paints during the day and parties at night."

"So you're the perfect child."

He stared out at a shrimp boat rocking its way up the coast near the horizon. "Right. At least my dad's version of it."

"He must be very proud of you."

Brett squinted at the sun. "He thinks the lab year was my idea for getting some extra experience so I can get my name in the literature so I can secure a professorship somewhere in academic surgery, just like he did. He has no idea how close to getting cut I really was."

"Give yourself some slack. There were at least four others who didn't even get lab spots, Brett."

"There were twelve interns and three guys in the lab, all competing for second-year residency positions. Two went into orthopedics, one switched to ophthalmology, and two ditched into radiology. That left ten. They chose the eight best for clinical spots and offered Sam Kowalski and me an extra year in the lab to see if we could produce. If we look like we're in the top eight next year, we might have a chance to get back into the pyramid. But remember, there's a cut to five spots the third year, and four for the fourth and fifth. A spot in the second year only means more competition, a chance to survive one more year."

"But certainly there are jobs in surgery somewhere, even if you get axed by Dr. Rogers' pyramid."

"A few, Claire, with emphasis on a few." He picked up a flat shell fragment from the sand and skipped it into the surf. "If Dr. Rogers thinks you will make it as a surgeon, he will see to it that he is the one to train you. If he thinks you can't make it and cuts you from his residency, most program directors look at you like you're damaged goods or something. They have a lot of respect for Dr. Rogers' opinion. They think if he doesn't want you, they won't either."

She didn't know what to say. "Great," she muttered.

"Knowing what little I know of you, I doubt you'll have a problem."

"You'll make it, too. We'll both make it." She hesitated, then added, "If we're supposed to."

"What's that supposed to mean?"

"I believe I'm not ultimately in control. God is. If he wants me to make it, I'm going to make it."

"So perform lousy, and if God wants you in, you're in. No sweat, is that it?"

"I didn't say that. But do the best with the raw materials God gave you, and he makes the right doors open."

Brett stayed quiet and seemed to quicken his pace. They had nearly reached the pier. It looked like only a few die-hard fishermen were left.

They spent a few minutes looking in the fishing buckets and asking about what was biting. The people were friendly, and a young boy missing his front teeth held up a fifteen-inch flounder for Claire to admire.

On the way back, Brett offered his advice. "If you want to make it, you've got to work hard. There are a few mistakes that are inexcusable. Lying is one. If you don't know something, it won't get you fired. If you don't know something and you make up an answer just to impress an attending, that's another matter altogether."

"That would be insane."

"Well, it happens, Claire. An intern has been working all night, and an attending asks for an X ray or a lab value. It's pretty tempting to guess and most of the time a good intern can guess right, but if they catch you guessing, you'd better pack your bags."

"Has anyone ever been thrown out for it?"

"Only one that I know of was two years ahead of me. He lied about a potassium value to one of the cardiac surgeons. The patient had a dysrhythmia that could have been prevented if the resident would have checked the actual value and corrected the potassium deficiency."

"Oh, man."

"The attending surgeon called the resident at home that night and calmly told him not to bother showing up the next day." He shook his head. "And he had already survived two pyramid cuts. He was two months away from the fourth-year level selections."

Claire picked up a shell. "Let's talk about something else. I don't want to think about the pyramid." She looked at the water. "I love it here. The ocean was one of the main reasons I chose Lafayette."

"Don't tell that to Dr. Rogers. He wants to believe that everyone came here to train with him."

She tucked away the fact without replying. "Have you always liked the ocean?"

"Yep. We went to the beach every summer when I was a kid."

"Ooh, the beach, too? Was that before or after Latin camp?"

He grinned. "Usually after."

"I saw the ocean for the first time when I was in high school. My father couldn't afford it, but my grandmother took me."

They talked about their families and family vacations until they arrived back at Claire's towel.

Brett's forehead was glistening. The temperature was still over eighty degrees in spite of the late afternoon hour. "Care for a dip?"

Claire looked at the water, then at the jersey covering her bathing suit. "Maybe I shouldn't. I didn't really bring a swimming, swimming suit. I wore more of a tanning swimming suit."

"What's the difference?"

Claire blushed. "Believe me, there's a difference."

"You went in earlier." He paused. "Uh, your hair was wet."

"You're right, but then I was swimming alone. Now I'm with you."

He shrugged and headed for the surf. "I just need to cool down."

She sat on her towel and watched him dive into a wave. He disappeared under the white surf only to reappear a brief moment later, shaking the water from his face. He walked back, his broad shoulders and chest glistening with water droplets. She didn't want to stare. *He's gorgeous. If only he was a Christian.* Claire looked down and tugged at the hem of the jersey, which had inched above her waist. *What am I thinking? I'm an engaged woman.*

She looked up and immediately diverted her gaze to the sand.

"Would you like to join me for supper? I'm not planning anything special. We could grill on my deck and watch the sunset."

"Brett, that sounds so nice, but I–I really should get home. I need to crash. I didn't sleep at all last night."

"I know the feeling well." He waved the back of his hand toward her, his fingers pointing down. "You run along. Maybe some other time."

She smiled, then took a deep breath and forced herself to pay attention to getting into her shorts and gathering up her textbook and towel.

"I'd better not get used to this," she said. "Next month I've got to baby-sit the open-heart patients. I hear those interns just live in the ICU."

They walked in silence back toward the parking lot, where Claire threw her stuff into the backseat of her aging Toyota. "Thanks for inviting me to the pier."

He nodded with nonchalance. "Have fun tomorrow. Friday nights always serve up something special for the general surgeons."

"I can hardly wait." She said it with sarcasm toward Brett's back as he turned to leave, but smiled to herself because she knew it was true.

Claire pulled into her driveway, surprised by the yellow cab parked at the curb in front of her house. What was going on?

She watched as the cabbie immediately hopped out and went around to the passenger door, where he began assisting an elderly woman onto her feet.

Claire walked up, squinting. "Grandma?"

"Good evening, Claire. I was beginning to think I'd be spending the night in this gentleman's cab. He's had the meter running for an hour." She fumbled with her purse and handed the gentleman a hundred-dollar bill. She waved her hand. "Keep it. You've been a good listener."

"Thank you, Ms. McCall," he said, handing her a little white card. "Call this number when you want to go back to the airport. I'll come right out." He set her suitcase on the street and closed the trunk, then insisted on carrying it into the house.

"What are you doing here?" Claire was incredulous. This was only the first week of internship, and she was on her second drop-in guest from out of town.

"Isn't an old woman welcome at her granddaughter's?" She embraced Claire with a stiff hug.

"Of course, Grandma. I just wasn't expecting you."

"Well, I wasn't expecting me, either. But we've got some things to discuss. I called you yesterday and left a message."

"Grandma, I spent the night at the hospital. I only just heard your message today."

"And I suppose I wasn't available to take your call, since I was on my way."

Claire smiled with relief. *She doesn't know I didn't try to call.*

"I am on my way to visit my cousin Hilda on Martha's Vineyard. It's no extra effort to stop here." She waved her hand in the air as if to downplay the unusual nature of her visit. She stepped away and studied Claire for a moment.

She was immediately self-conscious of her attire. Her short shorts were barely covered by the jersey she wore over her bathing suit. "I was off for the afternoon. I went to the beach to study."

"Of course." Elizabeth reached for Claire's hand and smiled at the ring on her finger. "John Cerelli came through, did he?"

Claire nodded.

"Strong family. I know his father." Her grandmother was immediately serious again. "Engagement is a tumultuous time for a young woman." She paused, then started up the brick steps past the smiling cab driver.

The old woman paused. "A tumultuous time indeed. I ought to know. I did it several times myself," she said, her face now locked on Claire's. "I suppose that's why I'm here, in a way. There are some things it's time for you to hear."

Chapter Thirteen

lizabeth inspected Claire's barren kitchen and immediately offered to buy pizza. "Certainly there's a delivery place available."

Claire walked toward the stairs. "The only place I've used is Luigi's. It's only two blocks from here. The number is on the refrigerator magnet."

"Got it," she called.

"Order whatever you want. I'm going to get cleaned up."

Claire showered, her mind busy wondering just what was important enough to prompt this sudden visit from Elizabeth.

Once she emerged, she found the table set and the pizza on the counter. She lifted the lid, taking in the wonderful aroma of cheese and pepperoni. "I didn't hear the doorbell."

"He only knocked."

"Was it the boy with a nose ring?"

"Yes," she said, shaking her head. "Have you ever seen the cooks?"

"I've never been in the place. It's probably better not to know." Claire giggled. "I always get takeout."

The two sat facing each other at the kitchen table. In spite of Claire's probing, Elizabeth would only make polite superficial conversation until she'd finished a generous slice of pizza. "It's never proper to engage in serious conversation until after eating. It's contrary to natural digestive processes." She gave her a look which implied that certainly Claire, being a medical doctor, should know such things.

Claire scrutinized her grandmother's face for clues. It had to be either money, the will, her own health, or Wally. Nothing else could have prompted such a trip.

Elizabeth pushed away her plate. "I want to talk to you about your father."

Claire nodded. "I thought so."

"That boy's been a heaviness on my heart for years, you know that. I've let him go his way. Since he was your age, I haven't had any control over him."

"He's a man, Grandma. He's made his own decisions."

"Certainly." She nodded. "We haven't been close, not for years, but your grandfather's funeral and your graduation forced us together again, and has started me thinking, wondering about a few things."

Claire fidgeted with her fork and fought the urge to interrupt.

"I know how you feel about the Stoney Creek curse. Your reaction at graduation was perfectly clear." She paused. "But when you called me the other night and asked me about your father, I, well, I just haven't been able to rest, thinking about this whole thing. You wanted to know if your father was adopted."

Claire nodded.

"What you really wanted to know was whether John McCall was Wally's real father." Elizabeth twisted the napkin in her hand.

Claire winced. Her mother was right. She shouldn't have brought this up to Elizabeth. She'd offended her and now her grandmother was upset. "Grandma, the last thing I wanted was to offend—"

"Let me finish, Claire. You didn't offend me."

"I'm sorry, Grandma, I—"

Elizabeth held up her hand. "I'm not done. I'm not stupid just because I'm old. I realized what you were worried about. You wanted to be sure that there wasn't some horrible inheritable disease that could affect you."

Claire nodded. Grandma had nailed it on the head.

"Well, I am concerned, too. But in a different way. I believe that the actions of one generation can affect subsequent ones." She halted. "God visits the sins of one man down to the third and fourth generation."

"Grandma, God forgives—"

"I want you to hear me, child. I've heard about generational curses on inspirational TV."

Claire looked away and rolled her eyes.

"A curse can be passed from generation to generation, Claire."

"Okay, Grandma. What does this have to do with me?"

"First, I need your word. This has to stay between us, okay? You're a doctor now. You should know about confidentiality."

"Of course I do." What could be so important?

Elizabeth's hand trembled. "I was once engaged to a man other than your grandfather. I loved him dearly, but my parents never approved. I was so young, only in high school. Eventually, I gave in to my father's demand that I break the engagement and see others. I started dating your grandfather, and my parents were thrilled. The McCalls were the richest family in the valley." She spoke slowly. "I learned to love him, too, and my mother convinced me that my life would be so much easier as a McCall."

Claire shifted uncomfortably. Talking about old boyfriends wasn't normally something a girl did with her grandmother.

"My first boyfriend would never give up. He came to me the night before I married your grandfather. He made one last effort at persuading me to cancel my plans. When I refused him, he flew into a jealous rage and—" She buried her face in her hands. Her voice broke. "He raped me, Claire."

Claire reached for her grandmother's hand. "Grandma, I'm so sorry."

Elizabeth lifted her head. "It's okay, Claire, it was a long time ago." Her eyes searched Claire's. "I've never shared this with anyone, not even your grandfather."

"But why? Why not share your pain? The man should have been punished."

"You don't understand, Claire. In those days women prided themselves in going to the marriage bed pure. I wanted to be a virgin for your grandfather. I know he was for me."

Claire felt a stab of remorse, then focused on her grandmother's words.

"I was afraid if he knew, well . . . I was afraid he wouldn't want me."

"But it wasn't your fault. It was rape. You said he forced you."

"I know." She hesitated. "But in my heart, I wondered. I kissed him that night, Claire. I meant it as a good-bye, but I ignited a passion that wouldn't be stopped. He forced me into the barn. I tried to stop him, but I never screamed out. I should have yelled for help, but I never did."

"Grandma, you can't blame yourself. You never intended for him to treat you like he did." Claire gripped her hand. "I've seen rape victims before, Grandma. There's often guilt. Women blame themselves. It's a common reaction, Grandma, but that doesn't lessen the crime he committed."

Elizabeth sniffed and forced a smile. "Thank you, Claire, but I didn't come here to pour out my problems to get your counsel."

"Why are you telling me this?"

"Because I think this man, Steve Hudson, is Wally's biological father. I've never had blood proof, but over the years, I've had my suspicions. And when I saw your father during your graduation, it all came pouring back. Your father stumbles around just like Steve Hudson did before he died." She sighed heavily. "Well, I knew about the rumors about the Stoney Creek curse. They abounded in Steve's family. His grandfather was the one who built the still."

"Harold Morris?"

"The same. And legend has it that he stumbled around and went crazy because of a curse placed by Eleazor Potts."

Claire nodded. She knew the rumor.

"I became convinced that your father must be under the same curse, either because he drank the still's liquor, or because he was in line for a generational curse."

"So why tell me now?" Claire shifted uncomfortably, aware of a gnawing anxiety about her father's parentage.

"Because you wanted to know about Wally's father. You were concerned about an inheritable disease. And I was concerned about a possible generational curse." She lifted her hands. "But I didn't think this disease you mentioned, this . . . Harrington's—"

"Huntington's," Claire corrected, her mouth suddenly dry. If Daddy's father wasn't Grandpa, then . . . The thought seemed to stick. She couldn't allow herself to continue.

"Huntington's disease, yes. Well, I didn't think it was possible that you could be right because I didn't think Steve's parents had any diseases like that."

"They did? One of his parents had Huntington's disease?"

She shook her head. "No. It certainly doesn't sound like it, but until I talked to Steve's brother, I was under the false understanding that I knew who Steve's real mother was. Evidently, the woman I knew as Steve's mother, who lived until a ripe old age, wasn't his real mother at all. His real mother died in childbirth. Steve lived, but his mother suffered a fatal hemorrhage."

"So his real mother was . . ."

"Evangeline Morris."

Claire was putting this together. "And Evangeline Morris's father was Harold, who was one of the two brothers that ran the secret still."

"Exactly. Anyway, the way I understand it, assuming Steve really was Wally's father, sins of the father can be punished up to the third and fourth generation. So if you count Harold's daughter as the first generation, Steve would be the second, Wally the third, and . . ." She paused. "You would be the fourth, so I thought you needed to know."

"Grandma, that's crazy. I'm not going to be cursed because of something Harold Morris did. That's so, well, so Old Testament."

"It's in the Bible, Claire."

"You came up here to warn me that I might be in line for the Stoney Creek curse?"

"I'm not crazy, Claire. This may sound upsetting to a scientific mind, but I'm convinced our sins have long-ranging ramifications to our children, and beyond. What I'm not sure about is what triggers the curse. I thought for a long time that it was the drinking that actually brought it on, that a person in line for inheritance of the curse may be able to dodge it by avoiding the devil's drink. I knew Steve's mother was a teetotaler, and she had no signs of any problems. But then when I learned that Steve's mother was a different woman altogether, well, I feared again that it may strike every generation regardless of the alcohol. But maybe if we pray, or take you to a priest perhaps, we can negate the curse's power."

"This isn't making sense, Grandma. Was Evangeline Morris affected?"

"I've thought about that. She didn't lose her mind, or stumble about like your father and Steve, but she did die a horrible death at a young age. It may be that her death was the way the curse was manifested. Perhaps if she'd have lived a bit longer, she would have lost control of her legs and arms as well."

"I am not believing this conversation." Claire stood and began to pace. Her worst fears, the very ones she'd been able to dismiss as improbable, were back, knotting her stomach into a tight fist.

"And I can't believe that you wouldn't be concerned."

"Grandma, everything you've told me concerns me. In fact, it terrifies me, but not because I'm scared of some mysterious curse." She walked to her desk and lifted a piece of computer paper from the printer. "In fact, you may have just stumbled on a solution to the mystery that's plagued our little town for generations."

"I know I have. But it's no mystery."

"Look, Grandma. Just consider the possibility that the manifestations of this curse, as you call it, are really symptoms of an inherited disease, a disease which doesn't manifest itself until midlife, and causes a deterioration of mental capacity as well as slurring of speech and an inability to control the muscles, making them appear intoxicated, and causing strange movements that some have even described as looking like a dance."

Her grandmother tapped her fingers on the table.

"Just look here." She wrote down Harold Morris's name at the top of the page. "Harold is here. He stumbles around town, loses his mind, and commits suicide." She drew a line down from his name and wrote *Evangeline*. "Evangeline Morris also has the gene, but since the disease isn't manifested until midlife, she never shows any sign of the disease, and dies before anyone realized she had it." She drew a line down and wrote Steve. "But she passed the gene to Steve, and—By the way, how did he die?"

"He committed suicide, Claire."

Claire nodded. "So he had the disease too. You said yourself he stumbled around like Daddy."

"Walked just like him."

Claire drew a line to her father's name and drew three lines from Wally's to Clay, Claire, and Margo. "Daddy gets the disease, but no one picks up on it because he's always been a drunk. All of his symptoms are attributed to alcohol intoxication or withdrawal, depending on whether he's bingeing or dry."

"And there is a disease like you're describing, I take it?"

"Yes!" Claire threw up her hands. "Huntington's disease, the disease of my patient in the ER that I told you about."

Elizabeth confirmed her memory of the conversation with a nod.

"Grandma, why did you ask me on the phone whether Huntington's disease could skip generations?"

"Because I wanted to be sure that my theory was the correct one, not yours. I knew, or at least thought I knew, that there was no evidence of Huntington's in Steve's parents. But when I talked to Steve's brother, and found out about Steve's real mother, it blew my little theory."

"And, unfortunately, it made mine a bit more plausible."

"Now look, Claire, you don't really know if any of this is right."

Claire began clearing the dishes, placing them in the sink. "This can't be happening to me." She shook her head. "I'm too tired to even sort this out. I didn't sleep last night, and I've got to be on my feet again at five tomorrow morning."

"Claire, we'll chat again tomorrow over supper. I'll take you out."

She shook her head. "I'll be in the hospital. I won't be home again until Saturday."

"Goodness me. They shouldn't work you like that."

Claire was too weary to explain the mentality of surgery training. "I know, Grandma, but they do."

"I'm supposed to be in Martha's Vineyard by then."

"You're welcome to stay as long as you like, Grandma. You'll just have to entertain yourself. I'm afraid my schedule as an intern won't allow me to be much of a host."

"I'll be fine. I'm used to taking care of myself. It's you I'm concerned about. I came up here to warn you about the future, hoping we could plan some intervention to change it. But all I've done is upset you."

Claire yawned. "I'll be okay, Grandma. I just need to sort things out in my head, work out a way to deal with this new information, that's all." She paused. "I need Daddy to get a blood test. A genetic test for the Huntington's gene."

Her grandmother approached and gripped Claire's arm. "Claire, I'm not sure it's best if Wally knew this information. It might devastate him to learn he may not be a blood McCall."

"Grandma, isn't it more important that he learn the truth?"

"Not if the truth is destructive."

Claire moved away and placed the leftover pieces of pizza into a Tupperware container.

"I'll put some thought into this, Claire. I'm sure there's some way around this problem. Just give me some time." The old woman raised her hand and pointed a bony finger toward Claire. "I may have been wrong about this all along. Maybe my suspicions about Wally are unjustified. Maybe he's really John's boy after all."

"But maybe not. You don't really know."

"And maybe it took the town's only woman doctor to finally solve the Stoney Creek curse."

Claire yawned. "I'm too tired to care right now."

She collapsed on the couch and snuggled against the pillow used by John Cerelli the night before. "I'm just too tired to care."

Chapter Fourteen

laire forced her eyes open and looked around in the dim light. She lay still for a moment, in that confused state between consciousness and sleep, wondering where she was and what day it was. Slowly a sense of orientation drifted over her. She recognized her living room and remembered eating dinner with her grandmother. She pushed away the blanket and realized she was still fully clothed. She had a dull ache in her lower abdomen, and she suspected it was her bladder that had forced her from slumber. Alarms sounded in her brain. *What time is it? Am I late for rounds?*

She jumped from the couch and stumbled over her surgery text, which sat in the middle of the floor. It was still dark. Claire took comfort in that. She breathed a sigh of relief when she saw the glowing digital readout on the microwave: 3:28.

She went to the bathroom and returned to the couch. There, she collapsed again and closed her eyes. Outside, Lafayette had begun to stir. Car sounds and the mournful song of a tomcat punctuated the night.

Slowly Claire began to sort through the clutter of her anxieties. She'd been a surgical intern for less than a week, at a program reputed to make or break the best medical students in the country. She'd ridden bareback on an emotional bronco, flying one hour with the joy of new discovery, and groveling in the dust of humiliation the next. She'd gone from being committed to John Cerelli, to tasting the bitter doubt about him which surrounded her attraction to Brett. She'd accepted a diamond ring in the middle of it all, and proceeded to forget her fiancé in her thrill of a surgical resuscitation. And to cap things off, she'd heard a tearful confession from her grandmother that confirmed Claire's worst fears: her father may have an incurable disease, the genes for which may be resting in every cell of her own body, just waiting for the right time to strike.

She felt as if there was a billowing black cloud looming above her, just waiting for the right conditions to electrify her life. It certainly wasn't raining yet, but to Claire, it looked like rain in the forecast.

At four, she cast off her blanket. She had a crick in her neck and knew sleep would remain elusive. She'd go to the ICU and get a head start on her Friday, a day notorious for bringing out the business for the trauma service.

She wrote her grandmother a note, dressed for work, and left for the Mecca. Maybe focusing on work would be her ticket of escape from the cloud over her head. Or maybe her grandmother was wrong all along, and her father was just a drunk. Oh, how she hoped that could be.

The idea struck Claire as ironic. The very item that seemed to be her biggest anchor—her hatred of her father's despicable habit, and the stigma that surrounded the family as a result—she now desired the most. "Oh, God," she whispered, "may it only be alcohol that Daddy has to fight."

By midafternoon, intern business on the trauma service had lulled, thanks to the work Claire had done before rounds at six. She'd been too busy to give serious thought to her current dilemma about her father, so she'd "back-burnered" the item. It was a technique she'd practiced since college, when she noticed that sometimes the best solutions would come at times other than when she was directly focusing on a particular problem. It seemed that when she pulled away from giving all of her attention to an anxiety, an answer would present itself. Invariably, if she stared directly at the problem, carefully inspecting every facet, her worries would multiply, blocking out even the most apparent answer.

She hung up the Dictaphone at the fifth-floor nursing station and began completing a discharge instruction page for patient Ricky Lemario, a thirteen-year-old who had ruptured his spleen in a skateboarding accident. She carefully wrote the instructions she had already given to Ricky and his mother. "No contact sports for three months. Come to outpatient radiology for a follow-up CT scan of the abdomen in six weeks."

She hurriedly filled out a discharge prescription for a pain medication and placed the chart in a rack to be processed by the ward secretary.

I can't just order a blood test on my father without his knowledge. And to obtain a genetic test for a serious disease without his permission seems unethical. So why not just get the test myself?

The idea seemed to have merit. It would provide a straightforward way of approaching her immediate concern about her own risk. After all, if she didn't have the Huntington's gene herself, she could at least go on with her career without worrying about coming down with some dreaded disease in the prime of life. It was a direct approach which appealed to her surgical personality. See a problem, solve a problem. There would be no mulling over eighty possible scenarios. That mentality was for internists and those with time for cognitive wheel-spinning. Surgeons like problems which can be solved with direct intervention. A chance to cut is a chance to cure.

She thought about Brett's warning to keep her concerns about HD quiet. She couldn't exactly have the program director knowing that she might start losing control of her hands, could she? No, she'd have to keep her intentions secret, at least from anyone affiliated with the residency program. She checked her watch. She had at least an hour before afternoon rounds with Dr. Fowler. Just enough time for a jaunt over to the basic science building which housed the department of genetic studies.

She took the stairs to the main lobby, then exited the air-conditioning into the muggy summer heat. She crossed the road, heading toward a modern rectangular building striped with blue window glass. Once inside, she studied a directory in the foyer, locating the department she desired on the third floor. She took the elevator and studied the door labeled *Genetics*. There were four physicians' names listed below the larger label, none of which Claire could pronounce.

She pushed open the heavy door and was greeted by a cheery receptionist. The woman, no older than twenty, had eyelashes too long to be real, and even longer red fingernails. She put down the phone. "May I help you?"

"Hi. I'm interested in finding out how I might obtain a genetic screening test."

"Oh, that's easy." She picked up a thick manual on the corner of her desk. "Our department handles all sorts of requests. If you have a specific test in mind, you'll have to give the patient the lab slip with your signature, with the name of the test and the date. Just have the patient register in the lobby so we can have their patient data recorded in the computer."

"No, I mean—"

The receptionist didn't seem to hear. She just kept on explaining. "Of course, most of our testing is done in conjunction with the counseling services. So, if that is required, we set up the sessions in advance of the blood test—"

Claire raised her hand. "No, I guess I didn't make a clear request. I'm interested in getting a specific blood test myself."

This seemed like new information for Ms. Longlashes. "Well, I, oh, I . . . I'm not sure I can help you with that. You have to be referred by a physician requesting a specific test."

Claire shrugged. "I'm a physician. Can I order a test on myself?"

The receptionist shook her head. "I don't think so. Just what test is it that you want?"

Claire saw a woman in a gray business suit step into the open doorway behind the receptionist. She had closely cut white hair and a trim figure. Claire looked back at the receptionist to address her question. "Huntington's disease."

The receptionist's expression was blank. She opened the manual and began paging. "I've heard of that before," she muttered. "Just what is Huntington's disease?"

Claire didn't really want to get into a clinical discussion with this clerical gatekeeper. Fortunately, the woman in the doorway stepped forward. She spoke softly to the secretary. "Don't worry about this, Kelly. I couldn't help but overhear. Perhaps I can assist you." She looked up at Claire and held out her hand. "I'm Dot Freedman, a social worker. I work in genetics counseling. Why don't you step into my office, Doctor . . ."

Claire took her hand. It was warm, like the woman's smile. "McCall. Claire McCall." She followed the woman into a small office with green carpeting and walls the color of sand. Pictures of birds—large, colorful prints with captions revealing the scientific genus and species—were evenly spaced along two walls. The third had photographs of young children, and several other family portraits. The last wall was completely covered, from ceiling to floor, with books.

The counselor lifted her hand. "Have a seat." Rather than sitting behind the large old desk in front of the books, Dot chose one with padded brown leather next to Claire's. "I take it you're a resident here at the university."

"A surgery intern." She took a deep breath. "For a whole week now."

Dot smiled. "And you want to be tested for Huntington's disease?"

Claire nodded. "Right."

Dot clasped her hands and leaned forward. "Do you have a parent with Huntington's?"

Claire wasn't sure where to begin. She shifted in her seat. "Not exactly. I think my father may have it." She watched Dot's expression. Her face registered concern and question, so Claire continued. "He has a lot of the symptoms, but he's never had anyone make a diagnosis."

"Are you showing symptoms yourself?"

"No."

"Do you have other relatives with Huntington's? Perhaps we know the family. We have a state genetics registry which lists all the known Huntington's disease families in Massachusetts."

Claire shook her head, and looked at her watch. She had to be in the ICU for rounds in forty-five minutes. "I'm not from here. I'm from western Virginia, the Apple Valley, from a town I'm sure you've never heard of . . . Stoney Creek."

Dot's eyes brightened.

"You know of Stoney Creek?"

"I've even been there."

"Nobody around here has heard of Stoney Creek."

Dot leaned back and laughed, her eyes lighting up like a delighted child at Christmas. "Our bird-watching club did a tour through the area. I spent a whole day tramping through the mountains west of Stoney Creek. In one day, we documented eighty-three different birds." She launched into a list of scientific names which were immediately lost on Claire. "Oh, my," she added. "I've gone on and on."

Claire smiled. "I had no idea the valley was so famous."

"Oh, it's a wonderful place." She fluttered her hands in the air, in a way which reminded Claire of the birds Dot loved so much. "Enough of that." Her face turned serious. "Tell me about Huntington's disease in your family."

"No one has ever made a diagnosis. But there is a curious legend in our town." Claire paused and looked at her watch again. "It's called the Stoney Creek curse." She watched the counselor for a reaction. If there was any negative response, Dot's face didn't show it.

Claire continued, explaining her situation by telling the story of Harold and Greg Morris and their still, and about the rumors of people in subsequent generations affected by a curse, stumbling about, losing control of their movements and speech. She hesitated when it became obvious that she would have to explain how this applied to her own family. Did telling this counselor constitute breaking her promise to Grandma McCall? She weighed the situation. Her grandmother's concern was that the information not get back to Wally or the family. Certainly she wouldn't mind if Claire shared the information with a medical professional. That shouldn't have any effect on her family.

She looked at the counselor. Dot seemed reliable and sympathetic. Trust seemed her only reasonable choice. "This is confidential, okay?"

"Sure. Everything we do here is."

Claire explained about the question of her father's paternity, and the possible family link to the Morris clan. "This is where it gets sticky, because Grandma has never told this to my father."

"Has your father ever seen a doctor?"

"Not often. My mother took him to a local emergency room, and the physician there just thought my father was experiencing alcohol withdrawal."

"Hmmm. And you just learned about this yesterday?"

She nodded. "My grandmother kept it a secret until I started raising questions about the possibility of a genetic disease in the family."

"And you think you may have solved the mystery of the Stoney Creek curse and discovered a previously undiagnosed pocket of Huntington's disease in one stroke."

"I'm afraid that's a possibility."

"So you thought the best approach to a diagnosis was to obtain a blood test yourself?"

"It certainly would answer the question for me. My whole career is at stake here."

Dot took a deep breath. "I see." She paused. "Have you stopped to think what a negative test would mean?"

"I wouldn't have to worry about HD."

"But it would still leave unanswered questions for your family. Just because you're negative doesn't mean that it's not something that your father and siblings might face." She sat up straight. "On the other hand, would you really want to know if you had a genetic disease, if there is no known cure?"

"I hadn't really considered that."

"You must also consider that with modern-day medical practice and detailed genetic databases like our own in every state, a population of people with Huntington's disease would be extremely unlikely. It would be much more plausible from a probability standpoint that the physicians who have seen your father are correct. He may just be suffering from the ravages of alcohol abuse."

"But what if he's not?"

"That's certainly a possibility, Claire, but it is up to your father to see a reliable neurologist who is familiar with HD before a firm diagnosis can be made." She paused. "Are there other people besides your father with symptoms? A relative perhaps?"

Claire thought about her conversation with Mr. Knitter back at Fisher's Café. He had mentioned several others whom he said were affected by the curse. "I think so, although I don't know them directly. There are rumors about the curse affecting people in our valley, but I don't know of a family link."

"So all you really have is a suspicion about your father based on his own symptoms, and the report of similar symptoms in a man who may or may not have been your father's father."

"Yes, but—"

"And was this man, the one who raped your grandmother, also an alcoholic?"

Claire nodded. "I think so."

"So there is another possibility. Alcohol could be responsible for their symptoms."

"Could be."

Dot made a clicking noise with her cheek. "Hmmm."

"What are you thinking?"

"Just that this is a very complicated and important issue for you. It is going to take some time to resolve this."

Claire frowned. This was starting to sound very much like a typical, I-feel-your-pain psychology gobbledygook.

Dot went on. "I think you must avoid focusing only on the negative possibilities here. You have to admit that there is still a good chance that your father does not have Huntington's, and that this is all a very unfortunate misdiagnosis."

"But it would be easy for you to test my blood, right?"

"A lab test is not physically difficult to obtain. You know that. But that's not the issue here. The testing process for someone at risk for HD is a process of three to four months that involves our whole team of genetics counselors, an exam by a neurologist, and maybe even a psychiatrist. It's not just a simple blood test. We do not take our responsibility lightly. Unloading information about a genetic time bomb like HD can have profound physical, emotional, and financial implications." She paused. Claire could feel her eyes boring in on hers. Claire looked away. "Claire," she continued, "this is an intensive process, and not an inexpensive one. And the unfortunate reality is that most people pay it out of pocket, not wanting their insurance carriers to know about the result." She shook her head. "Most fear losing their health insurance or their jobs, if their employers find out the information."

"That's discrimination."

"That's reality. Most people with Huntington's disease eventually require full-time nursing care, usually for years. It can be very expensive for a health insurer, so it's not the kind of patient they want to cover if there is any way out."

Claire never anticipated a blood test would be so complicated. "How much is the testing process?"

"Three to four thousand dollars."

Claire gasped.

"But I need to clarify something for you. We've never begun the testing process on anyone without a relative with a known diagnosis of Huntington's disease. It would seem premature to put you through an intensive evaluation only to find out that your father's problems were explainable by some other malady."

She sighed. "There is no other way to get a blood test?"

The counselor nodded. "Let's say a patient has characteristic symptoms of the disease. If a neurologist has a strong suspicion of HD, even in the absence of a family history, a blood test will usually be drawn. In that case the price is only about four hundred dollars."

"But that's not available to asymptomatic people at risk?"

"Right." She frowned. "Claire, it may not seem fair to you, but we feel we have an obligation not to hand out information about a person's genes without helping them understand what we're telling them. In essence, we're letting people see the future, predicting horrible circumstances like cancer or other serious illness. News like that changes lives, Claire."

Claire wasn't sure how to respond. She shifted uncomfortably in her seat and checked her watch. She'd never anticipated that things would be so complicated.

"Not everyone is emotionally equipped to deal with the kind of information we handle. We have some clients that, after the counseling process is over, decide they do not want the information that's available. They somehow make peace with not knowing, finding solace in the chance that they might not have Huntington's disease. They're more comfortable with that than finding out that they definitely will get it."

"Okay, I hear you. I had no idea how complicated this was. I only heard my grandmother's news last night, so maybe I just made a quick decision to get the problem solved." She smiled sweetly. "I think it's part of what my guidance counselor in medical school called 'the surgical personality.'"

Dot smiled in response, and Claire went on, "So what do you think I should do?"

"Find out more about others around Stoney Creek that may be having symptoms. Do a little digging to see if anyone has ever had a medical professional make a diagnosis. Find out if there are any relatives with this problem."

Claire stood up.

"If you find out more about your family, or if you'd just like to chat, I'm almost always right here."

"Thanks. You've certainly given me some things to think about." Claire held out her hand.

Dot received her warmly and cradled Claire's outstretched hand in both of hers. Her smile faded. "Claire, digging for family information like this can be frustrating. As you've already discovered, tracing a genetic line can be hindered by issues of paternity. Some people may not take so kindly to your questions."

"I'll be careful."

"You do that." Dot released her hand, but not before lifting Claire's left hand and admiring her ring. "Oh, my, you're engaged."

Claire smiled.

"Have you told your fiancé that you're worried about Huntington's disease in your family?"

Boy, this lady doesn't miss a trick, does she?

She grimaced. "Not exactly. I told him about a patient I had with HD, and told him that the patient reminded me of my father." She shrugged. "I haven't talked to him since my grandmother told me about the rape."

"You should talk with him, Claire. If it turns out that HD is actually confirmed in your family, and I emphasize *if*, then I'd be glad to talk with your fiancé with you. We have a wonderful video library of families discussing their struggles with HD. It can be a real benefit to see how others have managed."

"Hopefully, I've been too hasty. I could have just jumped to the wrong conclusion about everything."

"I'll bet that's true."

Claire turned to leave. "Thanks."

Hopefully, the counselor is right. I made a hasty decision based on circumstantial evidence.

But if I'm correct . . . Ugh! I can't think about that right now. I've got rounds to make.

Chapter Fifteen

Claire recognized the beeping noise without looking, the repetitive, obnoxious warning sound telling her the large truck in front of her Toyota was in reverse gear. The garbage truck backed toward her little Toyota, emitting a shrill warning. *Doesn't he see me? He's going to hit my car!*

The beeping continued, rhythmic, foreboding. Claire checked the rearview mirror. She couldn't back up. There was another car right behind her. She was trapped, and the ignoramus in the garbage truck was oblivious. She laid on the horn, but the beeping persisted. The truck edged closer and closer. Her Toyota would be a pancake.

Time to bail out! I've got to escape! Claire clawed for the button to release her seat belt. Where was it? Her fingers found the button and the belt popped free, but it was too late. She closed her eyes and braced for the impact ...

Claire's feet hit the floor with a thud. She opened her eyes, expecting the horrifying crunch of metal against metal. Instead, the emergency room trauma bay came into focus in the dim light. She rubbed her eyes. The beeping sound continued, the unrelenting noise, coming from the pager clipped to her scrub pants. Within moments, her orientation returned. There was no garbage truck. And the button to release her seat belt was on the side of her beeper.

She looked at her pager. The extension was a familiar one. The ER wanted her. Again. "I'm already here," she muttered to herself, plodding toward the central workstation. It was four A.M. and she'd been asleep on an empty stretcher for fifteen minutes. Brett's predictions about Friday nights on the trauma service had been only too accurate, and Claire had logged six new hits since midnight.

She addressed Cliff, the ward secretary. "What's up now?"

He handed her a chart. "Room eleven. College kid on a drinking binge. He has a beer-bottle cap in his throat."

Claire nodded. "And I thought I was having a bad night."

She entered the exam room to find a nineteen-year-old male sitting on the edge of a stretcher with a towel held up to his chin. He dabbed at the corner of his mouth. His eyes were wide, his cheeks flushed.

"I'm Dr. McCall." She looked at the X ray hanging on the viewbox beside his bed. Sure enough, a metal bottle cap seemed to rest in the middle of his neck. "Can you tell me what happened?"

The boy tilted his head back, trying to keep his saliva from running out. As he talked, he seemed to be fighting a rising tide of spit. "We were just playing around. We were unscrewing the caps with our teeth." He dabbed his chin again. "I can't swallow. Can you get it out?"

Claire nodded. "How much did you drink?"

He shrugged. "A few beers. That's all. Do you have to tell my parents?"

She looked at the chart. "You're not a minor. We don't have to tell your parents. But I think you should. They're almost certain to see the insurance papers."

The boy cursed.

"We'll have to let you wait a few more hours until your stomach has a chance to empty. Then we'll use a scope to remove the bottle cap."

"Doc, I can't wait! I can't swallow."

She didn't feel like arguing with him. "If we try to remove it before your stomach is empty, you could vomit into your lungs and die." She handed him a small basin. "Here, you can spit in here." With that, she left in search for the O-man.

She found him in the middle of a group of medical students, sitting on a stretcher expounding on his personal philosophies of medicine and life. It mattered little that it was time for normal people to sleep. This bay-windowed resident expected his students to hang on his every word. And what amazed Claire was that they actually did.

She smiled and listened for a moment as he carried them through an imaginary patient scenario, asking them questions and critiquing their responses.

"Okay," he summarized. "The patient has abdominal pain, tenderness in the lower right quadrant, and leukocytosis. What's your next move?"

The students called out their answers. "Ultrasound."

The O-man shook his head. "Two hundred dollars. And it won't change what you do."

"CT scan."

"Eight hundred dollars. And you still haven't helped."

"Barium enema."

Dr. Overby looked at Claire and muttered, "Wedges." It was his endearing term for medical students. The name was a physics word used to describe the simplest form of a tool. If you needed to get something done in the hospital, you used a tool. And the simplest tool, according to the O-man, was a third-year medical student, a wedge.

He looked back at the group and sighed. "I guess it's time for you to learn Overby's first rule of diagnosis."

The students groaned. Evidently they'd heard other such lists in the past.

The O-man raised his index finger. "Never let the skin stand between you and a diagnosis." He paused. "There is nothing wrong with proceeding straight to surgery with this patient. It's diagnostic as well as therapeutic. It's direct and efficient."

That's why I love this stuff so much, Claire mused. *If only all problems could be solved with a surgical approach.* She cleared her throat and caught the resident's eye. "I've got a case for us."

He nodded at her, then directed the students like a symphony conductor. "Remember, my little wedges, a chance to cut is—" He lifted his meaty hands.

The rest of the phrase was echoed in unison. "A chance to cure."

He waved his hands to dismiss the students from their teaching session, and turned his attention to Claire.

By noon on Saturday, Claire sat writing her last daily progress note, fighting back the fatigue that had become a normal part of her short intern life. She took a sip of lukewarm coffee and closed the chart. She felt physically and emotionally spent. In spite of her efforts to concentrate solely on her clinical work, the anxieties about her family seemed to lurk in the recesses of her mind, ready to pounce at any moment her attention wasn't demanded elsewhere.

She rested her forehead in her hands and had just closed her eyes when she felt hands touch her shoulders.

"Morning, Claire." The voice was Brett's. His hands remained.

Claire lifted her head. "Hi."

His fingers kneaded the tension from her neck. She allowed herself to relax.

He moved around and sat on the counter facing her. "Rough night?"

"Friday night on the trauma service. You warned me."

He chuckled.

"What are you doing here?" she asked. "I didn't think researchers came in on the weekend."

"I came in to enroll a patient in one of Dr. Rogers' clinical studies. I have to go over all the consent forms with eligible candidates."

"Hmmm." She sighed and laid her head in her hands again.

"Are you okay?" he asked quietly.

"I'm—" She halted. "Okay." She kept staring at the counter. She felt transparent, as if he would read her thoughts if she looked him in the eyes.

"You're quiet."

She yawned and looked up. "Sleep deprivation. I need to crash."

"I know about that."

She watched as he fiddled with a stack of papers on the counter. Her hands were under the counter now and she instinctively checked her ring finger. Her ring was in her locker, where she'd left it before the last case of the morning, a rigid esophagoscopy to remove the wayward beer-bottle cap.

Claire knew Brett would see the ring eventually. But why did she care? And why did her heart quicken at his gentle touch? She nibbled on her lower lip.

"Are you sure you're okay? Did the O-man make up a new tern rule just for you?"

She smiled at his teasing. "No." She pushed away from the counter. "I've just had some things on my mind."

"Want to talk to someone who's been there?"

She hesitated.

"I'll tell you what. Why don't you go crash for a few hours? Then head for the beach. My offer for dinner is good anytime. The sunset from my deck will do wonders for your mind."

She looked down. *It sounds wonderful. And I could use a friend to talk to.*

"Claire," he prodded. "I told you all about my dysfunctional family." He held up his hands. "You were a great listener. I can be too."

"I shouldn't." *I should tell him I'm engaged.* "I should catch up on—"

"I make wonderful shrimp kabobs."

She sighed. "How do I find your place?"

She could see his eyes light up. "Across from the beach parking lot. It's in the row of gray-stained cedar-siding town houses. Number 208."

Claire nodded her understanding as Beatrice Hayes walked up and lifted a chart from the rack near Brett. Claire watched as Beatrice made no attempt to hide her inspection, starting with Brett's tanned face and slowly gazing south.

I shouldn't be saying yes. But I love his persistence. Claire turned and walked toward the elevators. "I'll be there at seven."

Claire pried herself from her bed at five and studied herself in the bathroom mirror. She was wearing John's football jersey. *I need to talk to him.*

She dialed and waited.

He picked up after the first ring. "Hello."

"John." She could hear TV in the background and John asking someone to turn it down.

"Hey, Claire."

"Am I interrupting?"

"Nahh. Just some of the gang from work. We've got a softball game tonight."

She could hear a woman's voice. "A coed team?"

"What? Oh, yeah."

"I haven't heard about your trip to Boston."

"It was great. I think we'll be able to get our software into a large clinic on the south side of town. And if they like it, we'll have an inroad to some of the area hospitals."

"Great." She paused. "I'm sorry we couldn't spend more time together in Lafayette. I felt bad about our visit in the hospital. You were hurt."

The noise in the background disappeared. Claire imagined that John had walked into his bedroom. "I was just jealous of your time. I was disappointed, that's all."

She smiled. "I liked the porcupine kisses."

He laughed. "Me too."

"Do you have a few minutes? There's something we need to talk about."

She heard him sigh. "Sure. What's up?"

She launched into the story of her grandmother's surprise visit, and her confession that she wasn't sure who Wally's father was. She told him of Steve Hudson and his grandfather, Harold Morris, and how Harold, Steve, and now her father all seem to have the same malady.

The TV in the background became louder for a few moments, as if John was walking in and out of the TV room.

"Remember what I told you about the patient I had with Huntington's disease?"

"Uh, Huntington's?"

"Right. I told you the night we went out. About the patient who reminded me so much of my father."

"Uh, I guess I don't, Claire. I had my mind on the engagement, I guess."

She rolled her eyes and backed up to explain about her concerns that her father had symptoms of Huntington's, and now her fear that her father may actually have the disease, based on the new information her grandmother had shared with her.

"I'm not so sure why you're upset. It sounds to me as if you may have solved this whole town-curse mystery."

"John, you're not getting it. If my father actually has Huntington's disease, then I could get it too."

"Claire, you don't have a disease like your father. You don't act anything like him."

"Not now I don't, but Huntington's disease doesn't usually strike until midlife. It could be mid-thirties, maybe forties until I'd know."

"Oh." John paused. "Then you'd start acting like your father?"

"Not in every way, but most people with HD suffer a decline in mental capacity, in addition to a loss of ability to control their muscles. Their arms and legs move spontaneously to the point of having to be bedridden."

"You're nothing like your father, Claire. You don't seem to have inherited anything from him."

"I may have inherited more than I wanted." She felt like crying. "John, I might be beyond childbearing age before I know if I have it. And if I have it, I may have already passed it to our children by the time we know."

"Whoa, Claire. You don't even know for sure that your father has this, and already you're worried about our children?"

"John, this affects my future. Everything I've worked so hard for."

"Okay, I understand this is important to you. Why don't you have your dad tested? You're probably just overreacting."

"Maybe so, but this whole thing is very frightening. I keep praying that I'm wrong, that Daddy is just a drunk, and not manifesting some horrible genetic disease." She collapsed on the bed. "It's weird, John. The thing I used to hate the most is now what I pray for the most."

"So get your mother to take him in for a test."

"It's not that easy. Number one, Grandma has never told him about the rape, and number two, my father isn't crazy about going to doctors."

"Oh, great." He sighed. "Well, you're going to have to tell him, Claire. It's not right holding back something like this. You're just going to have to tell him."

"I can't. At least not now. I gave my grandmother my word that I wouldn't let this get back to my father."

"Talk to her, Claire. Make her understand how important this thing is."

Claire sighed. "That's not going to be easy."

She heard muffled voices in the background before John came back on. "Honey, this will work out, I promise." More muffled voices. "Look, I kinda need to run. Can I call you back later?"

She winced and thought about her plans to visit Brett. "I hope to be in bed early. We can talk some other time."

"Look, Claire, God wants you to be a surgeon, right? So he would never give you Huntington's disease."

The confidence in her voice belied her fear. "I guess not."

"Certainly not." He paused. "We'll talk later. I love you. Bye."

"Bye."

I wish I could be as confident as you.

Claire went grocery shopping, ran three miles, showered, and prepared for her evening with Brett. "Oh, God," she whispered as she put on some lipstick, "what have I gotten myself into?"

She dressed three times and finally chose a skirt and a blouse with a soft print. She looked at the shorts and jeans she had discarded in a heap by the bed, then checked the clock and decided to straighten her bedroom later.

On the way, she wondered how and when she should tell Brett that she was engaged. Maybe she was making too big a deal over his invitation. Maybe this was just his way of being friends with a fellow resident. He probably could care less that she was engaged.

So why was she so anxious to see him? Was she afraid of her feelings?

Twenty minutes later, she pulled into the parking area next to Brett's orange pickup. She walked across the street to 208 and knocked on the door.

She heard him yell from the inside. "The door's open."

She stepped into his town house and looked around. The furnishings were far from spartan. A large tan leather sofa dotted with blue throw pillows dominated the great room. "Brett?"

"I'm out here."

She walked through the great room and opened a French door onto a wooden deck. There, Brett was holding an imported beer with one hand and lighting a gas grill with the other. "Hi."

He looked up and smiled. "Wow. You look great."

"Thanks." She looked back toward his town house. "You've got a great place here. Not exactly your typical bachelor pad."

He shrugged. "It's really my parents' place. They bought it after I matched at Lafayette. They wanted to have a place to stay when they visited me. And they agreed to let me stay here for my research year." He held up his beer. "Can I get you a drink?"

"I'm fine. Can I help you with anything?"

"Can you make a salad?"

She followed him into the kitchen. As they worked together to prepare dinner, Brett urged her to tell him about her family.

"Being raised by Wally McCall was different than growing up the child of an academic surgeon."

"For your sake, I hope so," he joked, tossing her a cucumber.

"I dropped out of school and left home when I was sixteen."

She watched for a reaction. Brett was cool, not even showing a raised eyebrow.

She told of escaping her dysfunctional family, of caring for her grandmother Newby, of working for the rescue squad and earning her GED, and of being the first woman to go to medical school from Stoney Creek.

Brett listened, attentive to each story.

They ate grilled shrimp, hot buttered rolls, and Caesar salad on the deck and watched the sun escape beyond the horizon.

Finally, with Brett's prodding, she shared her concerns about her father, and about her grandmother's visit and the new questions about his paternity. She even shared with him about the curse of Stoney Creek, and had to scold him for laughing.

Unlike John, Brett had remembered the story she told him about the patient with HD. When she shared with him her fears about her father's possible diagnosis, he groaned. Then, she told him about her visit with the genetics counselor.

"What are you going to do?"

"What can I do? I guess I'll have to find out a bit more about the others in Stoney Creek that may have been affected by this so-called curse. I can't just sit around not knowing. My whole future is at stake."

He leaned forward. "You've overcome a whole lot in the past. Just look at you, Claire. No one from little Stoney Creek could have predicted you'd come so far."

"So?"

"So you'll get over this, too. You've never been one to walk around allowing a black cloud over your head to slow you down. Whatever you find out, I'm sure you will find a way to overcome."

"What makes you so optimistic?"

He shrugged. "It's always been easy for me to see the best for others."

She finished his thought. "But not always for yourself."

His eyes met hers before he looked away. "I guess."

Claire breathed deep and allowed a silent moment to pass. "You're easy to talk to, Brett. I like that."

He didn't respond.

"There's really something else I need to tell you. I'm not sure why I haven't told you this before." She paused.

He said nothing. He wasn't making this easy.

"I'm engaged."

"I know."

Her chin dropped. "You know? Why didn't you say something?"

"I was waiting for you to tell me. I was wondering if you would."

"How did you find out?"

"Beatrice Hayes told me this afternoon. I was kind of upset at first, but then, I took it as a compliment. I figure you'd have told me right off if you thought I wasn't worth your time."

"Brett, you're—" She began to protest, then stopped. "Well, you're right, I suppose." She shook her head. "But it wasn't right of me. I was leading you on. It's not that I didn't enjoy being around you. I did, and that was part of my dilemma. I—"

He silenced her with his finger on her lips. "Hey, you don't need to explain. I was nowhere near the picture when you began your relationship with your fiancé. You don't owe me anything." He held up his hand. "But I can be your friend."

She looked into his eyes, holding his gaze for a moment. "I'd like that very much." She kissed his cheek and stood up. "I'd better get home." She stepped into the kitchen. "Can I help you clean up?"

"I'll handle it. You need to be up early. I've got Sunday off."

She smiled. "Maybe I should do a research year. I'd like Sundays off. Think your parents would rent me their place?"

She stepped to the door and turned back to face him one more time. "I had a wonderful time. Thanks for dinner."

He nodded and closed the door behind her.

She inhaled the salt air and muttered, "Beatrice Hayes, you little wench."

Chapter Sixteen

laire set down her cafeteria tray and looked up to see Dr. Michael O'Brien approaching.

Bea was watching too. "Here comes a dream."

As a fourth-year resident, Michael O'Brien, MD, had made the final pyramid cut, and rumor had it that he was in line to be the next administrative chief resident, following the pathway of the colorful and respected Dr. Dan Overby. In that position, he would be the most influential of all the senior residents in providing evaluations of the lower-level residents' performance. He had already secured a coveted fellowship in transplant surgery, and had coauthored papers with six different surgical attendings. As an intern, the word was out: if you needed someone to go to bat for you, there was no one stronger to call to the plate than Dr. O'Brien.

Claire and Beatrice were exiting the hospital cafeteria when Dr. O'Brien came to a stop in front of them. "Well, if it's not the dynamic female trauma duo I've been hearing about."

"Hi, Dr. O'Brien," Beatrice gushed.

Claire nodded and smiled.

Beatrice put a hand on her hip. "Just what are you hearing?"

"Just that the O-man has unfairly stacked the teams in his favor. There are some benefits to being the administrative chief, I suppose." He ran a hand through his thick auburn hair and seemed to be studying Claire's scrub top.

Beatrice touched Claire's arm. "I've got to run down some X rays before rounds," she said as she scurried away.

Claire attempted to excuse herself as well. "I should run my lab list."

"Dan speaks highly of you, Claire. Your enthusiasm can take you a long way."

"Thanks." She hesitated. "Dan loves to teach. He's giving us a good start." She took a step away, and the upper-level resident followed.

"So you're on odd days this month?"

"Yes."

"Say, one of the Tagamet reps is throwing a barbecue at Dr. Jahn's pool house on Friday the fourteenth. I'd love it if you'd accompany me."

She tried not to cringe. "A date?"

"Sure. It will be informal. We do it every summer." He shrugged. "Everybody ends up staying up late. One year Dr. McGrath's secretary got so smashed she jumped into the pool with her clothes on."

Claire held up her left hand. "I'm not really on the dating scene. I'm getting married."

He stepped back. "But I heard, well, I thought you were still ... available."

She shook her head. "I'm sorry." She squinted. "Just who told you this?"

He shook his head. "It doesn't matter. It's just a misunderstanding."

"It matters to me."

"Well," he responded, "Beatrice told me you had a fiancé back home, but that your engagement ring hadn't apparently stopped you from seeing men around here."

"You were right," Claire responded, trying to quell her reaction. "It was a misunderstanding."

"Hey, your loss," he chuckled before holding up his hands in surrender. He smiled, revealing a row of white, even teeth. "Hey, can't blame a guy for trying, can you?"

"It's not your fault," Claire said, shaking her head and walking away. Then, to herself, she added, "It's mine."

She punched an elevator button and waited.

"This is my fault," she whispered. "And Beatrice's."

Claire tracked Beatrice from the cafeteria to the X-ray department, where she found her in a small reading room reviewing a CT scan with a radiology resident.

When she stepped into the hall in front of the elevators, Claire began. "I think you've gotten the wrong impression about me. I'm not dating."

Beatrice smiled. "Did Dr. O'Brien ask you out? He's handsome. If you like red hair."

"Yes, he asked me out, because you told him I was dating."

"I only told him you were seeing other men in the program, in spite of the rock you've been wearing."

"But, Beatrice, I—"

"You did accept an invitation to Brett Daniels', didn't you? He's gorgeous."

"But it wasn't really a date."

"I know the difference, Claire, and you don't have to tell me how the game is played. There's nothing wrong with using your looks to your advantage. And I hear that Dr. O'Brien will be the administrative chief next year. So you want him in your corner."

"I can't believe I'm hearing this. I don't think we're playing the same game."

"But it can be a minefield. I understand that some of the attending's wives are very jealous."

"I have no intention of using anything but my brain to stay in this program."

"You'd be a fool not to take advantage of what you have."

Claire's jaw slackened. "You're joking."

"Claire, I'd be the last one to condemn you for it. I just wish O'Brien would ask me. I've always had good luck with Irish men."

"Beatrice!" Claire yelled a bit louder than she'd intended. She lowered her voice and continued. "I'm not interested in dating. And I'm certainly not interested in sleeping my way to the top of this pyramid. Now I'd appreciate it if you'd not let anyone else think that I'm available."

Beatrice glared at her. "Touchy, touchy. Didn't you get enough rest last night when you were at Brett's place not on a date?" She laughed.

"I slept at my place, Beatrice, which is where I spend all of my nights away from this place."

"Suit yourself, Claire." Beatrice waved as she disappeared into an elevator.

Clay McCall loved weekends. The cabinet shop was closed, and he could spend the day as he pleased. He'd started his Sunday with two of his coworkers, with plans to take their dirt bikes up a logging road over to Mitter's Pass. From there, they'd pick their way across to Switzer Dam, and then back along the creek to Fisher's Retreat. All had started fine enough, but a flat tire after the first mile sidelined him, and after an hour and a half of pushing his Yamaha back to his pickup, the sweat poured from his back and face in hundreds of glistening droplets.

He sat on the tailgate of his truck and opened a large blue cooler. The beer had been reserved for the evening after the ride, but his thirst and disappointment changed his plans. He popped the tab on a cold Budweiser and sucked the can dry. Number two and three went down more slowly, but still too fast for Clay's empty stomach.

He wrestled his dirtbike into the back of the truck and secured it with red tie-downs. He then drank beers four, five, and six waiting for his buddies. Finally, bored from sitting in his truck, he decided to head into Carlisle to pick up an inner tube at the Yamaha dealer.

Driving out the gravel road was easy enough. He had to go slow there, because of the potholes. Driving on the highway was a different story. The lane just didn't seem as wide as it normally was. Clay wondered if they had been doing some construction to widen the shoulder of the road. It just kept getting in his way.

Clay first noticed the blue lights from the Fisher's Retreat police car a mile outside the city limit. He pulled over and slowed down to let the officer pass, but he just wouldn't do it. Finally, after he put on his siren, Clay rolled his window down and waved him on. *Can't he see it's clear to go around?*

Eventually, he realized he'd have to get all the way off the road. Curiously, the officer followed and parked right on his bumper, his lights flashing.

The reality dawned through Clay's fog. Quickly, he began throwing the beer cans out the passenger window. It wouldn't do for the officer to see these.

The police officer pulled a blue cooler from his vehicle. It had a large black mark across the side, and the top was askew. He plopped it down beside Clay's door. "This belong to you?"

Clay flinched. The officer was only returning his cooler. "Looks like mine. Only mine didn't look so bad."

"It pays to keep your tailgate up when you travel. Now could I see your license and vehicle registration?"

Clay made three attempts to get his wallet from his jeans pocket, before opening the door, standing up beside the officer, and retrieving it from his back pocket. "Here."

The officer read the information. "Are you Wally's son?"

"Yes, sir."

"You'll have to come with me." He motioned for the police cruiser and helped Clay into the back.

Clay looked around. He'd been inside a police car once, but never in the back. *Hey, there are no handles back here. How do you get out of this contraption?*

The officer pulled out a funny-looking tube and made Clay blow his breath into it.

Then he shut the door, leaving Clay in the police car, and went up to Clay's pickup and removed the keys.

Clay felt sleepy. The police officer took forever to fill out some forms. The car started moving, and just before Clay fell asleep, he heard the officer muttering, "A chip off the old block."

Chapter Seventeen

Days passed. Claire spent hours memorizing trauma protocols during the days, and hours at night acting them out. She could name five reasons for hypotension following chest trauma quicker than she could say her full name. She knew the different kinds of shock and how to manage them. She could put in a central line and a chest tube unassisted, and she felt certain she could assemble the rapid infuser and blood warmer in her sleep. On her eighth night of call she finally got her first appendectomy, and the team toasted her "first blood" on rounds the next morning. She loved her job. She disliked working with Beatrice, and she was actually looking forward to a month on cardiothoracic surgery.

She had been stymied in her search for answers about possible Huntington's disease in Stoney Creek. She felt bound to honor her grandmother's wishes that she not alert her father to her concerns, and until her grandmother returned from her cousin Hilda's place on Martha's Vineyard, Claire didn't have an inside contact in Stoney Creek to search out her suspicions.

Finally, on her last night off of the month, she decided to call her old family physician and mentor, Dr. Jenkins. If he was true to form, she'd find him at his office on Sunday evening sorting through the books in preparation for a new week.

He picked up on the second ring. "Dr. Jenkins."

"Hi, Doc. Doing the weekly books?"

It took him a moment to recognize her. "Claire? Uh, Dr. McCall?"

"Stop it. I'm Claire to you. Always will be, too."

"Are you in town?"

"Nope. Still in Lafayette. I've survived my first month."

"How is it?"

"I've been on the trauma service. It tends to be a lot of night stuff. So I'm learning what I can do without sleep."

"Medical school should have taught you that."

"Medical school was like kindergarten compared to this." She paused. "Well, maybe first grade."

He laughed. "Sanguines always exaggerate, Claire. I'm on to you."

"Me exaggerate? You're the one who always told me the stories about the worst cases you'd ever seen, every patient within a breath of death, within one red blood cell of exsanguination."

"Never let the truth get in the way of a good story."

She listened to his laughter for a moment before proceeding. "I guess my mother talked to you about my father."

She heard him sigh. "Yes."

"Listen, I need to run something by you. Something in complete confidence, okay?"

"Of course."

"My grandmother Elizabeth isn't sure Wally is John McCall's son. She was raped by a man named Steve Hudson just before her wedding. It's possible that he's my biological grandfather."

Claire pulled the phone away as a loud clattering noise penetrated her ear. She heard a scuffle followed by Dr. Jenkins clearing his throat. "I remember him. When did you find this out?"

"My grandma just told me. She's kept this a secret all these years. She never told anyone until now. And she shared it with me only because she wanted to warn me that I might be in a direct bloodline to inherit the curse."

Dr. Jenkins sputtered. "W–what? That's ridiculous. This stupid legend is—"

"Hear me out. Grandma tells me that Daddy's acting a whole lot like Steve did. Stumbling around, slurring his speech." She paused. "So when Daddy started acting the same way, Grandma started thinking about Steve and worrying that he might be Daddy's real father." She cleared her throat. "It all looks a lot like Huntington's disease to me."

"Steve Hudson was crazy. And he drank like a fish. I was away at college when he died. I can still remember my mom's phone call. She said he couldn't stand to see your grandmother with another man."

"Don't you see, Doc? The Stoney Creek curse may be nothing but an undiagnosed pocket of Huntington's disease."

"Claire, I've been the health care in this valley for over thirty years. There is no rare genetic illness stalking these hills."

"But how can you be so sure? Steve Hudson's mother may have had it, too. Grandma said she died at Steve's birth, so she could have carried the gene. And her father was none other than Harold Morris, the still owner who spawned the whole Stoney Creek curse legend."

"He was an alcoholic, too, Claire. He was addicted to the corn liquor he sold to half the men in this valley."

"How can you be so sure? My future is resting on this knowledge."

"You're being melodramatic, Claire. And may I suggest something else?"

"Well, I—"

"You're falling into a trap that many young physicians fall prey to. I call it ivory-toweritis. You go up to the big university medical center and see all the rare and unique cases, and have access to all the latest medical miracle machinery, and think that's the way medicine is practiced out here in the real world. Well, it just ain't so. Your attendings in the university may be able to look down from their ivory towers on the rest of us, but this is where most of the people in this county go for their care."

"No one's looking down on you, Doc—"

"Let me finish. We had a saying in my day. 'When you hear hoofbeats, think horses, not zebras.' So while you might see the rare diagnosis at the big referral centers, we go right on treating the bread-and-butter illnesses of the world. So when I see someone who loves the bottle stumbling around town, losing their temper, and slurring their speech, what do I think? Huntington's disease? No. I don't think zebras, I think horses. Your father is an alcoholic, Claire. And from the sounds of your grandmother's confession, his real father may have been, too."

Claire sighed. "I was hoping I could talk you into getting his blood screened for the HD gene."

"Well, I'm afraid I can't help you. Number one, your dad hasn't come into my office for care in a long time. And number two, even if he did, I'd be way out on shaky ground ordering a test like that. His insurance plan may never allow it, unless I could demonstrate a positive family history."

"That would be difficult to do."

He huffed. "Claire, you're a smart young woman. But my advice to you is to drop this search right now before you get yourself in the middle of a huge family tangle. You bailed out of your family at a young age, and for good reason, as I recall. Why do you want to go stirring things up so?"

"I just can't stop thinking about the patient I saw with HD. He looked just like my dad. What if we've been blaming him and his drink for his actions all this time, and it's really been out of his control all along?"

"Tell me the truth, Claire. You're not suddenly concerned about your father, are you? You stopped worrying about him years ago. You moved on. You made your own life. Why act as if you're so concerned about him now?"

His words stung. There was truth in them, Claire knew. She hesitated, then admitted softly, "Because now the issue is my life, my future."

"Stop worrying, Claire. You've got enough to do up there without obsessing over some rare genetic disease."

"You're right about that."

"I know I am. Drop this, Claire. I'm the one paid to worry about the people in this valley, not you."

"But I keep thinking that—"

"Claire. Listen to me. I've been a friend of your family's for a long time. Don't bring these kind of secrets out into the open with your curiosity. People could be hurt by this stuff."

"Maybe you're right." She yawned. "Ivory-toweritis, huh?"

"Exactly. Now follow my advice and I won't tell my old buddy Dr. Rogers that he's not giving you enough to do."

"You know better."

"You do too."

"Okay, Doc, I give. I'm gonna crash early tonight. I've got call tomorrow 'cause it's an odd day, the thirty-first. And unfortunately, when I switch services for August, I've been assigned the odd-day calls there too."

"So you've got two call nights in a row?"

"I told you medical school was kindergarten."

"So this is how they create surgeons. No wonder most of them are jerks."

"Doctor Jenkins!"

"Just a lifetime observation. Don't let 'em change you."

"I'll try not. Bye."

"Good night, doll."

Claire hung up the phone and collapsed on her bed. *I may have ivory-toweritis, but at least I have an open mind. Blindness is worse.*

Far worse.

I just want to be sure. Is that so bad? Why are there so many roadblocks to the truth?

Dr. Jimmy Jenkins set down the phone in its cradle and tried to quell a rising tide of panic in his gut. He walked to a large closet in the back hall of his office and opened the door. The shelves were lined with pharmaceutical samples, each arranged in neat rows according to alphabetical order. He reached for Valium and pressed two tablets from a bubble pack into his hand. He swallowed them dry and shuffled through the medicines to locate the Pepcid. He took forty milligrams, four times the over-the-counter dose, and returned to the phone, glancing first to be sure the door leading to his house was closed.

He called Della McCall. She answered after six rings.

"Hello." Her voice was cheerful, something that had always endeared her to him, but irritated him in his present mood.

"Della."

Her voice became immediately softer, stiff, and formal. "Yes?"

She must be with Wally. "Claire just called."

"And?"

"Della, I thought I told you to tell her to forget about this Huntington's disease notion."

"I did. I told her exactly what you told me. That you'd never seen the disease in this valley, so she shouldn't give it another thought. Why, what's the deal?"

"She talked to Wally's mother—"

"She didn't! I told her specifically not to do that! The last thing my family needs is to alienate Elizabeth with suggestions that she—"

"Della, calm down. She didn't accuse Elizabeth of anything. But Elizabeth confided in her that she'd been raped, and that she wasn't sure that Wally is really John's son."

"W–what? She never said anything to us!"

"She never told anyone, Della. She must have been too ashamed. But now, with Claire questioning the family tree, Elizabeth must have felt obligated to tell her. In fact, Claire said her grandmother wanted to warn her that she might be in the bloodline to inherit the Stoney Creek curse."

Jimmy heard the sound of a squeaky hinge and the slam of a screen door. He could imagine Della walking into the backyard.

"This is crazy. Did she say who did this to her? If John McCall wasn't Wally's father, who was?"

"She thinks it may have been a man by the name of Steve Hudson. Do you remember him?"

"Yes, but I didn't really know him. I was a teenager when he died."

"He killed himself, Della."

"I know. Everyone in Stoney Creek talked about it for weeks. He shot himself in the barn that belonged to Elizabeth's parents."

"I hadn't remembered that. I knew he committed suicide, and that rumor had it that he was lovesick over Elizabeth, but I didn't know he had killed himself at her home place."

"Right in the hayloft."

He shook his head to erase the mental image of Steve Hudson's corpse. "Anyway, Steve's grandfather was Harold Morris. Elizabeth evidently worries that some curse placed on him might be passing through the generations. And Claire has it in her mind that this might be Huntington's disease."

"And what do you think?"

"I think she's in left field, worrying about something so rare, when the real problem is staring her in the face. These men have all been alcoholics. The curse is nothing but the ravages of alcohol abuse."

"So why did Claire call you?"

"She wanted to talk me into having Wally tested. She wants to look for a faulty gene to blame for his behavior."

"What would be wrong with that?"

"Della, the last thing I want is to focus attention on Claire's gene pool."

"You're afraid for your own reputation, aren't you?"

"And what about you? You've been consumed with your own secrets, afraid that Elizabeth wouldn't keep the children in the will if she suspected—"

"I'm concerned about my children, yes, but also about how all this would affect Wally. He's a proud man, Jimmy. He wouldn't take this news quietly. He forgave me, but he never suspected that the children—"

"We don't know about the children," he interrupted. "It's never been proven for sure that—"

"You told me yourself that you knew. As soon as you saw Clay's hair, you felt it."

"It was only a stupid emotion, Della. We don't know. We never have. And we don't have any reason to suspect it now."

"Why are you so afraid? It was a long time ago."

"That's right. It was a long time ago. There's no benefit in bringing this up now."

"You're avoiding my question. Why are you so afraid?" Della asked.

"And you're not?"

"Maybe I am, but I asked you."

Jimmy looked at the closed door leading to his house. His wife, Fiona, was there preparing supper, soup or a fruit plate perhaps, just as she had for every Sunday evening as long as he could remember. "I've never shared this with Fiona. This would devastate her." He sighed deeply, exhaling into the phone. "Look, Della, I'm about to retire. News like this would taint my career. I've given my life to this town. Rumors spread like fire in this valley. I'd be ruined."

"And what about Wally? Aren't you concerned about him?"

"Sure, I am. But there's little I can do. The man won't see a doctor. And we know what his problem is. He's fried his brain on the same liquor that has been the undoing of too many men around here."

"So why did you tell me this? What can I do?"

"Talk some sense into Claire. Convince her to stop her crazy search."

"She won't listen to me. That should be obvious by now. I told her not to talk to Elizabeth, and she went right on. The girl has a mind of her own."

He cursed. "You can try."

"It won't do any good. And what am I to do with this information about Steve Hudson? I can't tell this to Wally. He's in no condition to deal with news like this. Yesterday he went to get the mail without his trousers on. And he peed all over the carpet this morning. I don't know what I'm going to do with him."

"He's going to need a nursing home."

Della started to cry. "He won't go. And how can I afford that?"

This conversation wasn't going the way he'd planned. "Della. Something will work out. Certainly Elizabeth would care for her own son, wouldn't she?"

"I–I hope."

"Don't cry, Della. Something always works out. I didn't call to upset you. I just, well, I just hoped we could keep Claire from asking so many questions."

"Claire's my daughter. And she's smart. Smarter than I ever was. Hopefully she'll avoid the mistakes I made." She sniffed. "If Claire has a medical explanation for this stupid town curse, maybe we should listen."

"Let her keep talking then, Della. People are going to get hurt. And not just in your family. These things have a way of ripping communities apart." He paced to the phone cord's limit, looking first into an exam room, and then back toward his desk. "And I don't need to remind you how jealous Leon McCall is over the McCall fortune. His lawyers would certainly find a way to keep the money away from anyone who isn't a blood McCall. And it sounds like Wally's going to need that money. He's gonna need that money soon."

There was an uncomfortable pause. "I'll talk to Claire, Jimmy. But I can't promise anything."

He heard a click. He laid the phone down and put his head in his hands before heading to the medicine closet again.

Chapter Eighteen

Sierra Jones was hit by a drunk driver while riding on her new bicycle on Claire's last night of trauma call. It was Sierra's seventh birthday. The bicycle was a gift from her father.

At eight-thirty, Claire stood anxiously awaiting the patient's arrival. The team had gathered after receiving notification by the Lafayette paramedics that an unstable patient was en route.

She glanced at the other members of the team. Nervous laughter punctuated their conversation. Everyone was pacing, milling around the empty stretcher, unable to still the anxiety that accompanied the knowledge that soon, very soon, a child's life would be in their hands. Claire sensed an unspoken heaviness that seemed to hover each time they cared for one so young. Adults, she supposed, mostly were in trouble because of their own choices. They drank. They took chances.

But children were different, at least for Claire. Their innocence captured her. Their cries, which rose from their ignorance and the fear of events unfolding around them, tugged on her heart like an adult's never could. And worst of all, there was little margin for error. Children bled to death quicker, occluded their small airways faster, and coded sooner than their adult counterparts.

As Sierra arrived, the team began a symphony of critical care. The paramedics had been unable to start an IV, and a quick assessment revealed her peripheral veins were flat.

"Should we do a cutdown?" Claire pulled a flexible plastic tourniquet off of the patient's arm. "There are no IV sites available."

"I'll do a central line," Basil offered. "I'll use the ultrasound."

Claire leaned over the little girl and smiled. "Hi, Sierra. I'm Dr. McCall. We're going to help you. Do you hurt anywhere?"

"My tummy hurts. And my arm."

Claire carefully explained everything that was happening to her young patient. "Don't try to move, Sierra. You're neck is in a brace until we know it's okay."

Basil inserted a large-bore central venous line while the O-man did a primary survey. "Her lungs are clear. Her heart is tachycardic. Her abdomen is distended and tender throughout. Pelvis is stable. Left arm is abraised, tender above the elbow. Knees are abraded. No malangulation of the legs."

Deb Parrish called out the vital signs. "B.P. sixty systolic. Heart rate 170."

Dr. Overby gave the orders. "Let's get a hematocrit, amylase, liver functions, and urinalysis. Type and cross for six units and give five hundred cc's of lactated ringers stat!" He looked at Claire. "She's going to need a CT of the abdomen. I want you to stay with her. Go over the scan with the radiology resident and call me. And arrange an ICU bed. She probably has a ruptured spleen, maybe a liver crack." He looked at an X-ray technician. "Get a portable chest and c-spine film before she goes to the scanner. "

The team responded. Claire squeezed the IV bag and watched the heart monitor. Sierra's blood pressure came up to eighty-five after the IV bolus.

"Careful," the O-man cautioned. "Let's not overdo it. Her normal blood pressure may not be much more than that."

Claire put her face close to the patient's. "Can you tell us what happened?"

"I was riding my bike on the sidewalk. A man in a red car ran into me." Her chin quivered. "He smashed my new bike."

"I'm sure it can be replaced, honey."

"It was my favorite color. Purple. And it had a bell and a handlebar bag."

"It sounds wonderful."

"I got it for my birthday."

"How old are you?"

"Seven."

"Happy birthday, Sierra."

"How did you know it was my birthday?"

"The men on the rescue squad radioed ahead, and told us about you. They said it was your birthday." Claire looked up to see Cliff, the ward secretary, standing at the foot of the bed.

"Her family is in the waiting room. Can you talk to them, Dr. McCall?"

Claire looked at Basil. He nodded. "You talk to the parents. I'll set up the CT scan."

She walked into a crowded waiting room where she met Roger and Celia Jones. Mr. Jones was wearing a blue workman's jumpsuit with his name embroidered on the breast pocket. His hair was blond, and he had black grease on his hands. He put his arm around his wife, and his other around two boys, who looked to be preschoolers.

Mr. Jones looked at Cliff, who had escorted Claire to the waiting room. "I thought you said you would bring out the doctor."

Claire ignored his comment. "I'm Dr. McCall. I'm helping take care of Sierra."

"You're a doctor?"

She nodded. "An intern." Claire watched as the parents exchanged glances.

The father spoke again. "How is she?"

"She seems to have stabilized. We need to do some tests."

Mrs. Jones frowned. "Tests?"

Claire nodded. "A CT scan of her abdomen. We want to check for internal injuries."

"I want to see her." The father stepped up, breathing down into Claire's face. "Now."

She stepped back. "Why don't you come back with me, and you can see her for a few minutes until she goes to get her CT scan."

Claire led the family back into the first trauma bay just as they were hooking Sierra up to a portable monitor for her trip to the scanner. Mrs. Jones rushed to her daughter's side. "Sierra, we're here, honey. Everything's gonna be all right."

Mr. Jones took his daughter's hand.

Basil Roberts, the second-year resident, spoke. "They're ready in the scanner, Claire. Josef will help you with transport."

Claire nodded. Baby-sitting trauma patients in the CT scanner was old hat to her by now. "Let's move." She spoke to the parents. "You can come as far as the radiology waiting area, then you'll have to leave her with us."

The father looked at Basil. "Aren't you going with them?"

"Sierra's in good hands."

Claire smiled. "She's going to be fine. Let's go."

Josef and Claire pushed the stretcher down the corridor toward the scanner, with Mom, Dad, and two younger brothers trailing. Once they were in the CT suite, Claire pointed to some chairs and a magazine rack. "You can wait here by the entrance."

Roger Jones gripped his daughter's hand. "Can't I go in there with her?"

The CT technician saved Claire from the confrontation. Shaking his head, he pointed to a radiation symbol on the door to the scanner. "Sorry, hospital policy. No family members can be in an area where they can be exposed to radiation."

"We'll be watching her through a glass window," Claire explained.

Her mother's hand went to her mouth. "She'll be alone?"

"We'll be with her, just a few feet away. And there's a speaker so we can hear everything she says." She watched them for a moment, understanding how hard this must be for them. "She's going to be fine."

Mr. Jones put his hand on his wife's arm. "Come on, honey. Sit down." He looked at Claire. "Take good care of our baby." He leaned down and kissed his daughter. "We'll be right out here, Sierra."

"Okay," Claire responded, wheeling the stretcher through the open door. She looked back at the parents. "We should only be a few minutes."

Claire, Josef, and Ron, the CT technician, hoisted the patient from the stretcher to the CT table. Josef positioned the IV pole at the head of the CT table, and Claire adjusted the monitor so it would be visible from the control-room window. She looked at Sierra, whose eyes were wide with fear. "Don't be afraid, Sierra. You will feel the bed move, but you shouldn't feel anything else. When you hear the instructions, you'll need to hold your breath. It won't take very long, I promise."

"I'm cold," Sierra complained.

Ron responded by placing a white blanket across her. "Here."

Claire checked the blood pressure again. It was down to sixty-five systolic. She adjusted open the IV fluids and looked at Josef. "Better run up to the blood bank. Bring me a unit of blood. If they haven't got her typed yet, bring O negative."

Josef nodded and jogged off.

Claire settled into a padded office chair on wheels in the control room. Beside her was Dr. Wendy Carrico, a third-year radiology resident, and in the control seat, Ron Burris typed in the patient information. Claire looked out at the cardiac monitor. Sierra's heart rate was 150.

After the initial adjustments, the scanner was ready.

A recorded voice filled the control room and projected into the scan room. "Hold your breath. Don't breathe."

The CT table whirred to life and moved the patient through the large circular opening at the end of the scan table.

Twenty seconds passed. The recorded voice returned. "Breathe."

As the images appeared on the computer screen, Claire looked at Wendy and rolled her eyes. They had shared many hours together since July first.

Wendy smiled. "What is it now?"

"Oh, you should have seen this girl's father sizing me up. When the ward secretary brought me out to meet them, he says, 'I thought you said you were bringing out a doctor.'"

"Chauvinists," Wendy mumbled, and poked the technician's ribs.

"That's why I send Ron here out to explain the scan results. I hate to keep saying, 'I am the doctor.'"

Ron grunted and mumbled something about being outnumbered, then pointed at the image on the screen. "Wowser! Look at this liver. It looks like this girl went a few rounds with the champion and lost."

Wendy and Claire looked carefully at the images, slowly bringing up consecutive pictures beginning at the lung bases and scanning all the way through the pelvis. Wendy put her finger on the screen. "Look here. This is at least a grade-four liver laceration. It looks like this crack goes all the way back to the cava."

"What's all this?" Claire pointed to an area of solid color inside the bony pelvis.

"It's fluid, Claire. And lots of it. And in the presence of that liver lac, I'd say we have to assume it's blood."

"How's the spleen?"

"Back up to the first few cuts." Wendy rubbed her chin. "It looks fine. There's fluid around here, but I don't see any evidence of splenic rupture. The fluid around the spleen is probably blood from the liver."

Claire picked up the phone and dialed 0. "Could you page Dr. Overby for me?"

She laid down the phone and studied the image on the screen for a few moments longer. "Can you tell if the kidneys are okay?"

Wendy pointed at two bright dots on the screen. "Yes, here's the ureters with contrast in them. That tells you the kidneys are getting blood flow."

The phone rang. Claire picked up. "CT. Yes. I think you'd better look at this scan. The girl has a grade-four liver lac." Claire held the phone away from her ear and whispered to Wendy. "I think he's upset." She heard a loud click. Claire shook her head. "The O-man must have been hoping for a quiet night."

Ron pointed through the window toward the cardiac monitor. "I think you better check that thing. Looks like a lead may have popped off or something."

Claire looked at the monitor. The EKG complexes were wide and rapid. She wasn't sure, but it certainly looked like ventricular tachycardia. She pushed past the technician and into the scan room. Sierra was blue and there was dark blood around her chest, darkening a circle on the white blanket and dripping on the floor in a crimson pool. "What's going on?" Claire yelled a little too loudly. Panic gripped her. She looked back to the control room and yelled, "Call a code!"

She looked for an ambu bag, then, seeing none, lowered her lips to the small girl's face and gave her four quick breaths. She felt for a pulse. Nothing. "Wendy!"

Overhead, the operator's voice began sounding the code. "Code blue, CT scanner one. Code blue, CT scanner one."

The door from the waiting room flew open as Claire started chest compressions. Dr. Overby bounded in, sweat glistening from his forehead. "What happened, Claire?"

"I'm not sure. After the scan, I walked in and found all this blood."

The chief resident pulled away the blanket so he could see. "The central line is disconnected from the IV tubing." He looked at the position of the IV pole at the head of the table. "You can't put the IV pole up there and expect the tubing to stretch this far! Weren't you watching?"

Wendy grabbed the IV pole and pushed it around the table so it would reach. She hooked it back to the central line.

Roger Jones was standing in the doorway, his eyes frozen on Claire. Behind him, his wife was sobbing. "No, no, no."

Ron gently put his hand on Mr. Jones's shoulder. "Come on, we'd better let the doctors work."

Claire was relieved to see the door close again. She wasn't sure she could stand to hear Mrs. Jones's agony.

"She's probably had an air embolism, from sucking air back into the disconnected IV," the O-man explained. "We need to put her back on the stretcher so we can tip her head down and put her on her side."

He scooped her in his arms and lifted her to the waiting stretcher. The members of the code team arrived as Claire resumed chest compressions.

Dr. Overby put a syringe on the central line and pulled back the plunger. Bubbles of air filled the syringe. "Bingo," he said. "Let's roll her on her left side. We've got to see if we can float the air lock out of her pulmonary outflow track." He tried the maneuver again. This time, he only withdrew dark blood.

"Get me an endotracheal tube," he barked.

Josef arrived with blood. The O-man slipped a tube in Sierra's trachea. Claire continued chest compressions. They gave blood. More blood. Lidocaine. Bicarbonate. Calcium. Multiple defibrillations. Minutes passed. Dr. Overby paged urgently for Dr. Walter Andrews, the pediatric surgery attending on call. Dr. Andrews arrived twelve minutes later and listened to the summary given by the chief resident.

They transfused more blood and continued CPR. For a full hour they worked, even inserting a transvenous pacing wire to try and capture the heart, to force it to beat normally again.

Dr. Andrews surveyed the scene with compassionate eyes. He pulled off a pair of disposable gloves and wiped the sweat from his brow. "You've done all you can, Overby."

Sierra Jones was dead on her seventh birthday.

"Let's call it." The O-man looked at his watch. "Time of death: 10:05 P.M."

Ron handed the chief resident a hard copy of the CT scan. He sighed and looked at the team. "Thanks."

Claire couldn't hold back the tears.

The chief resident put his hand on her shoulder. "She lost a lot of blood from the liver, Claire. Even without the air embolism, I doubt she'd have ever made it through surgery."

She couldn't respond. She was numb. Her patient had died because she hadn't been paying attention.

"Here," he said, handing her a tissue. "Wipe your tears. We have to face the parents."

She walked out behind Dr. Overby, who followed closely behind Dr. Andrews.

They found the family huddled together in the corner of the waiting room. They stood as they saw Claire approaching. "Well?" the father said.

Dr. Andrews grasped Roger Jones's hand. "I'm Dr. Andrews, a pediatric surgeon."

Celia stood beside her husband, her face ashen, her eyes swollen. "How's Sierra?"

Dr. Andrews shook his head without speaking.

"I'm sorry," Dr. Overby responded. "We did everything we could to save her."

"No!" Mr. Jones yelled. He pointed at Claire. "You said she was going to be fine! You went in there with her. She was alive. What have you done to Sierra?"

Celia grabbed her husband's arm. He shook it free.

Dr. Overby frowned and introduced his massive frame between the agitated father and Claire. "Mr. Jones, your daughter's liver was badly damaged. A drunk driver took the life of your child, not Dr. McCall."

Claire backed away. "I'm so sorry. So sorry." She pivoted and rushed from the room, her hand to her mouth. She found her way to her call room without thinking. There, she sunk to her knees and dissolved into tears.

Chapter Nineteen

laire washed her face, pushed the event aside, and completed the night with mechanical numbness. She managed to steal away to a call room at three A.M., but images of a purple birthday bicycle with a handlebar basket and bell prevented any hope of sound slumber.

In the morning, Claire's duties shifted. She walked with Beatrice in silence, looking for the O-man, their chief resident. They found him in the ER teaching a battle-weary group of medical students. She handed her beeper to him with a ceremonial salute. He patted her shoulder and held her gaze for a brief moment. "You've had a strong start, Claire. I've liked working with you."

She nodded. She felt like crying. She'd fought in the trenches side by side with this man, and in spite of his sometimes humiliating tactics, she'd learned more from him in a month than she had during a year in medical school. She wanted to grab his white coat and hang on, to stay with him another month, listening to his stupid rules, and watching him step in and rescue patient after patient. She didn't want to choke on her words now. "Thanks, Dr. Overby," was all she could say.

She turned and walked away, listening as the O-man said good-bye to Beatrice. As the doors to the ER closed behind her, she heard him joking about first blood.

She padded on heavy feet to the Cardiothoracic Intensive Care Unit, the CT ICU, where she was scheduled to meet her new team. She looked at her watch. It was almost six in the morning.

She was joined by fellow intern, Martin Holcroft, MD, PhD, a Harvard Medical School graduate. Martin was softspoken and geeky with a reputation for methodical slowness in completing his scut list. Scut, the grunt work on any hospital service, consisted of minor procedures like drawing blood or inserting IVs or running down the myriad of labs and necessary X rays for rounds. Scut work was usually handled by the medical students, which gave rise to the designation which most of them despised: "Scut monkeys."

Martin had on a white shirt and tie beneath his white coat. His pockets were filled with necessary accessories. Pens, a stethoscope, and several clinical manuals crowded his pockets. Claire had adopted more streamlined apparel. One pen, one stethoscope, and a pack of cheese crackers were the only necessities she carried.

Martin wiped his hand through his stringy brown hair before offering it to Claire. "Hi." He smiled, revealing a small gap between his front teeth. "I heard I'd be working with you this month."

She took his hand. "Hi, Martin. What service did you come from?"

"Plastic surgery at the VA." He frowned. "I haven't even seen the inside of an OR yet. How about you?"

"I was on the trauma service here at the university. I got to do a few cases, nothing too major."

They looked up as Robert Rosenthal approached. Robert was the cardiothoracic surgery fellow on the service. He was Dr. Rosenthal to the interns, as he had already completed his general surgery residency and was now in his second year of his CT fellowship.

Dr. Rosenthal looked at the intern duo and tugged on the lapels of his heavily starched lab coat. "Morning," he said. He held out his hand to Claire.

"I'm Claire McCall."

He nodded and held his hand out to Martin.

"Martin Holcroft."

Dr. Rosenthal pointed to an empty bed in the eight-bed CT ICU. "Let's sit down for a minute to go over the rules."

Martin and Claire sat on the bed. Rosenthal stood and seemed to be sizing them up.

Claire thought his jacket looked too starched. She wondered if he could sit even if he wanted to.

"We have two CT attendings. Dr. Lewis and Dr. Blanton. They are easy to please if you follow their rules. We will do morning rounds at six, starting here in the ICU. You will be on every other night." He looked at a notepad in his hand. "Claire, you've been assigned odd-night calls. All call is in house and you are expected to be inside the ICU for the night following any day we've done open-heart cases in the OR. We do open-heart cases on Monday, Tuesday, Thursday, and Friday. Wednesday is our clinic day. Scrub attire is permitted only in the OR. Dr. Lewis is particularly persnickety about this. If you are on rounds with Dr. Lewis, you'd better wear a white lab coat and a tie." He paused and looked at Claire. "Uh, in your case, you should wear a dress."

Claire looked down at her scrubs. "Uh oh."

Rosenthal made a clicking noise with his cheek. "Make sure you change by the time we round with Dr. Lewis after today's cases."

Claire winced. "This is all I have here. I just came off the trauma service. This is what we wore all the time."

"Well, this isn't trauma, it's hearts, and here, the attendings want you to look the part of well-dressed professionals." He looked at Claire for a moment longer and made a few more clicking sounds. "Can you get home and back in thirty minutes?"

"I think so."

"Good. After rounds, get home and get changed. If the interns aren't properly attired, it's my back that gets riding by the attendings."

Rosenthal lifted his hand and gestured toward the occupied beds in the unit. "These are our post-op open-heart patients. This is the pinnacle. Everything you've seen in general surgery up until now was just a warm-up. The CT surgeons actually cut and modify the human heart. Every open-heart case we do is actually an artificial suspension of life. We still the heart, and pump the patient's blood with a cardiopulmonary bypass machine. If you get your floor work done efficiently, you are welcome to come into the operating theatre and observe. But don't be hanging out in the OR if your scut list isn't complete."

Claire glanced sideways at Martin. She hoped he wasn't as slow as she'd heard. She wanted desperately to get in the OR where the action was.

"Questions?"

The interns shook their heads silently.

"There will be three students on this service, but, unfortunately, since this is August, it's the very beginning of the year for them, so they won't have had any practical experience. They are in an orientation until ten this morning. When they show up, you can divide up the patients on the service and assign them to the medical students. Since they are new, they're going to need a lot of help with case presentations. Work with them. Buff them up as much as you can. When they look good, the attendings think the interns are teaching them, and they like that. If the students look good, you look good. And if you look good, I look good. Got it?"

Claire nodded numbly. The only thing more worthless than an intern on her first day was a third-year medical student on her first day.

Dr. Rosenthal smoothed the front of his jacket. "Then let's have at it."

After rounds, Claire made a beeline for her house to grab a dress. While she was there, she listened to her phone messages.

Her mom had called. Clay had a court date for a DUI. Her mom wanted Claire to pray that the judge would be lenient and let him keep his license. The last thing she needed was to have to run him to work, in addition to caring for Wally. Claire shook her head. After watching Sierra Jones die, the last thing Claire felt like praying for was leniency for a drunk driver. Let Clay take his medicine like everyone else.

John called. Just wanted to hear her voice. Claire shook her head. How many times had she told him she was taking odd-night call? He should know she wouldn't be home.

Brett called. He hadn't seen her for a few days and was just wanting to see how she was doing. That was sweet.

She opened her closet and sighed. She hardly ever wore dresses. She had a few party dresses, but they weren't exactly the professional look that the CT surgeons wanted. She settled on a navy skirt and a white blouse and made a promise to herself that she would go shopping.

She changed, picked out a fresh blouse for the morning, and rushed back to the hospital. She wrote daily notes and went over the patient charts so she could present them on rounds to Dr. Lewis. By noon, the first coronary bypass patient was out of the OR and in the ICU, so Claire was expected to be at the bedside. "Here," Dr. Rosenthal remarked, handing her a small blue notebook. "These are the most common medications we use on the service. It also has all the protocols for most of the problems we encounter in caring for the open-heart patients."

She flipped through the pages of small print.

"Commit it to memory," he said casually. "But the best way to learn how the drugs work is to watch them in action when you are helping adjust the drips with the nurses."

Claire nodded, and introduced herself to Diana Strasburg, the nurse assigned to the first open-heart patient of the day. Diana busied herself adjusting the IV drips and recording the data from the monitor screen and the collecting chambers of the chest tubes and the urinary catheter. Claire took a seat on a stool at the foot of the bed and tried to concentrate on the small manual in her hand.

It was then that she realized she hadn't eaten since before Sierra Jones had died. And, other than a few catnaps after three, she hadn't slept. And she was supposed to sit in this ICU all night to take care of the open-heart service. "God help me," she whispered. Thankfully, the O-man had taught her something, and she found a pack of cheese crackers in her lab coat.

She had just finished the crackers when Martin Holcroft arrived. He was out of breath, and his tie was askew.

She looked up. "What's going on, Martin?"

"They need you in ER."

"Who?"

"They paged me to see a twenty-year-old guy with a pneumothorax. He needs a chest tube." Martin ran his hand through his hair. "I've never done one, so I called Dr. Rosenthal to help, but he's in the OR doing a mitral valve replacement with Dr. Lewis, so he suggested I talk to you. I guess he figured that since you've already done your trauma rotation, you'd be more comfortable with the procedure."

"He figured right. Shall I teach you how?" Claire stood up.

Diana spoke up. "Better not, Dr. McCall. Better not let the CT surgeons come through this ICU and not find an intern at the bedside of a fresh post-op."

"I'll stay here," Martin offered. "I'm sure I'll get the chance to do plenty of chest tubes."

"Okay. Where's the patient?"

"Room four. They should be all set up for you."

"Thanks."

Claire walked briskly to the ER, thankful for the chance to be on her feet again. It certainly made staying awake easier.

She found the patient in need, put in a chest tube, and wrote admit orders. She was just finishing up when she heard a familiar voice.

"I thought I might find you here, Dr. McCall."

She looked up to see Sierra Jones's father. He appeared to be wearing the same clothing as he had the night before. Black circles beneath his eyes highlighted sunken cheeks and a day's worth of prickly stubble on his chin.

He glared at her, his eyes intense with hate. Terrified, she pushed back, thankful that there was a counter between her and Mr. Jones. Her heart quickened and seemed to lodge in her throat. She calculated the time it would take to sprint to the exit.

She tried in vain to wet her lips with her parched tongue. "Hello, Mr. Jones," she responded, her voice barely above a whisper.

"Where are you from, Dr. McCall?"

"V–Virginia." Claire shifted her eyes to an empty chair to her right. Where was the ward clerk when you needed him?

"I'm gonna bury my daughter this week. She died on her birthday, did you know that?"

Claire felt her throat tighten. "I know."

"I heard what the other doctor, that man, said to you, when my baby was getting the CT scan." He raised a finger. "Don't think I don't know what went on. My baby went in there alive, but you didn't watch her. You let that tubing on her chest come apart. I heard the other doctor say so."

Claire stood and backed away. "Mr. Jones, I'm so sorry. You're daughter died because of internal bleeding."

"My daughter died because you made a mistake!" He jabbed his index finger in the air toward Claire's chest and lunged toward the counter.

Claire shrieked and jumped back. Thankfully, his loud voice had alerted the ER staff, and a crowd quickly gathered around Claire. A large African-American orderly stepped up beside her.

"Don't think I don't know what happened. I'll see to it you go back to Virginia where you belong," he shouted, his voice trembling. "You killed my baby." He put his hands to his face. "Someone's gonna pay." His eyes were wide with terror. He slowly backed away from the crowd and out through the automatic doors which opened to the outside.

Claire put her hand to her mouth. The scene around her blurred. Tears welled in her eyes and she steadied herself with her hands on the counter. A strong arm nestled around her shoulder, and she heard the soft voice of the head nurse, Gwen Thomas.

"Dr. McCall? Are you going to be okay?"

Claire sniffed and nodded. She slipped free from Gwen's supportive embrace and hurried to the door leading to the hall. She needed to go somewhere to regroup. She was frightened, exhausted, and alone.

I wish John were here.

She found little solace in a women's rest room, but she dried her tears with a paper towel, then wadded it up and tossed it at a trash can. Unable to suppress a fresh round of tears, she pulled frantically at the toilet-paper roll. She closed the door to the little stall and sat on the commode to dry her tears. When she heard the bathroom door squeak a few minutes later, she blew her nose and left the bathroom. She could see the sunshine through a window at thc end of the hall. *I just need some fresh air. And a strong shoulder. I need John Cerelli.*

She walked through the lobby and into the muggy afternoon heat. Swallowing the tightness in her throat, she crossed the street to the blue glass research facility. She found Dr. Rogers' GI lab on the third floor, and Brett Daniels alone in a tiny corner office. She knocked timidly on the door before letting herself in. She stood in the doorway for a moment before she started to cry. "Oh, Brett," she gasped. "I'm so afraid."

He stood and opened his arms, receiving her warmly, enveloping her gently, then more tightly as her body racked with sobs.

She pressed against him, burying her face in his chest and neck.

She felt his lips brush against her forehead, then move away, and come to rest against her forehead again. "There, there," he whispered, not moving his lips from her forehead.

She rested for a minute, then pulled away and looked in his eyes.

"What's wrong, Claire?"

She wasn't sure what to say. She didn't want to cry again.

She suddenly felt foolish. She thought of how silly she must look to Brett. *I'm supposed to survive this residency by being a man. So why am I bawling my eyes out over this?*

She sniffed and shrugged. "I've had a bad day."

Brett listened as Claire unloaded her story behind a closed office door. She held her head in her hands, looking at the floor. "What am I going to do, Brett? Mr. Jones might just be crazy enough to come after me."

"I doubt it. He's just trying to deal with his grief. Some people don't know any other way to deal with it, so they just lash out at the easiest target." He closed a book on his desk. "You just got in the way, that's all."

"He's gonna sue."

"I doubt he has the sophistication. He's just venting. It will all blow over in a few days."

"You know what bothers me the most?"

He shook his head.

"I think he's right. My negligence may have killed her. If I'd only been watching her, I'd have seen the IV pop apart. I could have run right in and reconnected it, and Mr. and Mrs. Jones might still have their baby girl."

"You can't know that, Claire. And you can't torture yourself over and over with the 'if onlys.'"

Her beeper sounded. She looked at the number. "CT ICU." She sighed. "I'd better run."

They stood and faced each other again. He smiled. "You're going to make it. Okay?"

She bobbed her head rapidly without speaking. Her throat tightened again.

He reached out and brushed her eyes with the back of his hand, then lightly tapped her mouth. "Stiff upper lip."

She forced a smile. "Okay."

He gazed at her a moment, his hand now on her chin, drawing her face to his.

She stiffened, and pushed her hand to his chest. "No."

He stepped away, yielding to her now extended arm. "Claire."

"Y–you can't," she stammered. "I can't. We're not like that."

"Like what? A couple?" Hurt registered on his face.

"I'm sorry, Brett. I didn't come to you for—"

"So what am I to you? A stand-in for your fiancé? You can't deny what I know you're feeling."

She looked down and shut her eyes. She took a deep breath before speaking. "You're a friend, Brett. And I needed a friend's shoulder to cry on. That's all." She shook her head. "Look, I shouldn't have come. I'm sorry that I've confused you."

She opened the door. "I have to go."

He nodded without speaking.

"Sorry," she added, her voice barely above a whisper.

Claire smoothed the front of her lab coat, cleared her throat, and walked away, glancing back only once to see Brett standing in the doorway with his head against the frame.

Chapter Twenty

Claire endured her first night of CT call by strict adherence to the O-man's second rule of intern survival: "Everyone teaches a tern."

Stephanie Dickson recorded the data from the pulmonary artery catheter and looked at Claire. "It gets easier once you've seen everything a few times."

Claire nodded. She understood that Stephanie knew what she was talking about. An ICU nurse for nearly twenty years, Stephanie had seen thousands of open-heart patients and hundreds of interns come and go. She knew the protocols. She knew when to ask for help. And if the rumors coming out of the surgery resident's lounge were correct, Claire would be crazy to question Steph's judgment.

At two A.M., the nurse pointed to a cardiac rehab chair. "That's your spot. If I have any problem you need to know about, I'll call."

Claire nestled into the padded leather chair and closed her eyes. She slept intermittently for four hours. She was awakened hourly with reports of patient's vital signs, potassium levels, mediastinal tube and urine outputs, and anything else that Stephanie thought important enough to tell her. The hourly updates fell into a comfortable routine. The nurse gave the report and looked to Claire to give the appropriate order in response, but kindly informed the intern of the most customary response desired by the CT surgeons for that particular clinical situation. Claire, in return, ordered what the experienced nurse suggested. It worked well because Claire understood what was needed for most of the situations, but to have the nurse clue her in on the particular likes and dislikes of the attending surgeons was very helpful.

In this way, Stephanie allowed Claire the feeling of being in charge, while subtly guiding her to make the right decisions. "Dr. Lewis gives blood to every open-heart patient with a hematocrit below thirty. Dr. Blanton waits until the crit is below twenty-five," she instructed. "Dr. Lewis uses crystalloid when the patient needs more volume. Dr. Blanton uses Hespan."

Since Wednesday was a clinic day, Claire and Martin were expected to write notes and finish the scut list in the hospital while the medical students helped work up the outpatients in the clinic. This arrangement was fine with Claire, as the new medical students only slowed her down. At noon, Claire and Martin headed for the cafeteria to obey Overby's rule number one: "Eat when you can."

At two, just when Claire had finished gathering the latest lab values on the CT ICU patients, her beeper sounded. Claire answered the unfamiliar extension.

"Risk management, this is Wanda."

"This is Dr. McCall. I was paged."

"Yes, Dr. Andrews would like you to meet him in our office. Is now a convenient time?"

"Now?" Claire looked at her watch. "What is this about? Who did you say this is?"

"My name is Wanda Miller. I work in physician support services, especially in the area of risk management."

"Risk management?"

"We often review clinical cases where there is a potential concern for medical liability."

"And Dr. Andrews is asking for me?"

"Yes. He's here in the office. We thought you should be made aware of our concerns. It would really be better to do this in person. I know this is short notice, but we've only just become aware of some potential problems regarding a case you were involved in. Can you come to my office?"

Claire felt a knot growing in her stomach. "Sure."

She followed Wanda's instructions and found the office on the second floor of the main hospital. She knocked on the door and entered. A secretary led her to a conference room with a large table. Seated around the table were Dr. Walter Andrews, the pediatric surgeon, another man Claire didn't recognize, and a short, plump woman in a business suit.

The woman stood. "Dr. McCall?"

Claire felt her throat tighten. "Yes."

"I'm Wanda. Thanks so much for coming." She pointed at the men. "You know Dr. Andrews. This is Peter Ondrachek, a hospital attorney."

An attorney? What's going on?

Wanda gestured to a chair. Claire sat, but didn't allow her back to touch the spindled support behind her.

Dr. Andrews smiled and folded his aging hands. "Hi, Claire."

"Hi." Seeing him here made her more comfortable. He looked like Walter Cronkite. Or maybe all Walters looked that way ... calm, wrinkled, with bright eyes.

"I'm sure you're wondering what this is all about. Let me put your mind at rest. You aren't being sued." She paused. "At least not yet. But Gwen Thomas, head nurse in the ER, told me you had been threatened by ..." She glanced down at her paper. "Roger Jones." She lifted her eyes to Claire's. "We like to get a record of everyone's memory of sentinel events as soon as we are made aware of them. That way everyone's memory is fresh."

"A sentinel event?"

Wanda nodded. "A term we use for any clinical event that results in significant patient morbidity or death or an event that results in significant risk of patient morbidity or death." She took a deep breath. "Since Dr. Andrews was the attending of record, he needs to be involved in the process. Mr. Ondrachek is here to represent the hospital's interest."

Claire's eyes narrowed. "What about my interests?"

Wanda smiled sweetly. "Any legal action initiated against a resident in this hospital is automatically against the university hospital. Mr. Ondrachek will also represent you." She glanced at her notes, then pointed to the hospital record on the table. "We've had a chance to review the legal patient record, and we've talked to Gwen, but we would like to hear from you. Did Mr. Jones threaten you with a lawsuit?"

"Not exactly. He approached me in the ER and claimed that I made a mistake responsible for his daughter's death. I don't remember his exact words, but I believe he said that someone was gonna pay." She felt her voice thickening. "He said he would see to it that I went back to Virginia."

Wanda and the attorney exchanged glances. "That verifies what Gwen told us."

Mr. Ondrachek smoothed the lapels of his three-piece suit and leaned forward. "Can you give us your version of the events that surrounded Sierra Jones's death?"

Claire shifted in her seat, feeling like she was on a witness stand. Mr. Ondrachek's legalese manner of speaking unnerved her. "Well, she came in with abdominal bloating and tenderness, and hypotension. She didn't have an IV, so Dr. Roberts started a central line."

The lawyer scratched a note. "Was that the line that was in her chest?"

Claire pointed to a spot beneath her right collarbone. "Yes. It was a subclavian line that entered into her subclavian vein and extended down into her superior vena cava. I took the patient to the CT scanner with a medical student with instructions to go over the scan with the radiologist and call the chief resident. The patient's blood pressure was down a few points again, so I sped up the IV fluids and instructed the medical student to go to the blood bank to get some blood. We got the scan, and I was going over the scan with the radiology resident when the tech called my attention to the patient's cardiac monitor. It looked like the patient was in ventricular tachycardia. I ran into the room and found that she had no respirations or pulse. She had blood on her chest and on the floor beside the CT scanner. I started CPR and called a code."

"What happened then?"

"Dr. Overby came and found that the central line had become disconnected from the IV tubing."

"You hadn't noticed this before?"

"No," Claire responded, looking down at her clasped hands. "The patient had complained of being cold, so we had covered her chest with a blanket, which hid the IV connection. After Dr. Overby came in, he pulled the blanket away and saw the connection had separated." She shook her head. "Evidently the IV tubing wasn't long enough to reach when she was moved through the scanner because of where the IV pole was positioned. The tubing must have popped free when the machine moved her into the scanner."

"Certainly you've watched patients in the scanner before. Have you ever placed the IV pole in that same position before?"

Claire nodded. "All the time. But we are normally scanning adult patients. They are taller, so the IV tubing reaches them easily even when they are in the scanner donut." She bit her lower lip to keep it from trembling. "I'd never watched such a short patient before."

"What did Dr. Overby do?"

"He immediately lifted her onto a stretcher so we could lower her head. He took a syringe and tried to pull air back out of the IV, because he feared that she had been able to suck air back into her venous system, causing an outflow blockage within the heart itself."

"What do you think happened?"

"I think she had a very low blood pressure from losing so much blood into her abdomen from her liver injury. So her central venous pressure was very low because of the bleeding, and therefore when her central line became disconnected, she sucked too much air into her central veins and died from a massive air embolism."

"Would she be alive if you had seen the IV become disconnected?"

Claire begin to sob. "I–I–"

Walter Andrews cleared his throat. He had been silent up until that point other than his greeting. "Claire, it's okay." He cast a fatherly glance at the attorney. "Easy, Peter." He reached over and laid his hand against Claire's arm. "We don't have an exact answer to his question, so it's unfair to ask it of you. The patient's liver injury appeared severe, and in the presence of so much blood in the abdomen, and with her hypotension before the scan, we assume she was still actively bleeding. All of these facts together make it highly likely that she would have died anyway."

"Am I going to lose my job?"

Dr. Andrews shook his head. "Of course not. This is an unfortunate event for your first month, but you will be forced to learn a lesson that all of us eventually learn. We do make mistakes because we're human. And patients suffer because we aren't perfect."

"Is Mr. Jones going to sue?"

Wanda spoke up. "We don't know. Other than the threat he made to you yesterday, did he say anything on the night his daughter came in?"

Claire sighed. "He was upset from the moment he met me. He saw that I was a woman, and assumed I wasn't even a doctor. Then, when we were going to the scanner, he asked Dr. Roberts if he was going along. Dr. Roberts assured him that his daughter was in good hands. Then, at the scanner, he wanted to go in with his child, but the technician wouldn't let him." She winced, remembering her words. "I tried to comfort them. I told the parents that Sierra would be fine." She looked up at Dr. Andrews. He was frowning, not appearing angry, just sad. "I'll know better than to make such assurances in the future."

Mr. Ondrachek stood up, signaling an end to the meeting. "If you get any further threats from this man, please let us know. And do not speak to anyone about this case. It would be best if you didn't mention it at all. Right now that's only a recommendation. If he sues, it will become a legal necessity." He nodded seriously. "And one more thing. If there's a memorial or funeral service for this girl, and I'm sure there will be, please don't show up. We've had residents in the past who have felt bad about deaths they'd caused, and they show up at the memorials in an attempt to show respect. But let me assure you, that's a bad idea. The attorneys for the other side will read that as remorse, presumed evidence of guilt. In addition, since the father has made a threat, showing up at a memorial service might result in some unpleasant fireworks." He raised his eyebrows. "Any questions?"

"No," Claire responded.

None for you. Only the ones I'll ask myself over and over. Would Sierra Jones still be alive if it wasn't for me?

By evening, Claire felt like a walking zombie. She'd been in the hospital, except for thirty minutes when she picked up her clothes, for sixty hours. She was in desperate need of sleep and a shower.

She trudged toward the hospital lobby, taking mental inventory. She'd arrived at six A.M. on July 31, enthusiastic, self-confident, and ready for her last night of trauma call. She was leaving on August 2, six P.M., defeated, threatened by a lawsuit, full of self-doubt, and confused about her feelings for Brett Daniels. She'd not had one spare minute to give to an anxiety over her family or the looming possibility of Huntington's disease. She smiled, nearly giddy from lack of sleep. *The one advantage to being so busy with my internship is I don't have any time to worry about my dysfunctional family.*

She was unlocking her car door when she saw Dr. Overby wave. He lumbered across the parking lot and wiped the sweat from his forehead. "I'm glad I caught you. I wanted to warn you about Friday. I had to post Sierra Jones's case for discussion for Friday's M and M conference."

M and M, the morbidity and mortality conference, was the weekly critique of all that went wrong from the week before. It was supposed to be a learning experience. For most residents it was a definite Maalox moment, as they had to be thick-skinned and prepared for questions. The chief residents were responsible to list all unexpected outcomes, complications, and deaths on their respective services. To not list a complication was risking discovery by Dr. Rogers and expulsion from the pyramid.

"Oh." She was too tired to care.

"You're going to have to present the case, Claire. I'll be there. I won't let you drown, but you're going to have to take whatever the attendings dish out. You should read up on air embolism and liver trauma. They are likely to ask you questions."

She opened her car door and threw in her call bag.

She knew the reputation of some of the attendings for chewing up the residents when they made mistakes. "Will it get ugly?"

"Probably not. Just don't make excuses. That just invites their attack. If you say, 'I screwed up,' it's more likely they won't be too excitable. The harshest comments usually come from other attendings who have specific bones to pick with the attending responsible for your case. So for you, that's good. Hardly anyone dislikes Dr. Andrews."

That seemed like little consolation. It had been bad enough going over the details for Mr. Ondrachek. Now she was going to have to confess her sins to the entire surgery department.

"Thanks for the warning."

"Sure."

With that, he turned and walked away. Claire sat in her car and began to cry.

Chapter Twenty-One

Once home, Claire forced herself to eat a nutritious meal, a microwave dinner. She consumed it in large bites, standing at the kitchen counter, knowing it would be faster that way, and less likely that she'd fall prey to the sleep which crouched ready to assault her at any moment. She dressed for bed and thought about returning a call from John, but decided she didn't have the mental energy to explain what she'd been through in the last few days. *I'll just have to call him Friday night.*

She slept the sleep of the dead, a motionless coma, aware of nothing until her alarm resurrected her at five. She rose and stared at her open closet and again promised herself that she'd go shopping soon.

She selected her only other skirt, a khaki material that fell just above the knee. She put on a white shirt with fine blue stripes, then sniffed the armpits of the white one she'd hung on the bedpost the night before. *This will have to do.* She hung it on a hanger, threw a pair of clean undies in her call bag, and headed for the Mecca.

Morning rounds with Dr. Rosenthal, the CT fellow, did not go well. Martin had given orders for Hespan on Dr. Lewis's patients, when he preferred crystalloid. He had transfused Dr. Blanton's patient with a hematocrit of twenty-seven, when Dr. Blanton preferred no transfusion for his patients until the hematocrit was below twenty-five. With each error, Dr. Rosenthal cleared his throat and appeared to be clenching his teeth.

Claire stepped back and stayed quiet as she observed Dr. Rosenthal's face reddening. Martin hadn't called the fellow when an open-heart patient had slipped into atrial fibrillation, a clear departure from accepted protocol. "When in doubt, Dr. Holcroft, it's always better to call." The CT fellow's face was within six inches of Martin's. "Do you understand?"

"Yes, sir, but the patient didn't have a drop in blood pressure and it was only an hour until rounds, so I thought I'd wait and—"

"Your job is to do what the attendings want. Your job is not to act on your own. Do you understand?"

Martin huffed. "Yes, sir."

Dr. Rosenthal backed away, then gave the nurse the appropriate drug orders to treat the dysrhythmia that Martin had ignored.

Claire followed along, herding the medical students to the next patient. Martin's shoulders drooped and he looked at Claire and rolled his eyes behind Rosenthal's back. Martin just wasn't getting it. Internship was more about keeping the residents above you happy than about learning to be a great surgeon. And keeping the higher-ups happy was more about following stupid rules than being an independent thinker. Claire suppressed a smile as she thought about the wisdom of the O-man and his third rule of internship survival. "If you don't know, ask."

After rounds, Claire cornered Stephanie Dickson, who was just completing sign-out to the nurse coming on for day shift. She kept her voice low, her tone that of a conspiring comrade. "What's the deal with Dr. Holcroft? Didn't you help him with the protocols?"

Stephanie glanced around the unit. "Of course I helped him. But he's a pompous jerk. I tried to tell him what the attendings would want, but his Harvard attitude got in the way." She shrugged. "So I let him swim on his own."

"Sink on his own is more like it."

"He didn't think so."

Claire put her hand over her mouth and tried not to smile. "He seemed so mild to me."

"He signed all his orders, 'Holcroft, MD, PhD.' You can't read the Holcroft part, but the initials are all in block letters that a first grader could decipher."

Claire looked for the cardiac rehab recliner, not seeing it anywhere. "Where did he sleep?"

"He didn't. He paced the unit like a caged tiger. He made Janice Turlington record vital signs every fifteen minutes on Dr. Lewis's stable valve patient, so she hid the chair in the storage closet."

Claire snickered. "You guys are brutal."

Stephanie pushed a strand of rebellious gray hair behind her ear. "Only when we have to be."

The intern nodded and picked up a chart to start her daily notes. *Boy, it pays to follow the rules.*

Claire settled into her new job of "sitting hearts" with little adjustment. As the open-heart cases were finished, she stayed at the bedside, watching the monitors, fascinated by the response of the blood pressure and cardiac output to her interventions. As she dialed up the pressor drips, the blood pressure rose. As she increased the fluids, the cardiac output increased, the response leveling out as the patient's heart reached optimal volume. This was cardiac physiology in real life, and Claire was in the driver's seat, loving the ride.

As the night passed, Claire's anticipation of the Friday morning's M and M conference grew from anxiety to dread. She'd had little time to prepare, and she knew she would arrive sleep deprived. In between hourly updates on the heart patients, Claire practiced her presentation and hoped for the best.

At five o'clock she stole away from the ICU to an empty call room. If she couldn't silence the sharks with her knowledge, at least she knew a little mascara couldn't hurt.

She showered, styled her hair, and applied her lipstick and mascara. "Oh, God," she prayed. "Please help me not to cry. The last thing I need is to run my mascara in front of the whole surgery department."

She studied herself in the mirror for a moment. She still had good summer color, although the tan she'd gained from her side trips to the beach was fading fast since she'd begun her indoor CT marathon. As a final step, she put on small pearl earrings, a gift from John, and smiled. She liked what she saw. She might be in need of sleep, but she wouldn't fail for lack of charm.

After rounds, she dutifully headed for the M and M conference room. She entered, surveying the audience for the best seat. M and M was always crowded. It was a required conference for the residents, but fortunately—perhaps the only thing Claire could find comfort in—it was closed to anyone outside the surgery staff. It was a place to air your dirty laundry in front of your colleagues without the threat that others would overhear.

There were donuts and coffee on a side table. Claire could tell which residents had to present cases. They were seated in the front, looking at their notes, oblivious to the joviality of the rest of the resident staff. No one on the front row was eating. There would be no coffee stains on the coats of the presenters. Claire took her place on the front row and silently noted that no other interns shared her distinction. *Great,* she mused, *Beatrice gets the First Blood award. I wonder what I'll get for being the first intern crucified in M and M.*

The nervous joviality ceased as Dr. Steve Acardi, a third-year resident, presented the first case of a thirty-three-year-old whose laparoscopic gallbladder surgery was complicated by an injury to the intestines. He successfully fended off questions from Dr. Denton, a vascular surgery attending, but got stymied by Dr. Garrison, an old-schooler who still thought laparoscopic surgery was newfangled and dangerous. To the resident's relief, Dr. Rogers, the GI section chief and chairman of the department, came to his resident's aid, called Garrison a dinosaur, and told the resident to sit down.

Dr. Wong Lee, a chief resident, was next, and presented a vascular case where the distal anastomosis of a femoral-popliteal bypass was accidentally hooked up to the vein instead of the artery. This brought a vigorous outcry from Dr. Denton, who proclaimed Lee to be the victim of a stupidity virus, and warned the audience never to get sick in July at a teaching hospital. Lee sat down humiliated, but breathing. He'd been through this too many times in his six-year stint to be defeated by the hot air of Dr. Denton.

Claire was next, and was thankful that the podium wasn't transparent. She presented the details of the case without faltering and admitted her mistakes quickly before any of the attending sharks had the chance to smell blood. "I made two critical errors. I didn't keep in mind how rapidly a pediatric patient can deteriorate." She looked down. "And I didn't keep my eyes on my patient at every moment. I was too distracted by my interest in her CT findings. I'd never seen a liver injury so severe, and I was caught up in going over the scan with the radiology resident rather than paying attention to my patient."

Dr. Stan Fowler stood up. Claire would have been surprised if he hadn't. As a trauma attending, he was obligated to speak out. She just hoped she'd have the answers to his criticism. But, instead of questioning her, he turned to the audience. "This illustrates a point I've made in this conference time and time again. The most dangerous place for an unstable trauma patient is in the radiology department. They don't have the proper equipment handy in case there is an emergency just like this."

Dr. McGrath spoke next. "Why did this patient need a CT scan at all? Wouldn't a portable ultrasound in the ER have been more rapid and given you the same information?"

Claire wasn't sure what to say. "Well," she began, just as Dr. Overby interrupted.

"The decision to get a CT scan was mine. An ultrasound would have given us information about free blood in the abdomen and could have shown the liver laceration, but it would never have shown us the additional information about her kidney function and could never have shown us the detail that a CT offers."

The group argued among themselves, pontificating over the virtues of CT versus ultrasound in the management of acute abdominal trauma.

Claire stayed quiet and tried to appear interested, and not just relieved at having the attention off of her.

Dr. Tom Rogers concluded by thanking Claire for bringing the case to discuss, pointing out the necessity of securing all central-line connections with care, and reviewing the steps to manage a patient with possible central venous air embolism.

Claire sat down and took inventory. She'd fielded one question that Dr. Overby answered for her. And she hadn't cried. Score one for the O-man. She looked over her shoulder and caught his eye. "Thank you," she mouthed.

He made a barely perceptible nod of acknowledgment before looking away.

She relaxed and wished there was an inconspicuous way she could get to the donut table. She was suddenly aware of her famished state and salivated at the aroma of the morning brew.

After waiting through two more presentations and Dr. Rogers' dismissal, she joined the throng at the refreshment table, listening quietly to Dr. Lee murmuring about the treatment he'd received. She picked up a donut and silently walked out behind him. He leaned toward his junior resident and complained, "If she'd have been a man, they would have taken her to task. But they sat there drooling like they were ready for dessert. I've never heard Dr. Rogers thank a resident before. He'd never treat a male resident like that."

The other resident laughed. "I'll bet she paid them in advance. Did you see how quickly the O-man took the heat?"

Claire shrank back and paused to let the dispersing crowd go around her, pretending to make a note on her scut list. She took a deep breath and counted to ten, attempting to shrug off their comments. *Chauvinist jerks.*

Dr. Lee was just jealous. But what did he care? He'd already made it to the top of the pyramid.

She looked up and waited until Dr. Lee disappeared around a corner. *I hope I don't have to work with him anytime soon.*

On Friday evening, Claire drove her Toyota up the alley behind Safeway, across Thompson Street, and into her driveway. She paused when she saw the items in the yard next door, the evidences of young children and their play. A wagon, a basketball and a bike, a purple one with training wheels, seemed haphazardly arranged, abandoned by the kids, likely in response to their mother's call for supper. The only occupant of the yard was a miniature schnauzer named Tiger, who ran up to say hello.

She knelt and scratched him behind his ears, receiving his wet greeting with gratitude while her heart sank. Why did it have to be a purple bicycle? Why not red or blue?

She blinked back the image that the bicycle evoked: Sierra's birthday party, shattered by a drunk driver and an incompetent intern.

A sudden weariness enveloped her as she pushed open the car door. Head down, she plodded toward the front door, lifted her key to the doorknob, and gasped. There, on her door, in orange paint, a vandal's message was scrawled in uneven letters. "DIE REBEL."

She stumbled back a step as the message sank in. She glanced around the neighborhood. No one was around, not a single person visible anywhere. Claire felt the hairs on her neck stand up, and fought the eerie feeling that she was being watched. She fumbled with her keys and unlocked the door, slamming it behind her and turning the dead bolt. She pressed her eye to the peephole, but the distorted, circular appearance unnerved her. She was alone, far from home, and someone wanted her to die.

She rushed to the phone and called the Lafayette police department. The woman on the other end of the line was friendly, but explained that this was a Friday night, and that most of the officers were responding to priority needs near the university campus, and she'd get an officer out to investigate the vandalism as soon as she could.

"Please," she begged. "Someone wants to kill me."

"Ma'am, stay inside and lock your door. I'll have someone out there as soon as I can."

She called Brett Daniels and got his answering machine. "Brett, this is Claire. Someone vandalized my house. I'm so afraid." She paused. "I didn't know who else to call. Can you come? I live at 201 Thompson Street, behind the Safeway."

She hung up the phone in frustration, then checked her watch and waited. It was seven P.M. She fixed a bowl of cereal and picked up a paperback, but couldn't concentrate. Every time she heard a car on the street, she was up, peeking through the closed venetian blind in the front room.

At eight-thirty, Brett arrived. He looked handsome even through the peephole. Claire unlatched the door and practically dragged him in.

"After yesterday, I was surprised to hear from you."

She frowned. "I know." She paused. "But can we just forget about that? I need you right now. As a friend." Her eyes were pleading. "I'm afraid to be alone."

He nodded his understanding.

"Did you see the door?"

"Hard to miss. Have you called the police?"

"Right after I called you. But they don't consider vandalism high on their list."

"Have you eaten?"

"Some cereal. And I made myself eat that. It's hard to have an appetite."

Brett sat on the couch opposite Claire. "What's your theory?"

"The obvious one, I guess. The only person that has threatened me lately is Roger Jones. He blames me for his daughter."

"But why would he do this? How would he know where you lived?"

"Anyone can look me up through information. Why?" She shrugged. "He's a loon."

"Striking out this way may be the only way he can cope."

"Wonderful. My first major clinical faux pas and it has to happen to a psycho's daughter."

A sharp rap at the door interrupted their conversation. A young officer, an African American with "Boone" on his name tag, was visible through the peephole.

Claire opened the door and poured out her story.

"Why 'rebel'? Are you from the South?"

"Yes. Virginia."

"How would this man have known this?"

Claire hesitated.

"He asked you in the ER where you were from," Brett said. "That's what you told me, remember?"

Officer Boone raised his eyebrows. "You told him?"

"Yes."

The officer made some notes. "Anything else I should know?"

"Can't you go get this guy? Lock him up?"

"It's not that easy. The department will do an investigation."

"But I don't want to stay here with this guy on the loose."

"People who do this sort of thing rarely act out violently. He's probably just trying to scare you."

Claire wondered if the young officer knew what he was talking about, or if he was just trying to make her feel better. "Well, he's been successful at that. I'd feel better if I knew you were watching the house."

"I'm sure you'll be safe with your husband here," he responded, looking up at Brett.

Brett pushed his chest out.

Claire shook her head. "He's not my husband. I live here alone."

"Oh. Well, just the same, I'm sure you'll be okay. He obviously did this in secret, knowing you'd be away. He's not likely to come back when you're home."

She looked at him without speaking.

The officer continued. "We'll be sending a detective over to take some pictures tomorrow. Don't have the door repainted until after that."

"I'll tell my landlord."

The officer left, and Claire closed the door and turned the dead bolt. She leaned with her back against the door and yawned.

Brett looked at her. "Now what?"

"Can you stay?"

"I've been waiting for an invitation."

"Brett! You know what I mean. I've got a sleeping bag. I can stay on the couch and you can have my bed."

"Forget it. I'd never agree to put you out. I'll sleep on the couch." He lifted his eyebrows. "Besides, your bed probably smells just like you do. I'd be crazy before midnight."

"Smells?"

He laughed. "A nice smell, Claire. I didn't mean it like a smelly smell."

She rolled her eyes. "It will only be for tonight. I'd feel a lot safer."

"Sure."

Claire headed to the bathroom to prepare for sleep. She took a long shower and tried without success to erase the tension from her body. She was standing in her robe, brushing her teeth, when she heard the phone ring.

John! I'd better get that.

She heard Brett pick up. "Hello. Oh, no, you've got the right number. She's just taking a shower. I'll get her for you. Claire?"

He tapped on the bathroom door. She opened it and took the portable phone from his hand. She closed the door again and sat on the edge of her tub.

"Hello."

"Claire, it's John. What's going on? Now you've got male visitors while you shower?"

"John, it's not what you think. He's just another resident here." She paused. She hadn't talked to John since before her last night of trauma call. So much had happened. Where should she begin?

"I called the other day. It's been a while since I've heard from you." She could tell by his tone that he was upset.

"It's been an unbelievable week."

She could hear John sigh. He obviously wanted to talk. She was exhausted and hardly knew how to explain.

"I'd like to hear about it."

She took a deep breath. "I was on call in house Monday night for the trauma service, and Tuesday night for cardiothoracic surgery service. I got home in time to crash on Wednesday night, then went in Thursday, spent the night, and just got home this evening." She paused. "On Monday night, a seven-year-old girl was hit by a drunk driver, and she died in the CT scanner when I was supposed to be watching her. Her father sought me out and threatened me because he blames me for his daughter's death. The hospital attorney met with me because they are worried about getting sued. I had to present my mistake to the whole surgery department in conference this morning, and when I finally made it back to my apartment this evening, someone had vandalized my house by writing 'Die Rebel' on my front door. The police just left. And I was too scared to stay here alone, so I invited one of the male surgery residents to sleep on the couch. Oh, and did I mention that my mother called to tell me that my twin brother is going to court for a DUI, my father continues to deteriorate, and his primary physician at home thinks I'm a fool for wanting him checked for Huntington's disease?" She paused and added with saccharin sweetness, "And how was your week?"

"Claire, I–I don't know how to respond. This all sounds terrible. And I don't know what I can do. I wish I was there. How are you holding up?"

"I wish you were here too." Suddenly, she felt like crying again. "I'm too tired to cry anymore. The only good thing about internship is that they work me so long that I don't have time to worry about all these troubles."

"Great," he replied with sarcasm. "A side benefit of being abused: They make you so miserable that you forget the other bad things in your life." He paused. "Would you like it if I came up for the weekend? If I left early in the morning, I could be there late Saturday night."

"I'd love to see you, honey, but it's hardly practical. I'll be back in the hospital tomorrow morning until midday on Sunday. I'd probably barely get to see you before you'd have to turn around and leave again."

His voice was soft. "I guess you're right."

"Are you mad about me having a man stay here?"

"Yes, but I understand. I don't think it looks good, but under the circumstances, I guess I understand. I'm jealous, but I understand."

"Thanks."

"Claire, I think we ought to pray."

"If I close my eyes, I'll be asleep."

"I'm serious, Claire. I mean like we used to do, when we first started dating, when we both seemed more concerned about what God wanted for us."

She nodded, even though he couldn't see. She knew he was right. It was the right thing to do, but she felt so spiritually dry. It had been months since she'd been to church, shoving her needs for fellowship and the Bible aside so she could pursue her career in surgery. "Okay," she said. "I'm listening."

John began to pray, haltingly at first, and then with fervor, words that he felt, asking God to protect Claire and put his arms of peace around her. He prayed for grace and for guidance.

Claire brushed back her tears. "Thanks, honey."

"I love you," he concluded. "Sleep tight."

She walked out of the bathroom clutching her robe and put the phone back in its cradle. She pulled a sleeping bag and a pillow from the closet and tossed them on the couch. Brett was watching TV.

"Don't you get cable?"

"Why would I want it? I'm never here."

"Good point." He paused. "I guess that was your fiancé?"

"Good guess."

"Was he upset about me being here?"

"Should he be?"

He nodded. "I think so."

"He's jealous. He's honest enough to tell me that."

"Should he be?"

She smiled. "I guess I wouldn't like it if he didn't care." She turned and walked to the stairs. "Thanks for coming over. I'll feel safer knowing someone else is in the house."

"Sure."

"Good night, Brett. I'll let myself out quietly in the morning so you can sleep. Saturdays off is a benefit you should cherish."

"Good night, Claire." He put his arms behind his head. "I'll be right here if you want me."

She turned and walked up the stairs, clutching the front of her robe. *Don't tempt me, lifeguard boy.*

Chapter Twenty-Two

The night passed without catastrophe, and in spite of her exhaustion, Claire tossed restlessly at any little sound. She awoke at two to the barking of the neighbor's schnauzer, suspecting that Tiger was responding to another prowler. She awoke at three to the sound of a Safeway bread truck, imagining a vandal's getaway vehicle speeding into the night. Each time, she stared at the darkness and listened, her ears attuned to every minute sound which could alert her to the presence of Mr. Jones, returning to exact vengeance for his daughter's death.

At four, she was sure she heard the floor creaking downstairs, and she had, but it was only Brett rising to use the bathroom. Then she started thinking how wonderful it would be if he would just disobey everything she'd told him and sneak upstairs and slip into bed beside her.

Ugh! I can't be thinking this way. She turned over and pulled the pillow over her head. *This is crazy.* She was actually looking forward to getting back to the hospital so she could get some sleep.

She rose and dressed at five, back to wearing her navy skirt. *I wish the CT attendings would enter the new millennium. What's wrong with a woman in pants?*

Claire left the house at five-thirty, with Brett sleeping soundly on the couch. At least one of them had slept well.

She closed the door quietly and looked at the jagged message printed there. She shivered and ran to her Toyota. Tiger barked again, and Claire escaped his wet greeting by ducking into her car.

Weekends on the CT service were a notch more relaxed than during the week, with no fresh hearts to sit. After morning rounds with Dr. Rosenthal, Claire spent an hour with the medical students, teaching them the basics of intensive care monitoring. They asked questions, took notes, and called her Dr. McCall.

"Call me Claire," she reminded them for the third time.

Martin walked by and whined. "I could use some help writing notes, Claire."

"It's the weekend, Martin. Why don't you skip out of here and I'll do all the notes today? Then tomorrow, you write the notes and I'll leave early."

Martin ran his hand through his unwashed hair and wrinkled his forehead. It seemed this was a new concept to him: working together, not simply competing. "Hmmm. I could use a nap."

And a shower. Claire smiled. "Get out of here, Martin."

"Okay, sounds like a plan." He pivoted and rushed from the unit, nearly running into Dr. Rosenthal as he exited the automatic door leading to the ICU. Claire listened to their conversation as she picked up her first patient chart.

"Leaving so soon, Dr. Holcroft?"

"Well, er, yes. It was Claire's idea. She'll do the notes today. I'll do them tomorrow."

Claire watched over her shoulder to see Martin backpedaling into the unit. "But I can stay if you want, sir. I really think maybe it's best if I do—"

"Relax, Martin," Dr. Rosenthal chided. "It's the weekend. The attendings don't care, as long as the work gets done." He opened his hand and gestured toward the double doors. "Have a nice day."

"Thank you, sir. I will, sir."

Martin disappeared and Rosenthal looked at Claire. "Where did we get him?"

Claire lifted her nose. "Harvard, sir."

Rosenthal laughed, then lifted a donut from a box on the counter. He held the donut with a paper napkin, appearing to carefully avoid touching the food with his fingers.

Only a cardiothoracic surgeon would eat a donut that way.

Rosenthal chuckled again, uncharacteristically jovial. He finished his donut and folded the napkin before discarding it in a trash receptacle beneath the counter. He studied a cardiac monitor for a moment before turning to leave. He paused at the door and looked back at Claire. "You might want to go easy on the Harvard jokes when you're around Dr. Lewis. He's an alum and he absolutely adores Harvard grads."

She tapped her pen on the progress note page and smiled before offering a mock salute. "Thanks for the warning, sir."

He shook his head. "Careful, Claire." He pushed a button on the wall to activate the automatic door leading from the unit. He disappeared with his words fading, "I'm on my beeper."

Saturday night Claire slept for five hours without interruption in a hospital call room. Five hours! She pried herself from the inadequate mattress and stretched, relishing in the amazing amount of time since her last page. She checked the beeper, fearing a dead battery, but it was fine. The service was stable, and she hadn't been needed.

She thought back to her last night at home and wondered how she would feel tonight all alone in her quiet house. She couldn't just invite Brett to move in with her. Sooner or later that would drive him . . . or her . . . to do something they'd regret. Or at least *she'd* regret.

She looked around the call room. And she couldn't exactly just live there, could she?

She back-burnered her concern during rounds, and left Martin Holcroft as the lonely front line for the CT service by nine A.M.

She traveled Devonshire Boulevard, noting the paucity of city traffic. She passed two large churches with parking lots crowded with cars. She felt an urge to turn in at the second, but dispelled the idea when she looked at her plain navy skirt and remembered her commitment to go shopping. She pressed on the accelerator and pushed aside a pang of guilt. *I feel guilty every time I see a church.* She tapped her fingers on the steering wheel, aware of the irony in her thinking. *I'm supposed to be in church so I can feel better, right? But I'll just end up feeling worse because I'll see how far I have to go.*

She'd find a church once she got through her internship. Certainly John would want to go somewhere after they were married.

Suddenly, she was thinking about Brett, about his lips on her forehead, and the way he gently nudged her face toward his. Her heart quickened at the memory. Why did she always have to think about Brett when she wanted to think about John? He was like a virus in her brain, lying in wait to attack, just when her defenses were down. What was it about him, that she had allowed him to get under her skin so effectively?

She looked down at her diamond solitaire, and she tilted it to reflect the sunlight coming through the windshield. *I'd better find another shoulder to cry on before I let him kiss me. I'm afraid I'd melt. I'd be putty in those masculine arms . . .*

She passed another church and felt guilty again. *I haven't even read my Bible in weeks.*

Claire pulled her car into the Safeway parking lot. She wanted to do her grocery shopping while the parking lot looked empty. *I'll read my Bible later today.*

Then I won't feel so guilty.

That afternoon, Della McCall cleared the dishes from the table and checked on Wally. He was watching TV with a glassy-eyed stare, sitting on the couch, but certainly didn't appear to be relaxing. His right arm flew up with a jerk into the air and landed on the seat back. His head twitched and he kept crossing and uncrossing his legs, seemingly unable to keep them in one position for any time at all.

"It wears me out just watching you."

Wally said nothing. He just kept staring ahead at the TV screen. He hadn't spoken two words since she'd returned from church. He may have belched once or twice, but he uttered nothing Della could understand. She stayed out of his way when he was like this. It was better just to let the cloud pass.

She went back to her dishes, filling the sink with hot soapy water. Della began to wash. Just doing something so normal brought a little comfort to her soul, as everything else around her seemed to boil. She caressed each plate with a drying towel and stacked them in a painted cupboard.

When the phone rang, she dried her hands and carried the receiver out into the shade of the back porch. "Hello."

"Mom, it's me."

"Claire." She sighed. "It's good to hear you."

"I hadn't talked to you for a while. I thought I should check in. How was Clay's court date?"

"The judge fined him 250 dollars and gave him a restricted license, but he has to attend an alcohol safety course of some sort."

"What's a restricted license?"

"He can only drive to and from his classes, to work, or to a doctor's appointment."

"Oh, man." She heard her daughter exhale into the phone.

"What?"

"Oh, I was just trying to imagine Clay not having access to all the things he loves to do: his motorcycle, fishing, whatever. He's not very content sitting still."

"He's going to have to be."

"I guess. How's Daddy?"

Della glanced back at the closed screen door. "He's the same, Claire. I'm getting to the end of my rope with him. I wish you could come home and see him. He needs a good doctor."

"Thanks but no thanks. He still won't see Dr. Jenkins?"

"No. He says he knows what he'll say. He thinks doctors are all the same. They'll just get on him for his drinking."

"Do you think it's all his alcohol?"

"No."

"So maybe someone is finally inclined to back my theory that Daddy needs a real doctor to see if something else is going on?"

"Claire, I've never doubted that he needs medical help. You're the one who insisted that he was a drunk and that all his problems stemmed from that."

Claire sighed. "I know, I know. But that was before I learned about Huntington's."

And that was before it was affecting your future, Della thought.

"You didn't want me to talk to Grandma about Huntington's disease. You thought I'd offend her."

"And you did anyway."

There was silence on the other end of the line for a moment. "How did you find that out? Did she tell you?"

"No. Dr. Jenkins told me of your concern, and why."

Claire huffed. "I told him those things in confidence! Why did he turn around and tell you?"

"Claire, it's not like he's spreading this all around. This is a family matter, and he thought I should know. Actually, he seemed concerned for you. He wanted me to reassure you that you didn't need to worry about this Huntington's disease or whatever disease you've diagnosed your father with."

"I'm not so sure what makes him so confident. Is he afraid he'll be looked down upon if he's missed an important diagnosis?"

"Dr. Jenkins is a very smart man, Claire. Perhaps you should believe him."

"Maybe he feels threatened by me. I've just finished medical school. He's been at it for a long time. I'm in a high-powered medical university. He's a country doctor. I come up with a diagnostic concern that I think he should check out, and instead of feeling grateful, he says I'm living in an ivory tower."

"Honey, he's one of your biggest fans. I'm sure he didn't mean to offend."

"Maybe it's not his fault. It's just all of Stoney Creek. No one can see past the end of their nose down there. Dr. Jenkins won't listen. You were too concerned that I would offend Grandma, and all she can think about is some stupid legend of an old curse. Is everyone just backwards, or does everyone have a skeleton in the closet?"

Della glanced in at Wally. He was still watching TV with a blank stare and still twitching. "Look, Claire, don't sell us all short. Stoney Creek may be small, but—"

"Dr. Jenkins told you everything that I told him? Even about Grandma?"

"Yes, even about Grandma's little secret."

"Ugh! I shouldn't have told him. Grandma was so concerned this would get back to Daddy. She didn't think he should know."

"Don't worry, Claire," she responded, lowering her voice. "I'm not about to share that with him, not in his condition."

"Good." Claire's voice lightened. "Have you talked to Grandma? How was her trip to Martha's Vineyard?"

"She stopped by this afternoon. She looks great. She's tanned, ready for another trip somewhere."

"She stopped there, by the house? What gives? I thought she never visited anymore."

"She doesn't. At least not very often. But since the summer rolled around, she seems to worry a lot about your father. I think she feels responsible for him."

"It's the curse thing, Mom. She's worried she passed along a generational curse."

"I'm not so sure. She may be coming around. She said that her cousin Hilda tried to talk some sense into her. She even mentioned that Hilda had known a person with Huntington's disease once, and said that in Hilda's opinion, you might not be so far out in left field after all."

"Thank you, doctor cousin Hilda."

Della heard the sound of the refrigerator door squeaking before Claire continued. "What about you, Mom? Do you think it's possible? Could the Stoney Creek curse be Huntington's disease? Maybe this is what's been wrong with Daddy all along."

Della shook her head. "I'm no doctor, Claire. And Dr. Jenkins thinks this is all hot air. I'm not sure how I can add anything."

"You can help, Mom. Dr. Jenkins said that he doubted an insurance carrier would ever even agree to pay for a test for Huntington's disease in the absence of a family history."

"I can't exactly remedy that, can I?"

"No, but you could snoop into this old legend a bit. The last time I was in town, I ate at the café over in Fisher's Retreat. The owner, Mr. Knitter, knows just about everyone. And he believes in the curse. We talked about it. He mentioned several people that he thought were affected by it."

"So what can I do?"

"Talk to him. See if you can find out if any of these people have similar family roots. See if this supposed curse can be traced by inheritance."

"Claire, I'd feel funny digging into other people's family business. Besides, Dr. Jenkins thinks this is a waste of time. You don't need to worry about this stuff, Claire. He says this disease is so rare that—"

"Mom, it's important to me. What harm can it do to check a few birth records?" She paused. "Mom, it's my future, can't you see this? If Daddy has HD, then I'm at risk too."

"Claire, don't you think you're out on a limb here?"

"Mom, I feel like someone is playing Russian roulette. And the gun is pointed at *my* head!"

"Are you overreacting? Isn't there any treatment for this disease?"

"A few treatments for symptoms, but no cure. Mom, a diagnosis of HD would be death to a surgeon's career."

"I understand. Look, maybe I can talk to Mr. Knitter, but I'm not about to traipse all over the valley snooping into people's lives, especially people I don't know. It just doesn't seem proper."

"Momma!"

"Claire!" She huffed. "Try not to worry about this. You've got enough on your mind with all your studies. But if I run into Mr. Knitter, and if I find out Dr. Jenkins is right, and there are no family links around, will you drop this and pay attention to your dream?"

"Dr. Jenkins has his eyes closed, Mom. Either that or he's embarrassed by missing a diagnosis, or worse. Why else would he be trying to get you to talk me out of my concerns?"

"He wants you to succeed, Claire, to be able to concentrate on your studies. Believe it or not, this whole little town that you think is so backwards, this whole town is excited for you. You're going to be the first woman surgeon to come out of these parts. Don't you think they're not proud. So quit worrying, okay?"

"I'll try, Mom."

"Residency is hard enough without getting paranoid that every disease you see is haunting your own family."

Claire's voice was monotone. "Okay, Mom, I hope you're right. I've gotta go. Tell Daddy hi for me." Della could hear the frustration in her daughter's voice. Claire always talked that way when she was trying not to sound mad.

Della pressed the "off" button on the phone, troubled by her daughter's comments. She put the phone down on the porch swing beside her and stared out at the Blue Ridge mountains. She felt so suddenly alone, threatened by an avalanche of memories she had hoped to bury. If she could only erase a month of her life, she'd delete the winter of 1972 and the images she couldn't expunge.

It was an unchaperoned house call to a lonely navy wife, an innocent exam which initiated desire, and led to the unthinkable, a lifelong regret. It was temporary ecstasy in the arms of someone she was never intended to love.

The sound of glass shattering startled Della back to the present. She opened the screen door and rushed to the kitchen. There, on the floor, Wally flailed his arms in a mess of peach pie, milk, and fragments of a stoneware plate. His face was blue, and his eyes bulged. A gurgling sound came from his throat, and as he retched, his head bobbed on his neck like a beach ball on a turbulent sea. After a moment, he was still. Was this a seizure? Was he choking?

Della ran back to her phone and dialed 911. "My husband's not breathing!"

Chapter Twenty-Three

The Wally McCall family sat together on the vinyl chairs in the corner of a crowded ICU waiting room. It was an awkward reunion, a forced gathering prompted by an unplanned emergency, as midnight vigils in hospital waiting rooms usually are.

Clay looked over the top of a hunting magazine. "You should call Claire."

Margo yawned. "She just tried five minutes ago. Claire's obviously not home."

Clay's head disappeared behind the magazine again. "Did you leave a message?"

Della blew her nose. "Of course."

"Did you tell her that her father's in the hospital, that he looks like he's gonna die?"

Della yanked the magazine from his hands. "Will you put this down?" She looked at the cover, a picture of a hunter with a large dead animal beside him. "I feel like I'm talking to a moose."

"It's an elk, Mom."

Margo stood up. "Would you guys call a truce?" She looked at a vending machine along the far wall. "Anyone want a soda?"

Della shook her head silently.

"Well," Clay whined. "Did you tell Claire he's hooked up to that breathing machine?"

Margo was searching through her jean's pockets, retrieving a handful of change. "That's not exactly the kind of thing that's appropriate to leave as a phone message." She sorted the coins. "Anyone have a dime?"

Della opened her purse and retrieved a quarter. "This is all I have." She paused and looked at Clay, who seemed to be eyeing the magazine that she still clutched in her hand. "I just told her that her father was in the hospital in Carlisle and that I'd call back later."

Margo accepted the quarter, then looked up and grabbed her mother's arm. "It's the doctor."

Della dropped the magazine and stood to face a middle-aged man with a starched white coat with neat embroidered lettering above a breast pocket: "R. W. Smuland, MD, Internal Medicine." He slipped a thumb beneath his ample belt and nodded his balding head silently as if to announce the importance of what was to follow. He had two chins and, in Della's opinion, was way too tan for a busy doctor.

Della gripped Margo's elbow. Clay kept his seat and folded his arms behind his head.

The physician spoke at a low volume, and glanced around at the others in the waiting area. "Can we speak here?"

Della looked around. No one else seemed to be paying attention. "Sure." She paused, angry that Clay had retrieved the magazine she'd dropped. She cast a disparaging glance in his direction before looking back at the doctor. "How is he?"

"Your husband has had a large aspiration."

Margo squinted. "What?"

"He vomited and choked some of the material back into his lungs." He wrinkled his forehead. "This is very common in alcoholics."

"He's not drinking anymore," Della responded.

"Mrs. McCall, your husband had an alcohol level higher than the legal limit for intoxication."

"No," she responded. "I'm with him most of the time. He couldn't have been." Her voice trailed off as the physician folded his hands across his chest.

Margo patted her mother's hand. "He was alone when you went to church."

Clay spoke up. "She's in denial, Doc. Tell 'er. My dad has 'er fooled."

Margo snapped, "Shut up, Clay. Let the doctor talk."

Clay huffed and lifted his magazine.

Della thought back over the day. Wally had done nothing but sit on the couch and stare at the TV all afternoon. He was there when she'd arrived back from the morning service, and he hadn't replied to her questions. "Will he be okay?"

"It's hard to say at this point. He is on the ventilator to assist his breathing. He was fighting the ventilator and jerking around so much that we've had to give him medicine to temporarily paralyze him."

"He jerks around like that all the time. He's been doing it for months," Margo reported.

Clay turned a page noisily. "How would you know? You're never around."

Della rolled her eyes. "I'm sorry," she whispered softly to the doctor. "But she's right. He jerks his legs and arms. He can't walk straight. It's like he's restless. Even in his sleep."

The doctor squeezed his lips together and shook his head. "I'm afraid what I saw may be evidence of brain injury. He may have had some brain damage from lack of oxygen after he choked." He unfolded his hands. "It may be a few days before we know."

"Can you help him?"

"I've started him on antibiotics. I'll support him with the ventilator. If he keeps fighting it, I'll have to keep him sedated or paralyzed until his lungs improve enough for him to breathe on his own again."

Margo tightened her grip on her mother's hand. "Could he die?"

The physician nodded. "That's a possibility." He held up his hand with three fingers extended. "There are essentially three outcomes. He could decline and die in the hospital. He could survive and be brain damaged, or, hopefully, he could recover and be his old self again."

Clay's voice came from behind a magazine. "Like that's something we should look forward to."

Della reached for the magazine and gave it a sharp tug, but this time, Clay held it secure. They struggled for a moment, the magazine bobbing up and down between them, before she emitted a frustrated huff and let go.

She looked at the doctor who diverted his eyes to the floor, obviously not caring to observe two adults fighting over a magazine. She looked at Margo. Her cheeks were flushed, and she had stepped away, looking at the coins in her hand.

Della then turned her eyes back to Clay. His fingers were blanched where he gripped the periodical, a vein on his forehead protruded, and he scowled at the elk on the magazine's cover.

She gathered the neck of her blouse beneath her chin and began to sob. She cried because she couldn't reach Claire. She cried because she'd embarrassed Margo. And she cried because her husband was lying between life and death and his own son wanted to read a hunting magazine.

He doesn't care if his father lives or dies.

Her next thought arrested her sobs, and came as an abrupt revelation, a horrible dose of reality which terminated her cries with the suddenness of a switching on of a lamp in a dark room. Suddenly, the things you deny are brightly illuminated, in plain view, and impossible to ignore any longer.

Della buried her head in her hands. *Wally is hanging between life and death . . . and* I *don't even care.*

Claire shopped all afternoon, carefully selecting two dresses, two skirts, a blouse, and a dress suit to use for more formal presentations. She took her time and gladly paid the purchases in cash with the money from her first paycheck as a real medical doctor.

She had borrowed money throughout college and medical school, but she knew her day of accounting was near, and she had sat down before starting her internship to plan a repayment schedule for all of her school loans. She couldn't afford to be extravagant, and her house rental took a fair share of the budget, but she saved on extracurricular spending, because she had too little time to spend money. Sunday, she made time, and judiciously made purchases out of need, not want, and had the rare insight of knowing the difference.

She ate supper at a local mall and seriously considered going to the beach to watch the sunset, but nixed the idea, knowing she would just end up at Brett's. Instead, she went to Foster Park and walked along the Danberry River and considered the options for the night ahead. She could return home to sleep and be mauled by an intruder. Or she could return home to sleep and invite Brett to protect her, and face the jealousy of her fiancé and the temptations that came with having a hunk sleep on her couch. Or, she could stay in a hospital call room with her beeper off, unavailable to the nurse's beck and call, and safe from vandalizing intruders.

She wondered about Roger Jones and how he was coping. He had dared to confront her with threats in a public place. What would restrain him from attacking her in private?

With her options analyzed, her obvious safe choice was the hospital. But what would a male intern do? She doubted they would cower in a call room. But then again, who would ever know?

She walked in quietly, hoping she wouldn't run into Martin or anyone else who knew she wasn't on call. She stole away into a small call room on the first floor and locked the door. She laid her call bag in the corner and sat at a small oak desk, the kind you might find in the homes of a middle-class high schooler.

She opened Sabiston's *Textbook of Surgery* and turned to a chapter entitled "The Breast." Finally, a subject where a female surgeon had a real advantage over her male counterparts, at least in the area of empathy. How could a man really understand what it meant to have a breast surgically biopsied or removed? She looked down at her own anatomy.

She read for a few minutes before remembering the promise she'd made earlier in the day, when just seeing the outside of a church made her feel guilty. She was going to read her Bible today, but she'd left it at home. She felt a pang of remorse and looked down at the massive book in front of her. But this was God's work for her. Surgery was her calling. She'd felt that ever since caring for Grandma Newby.

It's Sunday. I should have brought my Bible.

I'll be back home Tuesday night. Certainly I'll read my Bible then. She looked around the meager call quarters. Neat. Clean. Safe.

I'll read my Bible at home on Tuesday. If I go home.

By Monday morning at nine, with the CT fellow and the attendings in the OR, Claire and Martin slogged through the patient charts. There were transfer orders to write, progress notes to complete, labs and X rays to check, and medical students to teach.

Claire looked at the trio of students sitting at the counter writing notes. They were still a bit clueless, having just started their third-year rotations. Claire smiled. As hard as her job was, she wouldn't change positions with them for a million dollars. They worked hard, got no respect, and still had to study for tests.

The next thought made her smile. She realized her own life was almost the same. She worked hard, still took tests, and respect? Well, at least the nurses called her "Dr. McCall." The third-year medical students had to put up with their designation of M-3s. Claire thought that sounded more like a weapon than a title of a graduate medical student.

She remembered the O-man and his nightly teaching sessions with the medical students. "Wedges. The simplest tool to move a load."

Martin looked up. "What?"

She blushed, realizing she had verbalized her thoughts. "Nothing. I was just remembering what it was like to start the third year of medical school."

"Torture. Pure and simple."

"Oh, come on, Martin. I know you," she teased. "You'd do it again in a heartbeat."

He ran a hand through his unwashed hair. "I stayed up all night in the ICU. I haven't showered. I haven't eaten since last night. The nurses in the ICU don't appreciate the instruction I give them. And I think I'm getting an ulcer." He pointed to a stack of charts on the desk. "Ask me tomorrow, after your night on call."

Stop instructing the experienced ICU nurses, and they'd let you get a little sleep, Mr. MD, PhD.

Claire's beeper sounded. It was the operator. She picked up the phone and dialed "0." "Dr. McCall. I was paged."

The operator's voice was feminine, but monotone, almost mechanical. "I have Dr. McCall on the line, ma'am. Go ahead."

"Claire?" The voice was strained, but easily recognizable to Claire.

"Mom? What's wrong?"

"It's your father. He's in the hospital in Carlisle. He's on a ventilator, Claire."

Claire's hand went to her mouth, and she sank into a chair. "When? What happened?"

"After I talked with you yesterday, I found him in the kitchen. I think he choked on my peach pie."

"Oh, Momma."

"The doctor says he aspirated or something. He's afraid he might have brain damage."

"Brain damage?"

"He was jerking so. I told the doctor that he always does that, but he thought it may be signs of something serious, like maybe he didn't get enough oxygen while he was choking or something."

Claire sighed, unsure what to say.

"The doctor says that Wally was drinking. He had alcohol in his blood, Claire." She sniffed and started to sob. "He said he might d–die, honey." She blew her nose.

Claire pulled the receiver away from her ear.

"They had to paralyze him. He's just lying there all still, with all these tubes. He looks like he's dead already."

"I'm coming home," Claire mumbled. "I'll leave right away."

She said good-bye and hung up the phone.

Martin had obviously overheard Claire's intentions. He stood in her way as she picked up her stethoscope. "Just like that? You're going to leave me here by myself?"

She nodded and took a step toward the door of the ICU. "It's my father. He's on a ventilator. The doctor says he might die."

Martin shook his head. "B–but you can't leave me on this service by myself. They'll make me take call every night." His voice was pleading, desperate. "The nurses won't listen to me, Claire. I won't sleep."

She walked numbly to the exit. She turned and looked at Martin Holcroft, MD, PhD, his hair stringy, his shoulders stooped in defeat. "Get a grip on yourself, Martin. I'll talk to the program director. We'll work something out."

She stomped toward Dr. Rogers' office. She clenched her fists as she walked and quietly voiced her resolve: "My father needs me, so I'm going home."

Chapter Twenty-Four

Claire pushed her seat into a reclining position shortly after take-off and wondered how her life could get any more complicated. She'd been given one week off which she'd have to take out of her two weeks yearly vacation. Another intern, Brian McNeil, was pulled from his ER rotation to cover CT while she was away. In two hours, she'd gone from writing notes in the ICU to thirty thousand feet, flying home to a parent reported to be on death's door. She hadn't even stopped in at her rented brownstone for a suitcase. With her call bag packed, and her new clothes purchases carefully folded inside, she ought to have enough to make it until she returned.

She closed her eyes and reflected on the one advantage of her flight. At least she'd be away from Lafayette and out of Roger Jones's reach for a few days.

She thought of her father and wondered if her ideas about Huntington's disease were totally off the wall. She'd been accused of ivory-toweritis, and her mother implied that she was being paranoid about every disease she saw. She knew that was an exaggeration, but had known other students in medical school who always developed the symptoms of the disease they were studying. It wasn't so uncommon. A little hypochondria circulates in every medical school class.

Her father was drinking again. It wasn't so hard for her to believe. But did that mean nothing else was wrong? Were all his symptoms simply alcohol intoxication or alcohol withdrawal, or a combination?

She tried to close her eyes to rest, but the nagging feeling about her father's case wouldn't go away. She drank a diet cola and stared at the clouds.

Everything below her looked so small. Cars and trucks were ants. Buildings were blocks and the rivers were spaghetti. It was all a matter of perspective. All of the mountains that loomed so large when they were right in front of you looked like goose bumps from an airplane window.

Perspective. Maybe that's what she needed in her life.

Her problems seemed so big, but maybe that was because they were in front of her nose.

She was in an all-out competition with the best medical school graduates in the country. Her life was threatened by a man who blamed her for killing his daughter. Her father was on death's door in an ICU, and even if he recovered, he might still suffer from an incurable genetic disease, which he may have passed to her. She was engaged to a man she rarely got to see. She was attracted to a man she felt guilty for desiring. It had been months since she'd been to church, and weeks since she'd read the Bible.

Could things get any worse?

She looked at a man in a business suit next to her, busily typing on a laptop computer. He was a salesman, an attorney perhaps. If he made a mistake, someone might lose a few dollars. If she made a mistake, a mother lost her only daughter and a little girl would never ride her purple bicycle again. Claire felt her eyes begin to tear. She blinked and turned her head toward the window. Some perspective.

She landed in Pittsburgh, waited two hours, and then rode a puddle jumper into the Apple Valley Regional Airport in Carlisle. There, she contemplated her ride options. She didn't want to bother her mother. She had sounded too out of sorts. She didn't want to bother Margo. They really hadn't been close since Claire had left home. That would seem too awkward. And she couldn't call her twin, because his restricted license wouldn't allow him to pick her up. She was left with taking a cab.

She rode to the hospital with a talkative driver, watching out the window and offering minimal responses which never discouraged him from blabbering on and on. She didn't dare mention that she was a doctor. The man had already told her about his sickly aunt with stomach ulcers and a cousin with lupus simply because their destination was a hospital. She was sure he would pull over and ask her to look at a mole or some other hideous skin lesion hidden under his shirt if he only knew her occupation. She smiled sweetly and looked away.

At the hospital, Claire found her mother sitting in a corner booth in the cafeteria sipping cold coffee and pushing salad greens around a plate with her fork. Clay had gone to work at the cabinet shop. Margo was caring for her family of three girls. Della had stayed through the night catnapping on a couch in the ICU waiting room. They walked arm in arm, the way close families are supposed to do. As they trudged the long hall toward the ICU, Claire sensed a desperation in her mother's demeanor. The last months of life with Wally had taken their toll.

They visited Wally together, holding his hand, watching his chest rise and fall with mechanical regularity, the ventilator whooshing and humming in the background against a symphony of clinical noise. Electronic beeps and alarms, pulse monitors blipping, gastric tubes pumping, and the soft whirring noises of the inflatable air stockings all provided the medical music which Claire had come to love.

A nurse reported his progress. There had been no essential change. He started twitching again when the paralyzing agent was removed, so the medicine was resumed and the ventilator continued. Dr. Smuland should be around for evening rounds at nine. Claire should feel free to stay.

With some urging, Della agreed to return to Stoney Creek for the night. Claire would talk to Wally's doctor and keep up the vigil, sleeping, if she could, in the ICU waiting area.

Dr. Smuland arrived to see Wally at nine-thirty, and stopped, at the request of Wally's nurse, to see Claire in the waiting room. He looked tired. He had dark circles beneath his eyes, and his bald head was tan and glistening with perspiration. He stood at the corner of the waiting room and surveyed the crowd. "Claire McCall?"

Claire stood and greeted him with a handshake. "Dr. Smuland, I'm Claire McCall, Wallace McCall's daughter. Thanks for coming by."

He nodded. "I understand you're in medicine?"

"I'm a surgery intern at Lafayette University in Massachusetts." She paused. "How are things with my father?"

"His X ray looks like pneumonia. He is oxygenating better than yesterday. We tried to wean him from the ventilator, but when we took away the paralyzing medication, he had so much twitching and jerking that we had to put him back down again."

"What do you think is going on?"

"To be honest, I'm not really sure. I'm worried about ischemic encephalopathy." He seemed to be studying Claire's face for signs of comprehension.

She understood he was worried about brain damage from lack of oxygen.

Dr. Smuland continued. "It could be delirium tremens, alcohol withdrawal. I've seen some pretty remarkable tremors and twitching with that."

"Just what happened? My mom hasn't told me much. She seemed so depressed, I didn't want to drag it from her."

"Your father evidently choked while eating at home. Your mother did a Heimlich maneuver on him while she was on the phone with a 911 operator. She saved him, really. He started breathing, but was still having a lot of difficulty maintaining a good enough oxygen level, and his lungs sounded horrible, so after his arrival in our ER, he was sedated and placed on the ventilator."

"Did he get a bronchoscopy?"

"Yes. Dr. Cale did that. He sucked out a lot of particulate matter."

Claire winced. "Gross."

"Look, Claire, I don't want to scare you, but I don't really know how much of his function will return. We may have saved his heart, but his brain might be severely damaged."

"Can we get a neurologist to see him?"

"If we had one." He shrugged. "We're a small community hospital. A neurologist, Dr. Visvalingam, comes over from Brighton twice a month to run a clinic in Carlisle. If we have an emergency, sometimes we can get him to come for a consultation."

Claire recognized the neurologist's unique name. In fact, she'd done a rotation with him as a medical student. He was as eccentric as his name was difficult to pronounce. To the students at Brighton University, he was simply Dr. V. He was caring and brilliant. Oh, how wonderful it would be to have him see her father.

Dr. Smuland didn't seem inclined to pursue a consult. Claire thought of another diagnostic tactic. "What about an EEG?"

"We have a tech that can run the test, but in order to get it interpreted, we have to send it to the neurologist in Brighton."

"Do it."

Dr. Smuland's eyes widened. Evidently he wasn't accustomed to such directness.

Claire repeated her opinion. "If my father needs it, do it."

The attending took a deep breath. "I'm not sure how it would change things, exactly."

"It could show whether he has extensive brain injury from ischemia. Or if his twitching and jerking may be signs of something else entirely."

Dr. Smuland sighed. "True, but I'm not convinced we would do anything differently, at least not right away."

"Can I give you my theory?"

Claire watched as the muscles in Dr. Smuland's neck tightened. He tugged at the knot of his tie and looked at his watch. "Sure."

"I think my father may have Huntington's disease."

His eyes widened. "Is it in the family? Your mother didn't tell me this."

"It's not exactly in the family. In fact, I don't know exactly who my father's real father was. And nobody has diagnosed HD in the man who I suspect was his real father, but the way my father stumbles around, and jerks, and slurs his speech, and the way that the man who I think was his father acted is so characteristic of—"

"Dr. McCall," the attending interrupted paternalistically, "I think we'd better just work on getting your father over his pneumonia. First things first."

"My father has jerked and twitched for months. His symptoms are—"

Dr. Smuland put his hand on Claire's arm. "Claire, I hear your concern. But your father is an alcoholic. You know that."

Claire nodded quietly.

"He came into our hospital with an alcohol level of twice the legal level for intoxication. Before we worry about rare genetic diseases, don't you think we should concentrate on the things that seem to be more obvious?"

It didn't seem like a question that he wanted Claire to answer. "Couldn't we just send a blood sample for a genetic screen for the Huntington's gene?" she pursued.

He shook his head. "We can't send an expensive genetic test on a whim. We need a family history, some strong evidence . . ." His voice softened, and his eyes locked on Claire's. "Can I give you some advice, Claire?"

I bet I can't stop you. "Sure."

"You're Wally's daughter. That's why you're here. That's your role for now. You're not his physician. You really shouldn't get tangled up in treating your own family, not even if they want you to." He dropped his eyes to the floor. "I should know. I tried to treat my mother, back when I started. It was a disaster."

Dr. Smuland checked his watch again.

"Thanks for taking time to talk to me. It must have been a long day for you." She attempted a smile. "I keep hoping that when I get through training, my hours will get better, but look at you. I suppose you're here day and night too."

He smiled. There were light lines running from the corners of his eyes as if he'd gotten a tan while he was squinting. "Most days are better than this. But when a case like your father's comes along, my obligation is to be here." He stepped away, signaling his desire to end the conversation. "I'll try to update you tomorrow."

Claire didn't want him to escape. "Dr. Smuland, I certainly appreciate what you are doing for my father. He's not an easy man to take care of. He's avoided doctors for a long time."

He took another step to the waiting room exit.

"Would it be okay if I contacted Dr. Visvalingam, Dr. V, over at Brighton, to see if he'd consult on the case?"

Dr. Smuland covered his mouth as he yawned. His voice showed irritation, but control. "Yes, Claire, it's okay if you want to talk to him. It's your father's right to have a consult if you desire."

"Thanks."

Dr. Smuland backpedaled out of the unit. Claire knew she had been aggressive, perhaps overly so. She slumped into a vinyl chair. Maybe she shouldn't have been so forward. She should have known not to bring up her concerns about HD during her first meeting with her dad's doctor. She could have predicted that he'd take offense to a fresh medical graduate's suggestions.

She was being a thorn in Dr. Smuland's side; it didn't take a rocket scientist to realize that. She sighed and rested her head in her hands. But this was her father he was dealing with here. And her ideas may seem out in left field to Dr. Smuland, but they were important to her.

Claire shook her head and stared at the floor. She'd better have her ducks in a row before she asked for a university consultant. He would think she was crazy too, if she didn't do her homework.

She yawned and leaned her head against the squeaky maroon vinyl. Tomorrow, she'd visit Mr. Knitter at Fisher's Café and ask him about the Stoney Creek curse. She had nothing to lose.

Except her future.

Oh, God, I hope Dr. Smuland is right.

Chapter Twenty-Five

laire opened her eyes and unfolded her slender frame from the cramped couch which had served as her bed. She had a searing discomfort in her neck from resting her head against her call bag pillow.

It was five in the morning, too early for anything except strong coffee, but too late to spend another minute trying to rest in a public waiting room. The experience had been enlightening, to say the least. Around her were people with loved ones in crisis, people thrown into circumstances and pain not of their asking. These people endured a marathon of inadequate sleep, insufficient hygiene, and vending machine nutrition at its finest: chips, sodas, and candy if only you have the right change. Claire rose and stretched, massaged her neck, and sidestepped around the bodies of those who arrived after the couches were taken.

She found a women's room nearby, washed her face, and put on a new, slightly wrinkled blouse. After lipstick and mascara, she felt a notch closer to human. After her first cup of vending machine coffee, she actually thought she might be capable of rational communication.

With her call bag over her shoulder, she slipped into the ICU and into her father's cubicle. His heart rate was eighty-eight, his last blood pressure normal, and his oxygen saturation was hovering at ninety-one percent. She looked at his sallow complexion and his sunken cheeks. He'd been losing weight; the thin sheet stretched over his body couldn't hide that. He was unmoving, except for the rise and fall of his bony chest, forced to accept the air which the ventilator thrust into him.

She gazed upon him in awkward silence, father and daughter alone. She hadn't spoken to him in meaningful conversation since high school. Oh sure, she'd visited home since then, but infrequently, and their talk had been the polite conversation of strangers. She'd blamed his drinking, his irritable disposition, or any number of reasonable excuses for staying away. Her favorite scapegoat was the pursuit of her dream. She needed to study. She had a calling. She couldn't become a surgeon by staying close to her father in Stoney Creek.

In her mind, she thought there would always be time to reconcile later. She would bring him a grandchild or two, and she would gather the wisdom that he'd gained the hard way through life battles. Later, after her training, she'd return as a surgeon, and the daughter would have her father's approval at last.

But now, with his form appearing so lifeless in front of her, the sober realization grew: a cozy reunion with her father was only a fantasy. Her father was a drunk, and her idea of a relationship with him was a daydream.

She stroked the back of his hand, then slipped her fingers over the radial artery at his wrist, to assess the strength of his pulse.

What am I doing?

Why was it so difficult for her just to be his daughter for a minute? Why couldn't she shed the white coat and just be Claire, Wally's little girl?

Why did she care what his heart rate was?

Dr. Smuland was right. His words pierced the thick protection she'd laced tightly around her heart. "You're Wally's daughter. That's why you're here."

She hadn't been close to her father for years. So why did she carry on this charade and rush back to his side when he was on his deathbed?

Because she loved him?

Or because I'm worried about me?

Claire took her fingers from her father's pulse and simply held his hand. It was time to be his daughter again.

She sat in the cubicle at his bedside for an hour, trying to sort out the confusion of her emotions. She needed to find out the truth. Not just for herself. But also for her father. If he'd really had HD all along, it would put his life in perspective again. It would help to explain so much that they had all blamed on his drinking problems.

It's not just for me, God. I need to find out for my father.

The soft voice of a nurse interrupted Claire's silent prayer. "I need to give your father an antibiotic." She lifted a small plastic bag with a clear solution. "I really shouldn't let you stay. It's not visiting hours until ten." She smiled. "But you were being so quiet."

Claire stood. "I can go. Thanks for allowing me to be here with my daddy."

She walked away and made a silent vow. *Let him live, God, and I'll try to be a daughter to him again.*

Della met Claire at nine with hot cinnamon rolls and a thermos of coffee. Claire visited with her, giving her an update on Wally and her plans to contact the university neurologist, Dr. V. After an hour, Claire left Della to continue the ICU vigil, and drove her car to Fisher's Retreat, stopping at the café as the last of the breakfast crowd sat with the morning paper unfolded, separated into sections. The sports page was on one table in front of a gray-haired gentleman with a corn-seed emblem embroidered on a baseball cap. A man in a business suit drank coffee over the comics page, and the front page was being ignored completely, apparently discarded on the edge of the back counter. Claire glanced at the headlines while waiting for Mr. Knitter to turn his attention away from the grill.

"Well, looky here," he exclaimed, turning to pour her a cup of coffee. "Claire, what brings you back?"

She shrugged. "Couldn't stay away from your coffee, Ralph." She slid an empty cup on the counter toward him. He complied and filled it to the brim.

"Seriously," she began, "I came to talk to you."

He raised his eyebrows and winked at the man in the business suit. "It's not every day a man gets to talk to a pretty woman." He walked around the counter and sat on a bar stool beside her.

"I wanted to talk to you about the Stoney Creek curse."

Claire studied him. He hadn't flinched. "You seemed to think it was all plumb foolishness if I remember correctly," he said.

"Well, now I want to know what you know." She took a sip of coffee, then paused, counting the cups she'd had since she awoke. One from the vending machine, one with her mom. Okay, one more, and then she'd quit.

Her eyes bore in on Mr. Knitter's. "You mentioned you believed in the curse. Do you know of people rumored to be affected by this curse? People other than Harold Morris, the man reputed to have built and rebuilt the still Stoney Creek has been so famous for."

He squinted. "Why are you so interested now?"

She smiled. "I have a theory to test, that's all. I want to know if this curse is inherited."

"Maybe it is. Harold Morris started it, as far as I know. Harold went crazy, killed himself after the preacher cursed him."

"Who else? Harold's kids? How about his children?"

"Leroy's the only one I heard of. People say he went crazy too. I think he committed suicide, just like his father, and that revived the whole story of the curse affecting the Morris family."

"Did Leroy have kids?"

"Don't know."

"What about a sister? Harold also had a daughter, Evangeline. She supposedly married a Hudson, and had a son, Steve."

"Steve Hudson was Harold's grandson?"

"Did you know him?"

"No, but I heard the stories. He killed himself too, didn't he?"

"Yes."

"Wow. That's three generations of suicide." He nodded like an authority. "I'd say the answer to your question is yes. Sounds like the curse can be inherited."

"But what about others? Do you know anyone else with funny movement problems, slurred speech, people rumored to be affected by this curse?"

Mr. Knitter scratched his chin. "Peter Garret is one. I don't really know him, but his son Tony was telling me about his problems." He lifted his head and slowly and noisily blew his breath through pursed lips. "People do that to me, you know? They tell me their problems, just because I stand behind the counter and listen. I probably hear more problems than a doctor, eh, Claire? And I solve more of them, too." He laughed.

Claire wanted to keep him focused. "Who were Peter's parents?"

"Can't help you there. I have no idea."

"Any more people reported with similar trouble?"

"A cousin of mine, Bill Wampler III. My mother heard about his trouble in a Christmas letter. Bill's family moved down to Mississippi or somewhere. Bill was said to have problems with controlling his arms and legs, maybe his temper, and they are taking him to a specialist for help."

"Who were Bill's parents?"

He stood up. "Can you wait a minute? Let me call Lois; she's got the family tree in my mother's family Bible."

Before Claire could protest, Ralph was on the phone to his wife, and no sooner had Claire finished her cup of coffee than Lois came in and opened the book to the family tree. She slid it in front of Claire and stood back, her hands mounted on her generous hips in a defensive pose. Her eyes bulged. "Ralph tells me you're interested in the curse. It's about time a medical professional did a proper analysis of this situation. Old Dr. Jenkins certainly hasn't helped."

Claire put on a sweet smile and tried not to look at the large protuberant mole on the end of Lois's nose. "Thanks so much for your help."

"Where were we?" Ralph pointed a pudgy finger at William Wampler III. "William's dad is here, William Wampler Jr. It says he died in a farm accident. By the date he'd have only been twenty-five."

Claire started taking notes on a paper napkin.

He traced his finger up the chart. "Here's his father, William Wampler Sr. He was my grandfather, too. You see, Sarah Wampler is William Sr.'s daughter after his second marriage to Gloria Shifflett. William Jr. was his son by his first wife, Rachel Morris."

Claire's ears perked up. "Morris? Any relation to Harold?"

"Don't know. We've just got the Wamplers recorded here."

"Did she have any signs of a weird illness?"

"Hmm. Looks like she died young in a car accident."

Claire studied the note and the tree diagram she was drawing on the napkin.

So Rachel could have been a carrier of HD, but died too young to show any symptoms, and passed the gene to her son William Wampler Jr., who in turn died in a farm accident, also too young to show symptoms. Junior passed the gene to his son, William Wampler III, who was now possibly showing symptoms.

Now she just needed to find out who Rachel Morris's father was, and check out this Peter Garret to see if he was related too.

"Any idea where I can find out about Rachel Morris's genealogy, or this fellow, Peter Garret?"

Lois nodded. "Amy Stewart over at the county clerk's office could help you. They've been working for months to update their computer records in preparation for the bicentennial celebration over in Carlisle. She has all the birth records of people that were born in the county." She winked. "And that boy she has working for her in there is so cute. He's the spitting image of Brad Pitt and—"

Lois was silenced by a look from her husband. "Easy, Lois. The woman's engaged, if you haven't noticed the rock on her finger."

"My, oh, my," Lois gasped. "A doctor, and you're getting married?" She shook her head. "Pity the man that has a pretty wife who's never home. You'll drive him insane."

"Lois!" Ralph snapped. "Pity the man whose wife is always home, more like it," he mumbled.

She giggled. "Oh, I'm just teasin' her, Ralph. She knows that."

Claire looked at the mole on the end of Lois's nose. It was even in color, with a sharply demarcated edge, and had three hairs sprouting from its center. *All signs of a benign lesion, Lois. You won't need to have it surgically removed.* She diverted her eyes after her examination and picked up her napkin. "I've got to run," she said, laying a dollar on the counter. "Thanks for the information."

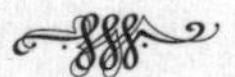

Claire freshened her makeup in the car before going in to meet Brad Pitt at the county clerk's office. And, surprisingly, Lois's judgment was strikingly accurate. In fact, Claire liked this one better than the movie star. She judiciously kept her ring finger below the counter and cleared her throat.

She introduced herself as Dr. McCall, explaining that she was doing some genetics research and needed to trace some local genealogies. Mr. Pitt was obviously impressed and practically stumbled over himself to promise full cooperation. He took down the names she gave him, along with approximate dates of their births, and promised to get back to her. He stood and stared at her for a moment before diverting his eyes to the floor.

"I'm only in town for a short while," she said, writing the number of her cell phone down on a small card. "Remember, I need parents, grandparents, and their parents if possible, with dates of births and causes of death if available."

"Sure thing." He glanced over his shoulder at a desk stacked with large manila folders. "This may take me a while. If we don't have the records on file, I'll have to fax down to Richmond to get them. Our records are pretty complete, but the state's are better."

"What's 'a while'? Are you talking hours, days, weeks?"

"Oh, not weeks, Dr. McCall. It depends on if someone put this data in the computer or not. We're trying to get a lot of this information updated on a database for Carlisle's bicentennial celebration. I may have the information in a few minutes. Or it might take a few days." His smile revealed a row of even white teeth. A dentist's child couldn't have looked nicer. He put a thumb in his belt and pulled his shoulders back an inch.

I'll bet he's practiced that pose a thousand times in front of his bathroom mirror.

"Call me Claire." She scribbled her name on the paper above her phone number and pushed it into his palm. "Call me anytime." She smiled. "I want to hear from you."

"Sure, Doc—eh, Claire. I'll call." He hesitated and spoke again. "I'll call soon."

She turned and walked out into the bright sunshine and looked up at a sky so blue it should have been on a postcard.

What was it with the Y chromosome, anyway? That guy was almost slobbering.

Wally McCall hadn't changed all day, so Claire pried her mother from the waiting room, drove to Stoney Creek for her grandmother, and took them to Chico's for dinner. Chico's restaurant was a quaint little place situated halfway between Fisher's Retreat and North Mountain, an Apple Valley fixture where the bread was homemade and the lasagna was fabulous.

Over dinner, the three most important women in Wally's life ate in awkward silence. Grandma Elizabeth had shared her secret with Claire, who had shared it in confidence with Dr. Jenkins, who in turn, blabbed it to Della. Now they all knew, but Elizabeth still didn't know that Della had found out.

Claire buttered a hot roll. "Confession time."

Elizabeth put down her fork. Della looked away.

Claire put her hand on her grandmother's. "Look, it's time we got some things in the open. Mom knows your secret, Grandma."

"Claire, you promised to keep—"

"Grandma, I kept your secret. I shared it with Dr. Jenkins. I told him in confidence because I had concerns over Daddy's health, over his family medical history." She paused, praying her grandmother would understand. "Dr. Jenkins is the one who broke a confidence by telling Mom."

Grandma McCall pushed her plate away and picked up a glass of tea. "So you know. Wally may never have been a blood McCall." She cleared her throat. "And you know I wasn't such a good Christian girl all my life."

Della sighed. "This doesn't change anything for us, Elizabeth. Blood certainly doesn't change fatherhood. Maybe at some biological level, but not in the real world, where it counts. John McCall was the only father Wally ever knew. And John treated him with the same love he gave Leon. It's that simple."

Claire looked at her mother with admiration and a bit of surprise. This from the woman who staked her whole reputation just on being beautiful? How could Claire have considered her to be a dumb blond? Had she changed since Claire left at age sixteen? Or was she just too stupid to look below the surface?

Della made eye contact with Claire before turning back to Elizabeth. "And what is this idea that you've not been a good girl. The way I understood it, you were raped. That wasn't your fault."

Elizabeth stared at her half-eaten plate of lasagna. "You weren't there, Della."

"Tell us. We're family. You can talk to us. You won't find any judgment coming from me, that's for sure." Della looked away. "I've never qualified for sainthood myself."

With the secret out, it seemed as if a well had been uncapped. Elizabeth began to vent the story which had been concealed for so long.

"Steve Hudson was my first love, before I met John McCall. He was a wild horse, not a safe catch like my John. His family was trouble, and my mother knew it. So when the McCalls came to town, and John started showing interest, she was eventually able to convince me to forsake my feelings for Steve."

She pushed a wide noodle into a dab of tomato sauce and looked over at Claire. "You know what young love is like." She blushed. "Steve used to kiss me in the hayloft. He'd come to my window at night and throw pebbles, just like in an old movie." Elizabeth's eyes seemed to sparkle when she talked. "I'd meet him in the barn and talk until the early hours of the morning. Oh, he'd kiss me, but I would never let him go further. But we allowed ourselves to talk about what marriage would be like, what it would be like to be together as a man and wife in the same bed. I promised him he would be the first to know me in that way." Her hand went to her mouth. "I can hardly imagine talking with him like that. It was so improper for an unmarried woman.

"Eventually, John came into the picture, and I pulled away from Steve. But he was heartsick and never gave up trying to win me back. On the night before my wedding to John, he came to my window again." She paused with a distant look in her eyes, unfocused, not seeing the present, but lost in a view of the past. "I was lying in bed, fantasizing of the marriage bed that soon would be mine. And then I heard the tapping on my window, pebbles from the hand of my first love." She shook her head. "I should never have agreed to meet him. I went to the barn, intending to say a final good-bye."

Claire looked at Della as she leaned forward, focused on the story.

"He cried when I told him it was over. He had tears in his eyes. He was crying for me, heartbroken and lost. I was so touched. I kissed him. I wanted it to be good-bye, but I felt more."

Elizabeth looked up, the memory bringing a fear to her expression. "He felt it, too. He knew that I was teetering. I pushed him away, but he pulled me into the barn. I resisted, but in my heart, I knew I'd led him on. I kissed him that night. I enjoyed knowing he wanted me so bad. It gave me such power." She thrust a napkin to her eyes. "It was so wrong. I tried to stop him, but I never cried out for help. I initiated his passion. I brought it on myself."

"Grandma, having feelings for someone is just being human. It's not a sin to be tempted."

Della nodded. "You can't blame yourself for this. A kiss, even if accompanied by desire, is not an open invitation for sex."

"What he did was wrong, Grandma. You can't blame yourself for what he did."

Elizabeth sniffed and blew her nose. "Oh, ladies, I shouldn't have dredged all of this up."

"I'm afraid it's my fault that you've been forced to bring this all up. It's because of my questions about Daddy," Claire said.

Elizabeth sighed heavily. "As much as I'd like to believe that, it's not really true. Just seeing Wally at your graduation brought much of this back to me. I'd kept it buried for so long, I didn't think it could ever bother me again." She shook her head. "But things have a way of catching up with you." She looked at Claire. "Don't blame yourself. I'm not so upset. I think it was good to get this out. But I'm not sure telling Wally that I don't know who his father was is such a good idea."

Della said, "I agree. He's in no shape to hear this news now." She dropped her eyes to her plate. "If he lives at all."

Claire reached for her mother's hand. "I have a feeling he's gonna make it, Mom." She offered a smile. "Something I feel as Wally's daughter, not as a doctor."

A chirping sound suddenly alerted Claire to refocus. Her cellular phone!

"Hello."

The voice on the other end was masculine. "Claire? It's Mike, from the clerk's office."

Brad. "Hi. Did you find out anything for me?"

"Plenty. You want to meet me for a drink? We can go over it."

Claire rolled her eyes at her mother and grandmother. "Oh, Mike, I can't make it. Can you give me the information over the phone?"

She heard him sigh. "Sure, uh, I guess so."

"I'm taking notes. Go slow."

"You asked me about Rachel Morris. Her mother was Lydia Treevy. Her father was Greg Morris."

"Greg Morris? How did he die?"

"Don't know. The records just list an accident, age twenty-five."

"Who was his father?"

"Ronald. And you know what? The other guy you wanted me to check into, Harold Morris? Ronald is his father too."

Claire felt her forehead begin to sweat. This was unbelievable. "What about Peter Garret?"

"Mother was Judy Dorman. She died age thirty-five of breast cancer. Father was Bill Garret. He's still alive."

So if Peter had HD, it didn't come from his father. He'd be too old. "Who was Judy's mother and father?"

"Mother was Lillie Dorman. Evidently Lillie had a baby out of wedlock. The name on the birth certificate for Judy was a man named Leroy Morris."

"Leroy?"

"Right."

"And this Leroy's dad was Harold, right?"

"Right. Hey, I thought you didn't know this stuff yet."

"I didn't. Not all of it anyway." She looked at the notes she'd scribbled. "You've given me exactly what I needed. If I need you again, can I call you at the clerk's office?"

"Anytime." He paused. "Call me."

"Bye." She clicked off the phone and stared at the information in front of her, then pulled out a second piece of paper. Elizabeth and Della's eyes widened as they watched Claire's frantic scribblings. Starting with Ronald Morris, she drew a line to Harold and his brother, Greg. From Harold's name, Claire drew a line to Steve, and from Steve to Wally. Then, she drew a line from Harold to Leroy to Judy to Peter, and finally a line from Greg to Rachel to William Jr. to William Wampler III.

She shook her head. "It's unbelievable. All of these people rumored to be affected by the Stoney Creek curse are related. It all traces back to Harold Morris and his brother, Greg."

"Sins of the fathers are visited to the third and fourth generation," Elizabeth spoke softly.

"It's not that, Grandma. This looks like genetics, pure and simple. Only people didn't realize it because too many carriers of the Huntington's disease gene appear to have died young. Look, this one here had breast cancer. She died before she could have symptoms of HD. Greg Morris died young of an accidental death. Harold died of suicide, but probably after symptoms started. Steve Hudson died of suicide, also likely after his symptoms started. Leroy died of suicide too. And here, Rachel Morris Wampler died in an automobile accident before she could have shown the disease."

"I'm not sure I get it." Della looked puzzled.

"Huntington's disease doesn't start affecting you until midlife, at least in the usual situations. People may not have any symptoms until their thirties, forties, maybe fifties. But that doesn't mean they aren't carriers of the gene responsible. In the cases around Stoney Creek, it looks like so many generations were skipped because the carriers died young of something else. These early deaths combined with the cases where the paternity was completely unknown, as in Wally's case, kept people from realizing that all of these people rumored to be suffering from a curse were actually related. It kept anyone from suspecting a genetic illness."

"So maybe all of Wally's problems can't be blamed on alcohol?" Della looked sad.

"Maybe not, Momma. Maybe not."

Claire folded the papers carefully and shivered. Now she had the information she needed to call Dr. V at Brighton University.

Elizabeth seemed to be grasping the implications of Claire's theory. "I hope you're wrong about this, Claire. For your sake, I hope you're wrong."

Chapter Twenty-Six

Late that evening, Claire called Dr. Visvalingam, professor of neurology, Brighton University, and asked for help. She explained her theory, and her father's symptoms, and asked him to come to Carlisle to consult on her father.

Dr. V's excitement grew as Claire told the story. The possibility of a previously undiagnosed family of HD patients fascinated him.

"Can you have the paralyzing agent removed so we can observe his movements?"

"I can ask Dr. Smuland. I think he's concerned that the jerking movements were evidence of his agitation, possible alcohol withdrawal. My father was also fighting the ventilator, so they kept him on the medicine for that."

"Hmmm. I really don't want to make the trip until your father is off the ventilator. It won't be a fruitful trip for me unless I can see him as he normally is."

Claire's heart sank. "I understand."

"Can you call my office in the morning? If he is able to come off the ventilator, I could make the trip tomorrow afternoon. And I'd like to bring one of my residents. If you're right, Claire, this will make the neurology literature for sure."

Claire took down his office number. "I'll call first thing in the morning."

She set the phone in the cradle and yawned. The Stoney Creek curse could make the medical literature? That was something that hadn't occurred to her. Her father's case, and the intrigue of discovery of a hidden pocket of HD patients masquerading as a town curse, would be important enough for publication. Claire shook her head and made a mental note to tell Dr. V to change her name if he reported a new HD family in the literature.

Now Dr. V was all excited about getting another paper published, and Claire was not completely sure her father had anything rare at all. Dr. Smuland could be right, and she'd end up looking like a fool.

Better to look like a fool than be at risk for Huntington's disease.

And if I'm right, it looks like a lot of people are going to find out about Stoney Creek.

Claire slept in her old bed and rose early, partly from her excitement to get back to Carlisle, and partly because the eerie stillness of her childhood home unnerved her. She made coffee and sipped it while looking at the Blue Ridge mountains. Fog had settled in the low elevations, but the mountain peaks above were clearly seen, poking through the pillowy cotton of the morning mist.

She was more peaceful here, sitting on her father's porch in Stoney Creek. The anxiety of residency life was far away, with the pressures it held seeming almost imaginary. She thought of the hectic ICU in Lafayette, and of her nights on trauma call, and of her disaster with Sierra Jones. It all seemed unreal and far away, shrouded in a haze like the Blue Ridge mountain fog. Had she really been away at all?

Intern life, the pursuit of a dream, had crowded everything else aside. Surgery was a bulldozer, forcing its way ahead, carving a path through Claire's soul. Her family life offered little resistance and had easily surrendered to the bulldozer's blade.

She found her mother's Bible on the porch swing. Somehow, it warmed her, knowing her mother also came to this spot, this shelter, for renewal. She lifted the book. Its leather cover was soft and worn.

It had been so long since Claire had sought comfort or guidance from these pages. She opened to the passages her mother had highlighted with a yellow marker. She paused, feeling hesitant to continue. It seemed like an invasion of her mother's private world, something Della did without thought that anyone else would see. Claire lifted her eyes to the mountains again wondering if she should proceed.

Claire shook away her apprehension. Sharing these words with her mother was the right thing, a way of restoration for Claire, a returning not just to her home, but to an intimacy with her mother that she'd long left behind.

She read in the Psalms, words of despair and longing, words of hope and confidence in a better life. She read from the book of Hebrews of men and women who overcame trouble with their focus on Christ. Claire lifted a small piece of notebook paper that was folded within the pages of the Bible. There, printed in her mother's small handwriting, was a quotation, perhaps written during a recent sermon: "We are not necessarily doubting that God will do the best for us; we are wondering how painful the best will turn out to be. C. S. Lewis."

Tears welled up in her eyes. She wasn't sure it was the message she read, or the realization that her mother had a depth she'd never appreciated. The image she had of a weak country woman trapped in a bad marriage, too insecure to leave and make it on her own, was not the woman Claire was seeing now.

The words her mother had often spoken in jest echoed in Claire's mind. "I know I'm pretty, but you're pretty and smart."

"No, Momma," she whispered, "you're the one who's pretty and smart."

Back in Carlisle, with some minor arm-twisting by Claire, Dr. Smuland agreed to remove the paralyzing agent to see how Wally would behave.

Within an hour, his eyes were open, and a facial twitch began. A few minutes later, the irregular jerking movements of his arms and legs resumed. It was nothing new for Wally. Della had seen it a thousand times before.

Two hours later, with Wally's oxygen level holding steady, Dr. Smuland instructed the respiratory therapist to remove the endotracheal tube which connected Wally to the ventilator.

After thirty minutes, Dr. Smuland seemed satisfied with the progress. He was uncharacteristically curt. "Call Dr. Visvalingam if you must. I think he'll agree with my assessment."

Claire watched the attending exit the ICU with stooped shoulders, obviously offended by her persistence at playing Wally's doctor. It bothered her, but she felt certain she needed to continue. She shrugged off the feeling and opened her cell phone, only to be stopped by a hand on her arm.

"You can't use that in here," a nurse informed her. "It interferes with our monitoring."

She shrugged and left in search of a pay phone.

She made the call and was transferred to Dr. V's clinic. Dr. V and a resident would make time for the consult later in the day. He'd had a cancellation, and late afternoon would suit his schedule. Claire hung up the phone and sucked in a deep breath. She was on the edge of confirming an anxiety she'd carried for a long time. A black cloud had hovered ever since she'd sutured Wilson Davis's scalp in the ER a month ago. Now she couldn't escape the feeling that she was seeding the clouds for rain. She had a dagger in her hand destined to slice open the thunderhead and release a torrent of water.

There was little to do but wait. Della wanted to stay with Wally, but the nurses were insisting on strict observance of the visiting hour limitation, especially since he had just been removed from the ventilator. So Claire and her mother found a corner booth in the hospital cafeteria and waited.

Claire worked on diagramming a large family tree, spreading her work over half the table. Across from her, Della sat in silence, paging through an old gardening magazine she'd borrowed from the ICU waiting room. Claire studied her with stolen glances, looking up from her work on the table. Something was eating her mother. She should have been encouraged by Wally's progress, but something seemed to prevent it from showing. Perhaps Claire was misreading her. There were certainly multiple reasons for her mother to be quiet. Della chewed the inside of her lower lip and haphazardly flipped the magazine pages. Claire yawned and brushed away the intuition that her mother was sitting on a secret.

At four-thirty, they met Dr. V and Dr. Nadienne Rice. She was tall, with shoulder-length brown curls and beautiful nails. She wore a flattering navy suit.

Claire shook Nadienne's hand before touching her own fingernails with her thumb, lightly caressing the nails she'd sacrificed for surgery.

Dr. V smiled. "Claire McCall," he said, reaching for Claire's hand, but eyeing Della. "One of my brightest students. I tried to talk her into neurology, but she was too stubborn."

Claire laughed and kept quiet. Sitting around figuring out chronic neurologic problems all day long sounded like pure torture to her. Give her a scalpel, where she could make a difference.

"She's been like that all her life," Della responded.

Claire lifted her hand to her hair, now above her ears in a feminine and practical style, and studied the neurology resident again. Boy, she looked rested. Nothing like the surgery residents at Lafayette.

They sat in a private consulting room just outside the ICU. There, for the next hour, Dr. V interviewed Della about Wally's symptoms and studied Claire's diagram of the family tree. "It all makes sense, Claire. But we still need to examine your father. Very likely, I will want him to come to Brighton in a few weeks when he is stronger, so he can undergo a battery of tests."

"Can you do a genetic screening for Huntington's?" Claire asked.

"If he looks characteristic enough," Dr. V responded, tugging at his bow tie. "Let's take a look at him."

Claire stayed with Della while Dr. V and his resident entered the ICU. She stood and paced in the little room. "Waiting is torture," she whined.

Della pushed a chair forward. "Patience is not a common characteristic of surgeons. Sit down, Doctor. You're making me nervous."

Thirty minutes later, the neurology duo returned. Dr. V raised his eyebrows. "He's quite weak now, as you might expect from all he's been through, but he is showing classic choreiform movements of HD."

Nadienne nodded. "He's doing the dance, all right."

Della wrinkled her forehead. "The dance?"

Dr. V explained. "Chorea is the type of movements we observe in a variety of neurologic disorders. They are involuntary, very complicated, and endless. It comes from the Greek word *choreia,* which means 'dance.'" He looked over at Nadienne. "So our residents have become fond of describing chorea movements in this way. They say, 'He's doing the dance.'" He flailed his arms to the side in imitation of typical choreiform movements. After a second, he added leg movements, then facial and head movements in a demonstration that would have been funny if it didn't look so much like Wally.

Dr. V stopped when he saw Della's horrified expression.

"Does this mean my husband has Huntington's disease?"

"Not necessarily. We see these dance movements in other diseases as well." He looked at Claire. "I think we're justified in ordering a gene test. I've instructed the nurses to do it."

To Nadienne he continued, "I'd like you to get a more detailed look into this family tree, with exact dates of birth and causes of death."

"You can get the information at the county clerk's office here in Carlisle," Claire volunteered. "A man that works there will be glad to help you. Just ask for Brad—er, Mike."

"Well, I've got to dictate a note for the chart. It will take a few weeks to get the results of the blood test. If you're right, Claire, our work will just be beginning. We'll need to contact as many relatives as we can and dig further back in this family tree."

Claire nodded soberly. *If I'm right, your work may just be getting started, but my life may as well be over. I could be doing the dance myself in a few years.*

That evening, Claire headed east over North Mountain on Highway 2, which snaked from Fisher's Retreat and the Apple Valley to Brighton. With her father's clinical improvement, she felt free to search for a respite in the arms of John Cerelli.

For this trip, her grandmother had offered her Buick. It was a boat of a car, but luxurious, and Claire felt out of character driving a vehicle which seemed to proclaim, "I've arrived." But, as her options were few, and Della needed the family car to get back and forth to Carlisle, Claire accepted the offer with graciousness. Now, as she maneuvered the massive car over the treacherous road, she longed for her aging Toyota.

Dr. V's consultation had been a small victory, the validation of her concerns which others had scorned. But with that victory had grown her concern that she too may be facing a genetic horror.

She hadn't talked to John since their strained conversation on Friday, when Brett had intercepted John's call. Her life was spinning so rapidly, and John seemed to be on the outside. She wore his ring, but she knew he had no idea what her life had become. Now, as she had begun a delicate reconnection with her family, she wondered what his response would be. How would John react to knowing that she may end up just like her father? Would it change his desire to commit his life to being with her forever? Did he have the depth that Della had shown to stick with a difficult spouse in the face of serious illness?

Oh, how she prayed that the test for HD would be negative, that her fears were unfounded, and that the worst outcome would be the humiliation of stirring up her family, and Dr. V and his resident. But somehow, she knew she needed to be prepared for the worst. If she expected the worst, and it didn't come to pass, she would have relief instead of disappointment.

She'd called John that afternoon, but declined to leave a message on his answering machine. Surprise would be the order of the day. He'd done it to her. Now it was her turn to reciprocate.

She stood on his doorstep dressed in a new skirt and blouse, a bit more formal than she would normally have chosen, but, given her options, it would have to do.

John opened the door wearing a faded pair of gym shorts, no shirt, and holding a slice of pepperoni pizza. "Claire?"

She smiled. "In the flesh."

"What on earth are you doing here?"

"Vacation," she said, glancing past the doorway into his front room, which was littered with pizza boxes, two-liter soda containers, and old newspapers.

"Vacation? You didn't tell me this, did you?" He looked over his shoulder. "It's kind of a disaster in here," he said, moving to obstruct her view. "When did you come down? Today?"

"It's a long story, Cerelli," she said, kissing his cheek. "Invite me in and I'll let you in on another disaster."

"Disaster?"

"Yeah," she said, moving past him into a room which smelled of old gym shorts. "My life."

Chapter Twenty-Seven

After ten minutes in John's apartment, Claire decided that surprising him wasn't her brightest idea. Giving him forewarning was definitely appropriate, and would have been better for her lungs.

"How do you guys stand it this way?" She picked up a pizza box in order to find room on the couch to sit down.

"Hey," John replied, "most of this junk is Mike's." He pushed a hamper of dirty clothes into the front closet and shut the door.

She peered into the kitchen and frowned.

John shook his head. "You don't want to go there. Trust me."

"Can we go out? Someplace casual where we can talk?"

"I need a shower." He picked up a towel from the stairway banister. "Give me ten minutes."

As he disappeared up the stairs, Claire could hear him muttering to himself, "I can't believe this. I can't believe ..." She giggled and braved a journey into the kitchen. There, she found plastic garbage bags beneath the sink and returned to the living room. She filled up a bag with pizza boxes, empty soda containers, and a few paper plates. Next, she returned to the kitchen and cleared the breakfast dishes, piling them into a sink of sudsy water.

She was placing the dishes in a drying rack when John appeared a few minutes later. "Ready?"

"This place wasn't like this when I lived in Brighton. What gives?"

"You were the reason we kept it clean."

"So, it takes a surprise visit to find out you're a slob."

"I'm not a—"

She halted his sentence with a flying damp dishrag.

He intercepted the cloth before it impacted his chin. "Okay, well, maybe I am a little bit of a slob. But we usually clean on weekends."

"I won't live with a slob, Cerelli. Surgeons don't tolerate dirt." She talked in jest, but knew he was getting the message. They were walking to his Mustang when she made a confession. "You want to know my secret, why my house in Lafayette is always spotless?"

John groaned. "Sure."

"I'm never there."

He took her to a Tex-Mex restaurant called D.C. Peppers, where she talked about her family and her experiences as an intern. When she talked about the possibility that her father may have Huntington's, he seemed nonplused.

"Why should anyone worry about what-ifs?" He shrugged. "Just live your life and see what comes. You said yourself that there's little to do about it."

"John, it's not like I'm talking about getting a flat tire on the way to the prom. This could affect my life. All my plans, everything I've worked for."

"All the more reason to sit back and trust. There's absolutely nothing you can do to change this, is there?"

"No." Claire sighed. There was a fundamental difference between John Cerelli and Claire McCall. His ability to just sit back and take life's bumps without getting upset had her puzzled. "But maybe you aren't understanding this. I'm talking about a disease that stays quiet until you're in your prime. Then it strikes, causing a slow deterioration until you die. And you die young, John, with your dreams shattered and unfulfilled."

"Bummer." He sipped on his Coke.

"Don't be cavalier about this, Cerelli. This would affect whether we could have a family. You've told me how you've always dreamed of a son to take under your wing. Think about how this would affect those plans."

"Claire, you don't even know that your father has this disease, right? And already you're worried about our children?"

"How can you not?"

John's face became serious. He leaned forward and took her hand in his. "Trust."

She was expecting more. "Trust. That's it?"

"Yes. Only trust."

"So I just sit back and live my life, trusting that everything will be okay? I'm not built that way."

"It's not trust that life will always be rosy. It's trust that when you encounter the thorns, that you're not alone, that you're not in control. You never have been."

She dipped a tortilla chip in a fiery salsa. "I'm not wired the way you are. You're type B."

"Even type A's need to learn to trust. Do you believe that God is sovereign?"

"He's all-powerful. All-knowing. I believe that."

"Do you think he's in control of your life?"

The discussion was making Claire uncomfortable. She wanted John's empathy, not a theology lesson. She looked down. "Look, John, I'm not sure. I want him to be in control. But I seem to have trouble letting him. I've made plans for my life. I've known what I've wanted to do for a long time. It just seemed right. And God seemed to be opening the doors. So is he in control?"

"Ultimately? Yes. We can choose to go our own way and sin. God's control isn't exerted in our life to make us do evil. But he allows us to go our own way. And he allows evil to touch our lives to accomplish his purposes. And regardless of our circumstances, our job is to trust. And it's trust based on knowing his character, his love toward us that never changes. It's a trust that believes, even in our darkest hour, God's love is just the same."

It all sounded nice, but Claire wasn't used to sitting back passively and letting someone else lead. Everything about her personality screamed, "do something," "take control," "make a goal and go for it." "I don't know, John. Maybe I just don't get it. I've heard words like this ever since I was a kid. But maybe I'm just not a good Christian like you. I have trouble trusting when things are looking bleak."

"Don't call me a good Christian. I've made plenty of mistakes." He looked up, and captured her eyes. "Some of them with you."

She nodded.

"Everyone struggles with doubt."

She watched him for a moment, wondering about the maturity she saw. When did everyone around her grow up? Why did everyone seem to have more depth than she'd credited them with? Her mother, now John. Had she just been so preoccupied with her own life not to appreciate it?

"It's funny, John."

"What?"

"Why is it that we never talked about this stuff before?"

"We've talked about God, Claire. And faith. Remember our Wednesday night study with Pastor George?"

"This feels different somehow. A Sunday school discussion is one thing. Applying this stuff in the thick of life is another."

John looked up. She followed his eyes to the waitress who was about to deliver their sizzling fajitas.

The portions looked huge. She raised her eyebrows in suspicion. "How much pizza did you eat before I came?"

"Only two pieces," he said, eyeing the feast. "I've still got room."

While they ate, Claire urged John to do something that she had successfully avoided all during their dating relationship. She asked him to come to Carlisle to visit her father.

"When are you leaving?"

"I fly back to Boston Sunday."

"I could come down to Stoney Creek Friday after work. Maybe we could go hiking or something."

It sounded wonderful. Except Claire didn't have any casual clothes. The next time she left Lafayette for a week it would be nice to have more than thirty minutes to prepare.

After an hour, Claire looked at her watch. "I need to be leaving."

John frowned. "I thought you were staying over."

"I feel like I should be in Stoney Creek while my dad is in the hospital." She sipped at the last of a diet soda.

"You can leave in the morning." His eyes were tender. "I'll sleep on the couch. You can have my bed."

"You know as well as I do that staying under one roof is asking for trouble."

"Claire, we did it at your place."

"That was different. You had no place to go. I have my home just an hour away." She pushed her lips into a pout. "Besides, having you in my house at night was pure torture. I'm not sure I should put myself through that again."

"Let me get this straight. It's okay for you to sleep in your house with a male resident, but not to stay in the same house with me?"

"Under the circumstances, I'd have been happy to have you stay. In fact," she added soberly, "I'm not sure what I'm going to do when I'm back in Lafayette."

He sighed. "I still wish you'd stay. An hour with you is so rare. We'll be good."

She shook her head. "I told my mother I'd be home, John. I'll see you Friday. I'll call you with directions."

He gave up his argument. "So I finally get to spend some time with the McCall family. I was beginning to think that Stoney Creek was a fairy tale, something you made up, but would never let me see."

She raised her eyebrows. "I think it's time."

"Why the change?"

She laughed. "Because I have your diamond now. It's too late for you to back out."

"Come on."

"I made a promise, that's all. A promise that I'd be a better daughter than I have in the past." She looked down. "Maybe it's time I let my family back in my life."

Chapter Twenty-Eight

Claire and Margo were on pleasant terms, not confidantes, but sisters separated by a silence that stemmed from pursuing separate dreams, and a desire to distance themselves from the stigma which surrounded being Wally's girls. Growing up, Claire resisted her sister's shadow, chose academics over boyfriends, athletics over Margo's choice of an after-school job, and college savings over following the latest trend in high school fashion.

Margo McCall Stevens lived with her husband, Kyle, just outside Carlisle. Margo eloped at eighteen with the twenty-eight-year-old manager of the McDonald's where she worked. She had married for love, thankful for an escape from an alcoholic father and the dysfunction that surrounded him. In the past twelve years, Margo and Kyle had had three daughters, Kelly, now eleven, Casey, eight, and an infant, Kristin, born just after Claire's graduation from medical school. They had forged a good life together. Hard work and long hours had brought Kyle a Wendy's franchise, a three-acre tract of land overlooking the Blue Ridge, two ponies, a minivan, a Cherokee Wagoneer, a four-bedroom house, and a membership at a fitness center.

By Thursday, Wally had improved enough to be moved out of the ICU, but he was still weak, and he tired easily after only brief visits by Claire or Della. And so, after her afternoon hospital visit, Claire headed for Margo's to see her new niece and reconnect with a sister she'd lost in the search of her own life.

Claire stood on the expansive deck listening to Margo complain of her husband's schedule and their incredible mortgage payment. Margo had given Claire a tour of her home, giving her a blow-by-blow account of the budget overruns on their house.

Claire sipped pink lemonade and smiled pleasantly, the smile she gave to strangers in the grocery store. Margo droned on. And on.

"I had to have the granite countertops in the kitchen.

"Kyle had to have the hot tub.

"The tile around the bath cost a fortune!

"Each of the girls have cable TV hookups in their rooms.

"We're getting a Kinkade canvas lithograph for over the fireplace. But of course you probably collect original oils, since you're a doctor."

Claire held up her hand. "You don't seem to understand. I'm a doctor, yes. But I make less than minimum wage when you consider my hours. My tastes are simple. It's good they are, because I couldn't afford one-tenth of the things you're enjoying."

Margo raised her eyebrows. "I'll bet your house is big."

"I rent a house. It's too big for just me, but I didn't want to live in the housing close to the hospital because it's too expensive, and I'd rather have a little yard. I've done very little decorating. I'd love to have the time to do what you've done so well, but . . ." She sighed before continuing, "I'm only there for a few hours every other evening, so I don't really care. There's too much else in my life to be concerned over my house."

Margo shifted in her seat. "There are other things in my life too, of course. Casey's in the Apple Valley children's choir. I have to cart her all over creation to sing. And with Kelly's traveling soccer team, Kyle is gone to a tournament almost every weekend. And if Kristin ever takes a nap, I like to work on my quilting."

"I don't see how you do it. I have trouble just keeping up with me. I don't think I'm ready to be responsible for children."

Margo shrugged. "You do what you have to do."

Claire nodded and looked out at the mountains. She was tired of polite, superficial chitchat. She felt like a stranger to her own sister. She sipped at her lemonade and cleared her throat. "I was hoping that our family could get together when John comes over this weekend."

Margo elevated her eyebrows. "Everyone?"

"Well, Daddy will probably still be in the hospital, but at least Mom, Clay, and your family could come. We could have a cookout in our old backyard."

Margo wrinkled her nose. "I don't know."

"It could be fun. I'd like you to meet John."

Margo shook her head. "Oh, I'd like to meet John, it's just that . . ."

"Just that what?"

Her sister stood up and began to pace. "It just that it seems so artificial. Like we're pretending to be something we're not."

"We don't have to pretend, Margo. It's okay for our family to get back together. It would be good for us."

Margo laughed. "Good for us?" She rolled her eyes. "I can't remember the last pleasant time I've had with Daddy and Mom. They've got their life." She turned and stared out at the mountains. "And I've got mine now. I don't really care to have a cozy little reunion with Daddy. I went to the hospital when they thought he was dying. I bet he wouldn't come if you or I were in the hospital."

"Has it ever occurred to you that things might change? That our father might actually like it if you'd come around and visit him?" Claire threw up her hands. "Did you know that Mom brought in pictures of your girls and taped them to the wall next to his hospital bed?"

Margo shook her head. "That's a joke. It's been a year since they visited. They've never even seen my new house."

Claire's hand went to her mouth. "No."

"Why should that surprise you? It's not like you've spent any time relating to our parents either. When did you leave home? Sixteen?"

Claire nodded.

"Well, don't act so surprised that the rest of us don't act any different than you. You left home and barely looked back, except to remind us of how great things were since you left us behind."

"I never said that."

"You don't have to. I hear it all the time. It's all I ever hear when I'm around anyone who knew you. 'How's Claire? She's a doctor now. I'll bet you're proud of your little sister,'" she mocked.

"Come on, you're the one with the family. I haven't done anything except study."

"And it gave you a great excuse to stay away from your family and Stoney Creek." She looked away. "Well, maybe I don't have as good a reason, but I'm doing just fine on my own without Daddy looking over my shoulder to tell me any different."

Claire looked down at the cedar deck boards. "I feel pretty stupid. I thought I was the only one isolated from Mom and Dad. I feel like I turned my back on them."

"And Daddy didn't do the same to us?"

Claire sighed. "Okay, I know things weren't great. But that doesn't mean things can't change. Daddy might need us more now than ever before."

"He's made his own bed as far as I'm concerned. He's going to have to sleep in it."

Claire wanted to protest, but the stern look on Margo's face silenced her attempt to speak.

"Kyle and I have made a life on our own, without any help from Daddy. I'm not interested in pulling together to help someone who chose the bottle over me."

"Don't you realize that he might never get better? That Mom is going to need a lot of support?"

"You are so idealistic. You march off to save the world, to become a doctor, a surgeon even, and now you want to come back here and save your family, too? Has it ever occurred to you that we might not want your help?"

Claire hadn't anticipated this bitterness. "Margo, what about a little grace?"

"A little grace? Look who's talking! I seem to remember Mom being quite upset that you hardly had time for your family after your med school graduation. You just ran off to Lafayette and your wonderful career in medicine." Margo paused and sucked noisily on the straw in her lemonade. "So what makes you think we should get together just because you want to?"

"Maybe I just started thinking of Daddy in a different light. It's taken me a long time to soften my opinion of his actions." She paused. "It might not be all Dad's fault, you know."

"Oh, right, and I guess you have some intellectual way of justifying his neglect?"

Claire leaned forward. "Mom hasn't told you?"

"Told me what? I talk to Mom about the weather and about the kids. We're friendly, but not friends."

"She hasn't told you about Huntington's disease? About the test they're running on Daddy?"

Margo's blank expression provided the answer.

Claire took a deep breath. "Daddy might be suffering from a rare genetic illness called Huntington's disease."

"Am I supposed to be upset? Excuse me if I don't cry right now."

"You don't seem to understand. If Daddy has a genetic illness, he could pass it to us."

Margo's eyes widened.

Claire slowly explained about her search to find the keys to unlocking the supposed Stoney Creek curse. She told about Huntington's disease, and what it would mean to her and Margo, and possibly Margo's three daughters, if Wally was confirmed to have HD. "So you see," she explained, "some of Dad's problems with irrational behavior, with irritability, even his explosive emotions could have been early signs of HD."

"You're making excuses for him."

"I'm not. I'm just making an observation. We may have misjudged him."

She shook her head. "He's a drunk, Claire. Don't sugarcoat it."

"This is serious, Margo. I'm not trying to justify how he treated us. But if it turns out that he does have HD, we're going to be facing whether or not we want to be tested."

"I don't want anything to do with this."

"We can't run from it."

Margo bit her lower lip and then spoke again, her voice low and steady, as if she was fighting not to let her voice waver. "I left home to get away because I thought that man was destroying my life. I've gotten along just fine without him. And now you want me to think about being cursed with an illness that will make me act just like him?" She shook her head and continued with sarcasm. "Oh, that's real sweet. I get away from him, and he still ruins my life by passing me some horrific gene."

"Margo, you may not have it. I may not have it. Dad may not have it. I could have been all wrong. But if I'm right, our family is going to have to pull together and find some support in each other."

Margo had a faraway look in her eyes. "I can't tell this to Kyle. He'd freak. He already hates Wally. I don't want to see what he'd do if he knew Wally had given me some dreadful disease."

"It's not his fault, Margo. A genetic illness is no one's choice."

Margo quickened her pacing. "Why did you have to start digging up all this stuff? Why couldn't you just apply your diagnostic skills somewhere else? Did you have to torture your own family?"

"It's not like I caused this. I just raised the questions, that's all."

"Well, stop. I like my life just fine the way it is. Has it ever occurred to you that digging all this up might upset everyone? Have you told Clay? He'll freak, too."

"I thought you'd want to know. Would you have rather I'd not said anything? Then what if Dad's test is positive? Then wouldn't you have wondered why I didn't say anything about my suspicions?"

Margo sat down on a deck chair and put her head in her hands. Just then, a baby's cry interrupted their conversation.

Margo stood. "Kristin's awake. Would you like to see her?"

"Sure."

They walked to the baby's room, and Margo filled the time by returning to chitchat about her daughters, never again mentioning the subject that she'd quickly shoved under the rug. Huntington's disease was obviously not something she cared to think about anymore.

Claire smiled sweetly and held a rattle up to her little niece. Claire didn't want to think about HD either, but getting lost in small talk felt plastic. She looked at Kristin, innocently cooing as Margo began changing her diaper. Claire did the math. If her father had HD, there was a fifty-fifty chance that Margo had it, giving Kristin a one-in-four chance of having the disease. Of course, if Margo was found to be a carrier, then the baby would have a fifty-percent risk of getting it, too.

It struck Claire as unfair. Here was a faultless child, incapable of intentional disobedience, and yet silently lurking within her every cell could be a gene capable of slowly destroying her mind and body. Certainly this couldn't be the workings of a loving God. At least not the kind of God that Claire understood him to be.

Claire looked at her watch. "She's beautiful."

"She looks like your baby pictures, don't you think?"

Claire shook the rattle. "My lucky little niece. You look like me."

"I hope she's as smart as you. Maybe smart enough to leave this backwards valley behind."

"Believe it or not, I miss this old valley." She touched her sister's arm. "And my family."

Margo ignored Claire's touch. "So will you bring John by so I can meet him?"

"Sure. He's coming in tomorrow night. Maybe sometime on Saturday." She paused. "Are you sure you wouldn't want to try a little family reunion?"

Margo stiffened. "I don't think so. Kyle isn't into it."

Claire nodded resolutely. That was it. No discussion. Margo wasn't going to budge. "I've got to get back over to the hospital. I told Mom that I'd bring her some supper. She's getting tired of the hospital cafeteria."

With the baby in one arm, Margo marched back into her living room and picked a book up from the coffee table. "Could you give this to Mom for me? She gave it to me months ago and I just haven't found time to return it."

Claire took the book, a thick volume on child development. "Why don't you come over to the hospital? I'm sure Daddy would like to see the girls."

"Claire, stop. I'm not into polite little visits and pretending we're some big happy family. We aren't, so I'm not going to act like we are."

"People can change."

"You've been gone a long time, Sis. I don't think you understand. Family gatherings are definitely not Daddy's thing. I'm surprised you'd want this anyway. Mom told me about the last time you visited Daddy at home."

"He'd been drinking. He's sober now."

Margo rocked Kristin in her arms. "Sorry, Sis. It's not going to happen."

Claire walked to the door. This was not going according to plan. Margo was supposed to be the easy one. "I'll call you when John's in town."

"Kyle usually works until noon on Saturdays. But we should be around after that."

Margo opened the door.

Claire stepped into the sunshine. The blue sky and peaceful setting belied the turmoil that she felt eroding her soul. Maybe Margo was right. Maybe it was too late for her family.

Maybe some things were best left undisturbed.

Leave her family undisturbed? Claire shook her head. It was too late for that.

They hugged politely with the baby between them before Claire turned to leave. As she walked across the manicured lawn, she glanced at the girl's bicycle which was cast aside, leaning against the mailbox. It belonged to Casey, Margo's eight-year-old.

Claire stopped in her tracks. It didn't take a second look to unsettle her stomach. One glimpse was enough to freshen the bleeding in her heart. *What is it with little girls? Why do they all have to ride purple bikes?*

The reunion Claire dreamed about never happened. It seemed everyone had their own agenda, and flexibility didn't seem to be a McCall trait. John arrived late on Friday, well after visiting hours at the hospital. Clay went off-road motorcycle riding with his buddies on Saturday, precluding any meaningful time with him. Margo's husband worked on Saturday until seven P.M. because a manager called in sick. John and Claire visited with Margo, and Claire endured another tour of her sister's new home and her litany of stories about their contractor and the costly overruns in their budget. Claire had "oohed" and "aahed" appropriately. *SITCOM,* she thought, amused at the medical field's love of initials and acronyms. If there was a summary of her sister's financial status, this seemed to be it. SITCOM: Single Income. Three Children. Oppressive Mortgage.

Saturday evening there was time for a short visit with Wally, but he was tired and seemed self-conscious. In spite of his obvious physical shortcoming, Wally was a proud man and was uncomfortable being the center of attention in such a vulnerable state. The visit was awkward. Wally's face reflected almost no emotion. There was no smiling, only a constant, rhythmic movement of his right cheek, which caused the corner of his mouth to pull to the side, as if tugged by an invisible string. He was pleasant to John, but Claire wasn't sure from Wally's nonreaction that her father even remembered John from her graduation.

Della was too concerned with Wally to prepare anything home-cooked, so after a thirty-minute visit where Della, Claire, and John sat around watching Wally twitch, they headed for supper at Denny's, hardly the reunion Claire had hoped for. At dinner, even Della, normally talkative, was subdued. It was as if her whole experience with Wally had finally left her drained of positive emotions. The only thing left for Della seemed to be a quiet resolution to plod forward, unsure of the future, and afraid. Claire searched her mother's beautiful eyes for clues. There seemed to be something more than fear. Something hidden, something Della held back, unable to express, or was too fearful to reveal. In John's presence, Claire knew not to probe. Della would never open up in front of him.

That night, with the sky salted with a million stars, Claire nestled her head against John's shoulder while sitting on the old porch swing. Her time at home was measured in hours. Tomorrow, half of her yearly vacation from the hospital would be over, and she would resume her other life as a surgical intern.

It seemed weird, in a way. Ever since her frantic flight from Boston, Claire had become so absorbed into her concerns about her family that other than a few snatches of memory, she had shelved her life at Lafayette. All her worries about the pyramid and the threatening message on her front door had been left behind. But now, as she realized her time in Stoney Creek was coming to a close, she turned her attention back to Lafayette and the pressures that awaited her there.

"This isn't what I'd wanted for your first trip to Stoney Creek," she began. "My family didn't exactly reach out and make you feel welcome." She felt a knot rising in her throat and her eyes moisten with tears.

She felt John's arm tighten around her shoulder. "It's okay, Claire. It's not like your family has time right now to drop everything and pay attention to me." He paused. "I had a wonderful time just being with you again."

"I guess I'm stupid for expecting anything different. I had imagined my family pulling together over my dad's illness, and putting to rest some of our old hurts." Her voice thickened. "Over and over on my trip down, I wondered what my father would say to me, his youngest daughter, returning to his side at his moment of tragedy. The last time I left him, he was in a rage, almost hitting me with a beer bottle. I wanted him to embrace me, to tell me how sorry he was, but . . ." Her words faded.

"He didn't apologize, did he?" John whispered.

She shook her head. "Mom says he doesn't even remember. He can slip into a rage, and ten minutes later it's like the storm has passed, and he acts like nothing has happened. For him, saying 'I'm sorry' isn't an issue. He doesn't remember hurting me."

They were quiet for a minute before Claire dared to ask the question that etched a deep crevice in the smooth highway she'd planned for her life. "So now that you've seen the McCalls at their finest, do you still think you want to be a part of the family?"

"I'm in love with you, Claire. I'm not exactly marrying your family."

"It's a package deal. I was wrong to shut them out of my life for so long."

His voice was gentle. "If it means I get to spend my life with you, I can put up with your family."

"But what if I end up just like Wally? Could you love me like that?"

"But you're nothing like him. It's not going to happen."

His reassurance did little to settle her thoughts. "If I'm right, and the curse that's plagued Stoney Creek for generations is Huntington's disease, I could end up looking just like him: lying in bed, unable to keep still, with my mind slowly deteriorating. You saw my father this afternoon. Could you deal with it if I ended up like that? You'd have to take care of me. And to boot, if we have children, they could end up suffering too. You might have to watch your own children suffer and die before you."

"Claire, stop worrying. This isn't like you. You've always been so optimistic about the future."

"That was before I learned about HD."

"You've said yourself that HD is rare. I can't see getting so worked up about something so unlikely to happen."

"Huntington's disease is rare, but it also runs in families."

"But so does diabetes. And so does colon cancer. My grandfather had that, and our family doctor told my mother that she is at increased risk for getting it, but it doesn't have to ruin her life. She doesn't go around worrying that someday she might get cancer."

"John, you're not getting it." She lifted her head from his shoulder to face him. "Huntington's disease is a dominant gene. Sure, diabetes and colon cancer can run in families, but the offspring are still unlikely to get it. A dominant gene like HD is passed to the next generation with a fifty-fifty chance of inheritance. That's one out of two, John. If Daddy has Huntington's, I have a fifty-percent risk of having it too."

"Fifty percent?"

"That's right, one out of two. It's a flip of the coin. Heads I win. Tails I lose. My career's over before it really gets going."

She watched John shift in his seat. He wiped his forehead with the back of his hand and made a clicking noise with his cheek. "How can it be that high?"

"It's simple genetics, John. We all have two sets of matching chromosomes, each of which contain thousands of genes. We get one set from our mother, and one set from our father. If Daddy has HD, that means he has one HD gene which he inherited from his father and one normal gene which he got from Grandma Elizabeth. He has to give me one or the other. That means that with normal probability, out of three children in my family, one or two of us will have HD."

John stared off at the outline of the Blue Ridge mountains, visible in the moonlight. Claire tried to read his face in the dim light. Could it be that he never really understood the risk that she was facing? Would knowing the real risk make him less enthusiastic about joining her family?

Finally, when John spoke, his voice echoed with nonchalance. "If your father has it, Clay's the one that should be worried. He's like a chip off the old block from what little I've seen. You're nothing like your brother or your father."

"Unfortunately, HD isn't linked to any other trait that can be measured. You can't say that just because Clay acts like Daddy, or looks like him, that Clay will or won't have the HD gene. It doesn't work that way."

John sighed and fell silent.

Claire laid her head back on John's shoulder. "Did you see the oak hutch in the dining room?"

He nodded. "Yeah."

"Clay made it at the cabinet shop. I used to think that Clay and I couldn't be any more different. But when I started looking at the hutch, I wondered."

"What do you mean?"

"Look at it, John. It has quality written all over it. All of the drawers have dovetail corners. The scrollwork on the top is perfectly symmetrical. When I saw what kind of care Clay put into it, I started seeing the perfectionism that has driven me to get where I am. I enjoy working with my hands in surgery. Clay loves to work with wood." She shrugged. "Maybe I'm not as different from my twin as I always thought."

"What does Clay think about HD?"

"I haven't talked to him. After bringing it up to Margo, I decided to wait until I knew for sure."

"Probably a smart move. Best not to muddy the water unless you know for sure."

Claire looked at her watch. The hour was getting late, and she needed to make an early flight in the morning. "I should go to bed. My flight leaves at seven in the morning."

"Back to the grindstone, eh?"

She nodded. "It's bizarre, John. It's like I'm heading off for another life. It's as if I've lived in two worlds. One here in Stoney Creek, a backwards little place with a dysfunctional family that believes in town curses. And one in the big city, pursuing my dreams and hoping against hope that I could leave my upbringing behind. In Lafayette, I have so many new pressures, a daily stress to do the right thing for my patients while their lives hang in the balance."

"But you haven't left Stoney Creek behind, Claire. You can't. It's a part of you."

"I'm learning that. But it has taken Daddy's health problems to make me come back. It's as if my two worlds are about to collide, threatening to destroy everything I've worked so hard to accomplish."

John smiled. Claire studied him for a moment. "What's so funny?"

"Nothing."

She elbowed his ribs. "Tell me."

He held up his hands as if he were holding two large balls, his palms up. He brought them together as he reiterated her words, "'My two worlds are about to collide.'"

"Don't laugh at me, Cerelli. This is serious!"

"I can't help it. I'm not going to let myself get all worked up over what-ifs."

She pressed her long index finger into his chest. "Admit it! Knowing that I could end up like my father scares you, too. And don't you dare say something to me about God's sovereignty. You aren't a human if you can't admit that a future with HD scares you to death."

His smile faded, and he looked away from her eyes. "Okay, I'm a little scared. I didn't realize the odds were as high as you said."

They sat quietly for a moment, the only noise being the crickets and the squeak of the old swing. He pushed his face into her neck and began to caress her with gentle kisses. "Let's think about something else."

Claire didn't feel like kissing. She shivered and kissed his mouth quickly, not receptively. It was definitely a kiss that said "Good night," not "I want more."

John groaned and stretched. "When do I see you again?"

"I don't know. I've burned up half my two weeks' vacation." She lifted her hand to cover a yawn. "So I guess it's up to you."

Claire thought about returning to her empty house in Lafayette. She wondered if her landlord had managed to repaint her front door. And wondered even more if Mr. Jones could find it in his heart not to blame her for his daughter's death. Here on her father's back porch, the pressures of residency seemed so far away, but as soon as she returned, she knew that she would wonder if her week away had only been a dream. Part of her wished she could stay in the Apple Valley. She wanted to marry John Cerelli and forget about the Mecca. But part of her knew she could never be happy without pursuing her goal of being a surgeon.

She thought about sleeping in her house in Lafayette alone. Could she ever feel safe knowing that someone had written a death wish on her front door? She had managed to push her fears about the situation aside while she tended to her family in Stoney Creek. But now the time was nearing that she would have to return to her other world and face the music that was being played there too.

She felt a knot welling up in her throat. She'd explained all of her residency trials to John earlier in the day. He was supportive, but Claire wasn't sure he understood the pressure she endured. She turned to John and buried her face in his shirt, not wanting him to see the tears begin to flow. He wrapped his arms around her as she released a sob, finally allowing her emotions to overflow.

She cried for fear she wouldn't make it through her internship, because someone wished she would die, because she had let down her team, and the university hospital could get sued.

She cried because she'd allowed a little girl to die.

She cried because she had to leave the man she loved.

She cried for her father and the disease that stole his body and robbed his mind.

And she cried because she might have solved the Stoney Creek curse.

And if she had, her life would never be the same.

Chapter Twenty-Nine

The next day, Claire resumed life in Lafayette and tried not to think about HD. She busied herself with internship life and waited for the call she knew would eventually come from Dr. V's office. After two weeks, she rotated off of the cardiothoracic surgery service and onto vascular surgery. She went from "sitting hearts" to watching over the agonizing sequence known to the residents affectionately as the "fem-pop, chop, chop," which referred to the process of performing an arterial bypass graft from the femoral artery to the popliteal artery to save a dying leg, only to watch the grafts eventually fail, necessitating higher and higher levels of limb amputation.

With new courage, she slept alone in her brownstone and downplayed her earlier fears that Mr. Jones was lurking, death wishes dripping from his paintbrush. She wouldn't let a little orange paint keep her away from her own house. Death threats, if they were real, wouldn't be broadcast out for everyone to see. No, she had a life to live, and she wouldn't let Mr. Jones interfere.

She longed for a friend to talk to. She talked to John, but the phone had a way of clamming him up. After sharing her heart with him, night after night, she'd hang up the phone and wonder if he'd really listened. Girlfriends were sparse. She had little time for developing relationships, and the few women in the residency didn't seem like appropriate confidantes. Especially not Beatrice, who always seemed to throw her shoulders back a notch and quote the surgical literature when Claire approached. Claire wasn't intimidated by this tactic, but she wasn't charmed, either. If she found a woman friend, it would have to come from outside the program.

And that left Brett. She'd fallen into a pattern of friendly visits, enjoying his company, all the while knowing that she was driving him crazy. She could see it in his eyes. She didn't really want to frustrate him, but she had to admit she loved his attention, and he was so easy to talk to. Besides, she really didn't have another friend who knew what she was going through as an intern. Brett knew it firsthand. He'd been there, and Claire appreciated his encouragement.

On one Saturday evening in mid-September, Brett and Claire sat across from each other at Claire's kitchen table. They were talking through the intern list, playing their own private version of "if I was the program director." It was an act they'd made into a joke, as a way to trivialize and cope with the decisions that would face Dr. Rogers as he selected the residents who would be advanced up the pyramid, and those he would drop.

"McNeil," Brett said, putting his thumb up.

Claire nodded, putting her thumb in the air. "A definite member of the top eight. He didn't even flinch when they pulled him from the ER and made him do my week of CT."

"Holcroft?"

"You mean Dr. Holcroft, MD, PhD?" She smiled and held up her hand before giving him a thumbs-down.

"No way," Brett responded, holding his thumb up.

"You'd promote him?"

"No, but Rogers will. He loves geeky Ivy Leaguers. I think it reminds him of his own lot in life. Besides, Holcroft has been hanging around Rogers' lab trying hard to get involved in one of the chairman's pet research projects. He wants to be too indispensable for Rogers to cut."

"Will it work?"

"Probably."

Dr. Bearss and Carter, the two remaining Harvard grads, both got two thumbs-up. Button got one thumbs-up and one thumbs-down. Wayne Neal got two thumbs-up.

"Beatrice Hayes?"

"If I had the choice, I give her the axe," Claire said, putting her thumb down.

"But you don't. You've got to vote like our attendings will." He paused and lifted his index finger. "She won the first-blood award."

"That can't really count for anything."

"Maybe not, but no one who's received it has ever been cut."

"That's ridiculous. It just means she was the first intern to do a real case."

"Yeah, but the attendings think it represents the type of go-get-'em attitude they're looking for." He held up a second finger. "Besides, the word is getting around the senior male residents that she is willing to do just about anything to keep the men on her team smiling."

Claire frowned. "You don't believe those rumors."

"I didn't say I believed it. But if it's true, Rogers is likely to keep her around for a year just to see."

"You've got to be kidding."

"I wish I was."

Claire huffed. "She won't get a thumbs-up from me. She's too cut-throat."

Brett gave her a thumbs-up. "Sorry, Claire, I'm only voting the way I think the boss will vote. Besides everything else Beatrice has going for her, Rogers knows it looks bad to have only matched two women. He won't be quick to get rid of them."

"Oh, so you think the women have an unfair advantage?"

"I didn't say that." He shrugged. "But it doesn't hurt."

"That's not the way I see it. He's from the old school, so a woman has to be twice as good as a man to make it through the program." She emitted a thin smile. "Fortunately for most women, that's not too difficult."

Brett rolled his eyes.

Crabtree and Rudy both got thumbs-up. It was common knowledge that Padgett wanted a spot in orthopedics and Griffin was looking for a urology spot, so both of them got thumbs-down.

"What about Kowalski? You have to decide whether he comes back from the lab into a second-year spot."

"I don't know him at all."

Brett held up his fingers and counted off. "Doesn't matter. We've already filled eight second-year slots."

"But we haven't even considered ourselves."

Brett mumbled a curse. "You're a woman. Rogers will probably keep you."

"Wait a minute, Daniels! You have no idea what it's like to be a woman in a man's world!"

He held up his hands, but Claire didn't stop.

"Do you know how hard it is to be noticed for doing excellent work in the OR instead of being noticed for how you look in a bathing suit?"

"Well, no, but—"

"Don't tell me it's an advantage to be a woman in surgery. Every attending looks at you like you should be in nursing. And don't even think about whining. If a male resident whines, it's okay. If I whine, I've got PMS!"

"Okay, okay, I get the picture." He slumped. "But I still say that if all other things were equal, I'd choose you over me any day of the week. Unless I get a big grant and get Rogers' name in a prestigious journal, I'm hosed."

"What if Mr. Jones sues the university? It's not likely that Dr. Rogers will want me if I'm a liability."

"Then you're hosed, too. But Mr. Jones hasn't shown signs of suing, has he?"

Claire sighed. She wasn't enjoying the conversation. "Other than what he said to me in the ER that day, and the paint on my door, I guess not."

The phone rang. Brett stood up as if he may pick up the phone. Claire didn't like that idea for two reasons. Number one, if it was John, she'd have to explain her friendship with Brett, which was, in her mind, just that—a friendship. And number two, she wanted her answering machine to screen her calls in case Mr. Jones might have weird ideas about harassing her.

"Don't get that. My answering machine will pick up."

"Why not?"

She flipped her hands over in nonchalance and attempted a smile.

"You don't want me to talk to your fiancé, do you?" Brett winked. "You're keeping me a secret from him, aren't you?"

She hardened her expression. "You wish," she responded, rolling her eyes.

After the answering machine picked up, she heard a female voice, "Claire? This is Dr. Nadienne Rice calling. I'm—"

Claire nearly stumbled over a kitchen chair in rushing to pick up the phone. "This is Claire."

"Oh, hi. I just wanted to get back with you about coauthoring a paper for *Contemporary Neurology.* I wanted to be sensitive to your feelings about this, but really the credit for solving the Stoney Creek curse mystery belongs to you, so I wanted to give you an opportunity—"

"Wait, Nadienne," Claire interrupted, her mouth suddenly dry. "I still haven't heard anything from my father's genetic test." She gripped the phone with both hands to try to keep it from trembling. "Are you telling me that his test results are in?"

Claire glanced at Brett and turned her back. She felt her heart quickening, pounding in her chest. She felt her cheeks flush. Was the news she had waited for so long finally available?

Claire heard Nadienne sigh. "Dr. V's office was supposed to call you earlier this week. His secretary assured me she would get you on Wednesday or Thursday."

"I've been at the hospital most of the week." She paused. "I suppose you understand, being a resident." She lowered her voice and walked away from Brett. "Is my dad's test positive? Does he have HD?"

"I didn't think I'd be the one to tell you."

"He does? He has it?"

Nadienne was quiet for a moment. "Yes."

Before Claire could respond, Nadienne added, "Dr. V is so excited about working with your family and searching out the family tree. He wants me to go back out to Stoney Creek this week and do some of the legwork. He was so impressed that a surgery intern could make such a rare neurologic diagnosis."

Nadienne's insensitivity made Claire's jaw drop. *How can you researchers be so out of touch with a patient's feelings?* She shook her head and closed her mouth. *Wonderful. I've made my first impressive diagnosis. And I've never been so unhappy to be right.*

Finally Claire mumbled "Thank you" before quietly promising to call back. She dropped the phone in its cradle and avoided Brett's eyes.

How would our little game have gone if Brett knew I might be carrying a gene for Huntington's disease? Training someone with HD to hold a scalpel could be a disaster!

Claire had suspected this moment was coming for weeks. Ever since she first saw the patient with HD in the ER, her gut had not allowed her to completely rest. Well, now she knew. The waiting was over. Her father had HD.

She reached up and pronounced the judgment which summed up her own feelings about her chances of climbing the pyramid. She held out a silent "thumbs-down." She turned and walked back into the kitchen, where Brett studied her face.

"What's going on, Claire?"

"Nothing." She shook her head.

"Nothing?"

She shrugged. "My father isn't well." She looked down. "He drinks too much."

Brett nodded and reached out to touch her shoulder. "You okay? You look like you've seen a ghost."

"I may have, Brett," she muttered. *The ghost of Stoney Creek.*

Part Three

Chapter Thirty

For the next month, the already worn fabric of the Wally McCall family began a slow unraveling. Coping with the news that one is at fifty-percent risk for a disease that will destroy you in your prime affected each one in different ways.

For Claire, immersion into work became an umbrella which shielded her view of HD, the risk she privately referred to as "the cloud." She shared the news with no one in Lafayette, for fear that the knowledge of her risk would buy her a quick exit from her dream. With competition at a premium, a program director would be silly to train a surgeon who was likely to develop an illness which would end a career as it began, and put patients in jeopardy if the surgeon twitched while holding a knife. One thing became clear: The more she wanted to know if she had the HD gene, the more she feared the result and the future a positive result predicted. To have the genetic test would remove all uncertainty, but she couldn't face knowing she had the disease. If there was no cure, what was the point in knowing? On the other hand, if she was disease free, she could proceed with her life without the cloud which hung over her head like a threatening storm. But for Claire, at least for the present, not knowing if she carried the HD gene was more comfortable than finding out that she definitely had the gene, and so she opted to work forward and live life as if the cloud wasn't there. That, however, became increasingly impossible. Every day, it seemed, brought some new reminder that the horizon looked bleak. Frequently, it was the every-other-night rundown of her phone messages, each bringing new news from Stoney Creek as Huntington's disease impacted the McCalls.

The calls were always from Della, who kept Claire informed of each new family tragedy. "Please call your brother and convince him to get tested. He's started racing his motorcycle, and last week he took up skydiving. He's convinced he's going to die young because of Huntington's, and he says he wants to live a full life while he can." Della sighed. "I'm afraid he's going to kill himself with all these dangerous activities. Please call him."

Claire avoided the call, not because she didn't want to please her mother, but because she didn't know how she could convince Clay to do something that she herself was unwilling to do.

Margo, in a desperate attempt to put the HD question to rest, began the genetics testing immediately upon hearing the news of her father's diagnosis. She traveled to Brighton for weekly visits with a genetics counselor, a required part of the testing process. Kyle agreed to go once, but after that, feigned disinterest and cited his business obligations. After Margo's third visit, she returned to Carlisle to find that Kyle had packed his bags and moved in with a college coed who had been flipping burgers part-time at Kyle's restaurant. Kyle cited a loss of love, the pressures of business, and a sudden realization that he and Margo had drifted apart. He refused to acknowledge a fear of Huntington's disease, but Margo and Claire suspected a different story. Sadly, Margo blamed Claire, citing the origins of her problems when Claire revealed the family curse.

Ironically, Wally and Della seemed to fare the best. Finally, they had a real reason to explain Wally's symptoms. Even the news that his biological father was not John McCall failed to devastate him, a fact that Della thought would surely push him over the edge. In fact, after surviving his hospitalization, Wally seemed nonplused that the father that he'd been estranged from for so long before his death was not his father at all. "I knew I was different. I never felt like a McCall," he said.

The biggest improvement came with the beginning of an antidepressant medication, and some appropriate counseling which helped Wally to reach for something other than a whiskey bottle to cope with the stress of a body no longer able to cooperate with his mind.

For Claire, the cloud was the beginning of a downward spiral. She had always been such an optimist, looking forward to her future in medicine with a near invincible attitude. Now, it seemed, the future carried an uncertainty that threatened her confidence and made her question the calling she had clung to for so long. And now, instead of digging deeper into her Christian faith for help, she faltered, unsure if God had really been watching. For years, she had fled from her roots, spiteful of the reputation of being the town drunk's daughter. Now, the very roots she had pridefully ignored were back, firmly attached, creating a link which Claire would have given anything to shed. To Claire, it all seemed a huge cosmic mistake. God couldn't possibly have given her such a strong desire to be a surgeon and infused every cell in her body with a gene that would make that dream impossible. Or could he?

And if he had, could she trust him? How could the loving God she'd learned about in Sunday school be the same one apparently orchestrating this family disaster? And if he wasn't in control, who was? And if he had given her the HD gene, he'd have known about it since before her birth. And since she hadn't done anything to deserve such a terrible fate, how could he ever be considered good and loving? There could be nothing loving about a God who could predestine her to a life of suffering.

Slowly, Claire's image of God began to change. It had been months since she'd darkened the doorway of a church building, weeks since she'd embraced meaningful prayer. The only one she dared share her feelings with was John, and he didn't seem to be comfortable with her doubts. Coping with the unknown was accomplished by working harder and longer hours at the Mecca. If her head was in surgery, she couldn't be worrying about HD. She worked long hours on the vascular surgery service, memorizing patient data and ignoring "the cloud." After a month of vascular surgery, she rotated onto surgical oncology, where she poured every spare moment into memorizing cancer staging and treatment protocols. So her internship standing seemed strong. Her secret was intact. And her spiritual life was a joke.

It was a Friday evening after a long week on the oncology service when she spoke to her fiancé by phone.

Claire thoughtlessly stirred the pan of instant macaroni and cheese and balanced the phone against her ear. When John mentioned getting a test for HD, she pushed the pan to the back burner and began to pace. "John, we've talked about this before. I'm not ready for any test. I'd rather not know than know I'm going to get HD."

"It's not just for you, Claire. I think I have a right to know."

"You do?"

"I'm going to be your husband. I should know."

"I don't want to know the future if the future is bad."

"It may not be bad, Claire. We have to know, so we can plan."

"I'm afraid to know. I don't want to think about it."

"Claire, you just can't go through life with this thing hanging over your head. It affects you. You've let it change you. Why don't you just get tested so we can put this thing to rest?"

"Because I'm not ready to face a future with Huntington's disease. The thought of ending up like my father terrifies me."

"But you might not have the gene."

"Right. And I don't want to know if I do."

"So what do you do? Just pretend it's not there?"

"Maybe. For the most part, that's exactly what I'm trying to do. Fortunately, I love my job, and there's practically an endless number of hours I can spend doing it. So I work and try not to think about HD."

"You can't live life that way. It's running you. Someday you're going to need to get tested, so you can forget this, or learn what it means to leave it in God's hands and trust."

"I can't."

"You can't get tested?"

Claire paused. "Look, Cerelli. You've always been the laid-back one. Take life as it comes and don't worry about the what-ifs, remember? So why is it you're the one who suddenly has to know? Why aren't you sitting back and trusting just like you're preaching to—"

"I'm not preaching—"

"And I'm not trusting!" Her voice ended in a sob.

"Claire, I—"

She inhaled sharply, rhythmically, in a gasp, a sucking sound stopped only by her hand over her mouth. She'd never verbalized it before. But it was pretty obvious by her anxiety. She wasn't trusting God, wasn't even sure if she thought he was trustworthy anymore.

"How can I trust him?" she cried. "I feel so betrayed."

"Regardless of your feelings, God still loves you. Even if he allows you to get HD, that doesn't change anything."

"I hear the words with my brain, John, but unfortunately, my emotions can't seem to comprehend. All I've wanted to do, what I *thought* God wanted me to do, is in jeopardy. Having HD means giving up everything I've worked so hard for. How could God do this to me?"

"Claire, God is not 'doing this to you.'"

"It feels like it. It sure doesn't feel like love." Her eyes began to sting.

"Remember back at Brighton, we talked about the problem of pain with Pastor George. You wanted answers for your patients. What did he say?"

Anger welled up as a bitter gall in her throat. She hadn't intended on dumping it all out on John, but he asked for it. "Yesterday I saw a thirty-six-year-old with inoperable pancreatic cancer. He was holding his Bible, so I smiled and told him I was a Christian, but even while I said it, I felt like such a hypocrite. He looked at me and asked me why he had to suffer." She halted. "I didn't know what to say. I know all the pat theological answers," she snapped before continuing in a mocking tone, "'God's ways are not our ways.' 'In all things God works for the good of those who love him, who have been called according to his purpose.'"

"That's true, Cl—"

"Well, what if I don't love him? What if I'm not called?"

"Claire, uh, honey, uh—"

"What if he's getting me back for abandoning my family when my father was sick?"

"He doesn't work like that. It's not tit for tat. Evil touches the righteous and unrighteous. It's part of the Fall."

Claire didn't want to hear it. She didn't want theological arguments. She wanted to cry on John's shoulder. She fought the urge to hang up. She took a deep breath and counted, trying to slow her racing heart. When she reached ten, she responded, "All of the things we studied seem shallow when you're the one facing pain."

John stayed quiet. She'd unloaded things that she'd never had the nerve to express, the quiet doubts that people in pain are too afraid to confess.

Finally John sighed and cleared his throat. "So what did you tell your patient?"

"I put on my sweetest Sunday school smile and I said I'd pray. Then I practically ran out of there to a call room for a good cry. I felt so plastic. All of my practiced theological answers fell short when I looked at the pictures of his children on his hospital tray table."

"We don't understand it, but God allows evil to touch us to accomplish his purposes. He even allowed evil to touch his only Son, so why should he—"

"John! Stop!" Claire felt like screaming. Instead, she restrained her voice and took a deep breath. "My patient didn't want theology. He needed someone to hold his hand."

"But there are answers, Claire. The Bible—"

"There is a time for theological analysis, answers to the why questions, but, unfortunately, everyone affected by pain experiences it emotionally. All the intellectual arguments in the world do nothing to ease the initial emotional upheaval."

"Come on, honey, it's got to be an encouragement to know that all things work together for good." John raised his voice. "You can't make a mockery of the Bible."

"I'm just telling you how I feel. And I've started looking at all my pat answers, and once I was the one facing the trouble, they all seemed a little silly."

"So now you think the Bible is silly?"

Claire sighed. "I didn't say that. I just said all my pat answers, my favorite verses, *seemed* too silly to speak to someone who has three months to live and will never see his children grow up."

"You didn't say that. You were talking about yourself."

"Me, my patient, whatever! That's what I meant."

She shook her head. She and John had rarely raised their voices to each other. This didn't feel good. The phone had a way of making everything more difficult. She wanted to see his face, to see his emotions, and be seen. To only hear the tension in John's voice added to Claire's frustration.

She fought the urge to cry. "I'd rather not argue, John. But I don't have anyone else to dump this on."

"Claire, I'm concerned. I don't like how this is getting to you. You've always been such an optimist, so open and full of faith."

Her voice dripped with sarcasm. "What can I say? I'm sorry? I haven't ever been in these circumstances before."

He paused for a moment, then continued with his voice sober. "I've never heard you question God's love."

"Well, now you have."

"Claire!"

"Look, I'm sorry if that upsets you, but I'm just being honest."

"And I want you to be, it's just—"

"Just what? If I can't share my feelings with you, where will I go?"

"I want to know how you feel. It's just that I want the old Claire back. The one that swept me off my feet, the one who couldn't stop talking about how great our future was going to be."

Claire sniffed. "I want the old Claire back too." She looked back in the kitchen, and then at her watch. "I should let you go. It's getting late. Let's talk about this some other time."

She could hear him exhale into the phone. She had frustrated him. She wanted his arms around her. She didn't like the telephone at all. "Okay," he responded, his voice near a whisper.

"I love you, Cerelli. Good night."

"Night, Claire."

She listened for more. He always said "I love you" when they ended a phone conversation. Always.

But not this time. After a click, the line went dead.

The next morning Della followed Dr. Jenkins' nurse back down the hallway to his private office. She opened the door and pointed to a chair. "The doctor will be here in a few minutes."

"Thanks, Greta," Della responded, trying desperately to maintain an air of nonchalance in spite of the knot of anxiety in her abdomen. "I'll just read a magazine."

She sat in the cluttered office and stared at the desk. She wondered when the last time was that anyone saw the color of the wood underneath the stacks of charts, magazines, and mail. After a moment, Jimmy appeared and shut the door behind him. Della didn't stand. She merely lifted her eyes and offered him a nod. "Morning, Jimmy."

He frowned and spoke softly. "I'm sorry about Wally."

"I guess news around Stoney Creek travels fast."

"You knew this one would get around. That neurologist from Brighton has asked for my records on a half dozen of my patients." He ran his hands through his graying hair. "Claire sure has opened a can of worms."

Della nodded. "I want you to talk to Clay."

He raised his eyebrows and walked around his desk. He sat on the edge of his chair, partially hidden by a large stack of medical periodicals, and unwrapped a peppermint candy. "What for?" He popped the mint into his mouth.

"I want you to convince him to get genetic testing for HD."

He clicked the mint against his front teeth. "He doesn't need to worry, Claire."

"He doesn't know that."

"I don't think that's a good idea. They are bound to find out things he won't want to know."

"I don't think so. Besides, that kind of information has to be kept quiet."

"But they have to look closely to do a mapping study for a specific gene. That has to be expensive, and I'll bet they do a paternity screen first, just to be sure the test is necessary."

"You don't really know that, do you?" She crossed her legs. "I think you're bluffing."

"And I don't think you or I really want to know." He stood and came around the desk, pushed aside a stack of charts, and leaned against the desk directly in front of her. He looked down at her and spoke again. "Why in heaven's name would you want to bring this all up again?"

"Jimmy, Clay is falling apart. He won't listen to me. Claire seems too preoccupied to talk to him. And he definitely won't listen to Wally. I hoped that maybe he'd listen to you. He's always looked up to you." She was tempted to add "God only knows why" but thought the better of it and shut up.

"Convincing Clay to have a genetic test isn't the answer. It's expensive, he's at low risk, and he—"

"Jimmy, he isn't able to handle being at risk for HD. Yesterday, he drank himself silly and climbed to the top of the water tower on Adam Hill Road. He made it all the way to the top before a county deputy arrived. It took him an hour to talk Clay into coming down. He sat up there swearing like a sailor, threatened to jump, then broke down and cried like a baby." She reached out and took Jimmy's hand. "I'm afraid for my son. He's got to know the truth. He's convinced he's destined to end up like Wally. He doesn't even see the value of the test."

"He's acting like Wally." He smirked. "Drunk in public. A chip off the old block, I'd say."

Della quelled the urge to slap him. She dropped his hand and tried a different tactic. "Jimmy. I'm afraid for *our* son."

Jimmy's eyes darted to the closed door. "Don't say that, Della. You don't really know."

"Stop playing games, Jimmy. Maybe it's time I threw this secret into the town's rumor mill myself."

He blanched. "You wouldn't! We decided a long time ago that this wouldn't do anyone any good. If people found this out, my reputation would—"

"Who cares? I care about helping my son." She stood up. "In fact, maybe I should just tell Clay myself. I don't guess he'd go spreading it around." She shrugged. "Not that I have much of a reputation to protect anyway, being the wife of a drunk!"

"Della!"

She stepped toward the door. He grabbed her arm. "Don't do this. Think it through."

She pulled free. "I'll do whatever it takes to help Clay."

"And do you think Elizabeth is going to let the McCall money slip into the hands of anyone who isn't really her blood at all?"

"I don't care about money. I care about saving my son." She locked eyes with her former lover and fought back the tears. Tears were to be plan three, if her bravado failed.

He exhaled sharply. "Okay," he replied, shifting his eyes to the floor.

"Okay, what?"

"I'll talk to him. I'll try to convince him to go to Brighton. Maybe talking to the genetics counselor will do him some good."

Della took a deep breath. A deep, cleansing breath. "Thanks." She took a step to the door and pulled it open before speaking again. "I had a feeling this would come back to haunt me."

With that, she let herself out, walking down the hall, then out through the waiting room crowded with people. She recognized Mrs. Miller, Amy Johnson, Keith Summers and his boy, Jake. Barb Grable and Bonnie Bratton were holding their new babies. Glen Atkins, one of Apple Valley's oldest fiddle players, hacked into a Kleenex, sounding all the world like he had a death rattle. Linwood Weaver sat next to the door and tipped his hat as she passed. For once in her life, she wished she wasn't so recognizable.

"Morning, Mr. Weaver," she spoke softly as she passed.

"How's Wally?"

He's going downhill fast. He can't seem to control his legs. I need to find a wheelchair with some good Velcro straps to hold him in. He choked on breakfast. Again.

She forced a smile, then looked away before her eyes could betray her. "Fine."

You can't hide your troubles in a small town.

Claire hurried through her daily notes, turning her attention on the twenty-two cancer patients on the oncology service. The service was made up of mainly postoperative patients, people who'd been operated on for breast, colon, esophageal, pancreatic, and thyroid cancers. Each one had a different story to tell, and Claire spent hours listening to their tears, rejoicing with their small triumphs, and encouraging them in the battles they waged together. It helped to focus on someone else's problems. It helped her keep perspective, and kept her from being overwhelmed by her own circumstances.

But when she hit a work lull, her mind inevitably returned to her concerns about her own personal genetic makeup. To get tested, or not to get tested? The question swirled with a thousand little variations. Claire imagined them all. Get tested, find out she's negative, and stop thinking about it. Get tested, be positive, and risk being discriminated against, lose her job, and give up her dream. On the other hand, if she found out she was positive, she could make appropriate plans for the future. She and John could decide together about bearing children. That assumed, of course, that John would even want to follow through on the wedding if he knew his bride might someday dance like Wally. That thought, particularly in light of their last strained conversation, scared Claire even more.

Don't get tested, and face the daily anxiety of the unknown. But at least she wouldn't have to face the horror of a positive test. And what good was predicting the future if you couldn't do anything to change it, anyway?

And what did God think about finding out in advance a course that he had predestined by a genetic code?

Claire pushed herself away from the counter, having finished her last note. She glanced at her watch and considered her options. She had an hour before attending rounds. She could join the upper-level residents in the OR, read, or gather the med students for a teaching session. Instead, she decided to slip away to talk to Dot Freedman, the genetics counselor she'd met back before she knew her father really had HD. Perhaps she could shed some light on Claire's confusion. It was definitely time to get an outsider's perspective on her family secret.

She found Dot wearing the same gray business suit she'd seen her in last. Her white hair was perfect. Claire guessed her age at fifty-five and found herself wondering if she'd be as fortunate to maintain her figure like Dot had. *If I live past midlife.*

Claire rapped softly on the door frame. "Can I interrupt you for a few minutes?"

Dot looked up and smiled. "Sure." She looked puzzled.

"Claire McCall," the intern responded. "I'm a first-year surgery resident. I spoke to you a few months ago."

"Of course. I remember." She pointed to a chair. "Have a seat."

Before beginning, Claire looked up at a picture of an eastern bluebird. "I took your advice. I did some digging into the history around Stoney Creek."

"Stoney Creek." Her face brightened, and a fine spray of wrinkles extended from the corners of Dot's blue eyes. "I saw four different woodpecker species there in one afternoon."

Claire nodded. "Is everything I say to you in strict confidence?"

Dot leaned forward, her smile evaporating. "Of course."

Claire took a deep breath. "My father has Huntington's disease."

Dot seemed to be studying Claire's face. She just looked without talking. It was a look that seemed to bore right through her outer coverings down into her soul.

There. She had admitted it. For the first time, other than to John, Claire had revealed the mystery of the Stoney Creek curse.

She looked at her trembling hands and twisted her diamond in a small orbit around her ring finger. She felt like crying. She closed her eyes for a moment to collect herself. She hadn't anticipated this sudden urge to fall apart. As a surgery resident, she prided herself in being cool under fire. Now, simply with the admission that her father had HD, she found herself choking up.

Dot nodded. "I'm sorry."

Claire sniffed and looked back at the kind face which was still focused on hers. "I haven't told anyone else. Except my fiancé."

"How has he taken it?"

"I'm not sure." Claire dropped her eyes to the floor. "He's back in Virginia, so I've only talked to him on the phone. He's been supportive all during the time I told him I suspected HD might be in my family. He always encouraged me to trust God that everything would be okay. But that was before he saw how bad my father has gotten." She paused. "And before he realized there was a fifty-fifty chance that I might get the disease."

"And now?"

"He wants me to get tested. He says he has a right to know, because he's going to be my husband. I'm not sure he understands."

"How do you feel about that?"

Claire pressed the side of her index finger to her top lip. "Scared. The idea of testing positive scares me to death."

"How are you with not knowing?"

She shrugged. "Not so good. I worry about it all the time. The only way I've gotten along is by keeping myself busy with my work." She released a nervous giggle. "Fortunately, as an intern, that isn't difficult."

"Do you have brothers or sisters? Anyone you can talk to?"

"One brother, my twin. I haven't even spoken to him since we found out. We haven't really been close since I left home as a teenager." Claire shook her head. "My mom says he's certain he's going to get it. Everyone has always said that he's a chip off the old block."

"Hmmm." Dot brushed back her white bangs.

"He's pretty freaked out about it. He's doing all the risky things he's talked about doing for a long time. Skydiving, motorcycle racing. I guess he thinks, 'What the heck? I'm going to die young anyway.'"

"It's really not that uncommon a reaction. I've seen it before."

"Really?" Claire nodded, relieved to see that Dot seemed to understand. "I have a sister, too. Her husband left as soon as he heard about the diagnosis. She has three girls. She wants to get tested. She's in the process, getting some counseling down at Brighton University."

"Can you talk to her?"

"Not really. She's pretty upset with me. She blames me for discovering all this."

Dot nodded. "That won't last. I'll bet she comes around. Sisters usually do."

"I'm not so sure." Claire attempted a smile. "But I hope you're right."

"So you've got a fiancé you're not so sure understands, and you don't really have any support from your sibs. What about your mother?"

"She's okay, but she's pretty overwhelmed just taking care of my father."

Dot pursed her lips and patted her hand gently against the desk. She appeared to be thinking, sizing up the situation. "You mentioned that your fiancé wanted you to trust God. Are you a Christian, Claire?"

Claire nodded. "Yes," she replied quietly. "I try."

"You don't have to tell me about that," she said. "I'm just trying to figure out if you have some intact support systems. You've got a lot to think about. It's important to have someone to talk to."

Claire stared at the carpet. "I haven't gone to church in Lafayette since I moved. I've been so busy."

"I've seen how you residents work. You don't have to explain."

"You are a Christian?" Claire asked.

"For a long, long time." She leaned back. "I made a commitment to serve Jesus after my youngest son died in a car accident."

Claire lifted her eyes to study Dot's face. Was she serious? Certainly she wouldn't joke about something so tragic.

"Does that strike you as odd?"

"Well," Claire stuttered, "I just wasn't expecting you to say that. And it does seem a little strange to become a Christian after something that must have been so horrible."

Dot smiled. "I suppose so. It was a horrible time for me."

"Most people would doubt God's love if they lost a child."

"I did. At least for a while. But it was watching my husband, who was a Christian at the time, and seeing how he dealt with the agony we found ourselves in, that eventually opened my heart to God's love."

Claire felt a stab of guilt and looked away.

Dot continued. "How has finding out about HD affected your faith?"

Claire took a deep breath. "I don't know," she said.

Dot stayed silent. It was a silence that screamed, "You're holding back."

Claire shifted in her seat. *What am I? Transparent? I can play this game, too.* She raised her eyes and met Dot's gaze, determined not to be the one who looked away. After a moment, Claire lost. She *had* to look away before she burst into tears. She looked at her watch and checked her beeper. *Why doesn't this thing go off when I want it to?*

Dot finally spoke. "This has to be a major disruption for you. If you're anything like other surgeons I've met, I bet you've been focusing a whole lot of attention on your career."

She nodded. "It's all I've thought about for a long, long time."

"Are you a control freak?"

Claire wrinkled her brow.

"You know, most surgeons are off the scale when you measure their need to control their environment. They want things to be done according to plan. Their plan, mostly."

"That's a stereotype."

Dot shrugged. "It's an observation."

"I like to have things planned out. I've known what direction I was headed for a long time. I've worked extremely hard to make my dreams happen."

"I admire you."

Claire coughed. It wasn't the comment she was expecting.

"I'm serious. You obviously haven't let much stand in your way. You don't get invited to Lafayette unless you've excelled. Coming from a small town like Stoney Creek, I doubt you had many female role models. You've paved your own way. You've made it to a level that most women don't even dream of. Look at you," she said, holding up her hand. "You're on the edge of a career in surgery. How many women ever get that chance?"

"But suddenly I feel like it's all for naught. HD is like a time bomb ticking away inside me, waiting to strike as soon as I reach my prime. I could be jerking like my father before I ever get to realize my life's dream."

Dot tapped a pen against the desktop. "Why did you come to see me?"

"I needed to talk to someone. Holding this in is driving me crazy. I need to figure out whether I should get tested or not."

"Fair enough. But it's not likely something you'll figure out in one day."

Claire nodded her assent. "Really."

"So what are the issues on the table? If you get tested, you'll know, and be spared the agony of not knowing. You can plan for the future." She paused. "On the other hand, if you test positive, there is a chance that you could be discriminated against. I don't think you should share this with your attendings. It could cost you a position in surgery."

"That would be illegal."

"Well, I'm sure no one would admit that you are being ousted because of HD, but it certainly couldn't help."

"I've thought as much. So far, I've kept it a secret."

"Good. There are some financial concerns. Testing can be expensive, and again, I doubt if it's something that you want to submit to your insurance. They would not want to insure you if they found out you tested positive for HD."

"I don't think the money would be a problem. I suspect I could talk my grandmother into paying for it. The HD came through a man she had a relationship with, so I think she feels responsible, in a way. Helping me might ease her conscience."

Dot began writing notes. "What are the implications of HD on your selected occupation?"

"Obviously, I couldn't practice surgery once the HD was symptomatic. That could happen anytime, assuming I'm HD positive."

"So, is it fair to your patients not to know? Is it possible that you could jerk or twitch during an important surgery, and actually hurt someone?"

Claire looked at the carpet. "Maybe."

Dot spoke again, more softly. "Listen, I'm not trying to talk you into being tested. I just want to help you explore all the issues."

"Right."

"Maybe you can find a neurologist you can confide in. If you decide not to be tested, at least you could get periodic examinations to see if you are showing any signs of HD. I think a surgeon would owe her patients that much, at least."

"Fair enough."

"You're going to have to think of the implications of a positive test on your relationships. Could your fiancé handle you testing positive?"

"I think so. I don't know." Claire ran her fingers through her hair. "He wants me to be tested. And I'm sure he won't like it if I decide not to be tested. And I'm even more sure he won't like it if I test positive."

"Could he handle it?"

"Meaning, would he stay with me, take care of me?"

Dot nodded.

"I think so." She sighed. "But he's not so comfortable with not knowing. And right now, this whole HD thing seems to be bogging down our relationship. I can't seem to understand how God could have allowed all of this. Everything in my life was sailing along so smoothly, until I discovered HD." Claire shook her head slowly. "I've started questioning everything. I've always felt that I understood what God wanted me to do. I felt as if he wanted me to be a surgeon. He called me." Claire looked up. "Does that make sense?"

"I think so."

"But now, I find myself wondering if I just manufactured that idea on my own. If God wanted me to be a surgeon, he wouldn't have put HD in my path, would he? And if he did, it kind of blows my whole concept of him." Claire shook her head. "I can't see how a loving God could do this."

"How does your fiancé feel?"

"He isn't comfortable with my doubts. It upsets him when I question my faith."

"I see."

Claire looked at her watch. She still had a few minutes before she needed to get back to the hospital. "Do you think it's okay to know the future?"

"What do you mean?"

"Does God hide things from us intentionally, not ever wanting us to know our own future? Is getting a genetic test to see if I have HD treading on ground he never intended for me to cover?"

"Claire, I can't answer your questions directly. I think the correct answer might be different for different people. There is no biblical absolute to guide us here." She paused and folded her hands. "I think you're on the right track."

"The right track? I've never been more unsure of myself."

"Yes, but you're asking questions, seeking advice. That's a good start."

"Maybe." Claire stood up. "But the answer scares me more than the question." She pinched the bridge of her nose and sighed. "Not knowing runs against my scientific, objective approach to life. Surgeons are trained to find the answers, not conceal them."

"True."

"But I'm not sure I could handle knowing I'd get HD if I tested positive. At least this way I have hope."

Dot shrugged. "Hope is good."

Claire frowned. She could see that Dot wasn't about to give her an easy answer. "I need to go." As she turned to leave, the social worker touched her arm.

"You might find it helpful to just mentally give yourself permission not to know. At least for now, when you're not so sure if you want to know or not, tell yourself that it's okay not to know everything, even though everything in your scientific worldview is demanding knowledge. Use it as a springboard to walking in faith. It doesn't have to be something that destroys you. If you knew everything, where would trust come in?"

Claire nodded slowly.

"So give yourself permission not to know. And if you change your mind later, it's okay too."

Claire looked away silently. The scientist, the physician in her screamed to know. Getting comfortable with not knowing would take iron determination. But she desperately needed to come to a place of peace, a place of rest, and right now, she didn't feel capable of dealing with the results of an HD gene test. So the only alternative was to come to peace with not knowing. "Thanks, Dot. I'll think about what you said. I–I know I need to trust."

"Come back if you need someone to talk to." She lowered her voice as she stepped with Claire into the hall. "Do not let this information out in an uncontrolled manner, Claire. You have a right to keep this to a trusted few. You'll know when it's right to share."

"Okay." She looked at her watch. "I've got to run." She turned and accelerated to a brisk walk, her foot catching on the floor as she crossed from the padded carpet to a linoleum hall. She stumbled forward and regained her balance. She looked back and shook her head. Thankful that no one saw her klutzy move, she resumed her walk at the harried pace normal for a Lafayette surgery tern.

As she walked, she remembered the ribbing her brother, Clay, used to dish out whenever she showed a rare sign of clumsiness: "Smooth move, Grace." She smiled at the memory until a new thought assaulted her: *It could be Huntington's disease.*

Chapter Thirty-One

Tony Broderick sat in a corner booth facing the front door of the smoky little bar. His eyes were on the door, but he wasn't seeing the peeling paint or the windows, which were in desperate need of cleaning. Tallyho's wasn't known for its decor, which started as a nautical theme a decade ago, and had degenerated to something that reminded Tony of an old version of a fifties soda fountain that had survived a time warp. An oar still hung above the door as a vestige of the first owner's attempt to link it with the nearby sea. Overhead, old vinyl LPs from popular fifties groups dotted the ceiling. Tallyho's served beer, and plenty of it, mostly to sweaty dock workers, and the others from the Lafayette shipyard a block away.

Tony gulped his drink and looked at his watch. He hated waiting. Especially waiting for lawyers. In fact, he hated lawyers in general. He hated the way they dressed, the money they made, and the way they talked in big words which he didn't understand. Mostly, he hated Jeremy Pinkerton, the fast-talking attorney that his father had insisted upon. His father knew Mr. Pinkerton from multiple previous scrapes with the law. Tony's father loved Mr. Pinkerton. That, in itself, was reason enough for Tony to despise the man.

But Tony had never been in more trouble in his thirty-five years. He had been enthusiastic about Jack Daniel's whiskey for a decade, and even more so since his wife left two years ago, taking his two sons, Jimmy and Garret, with her.

Murder. It seemed implausible that he could be facing such an accusation. He wouldn't hurt a bug, if he had a choice. When his uncle took him hunting as a boy, he couldn't stand the thought of killing anything. All he remembered was sitting in the cold woods praying that a deer wouldn't come his way and show him to be the softy his uncle would claim him to be.

But alcohol had changed all that. He'd had one other DUI before. He couldn't imagine a jury would feel too sorry for him now.

He closed his eyes and tried to erase the memory of her shrill cry: a little girl, afraid, and in pain, screaming about her purple bicycle.

He'd only had four drinks. Four measly drinks. His liver could handle far more than that without affecting his brain. At least that's what he thought before the fateful July evening that threatened to change his life forever.

A little girl was dead. And the prosecuting attorney was eyeing a judgeship and was certain to push for a harsh punishment. The charge leveled against him was a second DUI and vehicular homicide. He was staring down some serious jail time. He'd never see his sons play Little League again. So now, he had little hope but to rely on the slimy lawyers to try to get him off.

At ten after seven, after Tony had devoured three beers, Pinkerton arrived. He was wearing a dark suit and tie combination which emulated Regis Philbin. Immediately, he scowled at Tony. "I told you not to drink in public. We need you to be clean as a whistle by trial."

Tony lifted his eyes and didn't smile. "You invited me to meet you at Tallyho's. What am I supposed to do while I'm waiting?"

Pinkerton lit a cigarette and sat across from the shipyard worker. He touched his graying temples and blew smoke at Tony's face. "I have good news."

Tony didn't respond. After a few moments' delay, he looked up. "Well?"

The lawyer lowered his voice and leaned forward. "I may have just the information that will give the jury reasonable doubt about convicting you of murder."

Tony huffed. "Right. Like I wasn't really driving my car."

Pinkerton held up his hand. "A rumor is circulating around the office about Roger Jones."

"A rumor?"

"A well-substantiated fact, actually. Ramsey Plank's paralegal told me that a tribunal has met and approved a malpractice suit on behalf of Sierra Jones."

"What?" Tony sipped his beer and wiped his mouth with the back of his hand. "What's that got to do with me?"

"If Ramsey can nail the university with malpractice, we'll have another avenue to convince the jury that Sierra died because of faulty medical care, not because of the injury you caused her. It will go a long way toward getting a more reasonable charge. If they think that Sierra would still be alive unless some doctor screwed up, I'll bet I can convince them that you can't be held responsible for her death."

Tony's heart lifted. "Really?"

"It's a hope."

Tony smiled. Maybe old Pinkerton wasn't so bad.

"Ramsey is the best. He specializes in nailing doctors' hides to the wall. Malpractice insurance carriers have all heard of him." Pinkerton straightened his shiny solid blue tie. "Ramsey can make a doctor's life misery. He can make 'em confess anything."

Tony snickered. "Doctors make too much money."

The attorney nodded. "Really." He grasped Tony's hand. "I'm going to do everything I can to get your trial delayed until after the malpractice trial. If they rule against the doctor, your jury will be much more likely to vindicate you."

"Buy you a drink, Jeremy?"

Pinkerton frowned. "No!" He stood up and jostled Tony's chair. "Come on, I'll give you a lift home. We can't have you getting another DUI now, can we?"

Tony stumbled out behind Pinkerton and laughed at the thought of a doctor being nailed, and how that might help his own cause. Tony hated doctors. He hated the way they dressed, the money they made, and the way they talked in big words which he didn't understand.

Maybe slimy old Pinkerton wasn't so bad after all.

Claire opened her eyes and squinted through the darkness at her bedroom ceiling. The night wasn't over, but her mind wouldn't let her return to sleep. The red numbers on the clock face seemed to mock her. Four-thirty. She would be on call the next night, and the knowledge that she might not get to sleep for another forty hours frustrated Claire even more. She rolled over and gripped her pillow. In another minute, she rolled back again and threw her pillow to the floor.

Sitting up, she rubbed her eyes and listened. All was silent outside, a fact that stood out in stark contrast to the lack of inner quiet in Claire's soul. *Early awakening. Insomnia. It's a classic sign of clinical depression.* She got up and walked across the cool, creaky oak floor. *It's a curse to be an intern. You know just enough to torture yourself. Every time you have a common symptom, you're sure you have some pathologic diagnosis.*

She turned on the bathroom light and stared at herself in the mirror. She stuck out her tongue, then carefully ran her fingers over her neck and swallowed so she could feel for nodules in her lower thyroid. It was the week after her menses, so she proceeded with her monthly self-breast check. She pulled off John's jersey and watched carefully in the mirror so that she wouldn't miss anything. She would repeat the exam a few minutes later in the shower, so a soapy lubricant could heighten the sensitivity of her exam.

It was a routine that Claire had followed since medical school. She was vigilant about her own health, wanting to practice appropriate self-examinations both as a part of proper health maintenance and as an example to her future patients. She'd started examining her own body parts as a way to learn what normal was supposed to feel like. She knew every inch of her well-built frame, and comforted herself in the even, firm texture of her own flesh beneath her fingers.

She checked her resting pulse rate. It was sixty-eight. She had been inconsistent with her running lately, but frequently avoided the elevator at work to raise her heart rate for a few minutes.

She looked at the dark circles beneath her eyes and yawned. The anxiety that had driven her from sleep was a cancer beyond her detection. A change in a mole could be detected by sight, prompting a biopsy. A colon cancer might cause a change in bowel habits or blood in the stool. A subtle change in a breast examination might hint at pathology lurking beneath the skin surface. But the thought that within every cell of her normal-appearing body, an abnormal sequence of DNA could be invisibly responsible for some horrible genetic illness seemed to be a deviation from the level playing field. It didn't seem fair somehow, that something so horrible could lurk undetected for so long, only to raise its ugly head in midlife right when your life's work was beginning.

Claire turned on the shower and waited for the steam to start clouding the mirror in front of her. She kicked John's football jersey into the corner and stepped into the shower. There, she finished her monthly self-exam and tried to rinse away her obsession with her genetic future. She tried to concentrate on Dot's advice. *"Use it as a springboard to walking in faith."*

As the water fell, she began to pray. "Please, God," she whispered, "help me to trust. Help me to keep my mind on my work and be satisfied with not knowing."

As Claire finished her preparations for the day, she thought back to all the other battles she'd waged in her young life. She'd slaved to get her GED, worked through college and medical school, and had matched into one of the most sought-after surgical residency programs in the world. In the past, she'd always tried to find a silver lining in every dark cloud. A stumbling block could be a stepping-stone, a sharpening tool to make her sharper, stronger. A lonely hilltop tree which meets the adversary of the wind is always stronger than one in the forest. These were the attitudes that had helped her win. Now, she wanted to summon the same attitude to help her deal with the threat of HD.

But how could her risk for HD make her better, stronger? Claire dried her hair and decided to make a plan. If she wasn't in control of the situation, at least making a plan would help satisfy the surgeon in her, and give her a feeling of power, even if it was an illusion. For starters, if anxiety about HD robbed her of sleep, she would use her waking hours efficiently. She could always study for her boards. And if her life was destined to be a short one, she would make the most of every day so she could accomplish everything she wanted to before it was too late.

She picked up John's jersey and thought about her fiancé. He missed "the old Claire." Claire the optimist. Claire wondered if she could recapture her optimism to fight her current trial. She folded the jersey and put it under her pillow before making her bed.

She made coffee and sat down at her desk, pushing aside her Bible and opening Sabiston. She did it with a twinge of discomfort, but thought about her commitment to being the very best resident she could be. Life may be short, so she couldn't afford to slack off while she had her health.

Claire spent the next hour scribbling down facts about the dangerous skin cancer, melanoma. At five-thirty, she packed her call bag and headed for the hospital.

She met her chief resident, Drew Tripp, in the cafeteria. She approached his table. "Hi, Drew. You're up early."

Drew grunted and took a long swig of coffee. "Our liver resection decided to bleed at midnight."

Claire looked at his unshaven chin and stared at the plate of eggs and bacon. *I hope you've got good cholesterol genes.* Claire knew the "liver resection" to be Lawrence Smith, a fifty-two-year-old asparagus farmer who had just returned from a cruise in the Caribbean, where he and his wife, Mary, had celebrated their thirtieth wedding anniversary. He didn't recognize the jaundice right away. He thought he'd just gotten a good tan on the ship. By the time his wife's tan had faded, he'd begun to itch from his deepening yellow color. He'd gone to his family doctor, who'd found cancer in his bile duct and referred him to the university for surgery. The chairman, Dr. Rogers, had resected the invasive cancer, along with a portion of Mr. Smith's liver. Mr. Smith had endeared the house staff with his doctor jokes, and his constant complaining about the hospital food, and the green Jell-O that he called "cruel and unusual nourishment."

She wrinkled her forehead and sat down with her breakfast, oatmeal and coffee. "Did you have to explore him?"

Drew shoved in a large bite of ketchup-laden scrambled eggs. "Yep. He bled from a portal vein branch. We stopped the bleeding, but not before he had a massive MI. He coded and died in the recovery room." The chief resident shook his head. "Bummer."

That delightful man dies after an operation you participated in and all you can say is "Bummer"? Will I ever get that callous?

Or is that what being objective is all about?

"That's horrible."

"Yep. And Rogers was already in a bear of a mood. He called a special meeting with all the senior residents later today to lecture us on legal risk management."

"Risk management?"

The solemn surgeon nodded. "He always gets this way when the university hospital gets sued."

Claire felt a knot tighten in her stomach. "Sued?"

"Oh, I'm just guessing really. But I've been here long enough to recognize a trend. Every time the surgery department is threatened by a lawsuit, he briefs the house staff on damage control."

"What do you mean?"

"The need for adequate chart documentation, confidentiality, never spilling any story about patients outside the hospital, etc." He chuckled. "Mostly he'll just want us to keep the interns from talking to the ambulance chasers."

Claire stirred her oatmeal and replied quietly, "Oh."

Drew tipped his head toward a man in a three-piece suit at a corner table. "See that guy?"

Claire nodded.

"He works for Ramsey Plank, attorney-at-law. He worms his way into the trauma patients' rooms to convince them to file lawsuits because of their injuries."

"What a leech."

Drew sipped his coffee. "Really."

"Why would an intern talk to him?"

"Medical malpractice suits in this state can result in huge profits for plaintiffs. And that means huge profits for their lawyers. The lawyers, in turn, don't hesitate to pay handsomely for information that will result in big payoffs for their clients."

"Hmm." Claire's oatmeal seemed too thick to swallow. She feigned nonchalance. "Any clue what a suit could be about?"

Drew seemed to be surveying Claire's blouse. "Hmm?" He looked up. "Nadda. I don't even know that there is one. I'm just making an educated guess, that's all."

"Oh."

Drew rubbed his chin. "I need a shave." He stood up. "I'll see you in a few minutes for rounds."

"Sure." Claire looked down at her oatmeal. *Cruel and unusual nourishment.* She smiled to herself and shook her head. *Mary's going to miss you, Lawrence. I know I will, and I only knew you for a week.*

Claire pushed her oatmeal aside and looked over at an adjacent table of female medicine and pediatric residents. They were laughing and talking about men. She heard one of them complain about being on call every third night.

Good grief, girl. Try a surgical internship and we'll show you what a real schedule is like, where the only thing wrong with every-other-night call is missing half the good cases. She frowned and felt lonely. Only a few women from each medical school class decide to do general surgery. *It's no wonder,* Claire mused. *It is almost impossible to pay attention to anything else during your training. Just look at me. I'm engaged, but I never see my man. And now that he knows my father has the dance, I'm not sure he'll want to be my fiancé for much longer.*

She stood and plodded toward the ICU so she could review a few charts before rounds.

A half hour later, Chris Bearss, the other intern on the service, arrived, looking as if he wore sleep as a cloak. His hair was combed, but his scrubs were wrinkled, and he carried a Dr. Pepper, his preferred breakfast beverage, in his left hand. He took a long swig of soda and stared blankly at Claire. He formed a word with the stomach gas which escaped as a belch. "Ralph," he bellowed.

Claire rolled her eyes. "For a Harvard grad, you show remarkable talent."

"My brother can recite the entire alphabet with one burp," he responded, his voice showing hints of awe. "He's one of the great ones."

"You don't get out much, do you, Pepper?" It was the name the O-man gave him when he rotated on the trauma service. It had stuck, and Chris didn't seem to mind. In fact, nothing seemed to bother him. Once, during his first month of internship, on the neurosurgery service, he had eleven admissions in one day. He never even flinched. His resident just kept feeding him Dr. Pepper and pointing him toward the emergency room.

"None of us get out much. We're terns. We're not paid to get out."

Claire nodded. "Rough night?"

"The usual." He sighed. "Mr. Smith boned it."

"I heard. I ran into Dr. Tripp at breakfast."

"He had the gall to page me to the recovery room to dictate a stat death summary after the patient coded. Then, he stood over me, coaching me how to phrase everything, wanting everything documented, in case the chart is picked apart by an attorney someday." He slurped his Dr. Pepper. "I'm not sure what's going on at the top, but the sphincter tone is pretty tight in the chairman's office right now, and that pressure is going to roll right down the pyramid."

"So I hear."

Claire thumbed through the bedside clipboards on the ICU patients while the rest of the team gathered. Claire and Pepper anchored the scut team with support from three medical students. There was one third-year resident and a chief resident over them, and four attending surgeons on the oncology service, including the chairman, Dr. Tom Rogers.

After a few minutes, Dr. Drew Tripp arrived to begin rounds. Lynn Nio, a third-year student, handed the chief resident a cup of coffee. He nodded. "Glad to see we've got at least one honors student among us."

He walked to the first bed where a sixty-two-year-old man was recovering from an abdominal perineal resection, a surgery performed to remove the rectum for colon cancer. Claire picked up the chart to begin her presentation, but before she could speak, Drew tugged on the clipboard.

"Let Pepper present the patient."

"Well—" Claire registered her surprise, but was cut short by Drew's serious expression.

Claire tried to read him, but the chief resident quickly looked away. "I almost forgot. Dr. Rogers wants to see you in his office." He pointed with his head toward the automatic doors leading from the ICU. "Now."

"Why?"

"I'm not sure, Claire."

"But it's seven in the morning."

"I know, but he's likely been here all night. We didn't finish in the OR until quite late." He lifted his eyes from the floor to meet hers for a moment. "You'd better not keep him waiting."

Pepper lifted an unopened soda can from the pocket of his white coat. "Take him a soda. No one can be too mean when they're enjoying a Dr. P."

Claire wasn't humored. She shook her head and turned to go. Behind her, she could hear Pepper's last-minute advice. "You're okay if he starts out by saying you screwed up. If he starts with 'You're doing a wonderful job,' watch out for the slam."

Claire hit the button activating the automatic door.

The doors were closing as she heard Dr. Tripp's laugh. "Shut up, Pepper!"

A few minutes later, Claire walked down the dim hallway of the surgical staff offices. Dr. Rogers, the chairman, wasn't the only one in his office this morning. She also saw light coming from the open doors of the trauma attendings, the night owls of the surgery department. Dr. Rogers' door was open, and she could smell coffee brewing from a pot in the hall just outside his door. He wasn't alone. She could hear voices. One, a female, was a voice she had heard before, but couldn't place.

She approached the doorway and cleared her throat.

Dr. Rogers looked up. In a chair opposite the chairman's desk, a plump woman in a gray suit sat with her legs crossed. Next to her, a gentleman in a three-piece suit looked up without smiling. Next to him, Dan Overby sat with a large cup of coffee in hand. "Claire, come in. You've met Wanda Miller from risk management, and Peter Ondrachek."

That's where I've seen them before! "Of course." Claire held out her hand. The attorney shook her hand limply.

"Thanks for coming by." The chairman got up and closed the heavy oak door behind her. "First let me make something very clear. I think you're doing a wonderful job as a surgical intern."

Claire tried not to show her negative reaction. The only thing she could think of was Pepper's advice.

Rogers continued. "We're being sued, Claire. A Mr. Roger Jones has sued on behalf of his daughter, Sierra, who died in our hospital on the last day of July."

"I remember the case well."

"In Massachusetts, a potential malpractice case has to go through a tribunal before it is allowed to go forward," the hospital attorney interjected. "We had hoped the case would never get this far."

"We never really thought it would get this far," Wanda echoed. "Ramsey Plank requested hospital records a few weeks after the incident."

Claire leaned forward. "Why wasn't I told?"

"There was no need to worry you. We had reviewed the record, and there did not seem to be a real case," Wanda responded. She nodded toward the O-man. "Dan had done a super job on the records, and it really looked like they had no case at all. As far as the official record reads, Sierra Jones died from massive internal bleeding."

"Basically that's true," Claire responded.

"We know that, Claire." Rogers' eyes shifted from one person in the room to the next before coming to rest on Claire's. "But we think that the prosecution must have had some help outside the official record." His eyes bore in on Claire. "Have you been talking about this case to anyone?"

"No."

Wanda uncrossed her generous thighs. "But our conversations with the judge from the tribunal indicate information has passed that was not in the official record. Mr. Jones's claims that you did not properly monitor the central IV line has been verified by a direct witness."

Wanda uncrossed her legs and leaned forward. "I specifically remember requesting that you not talk to anyone about this case."

Claire locked eyes with the administrative assistant. "I told only my family and my fiancé, back in Virginia."

Rogers shifted in his leather chair. "Claire, we understand if you thought you were talking off the record, but—"

"I haven't talked to anyone involved in the case, Dr. Rogers," Claire interrupted. "Is that what this is about? You thought I'd incriminated the university?"

The O-man spoke up. "Somebody did, Claire. If it wasn't you, where did the information come from? I know you felt bad about that night. Did you apologize or something?"

"No." Silence hung in the room for a tense moment. "You think I'm lying?"

Wanda shook her head. "Of course not. We only want to remind you that as this process starts, you mustn't talk to anyone."

Claire clenched her teeth. "Of course, I was asked to present the case at the M and M conference. Did you ever think that someone else might be talking to the prosecution?"

Claire watched the O-man and the chairman exchange glances.

Dr. Rogers rubbed his chin. "The residents should understand that the contents of that conference are confidential. But still . . ." His voice drifted into silence.

Claire dropped her face to the floor. "Of course."

Dr. Rogers snapped back to attention. "We will need you to dictate a full recollection of the events of that day. We will forward your report to your malpractice carrier. They will assign an attorney to the case who will defend you."

"Am I the only physician named in the case?"

"No. The university is named. They're the ones with deep pockets. You are named because you were the physician in charge at the time the patient deteriorated."

Claire looked up at the O-man. She had loved working for him. He taught her so much. And now she felt she had let him down. She caught his eye. "I'm so sorry."

He nodded and sighed.

Claire looked back at Dr. Rogers. "What are they seeking?"

"Twenty million dollars."

Claire gasped.

Wanda pointed at the medical record on the desk. "Review the chart and dictate a full summary."

Dr. Rogers stood up. "I want to see it by noon today. I've instructed Drew to relieve you of your duties until the report is done."

She nodded and looked at Peter Ondrachek. "Does this happen often?"

"Unfortunately, in a university this size, once or twice a year."

"Does the university ever lose?"

"They've settled a few times. But only once before did a resident go to trial."

"Dare I ask the outcome?"

"We lost," he admitted soberly. "To Ramsey Plank."

Chapter Thirty-Two

or the next four hours, Claire sat in an empty conference room beside Dr. Rogers' office and pored over Sierra Jones's record, hoping to clarify the events in her own mind, trying desperately to uncover something that would offer her an inkling of hope. Instead, the experience was like debriding a scab, leaving the wound fresh, oozing, and painful.

She made notes to herself, jotting down times and lab values, and chronicling the last moments of the life of Sierra Jones. Somewhere there had to be a fact that could be gleaned from the record, something that could be useful in her defense. She wrote down everything, trying to recall exact words or phrases from the moment Sierra hit the ER door until the time she died. *It was the medical student who positioned the IV pole at the head of the bed. Not me.* She frowned. *Oh, like that's going to help me. "It wasn't my fault, it was the medical student's," isn't going to cut it as a defense. I was still supposed to be watching.*

Claire sighed and dropped her head in her hands. How could her life get any more complicated? She wasn't sure how much more she could take. She felt so alone.

She started taking inventory. Her status as an intern was on shaky ground. Her social life was in the pits. She was wearing an engagement ring to a man she rarely saw.

Worst of all, God seemed to have betrayed her. She thought he'd called her into surgery. But that all seemed like wishful fantasy now. Why would he call her and then make the way so rough? She felt spiritually dead. The last time she prayed was . . . well, this morning. She tried to capture the memory of her early morning shower. What did she pray? That God would help her concentrate on her work and trust in him? She looked at the stack of notes in front of her. *If this is your answer to helping me focus on my work, God, you've got quite a sense of humor.* She brushed back a tear and rearranged the papers in front of her.

Carefully, haltingly, with Dictaphone in hand, Claire spoke through the events of Sierra's last hour. Back up. Retape. Back up again. Shuffle through the notes to get every fact, every word, correct. Thirty minutes into her effort, a gentle tapping interrupted her train of thought.

She watched as the door pushed open. Brett's face appeared. "Hey. I had a hunch I'd find you here."

"A hunch?"

He shrugged, came in, and shut the door behind him. "I asked Dr. Rogers' secretary."

"Why?"

He held up a white bag from behind his back. "I thought you could use a break. I brought some lunch."

"But how did you know about—"

"I overheard Dr. Rogers talking in the lab this morning. I knew something was up, the way he was moping around. I just kept my ears open, that's all."

"You're a busybody," she said, trying to suppress a smile.

"If you'd rather I'd leave, I could—"

"Hold on, there. You haven't shown me what's in the bag."

He smiled. "I've got Mr. J's bagel sandwiches."

She reached for the bag. "You can stay."

He handed her the bag and sat down at the conference table opposite her. "You're just using me for my lunch."

She laughed. "Yep." She held up a bagel sandwich, wrapped in white paper. "What'd you get?"

"One tuna fish salad, and one turkey and Swiss."

She sniffed the wrapper and handed it to Brett. "You like tuna salad?"

"Sure, I love seafood."

"Tuna salad is not seafood."

"It is if you're a resident. I can't afford anything else."

Claire paused, grateful for the break. She looked up at Brett, who was already devouring his sandwich. "Thanks, Brett."

They made small talk while they ate. After she finished her bagel, Claire hoisted the medical record in front of her into the air, up and down, weighing it in her hand. "What do you think, Brett? Is this going to be my ticket off the pyramid?"

"I don't think so. The way I see it, it's probably neutral."

"Neutral? Certainly they won't want to keep me around if I cost the university twenty million dollars."

Brett shook his head. "Look at it from a defense viewpoint. It would look bad for you to lose your job now. It's like an admission that you're a bad doctor. If they hold on to you, it shows they are confident in your skills."

"Oh, great. So they keep me, not because they want me, but because they have to."

Brett wrinkled his forehead. "I don't think Dr. Rogers will let this influence him. He has a ranking system based on clinical performance on the wards, and your in-service training exam." He held up his hands. "But, if in the discovery process, it looks inevitable that the university is going to lose the suit, they may cut you to save face, and appear that they do have the patient's best interest at heart."

Claire pouted. "You're encouraging."

"Hey, I'm just telling you the way I see it. But for now, I think you're safe. They can't cut you if they want the jury to think you're competent."

"But this can't help me. It can't be beneficial to be the center of what will undoubtedly become a media frenzy. I can see it coming. They're going to be all over the hospital criticizing residents' training hours, the danger of medical care by sleep-deprived resident staff." Claire felt her voice thicken. She didn't want to cry.

Brett's voice was steady, quiet. "Hey, now, try not to let this get to you. You've fought bigger battles in the past. You'll get through this."

He walked around the table and sat next to her, placing his hand on hers. "What else is going on, Claire?"

She gazed into his blue eyes for a moment before looking away. "Am I that transparent?"

He stayed quiet.

She answered her own question. "I guess so, huh?"

"Trouble at home? Trouble with your fiancé?" He paused. "As if residency pressure isn't enough to steal your pretty smile."

Her eyes met his again.

"Hey," he responded. "I'm just offering a shoulder to cry on, that's all."

She pushed her fists into her eyes in one last attempt to keep from crying, but she'd let her guard down. She wasn't playing the steel-nerved surgeon role now. She was just plain scared and lonely. She began with the story of her suspicions about her father and the Stoney Creek curse, the surprise about her real grandfather's identity, and how she made the diagnosis of Huntington's disease in her own father. She unloaded her fears about being at risk and how the risk was destroying her family, her sister's marriage, and her brother's outrageous risk-taking. Lastly, she cried about her separation from John and her fears about how being at risk for HD might affect his feelings for her and of his seeming intolerance to her doubts about God's care.

"Now every time I do anything klutzy, even a minor misstep or stumble, instead of just going on, the first thing on my mind is Huntington's disease. It's like a bad dream, and I can't wake up."

He held her hand, then slid his chair close to hers. He turned toward her and coaxed her into his arms. "Come here," he said, standing and pulling her gently to her feet.

She stood and allowed him to lead. She slowly placed her head against his chest and cried. He patted her back before letting his hands and arms rest around her, gently but certainly pushing their bodies into close contact. She felt his breath, then his lips brush against her forehead. "It's going to be all right, Claire. You are so strong. You'll make it."

She sniffed and blinked back the tears. "I don't feel very strong." She turned her head and clung to his broad shoulders. She needed the support. Brett was offering it freely. So why did she feel on edge? She could sense his breath quickening. Slowly, softly, he was applying pressure on her lower back, edging her even closer.

Her thumb felt for the diamond on her ring finger. She spun it around and closed her fist. She felt his breath on her hair, on her ear. The hairs on her arms stood up as she tilted her neck to allow his face access to her neck. He nudged her earlobe with his nose, then his lips. "Everything's going to be all right."

Claire closed her eyes and tried to push aside her hesitancy. She longed for comfort, and his arms felt strong and secure. She shifted her upper body against his, her skin fully aware of his warmth.

She pinched her eyes closed and put her palms on his shoulders. She pushed back and avoided his gaze. His fingers drew across her back and arms, lingering, tracing a meandering path down her arms as she backed away. His touch electrified her. His hands were lightning, warm, and full of energy. With her throat suddenly parched, her breath came in short gasps. As much as she wanted to surrender to the comfort he wanted to give, resting in his arms felt like a betrayal. "I–I should finish this dictation."

Brett took a step forward and swept her into his arms. In a moment, his mouth was on hers, kissing, searching. Her movement was firm, more decisive than she felt, her hand against his chest pushing forcefully until her arm was at full extension.

"No."

She saw a flash of fire in his eyes. Hurt? Passion? Anger? She watched as he pumped his hand into a fist.

"Claire—"

"I can't. I—"

"You can!" Brett stepped away, still holding his hand in a fist. "You talk with your lips, not with your heart."

Claire shook her head. "No."

"Claire, listen to your heart," he pleaded.

"Don't do this to me. I need you. I need you as a friend, a confidant. No one else in this department has heard the story I told to you."

Claire watched as Brett took a deep breath and blew it out through pursed lips.

"Sometimes I think I should just quit the program." It was an admission that shocked her, even as she spoke. "Just one more straw on this camel's back, and I'm outta here, back to Stoney Creek and a simple life." She dropped her eyes to the table. "The Lord knows my mother could use the help with my father."

"You wouldn't quit. You've lived for this."

"What makes you think you know what I will do? And how can you presume to know my heart?"

"I—well, I—" He threw up his arms. "Vibes, I guess."

"Vibes?"

"Good vibrations. I thought you felt what I felt." He looked down.

"Brett, the last thing I want to do is hurt you. If I'm sending you vibrations, it's out of my own confusion."

Brett looked at his watch. "I'd better leave you. I know Rogers has you on a tight schedule." He took a step to the door. "I'm sorry."

"Brett, I'm the one who's sorry."

Brett gathered up their trash from lunch. "I've got to get back to the lab." He opened and shut the door without saying good-bye, leaving Claire alone. She sunk to her chair and stared at the Dictaphone.

I must be see-through. If I have an ounce of desire for that man, he can sense it like I've shouted it from a stage. She paused. *I'm just like Grandma, inviting unwanted advances . . . or are we getting what we want?*

"God," she whispered. "I finally decide to share my problems with another resident, and I just seem to end up with one more problem."

Looking at her watch, she shook her head and backed up the Dictaphone to listen to what she'd just recorded.

Then, picking up where she'd left off before Brett's interruption, she took a deep breath and continued.

The blue rental Dodge Durango SUV wove across the double yellow line as Billy Ray Davis squinted at the map. He swerved back and muttered a curse as the driver of an eighteen-wheeler loaded with turkeys laid on the horn. A feather lodged momentarily on his windshield before flying off toward a field of corn to his right. "Blasted poultry trucks!"

He pulled out a cell phone and started to dial with his thumb, but when the road curved sharply to the right again, he lost his place and decided it was time to find a place to stop.

He found a gas station in Berryville and pulled in for gas, a six-pack of Heineken, and a large bag of jalapeño nuts. He'd found the delicacy on a recent trip to the South, and loved the peanuts seasoned with peppers enough to endure the heartburn he was sure to experience. That's why he bought the Heineken. Not that it made the heartburn better; in fact, it made it worse. His physician had said something about relaxing his gastroesophageal sphincter or some such fancy doctor-speak. But the Heineken would cool him down enough to sleep, even if the peanuts tortured him.

Ramsey had insisted he leave right away. "We've got to do our groundwork early, before everyone is on their toes," the attorney instructed. But now, Billy Ray was lost on a country road, buying beer at a mom-and-pop gas joint, with a map that didn't even show a town by the name of Stoney Creek.

He found the nuts without a problem, but settled for an American brew when he discovered that the store didn't sell imported beer. He placed a case of Michelob on the counter and smiled at the woman behind the counter. He knew she had been admiring his new vehicle, and he had dressed the part of a professional, so he opened his wallet and told her it handled a little rough, but was much more fun than his Mercedes at home.

The woman appeared to be in her forties, fifties maybe, pretty well preserved for a hardworking country woman. She eyed the beer.

"Want to see an ID?" Billy winked and lifted his hand to his temple. "Prematurely gray."

The woman smacked her chewing gum. "Whatever." She smiled back and whistled between the gap in her front teeth. "I earned every gray hair I own."

Billy Ray stared at her big hair for a moment before asking, "Ever heard of a town called Stoney Creek?"

She eyed the man suspiciously. "Are you a reporter?"

Billy Ray pushed his shoulders back. "Me? No." He snickered. "Why?"

"'Cause just last week some feller driving a vehicle just like yours came through asking about Stoney Creek. Said he was writing about solving the curse or something. Seems our little Stoney Creek has caught the eye of some of the doctors over at Brighton University."

Billy Ray leaned forward to study the gap in her front teeth. Every time she said an "S" sound, it came spraying right through her front teeth, whistling as it sailed past her ruby red lipstick.

"Hmmm. So you know of it?"

"Sure. Just take this road south to bypass Brighton. Then head west on Highway 2 toward the Apple Valley. First town is Fisher's Retreat. The second is Stoney Creek."

He paid for his purchases and settled back into the rental. He opened the nuts and buried his bulbous nose into the foil container. After inhaling deeply, he moaned. The heartburn would be worth it. He tossed his first handful into his mouth and pulled back onto the road.

He reviewed what he could remember about the extraordinary woman he knew only by name and the data he'd collected. Born a twin, Elizabeth Claire McCall had risen above the normal dismal heights of her small-town roots. Billy Ray had focused his early search on Claire's academic records, hoping to find something that could be exploited to their advantage, hoping to uncover a fact that could paint a picture of the young doctor as less than studious, less than dedicated to her craft or the patients she served. But, so far, every academic rock he overturned revealed her to be a stellar example of what every patient wanted. She was consumed with excellence, and her nose seemed to be pointed straight toward her goal. If he could find a flaw, it wouldn't be in the grade book.

Ramsey had made him tail her for a week, back in Lafayette, hoping to find a drinking problem, or a tawdry affair with a married attending, or anything which could make a jury understandably concerned about her judgment. But other than one stop at a grocery store, the young intern spent all of her waking hours at the hospital. If there was a weakness, it was that the poor girl never got out. Maybe the overworked, sleep-deprived angle would work to their advantage. It had worked for Ramsey in the past. Maybe it could work again.

Billy Ray sighed. The nuts were burning the back of his throat. He eyed the Michelob. Maybe just one on the road wouldn't be so bad. He checked the rearview mirror and carefully screwed off the cap of a cold beer. He took a long swallow before shoving the bottle between his legs to hold it steady. He turned right on Highway 2, and soon discovered that he needed both hands for adequate control on a road he swore was designed by an engineer with a tremor.

Why couldn't Ramsey just be content to play the sleep-deprived intern angle again? No, Ramsey always had to have a backup plan. "There are skeletons in everyone's closet, Billy Ray," the attorney proclaimed. "It's our job to bring them out so the jury has a chance to judge for themselves." It seemed relevancy to the case had little to do with Ramsey's exhaustive searches. Anything and everything which could create an environment of mistrust of the accused would be used to his advantage.

On the first straight stretch of road, Billy Ray grabbed the rearview mirror and adjusted it so he could see his face. He smiled at himself, then picked a nut fragment from between his teeth.

"Hello, ma'am," he practiced. "I'm Harvey Bridges with the Great South Health Plan. May I have a moment of your time to show you our policies?"

That evening during attending rounds, Dr. Rogers treated Claire as if their encounter earlier in the day had never happened. She followed his example, obviously meant to instruct her that she was never to mention the suit outside a carefully monitored situation.

After rounds, she sent Pepper home and proceeded to slog through the scut list. There were two central lines to change, one new admission from clinic to pre-op for a gastric resection, and a few X rays to follow up. She changed the first central line and talked a medical student through the second one. She had been brought up at Brighton University Medical School to observe the philosophy "see one, do one, teach one." It made her extremely popular with students who were normally relegated the lowest scut jobs on the ward.

By seven, she made it to the cafeteria for a bowl of cooling vegetable soup and a grilled cheese sandwich. She sat at a table with Beatrice Hayes and her senior resident on the neurosurgery service, Dave Barnum. "Hi, guys," she offered with a smile.

"Evening, Claire," Dave responded.

Beatrice looked up and moved her tray an inch closer to Dave's. "Oh, hi, Claire."

Claire stared at her plate for a moment and thought about praying. *I feel like such a hypocrite, God. I'm not pious at home. Why should I pretend to be here?* She picked up her spoon and lifted the soup to her lips.

Dave looked like so many neurosurgery residents; working long hours was taking its toll on his demeanor. He tapped his fingers against his furrowed brow. "Whose service are you on?"

"Oncology."

Beatrice lifted her eyebrows. "Ooh. Getting a chance to impress the chairman?" She pushed back from the table and crossed her legs. "I hear he's been in a bear of a mood lately. I hear he's in a funk about a lawsuit."

Claire didn't flinch. "Really?"

Claire watched them exchange glances. Obviously they expected something else. They must know about the suit. They were just baiting her.

"Come on, Claire, I know you've heard something."

She held her ground. This was just a test. "I really shouldn't say," she responded quietly. She locked eyes with Bea's. "Just what do you know?"

"Nothing, really. I just heard someone is suing the university over some resident screwup. Pity the poor resident that has to take the fall for a department that Dr. Rogers heads up. He's not likely to let the blame get too close to him or his department."

Claire tried to swallow the bite of grilled cheese sandwich in her mouth, but she seemed suddenly short of saliva. She reached for a soda for assistance. She stayed quiet for a minute, focusing on sipping her soup, but not really appreciating its taste. Her mind was on a little girl with a purple bicycle.

After a few more minutes, she watched Beatrice brush a few crumbs from Dave's thigh and smile. "I guess we should go. I hope you have a quiet night."

"Thanks. You too," Claire responded. She watched the duo walk out, shoulder to shoulder, barely a molecule of space between them. *Watch out, Dave. She only wants to climb the pyramid.*

After supper, Claire made post-op rounds on the patients who had undergone surgery that day and retired to a call room for a date with her Sabiston text. By eleven her eyes were heavy and she drifted into a fitful slumber. At one, she responded to the emergency room to see a colon cancer patient with a bowel obstruction. It had been twenty-four hours since the patient had passed any flatus and the X ray showed dilated small intestine. It was time to summon the chief resident.

They had the patient in surgery by three, finished by five, and had an hour and a half to sleep before rounding again. Drew Tripp, the chief resident, looked whipped. He'd had two nights in a row in the OR. Claire studied his unshaven chin for a moment and pondered her own plight. At least an intern got every other night off. The chief residents, with the exception of the trauma service, had to respond to their service's demands every night.

After rounds, Claire helped with the daily notes, missed lunch while pulling on an abdominal retractor during a gastrectomy, and attended an afternoon tumor conference. During the gastrectomy, she wedged her slender frame between the operating surgeon, Drew Tripp, on her right, and the board supporting the patient's arm, on her left. Surgical procedures, she had learned, forced the team together, bodies in close contact in order to concentrate on the same small field. Right Guard, peppermint gum, and a tolerance to having your body pressed against your assistant's were prerequisites. Whenever she relaxed her grip on the hoe-shaped metal retractor lifting the abdominal wall out of the surgeon's way, the chief resident would repeat, "Ski, baby, ski," making reference to the leaning-back motion used while holding a water-skiing towline. She must have heard it thirty times. Every time she changed her position to relieve her forearms of the cramps, the phrase was the same. "Ski, baby, ski."

She thought Drew was acting sexist until he repeated the same phrase to a male medical student who stood on the other side of the table. Then she just thought he was boring.

After the tumor conference, she assisted with the remaining scut, plodded through attending rounds, left Pepper the on-call pager, and fled from the hospital. She was weary of the hospital, sick people, and bloody socks. She was weary of medicine. Even baseball players destined for the Hall of Fame needed a break from the game once in a while.

Mechanically, she guided her Toyota to her rented brownstone. The sun had set on another day of internship, and she was glad to be a survivor. She was too tired to worry about HD, too tired to worry about making it up the pyramid, and too tired to care about the lawsuit. She opened her front door with two things on her mind: food and a bed.

She tossed her white coat on a chair and headed for the kitchen. She stared blankly into her refrigerator. The middle shelf was empty. The top shelf housed a quart of milk and a head of lettuce. She sniffed the milk and scowled. As she dumped it into the sink, the phone rang. Her heart lifted. One voice could satisfy her more than sleep or food: John Cerelli.

Be John. Be John. Be John.

"Hello."

The voice was distant, almost like it was coming from the inside of a box. It was male and gravelly. "I'm going to make sure you pay for what you did."

A shiver passed over her back and arms. "Who is this?"

"Doesn't matter. I hear you killed a baby."

"What? Who is this?"

"You're going to pay. Might as well admit what you did. It's gonna come out. You know it will."

"Wh–what?"

"Don't call the police, Doctor. I'm watching. And don't run away. I can follow you." She heard a low laugh. "I can see your pretty face now."

Instinctively, she looked up to the window over the kitchen sink. Seeing only her reflection, she quickly backed away and pawed frantically at the light switch next to the refrigerator. Darkness greeted her. Was someone really watching? Or just playing a cruel game?

She squinted toward the window and the side yard beyond. From where she stood, she could just see a short section of the street. She could see her neighbor's van parked against the curb. Was there a vehicle on the other side, in the shadow of the van? She pressed her face against the window for a better look. It was no use. The van obscured her view. She realized she still held the phone and could hear an insidious laugh. "Yeah, baby, I think I'll watch you all night."

Claire slammed the phone onto the counter as the screech of tires peeling against the pavement outside echoed through the neighborhood. A vehicle was speeding into the night with the headlights off.

Her heart pounded in her chest as she ran from the kitchen to the front door, and then to the back. The locks were secure. She selected the largest butcher knife from the utensil drawer and retreated to her bedroom with the phone. As she did so, she imagined how silly she looked. Just what protection would a kitchen knife offer? And did she really think that the man on the phone was about to attack? Still, the phone call had unnerved her, and no amount of reasoning made her feel better than the feel of her firm grip on the butcher knife. She slowly opened her closet door and checked under her bed. Then, satisfied that she was alone, she locked her bedroom door and called John Cerelli.

After two rings, his answering machine picked up, and her heart sank. After a beep, she left a frantic message. "John, this is Claire. I need you to answer." Her voice cracked with a sob. "We need to talk." She didn't exactly feel like explaining her predicament to an answering machine. She prayed he was home and would pick up when he heard it was her. After a moment's silence, she quietly put down the phone and cried, "Oh, God, what should I do?"

She walked from her bedroom to the stairs, acutely aware of the quiet of the old house around her. She paused and listened. Then, hearing nothing, she descended the stairs. Her auditory senses were on alert, and every sound seemed magnified. The stairs creaked beneath her, and her footfalls seemed like hoofbeats. Even the refrigerator emitted a low hum, an irritating noise that Claire had not previously noticed. At her desk, she paused and traced the butcher knife over the calendar to today's date. She read, "John in Baltimore."

She'd written the note a month ago when her fiancé gave her his business travel schedule. A knot in her stomach tightened. John wouldn't be home until the following evening to get Claire's message.

She paced a path between the front living room and the kitchen, contemplating a course of action. She could leave and go sleep in the hospital. She could call the police, but the thought that her caller might see them and retaliate scared her more than doing nothing. She could try to ignore the phone call and sleep in her house alone. Or she could call Brett. No, that was out. After yesterday, she couldn't exactly ask him to sleep over. She'd be driving the boy crazy. Maybe even driving herself crazy.

She paced the house for a few minutes more, listening to every sound. This was crazy. She'd never get any sleep here. As much as she hated going back to the hospital, at least she could find a safe call room to sleep.

She walked back to her bedroom and unfolded her whitened fingers from the butcher knife. She placed it on the dresser by the door. She pulled a fresh outfit from her closet and packed her on-call bag. She'd have to be ready to spend two nights in a row back at the hospital. What to do after that would have to be decided later. Fatigue was catching up with Claire, and she didn't want to think that far ahead. What mattered was now, and her first priority was a safe place to get a night's rest before the next day's call.

She finished her packing and was just zipping her bag when the doorbell rang. She froze for a moment, then picked up the knife and ran to the bathroom window which overlooked the front stoop. Who could be ringing her doorbell at this hour? Was it her caller, trying to further convince her of his ability to get close to her? She eased her head up to the window and gently lifted the white curtain. Expecting to see no one, she gasped with relief. It was Brett!

She stumbled down the stairs, knife still in hand. She jerked open the front door and pulled Brett into the house.

"Whoa!" He stood back and laughed at her enthusiastic reception. "Uh, hi." He leaned forward and wrinkled his forehead. "Are you okay?"

Claire slammed and locked the door behind him. "Am I glad to see you!"

"C–Claire?" Brett stammered and backed away, looking at the knife.

She glanced at her hand and thought about telling him she was just working in the kitchen. Instead, she smiled sheepishly and shrugged. "I thought you were threatening me."

"Me?"

"Well, not you," she said, still waving the knife. "I mean I thought the person at the door might be someone who just threatened me."

Alarm spread across his face. "Threatened you? Would you mind telling me what's going on?" He paused, his eyes still on the knife. "And would you mind putting down your weapon? You're making me nervous."

Claire's cheeks felt hot. "Sorry." She put the knife on her desk. "Someone just called here."

"Who? Someone threatened you?"

Claire slumped to the couch and spilled her story.

Brett's eyes widened. "Did you get a look at the vehicle?"

"No. It was hidden by the van." She felt her eyes begin to sting. "Brett, who would do this?"

He shrugged. "Someone who really wants to win a lawsuit is my bet."

She sat quietly for a minute while Brett looked around the apartment. She watched him as he sauntered back into the room. "By the way, what are you doing here?"

He sat down in an old easy chair across from the couch and leaned forward. "I came to apologize for being such a jerk yesterday. I had no right to treat you like I did." He opened his arms, palms up. "Sorry, Claire."

The simple act touched her. He'd come to apologize, yet he sat quietly listening to her entire story first. Part of her wanted to jump right into his arms again and let him tell her everything was going to be all right, just like he'd done the day before, after she'd shared all of her fears about HD. But she refrained, telling herself that she'd just complicate their relationship with unnecessary temptation. She smiled. "It's okay, Brett. I'm glad you came over. Thanks for apologizing."

She twisted her engagement ring and inspected the setting. "It's hard to keep this thing clean at the hospital. I'm constantly getting glove powder down beside the stone."

"Let me see," Brett responded, leaning forward and taking her hand. He held it up to the light and nodded. "I can clean it for you in the ultrasonic tub in Dr. Rogers' lab. It's great for jewelry."

"Really?"

"Sure. If you trust me, let me have it, and I'll take it in tomorrow."

She shrugged. "Sure," she said, twisting off the ring. She put it in a little velvet box that she kept in her desk drawer. "Here." She dropped the box in his hand and looked away. "I should let you go."

"Are you afraid to stay by yourself?"

She shook her head. "I'm not sleeping here alone. I'm going back to the hospital to a call room."

He shook his head. "Don't do that, Claire. That means you'll be there three nights in a row."

"I can't stay here. That creep might be watching me. He said so."

"That was probably just a threat to scare you." He paused and shuffled his feet. "I'd be glad to stay."

She lifted her eyebrows and stared up at his tanned face. "I can't expect you to do that."

"I did it before. I'll take the couch." He smiled. "I'll behave myself." He motioned his head toward the stairs. "You need to get some sleep. I ran into Drew this afternoon. He told me about your night."

She nodded. "You know what they say. 'Never let the sun come up on a bowel obstruction without an operation.'" She walked to the hall closet and retrieved two blankets and a pillow.

She watched Brett's eyes light up.

"I guess I'm invited?"

She laughed nervously. "To sleep on the couch."

He spread out the blankets and threw the pillow at one end of the couch. "Where's your Sabiston?"

She pointed to her desk. "Need to study?"

"I need something to help put me to sleep." He hoisted the heavy book into his hands. He looked up at Claire and responded soberly, still weighing the book in his hands. "You know, I love this stuff." He shook his head slowly. "It's crazy, the life we put up with, but . . . I really love this."

She nodded. "I know exactly how you feel." She started up the steps. "Thanks for staying. I'm going to be leaving at six in the morning. Feel free to sleep as long as you want. There's an extra house key in the top drawer of the desk. You can use it to lock the dead bolt when you leave."

"Don't I get breakfast in bed for protecting you?"

"You can have what I'm having. Coffee. Strong. With French vanilla creamer if it hasn't spoiled in the fridge."

He wrinkled his nose. "Sounds great. If you need me, I'm right here," he added, opening the surgery text.

"Good night, Brett." She climbed the old stairway and shook her head. *Just when I'm in a panic, Brett shows up. God, are you trying to tell me something?*

Chapter Thirty-Three

The next evening, John Cerelli's flight into Brighton was delayed an hour because of heavy rain. When he finally arrived home, the odor of stale pizza greeted him. He flipped on the light and grumbled to himself about his roomie. He grabbed a can of Pepsi from the refrigerator and listened to his phone messages. The third one grabbed his attention.

It was Claire, and she sounded distressed. Frightened, maybe? Her voice carried an urgency and cracked with a sob. "John, this is Claire. I need you to answer. We need to talk."

He whispered a quick prayer. Claire had been so upset by the news about her father. She probably just needed an ear.

The news about HD was taking its toll on John as well. The visit to Stoney Creek to meet Claire's parents had been an eye-opening experience. Since his visit, John had spent hours searching out everything he could find about Huntington's disease. He had bookmarked at least six different Internet sites so that he could get his hands on helpful resources for himself, and for Claire.

He wanted Claire to be tested for the HD gene. He wanted to know so he could be prepared. But life with HD looked like certain agony, so he understood how years of waiting for the disease to strike could ruin what good years a person might have, if the person at risk tested positive. In the end, he would have to let Claire make the decision. He wanted to marry her anyway. He felt certain of that. He was willing to pay any price to have Claire as his bride, even if he was only to have her at his side for a few good years.

He'd started keeping in contact with Della. Talking with her, seeing her strength in the face of having to care for Wally, gave John hope that he too could summon the fortitude to care for Claire if she had the Huntington's gene. In fact, knowing the diagnosis seemed to bring Della to a new calm. Finally, she had a name for the problems she'd been facing. Finally, there was a reason. The enemy had a name. It wasn't her husband. The enemy was acting through him. The enemy was Huntington's disease.

John dialed Claire's number and stuck his head in the refrigerator. The only thing he found was a half-empty can of Spaghettios. He sighed and shut the door.

After ten rings, he checked the calendar. Of course, it was an even day. Claire was in the hospital tonight.

He called Della to see if she'd talked to Claire. She hadn't, and sounded more upbeat than the last time he'd talked to her. She was excited that an insurance man had stopped by, and when she told him about Wally, he promised to look into a policy that could cover nursing home costs in the future. "He was such a nice man," Della proclaimed. "He seemed so interested in everything about our family."

"That's great," John responded. He said good-bye and promised to call again if he heard from Claire.

He walked to the den and pushed a pizza box away so he could plop on the couch. He felt helpless. It had been too long since he'd seen Claire. He hadn't even seen her face-to-face since she'd gotten the news about Wally's diagnosis, the news that seemed to be beating Claire down and pulling them apart. She needed him. How could he help her from so far away?

He prayed again and made a sudden decision to leave for Lafayette in the morning. His boss wouldn't mind. John had a few extra days coming to him anyway, and he'd just signed on the biggest clinic in Baltimore to use their software. If his boss wouldn't let him go, he'd tell him to take a hike. Claire was more important than any job.

He felt excitement rise within him. The decision seemed right. He would get an early start, take a thermos of coffee, maybe pack a few snacks, and take the tape series on the book of Galatians that Pastor George had been teaching. It would be a long drive, but if he left early enough, he'd be able to take Claire to dinner.

He smiled to himself. He would surprise his fiancée tomorrow.

The next day, John Cerelli spent the lonely hours on the road in a quiet search of his own soul. His relationship with Claire had blossomed in such a wonderful way when they were together back in Brighton. Now the miles between them were straining their commitment. Her absence from him made his heart ache. All he could think about, all he could dream about, was being with her again.

He'd never been a great communicator. That much he knew well. But writing and phoning were definitely not his forte. He wanted to tell her how he felt. He longed to unload his emotions, but he seemed to clam up and freeze whenever he had to speak into the phone. His father said that it was a "man-thing," that the same thing happened to him. "Go see her," he constantly urged. "Let her see you face-to-face."

John hoped a face-to-face encounter would help, but memories of his last visit to Lafayette seemed to haunt him as the miles on the way to Lafayette went by. Life as a surgical intern made a normal relationship impossible. The last time he visited, he spent more time waiting to see Claire than actually seeing her. This time, he was committed to staying longer, at least through the weekend.

While he drove, he imagined his own relationship report card. He gave himself a "C" for communication, an "A" for compatibility, and a big fat "F" for their physical relationship. He'd satisfied his own lust, and came away feeling as if he'd forced Claire into a compromise she'd regret forever. Sex was supposed to be such a wonderful blessing to a married couple, and now it had become a point of contention. He cringed at the memory. Oh, it had been fun, but it had come at an expensive price. Now he wondered if their honeymoon could ever be what he'd always dreamed it would be. He'd ruined the excitement for himself, and stolen something from Claire that she'd never be able to give again. He was supposed to be the leader, and lead her he had, right down the wrong path. And even when he'd come to realize how wrong he had been, he'd counted on Claire to be the strong one. During his last visit, he'd forced her to be the strong one. It was only because Claire had said no that he hadn't tripped up again. This time, he promised himself, he'd talk it out with Claire, apologize for the way he'd treated her, and start again with a clean slate.

So, as the hours passed, John Cerelli repented. And then repented again, just to be sure he meant it. He felt better and reminded himself of God's grace. He chugged a Pepsi and burped loudly. Why not? He was alone, and God didn't care.

He stopped for lunch at McDonald's and lowered the top to his Mustang. The sun was shining. His past was forgiven, and he was going to see his girlfriend. Nothing could be finer.

During the last hours, he listened to Pastor George on tape, chugged two more colas, and ate a bag of Cheetos. Life was good.

He stopped twenty minutes south of Lafayette to freshen up at a rest area. He changed his shirt and brushed the Cheetos from his teeth. He stopped again in Lafayette to find a florist and bought a bouquet of pink roses, Claire's favorite. He arrived at her house at six, prepared to wait for Claire's return. As he pulled up, he noticed an orange pickup in the driveway. He didn't see Claire's Toyota, but smiled to see a light on in the front room.

He knocked on the front door. Claire was going to freak!

A man pulled open the door. He was tall, an inch or two above John, tan, and blond. John stared for a moment at his muscular build before speaking. "Uh, I'm here to see Claire."

The man shook his head. "She's not home." The man stood in the open doorway, but didn't seem to want to move aside.

"Well, uh, mind if I come in and wait? I guess she'll be here in a few minutes, right?"

"Hard to say. Interns lead a strange life." The man moved aside an inch and allowed John to squeeze in. The smell of grilling red meat greeted him. In the kitchen, John could see a table set with two plates and candles.

John felt suddenly awkward. He looked at the flowers in his hand and at the preparations under way in the kitchen. John extended his hand. "John Cerelli."

"Brett Daniels."

John squinted at Brett. "Do you mind telling me what you're doing at Claire's?"

He shrugged. "What's it look like? I'm preparing dinner."

"Where's Claire?"

"Hospital."

"How did you get in?"

"With my key."

"You're staying here?"

"Well, not all the time. Just when Claire asks me." Brett eyed the flowers. "Who are you?"

"John Cer—" John blushed. "Er, I already told you that. I'm Claire's fiancé. She's wearing my diamond."

The tanned occupant nodded, but didn't smile. "Oh, sure, the diamond. Nice ring. I've admired it." He lifted his eyebrows. "She keeps it around here somewhere, I think." He walked over to the desk and picked up a velvet box. He popped it open and held it up to John. "This the one?"

John hung his head. "That's the one."

"Say, if you don't mind me asking, I don't recall Claire mentioning that she expected you tonight."

John gritted his teeth. "It was a surprise."

Brett smiled. "Quite."

John eyed the kitchen again. He looked closer. A wine bottle was chilling in a small cooler beside the table. Maybe this guy was just using Claire's kitchen to entertain a friend. "You expecting a guest for dinner?"

"Just me and Claire."

"Claire left me a phone message. She said she needed to talk to me. She sounded so upset." He shook his head as a knot began to form in his stomach.

"Look, I don't want to be out of place here, but I've made plans here, and maybe you should have called ahead. If Claire said she needed to talk, maybe you should have tried just that. It looks like you guys have plenty to talk about."

John looked around the room, incredulous. He'd driven all day to surprise his fiancée, and instead, he'd stepped into a nightmare. This didn't seem real. It was as if he'd set foot in the wrong house. But the stuff in the room looked like Claire's. He recognized her furniture, her desk, her Sabiston's textbook. He looked back at Brett. *This is unbelievable. Maybe this is why Claire was crying. She needed to tell me about her new love.*

He shook his head and stared at the ring box on the desk. He thought for a moment about taking it with him, but decided it might appear tacky.

Brett prodded. "Look, pal, it's going to be awkward if Claire shows up. I'm sure she'll want to talk to you, but . . ."

John didn't let him finish. He dropped the flowers on the desk and bolted through the door.

He couldn't think. His mind was blank. With his heart exploding, he stumbled back to his Mustang and found himself driving through Lafayette, taking a right here, a left there. He didn't care where he ended up. He just knew he had to drive. He was on automatic. This situation was unthinkable. Claire and John had been inseparable just a few months ago. She'd accepted his ring. And now his world had come to an end.

He passed a strip mall with a grocery store, went through two intersections, then turned right again beside a rescue squad building with a sign out front: "We save lives with donations." John muttered the words without comprehension. Then, on the left, he saw a familiar marker for the interstate system.

In another minute he was back on the highway heading south. He put the Mustang on cruise so he could prop himself up to get his head into the wind above the windshield. His eyes stung, instantly blurring with tears.

He shook his hair and opened his mouth to pray, but as he spoke, the wind seemed to tear the words from his mouth and scatter them silently behind him, unseen and unanswered.

So much for surprising his fiancée. He dropped back onto the seat and pounded the steering wheel, unsure if he still had a fiancée anymore at all. He drove numbly, unaware of anything except the agony of his soul. Slowly, his thinking turned from shock to sorrow to self-condemnation.

Surgery had stolen his fiancée away, weakening her with long hours away from support. Huntington's disease had made her doubt God's love, and John hadn't been there to hold her.

He turned on the headlights as the sun sank beyond the horizon and dusk settled upon his soul. And, in the darkness, he began to weep, wondering if he would ever feel Claire's love again.

Claire wasn't in a hurry to be home. At six, she left the oncology service to Pepper and headed to the grocery store. Because she loathed the idea of another dinner of mac and cheese, she loaded her cart with microwavable dinner entrées and boxes of fiber-laden breakfast cereal. She paused briefly at a display of cutlery, staring at a large meat cleaver, and wondered if keeping it on her nightstand might make it easier to sleep alone. She shook off the idea. A handgun would be better. It wouldn't be so messy. She shivered at the thought of actually taking a hack at someone with a meat cleaver.

As she loaded her purchases into her car, she caught a glimpse of a passing red Mustang convertible. Just like John's. *Man, what I wouldn't give to have him with me again.* The thought filled her with longing and intensified her feeling of isolation.

She drove home trying to decide between linguini with beef and mushrooms and vegetarian lasagna. Once on her quiet street, she saw a familiar sight. An old orange truck was parked in her spot. She smiled and pulled to a stop at the curb. Brett must have used the key she'd left him.

She opened the door and surveyed the scene. Her den was immaculate, her desktop uncluttered, and a delicious aroma beckoned her toward the kitchen. Brett stood in the middle of the front room and immediately relieved her of the burden of her grocery bags.

"Allow me, Dr. McCall," he responded.

Her eyes widened as she walked without speaking toward the kitchen. Candles were in place, wine was chilling, and pink roses adorned the center of her small table. Her favorite roses!

She spun around and locked her eyes on Brett, who stood behind her, his arms laden with groceries. He wore a white shirt, a stark contrast to his tan. It had no collar, and buttoned up the front, and was open across his chest. A small nautical insignia on his shirt matched the one on his blue jeans. His hair was ruffled, and he smiled with a boyish grin. She didn't know what to say.

"I–I–," she stammered. "What's the meaning—"

"Don't read anything into this," he interrupted. "I knew you needed a lift. That's all." He set the bags on the counter and busied himself with putting away her purchases.

With that accomplished, he uncorked the wine, poured a glass, and led her to the couch. "Here," he instructed. "Prop your feet up. Dinner will be served momentarily." He handed her the glass. He pointed a finger at her nose and snapped, "Relax!"

She took a deep breath and sipped from the goblet, while Brett retreated toward the kitchen, still pointing at her like a stern high school instructor. She lifted her feet to the couch and slipped off her shoes, allowing them to drop to the floor with a thud. She wiggled her liberated toes and yawned. She listened to his final preparations in the next room while she sipped the wine and closed her eyes. In a few minutes, with her head already a bit fuzzy, she rose in curiosity to view her host. She watched as he tossed a green salad and pulled steaming biscuits from the oven.

"Scratch?"

He laughed. "I'm good, but not that good." He lit the candles and turned off the overhead kitchen light. He refilled her wine glass and pulled out a chair. "Here, Dr. McCall, dinner is served."

She glanced at her phone answering machine. No messages. John hadn't even returned her frantic phone message. She pushed her disappointment aside and inhaled the aroma in the air. "What's for dinner?"

"I grilled some sirloin." Brett sat across from her and shrugged. "Hey, I know what it's like to be an intern. I went weeks without eating a decent home-cooked meal."

She paused for a moment, accustomed to a prayer of thanks. But she watched Brett quickly diving in, so she picked up her fork to begin.

They talked of their common love of surgery, of the cases Claire had assisted with, and the oncology attendings. Claire listened as Brett told of his first experiences following his father on rounds and in the clinic.

"As much as I disliked his perfectionism," Brett reflected, "I've always wanted to be a surgeon just like my father."

Claire forced a smile as Brett refilled her glass. She thought of Wally. She couldn't remember ever wanting to be like him. She ate quietly as Brett ran through the list of the other interns. Brett worried he wasn't going to make the top eight.

"What are you going to do if you don't make the cut?" Claire asked.

"I have to make the cut." He shook his head. "I don't want to do anything else."

"What if it comes down to you or me for the final spot?"

"That's not likely. I have a feeling you won't have to worry."

"Right. All I have to worry about is being the only intern to be named in a lawsuit, and the only intern with a family history of HD. You think Rogers would keep me if he knew that?"

Brett sighed and stayed quiet. That was answer enough for Claire.

She pushed him further. "Seriously, I want to know. What would you do if it was down to me and you?"

He squinted and sneered. "I'd have to kill you." He stayed serious for a moment, before showing a hint of a smile.

"You'd never get past my butcher knife," she sneered back, before giggling. She wiped the back of her mouth with her napkin and lifted her wine glass again. She looked at the empty glass and found it just a little hard to focus. The combination of sleep deprivation and her alcohol intolerance were showing. She giggled again.

"What are you laughing about?"

"About protecting myself with a kitchen utensil." She shook her head. "What was I thinking?"

"Claire, you were scared and alone. It's not really so silly."

"I was s–cared," she slurred.

Claire finished the meal and fought the urge to close her eyes. "I always hated my father for drinking too much," she confessed, before laughing again. She lifted the empty bottle of wine. She tried hard to remember how it had gotten that way. "You must have hogged the last glass."

She stood up and steadied herself against the counter, looking again at the phone. "My fiancé didn't call me. He knew I needed him, and he didn't even call." She frowned. "I was scared to be alone." She paused. "What if that man calls again? Is he still watching?"

"Come here," Brett coaxed, taking her by the hand. "You've had a little too much wine."

He led her to the couch, where he took her in his arms. She laid her head against his chest and started to cry. She wasn't sure exactly why. All her emotions seemed to want to come out in tears. She was mad at John for not responding. She was embarrassed at her own intoxication. She was afraid of men who called in the night to call her a baby killer, afraid of men who painted hateful messages upon the door of her house. She was mad at God for putting HD in her family.

But more than anything else right then and there, she hated herself for wanting so much more than just Brett's arms around her.

He stroked her shoulders and her hair, and told her everything was going to be all right. He promised to stay with her, even when she insisted that he'd done enough and needed to leave.

Minutes passed and her sobs subsided, and in the comfort of Brett's arms, she slept.

John drove on in a daze, not stopping until one in the morning at a Motel 6. He unlocked the door to his room and collapsed on the bed. Nothing seemed real. His excitement over seeing Claire had been exploded by an unseen land mine. He opened his suitcase and laid a stack of papers on the dresser, resources on Huntington's disease that he'd downloaded from the Internet to give to Claire.

In his exhaustion, he began to question reality. Maybe this was all some bad dream. He'd been inseparable from Claire for years back in Brighton. He knew her. Maybe what he'd seen didn't reflect reality. Maybe he'd misunderstood. Maybe this whole mess was a big misinterpretation.

He looked at the phone, and, in spite of the hour, he needed to hear her voice. He wanted to hear it from her. Who was this Brett, and just what did he mean to her?

The phone rang once, twice, six times before he heard an answer. "Hello."

John's heart dropped. The voice was male. He was spending the night.

The voice on the phone continued until John was sure he recognized it. "Hello? Hello?"

John returned the phone to its cradle without speaking. He wanted to tear it from the wall. Instead, he picked up the papers he'd just set on the dresser, slowly crumpled them into a large ball, and dropped them into the wastebasket.

Then he undressed, crawled into bed, and pulled the pillow over his head to shut out everything the world was dishing out.

Oh, God, he prayed. *Let me wake up from this nightmare. What has happened to my Claire?*

Chapter Thirty-Four

laire pried open her eyes at five, jolted into consciousness by her clock radio blaring the weather forecast for Lafayette, Boston, and Cape Cod.

She rose slowly with two sensations battling for prompt attention. Her bladder cried for relief, and her head pounded with every stroke of her pulse. As she looked around the room, a hazy memory of the night before stayed just beyond sharp focus. How had she gotten to her bed? She clutched her clothes. *John's jersey.* She pinched the bridge of her nose and tried to remember changing her clothes. Had Brett helped her undress? Did he see her naked?

Her heart quickened and that made her head pound harder. She attempted to concentrate on what she did remember. A delicious meal, too much wine, conversation and tears, being cradled in Brett's arms. She felt so confused. How did she get to her bed? How did she change her clothes? Was he with her? Was he longing for her like she yearned for him? Did they . . . ?

She touched her undergarments, anxiously searching for evidence of her actions during a night which remained in the blackness beyond memory.

Brett wouldn't have touched her without invitation . . . would he? But she'd had so much to drink . . . and she just couldn't quite remember.

She crept down the stairs and looked at the couch. Brett was sleeping with a blanket pulled up under his chin. Dare she peek to see if he was clothed? But what would it mean if he wasn't? She took a step toward him in the dim light and stepped on an article of clothing. As she reached to pick it up, she felt a stab of dread. It was her bra. Had she undressed in the living room?

Certainly, he would have stayed in my bed, if we had . . . She shook her head. The idea was unthinkable. She'd made a promise to God that she'd remain pure. She massaged her temples. *But alcohol can make you lose your head.* The thought struck as a stone of anxiety crystallized just below her chest.

Claire's thoughts raced. Would Brett have taken a liberty uninvited? Or did she invite him in her intoxication? She was not on any birth control. A pregnancy would ruin her chances at being promoted. As if Dr. Rogers needed another reason to cut her from the program.

And of course family planning for someone at risk for HD was complicated by her children also being at risk. Any child of hers had a one-in-four chance of HD.

She rummaged through her on-call bag to find the ibuprofen. She swallowed four tablets and added two Tylenol for good measure.

She climbed the steps, pulled off John's jersey, and stepped into the shower. A pregnancy would be so unlikely. She doubted that she'd shared a bed with Brett, but a nagging worry remained. *It's not the right time of the month. I couldn't be. Could I?* She held her face up to the water, hoping to wash away her fear, but soap and water didn't have the power to bring back her memory, and no amount of reason could relieve her runaway anxiety.

She'd feel so foolish asking Brett.

And how could she ever share this with John?

A pregnancy would ruin her life. She couldn't handle a baby now. And no one would want to adopt a baby who was at risk for a catastrophic genetic illness. She pushed the thought aside and tried in vain to concentrate on her preparations for work.

There's another good reason to be tested to see if I'm carrying the HD gene. If I am, I should understand that my children may see a little hell on earth.

Claire plodded through the next two days on the Lafayette oncology service, pouring her efforts into patient care and trying not to concentrate on her complicated social and family problems. She felt like a circus juggler, tossing her worries into the air and focusing only on one thing in hand at a time. The balls of her worry were manifold: making it through the pyramid, her risk of HD, her guilt over Sierra Jones's death, her relationship with John, her relationship with Brett, a threatening phone call, defending a malpractice suit, and a possible pregnancy. Anytime any one worry would surface, she would toss another in the air, unable to handle or deal with more than one at a time. It was an unhealthy practice, she realized, and she silently feared that all of the balls would come crashing to the floor at any moment.

On Friday, she met with a malpractice attorney for three hours, going over every possible angle of defense in the Sierra Jones's case. Mr. Peters, the attorney assigned to her case, was a pleasant man in his fifties. He had snow-white hair and his face was overly wrinkled from too many night-time vigils practicing law, and too many hours perfecting his golf swing in the sun. She liked him, but not what he told her. The judge assigned to her case also had to decide the vehicular homicide case against the drunk driver that struck Sierra Jones. The criminal defense for the drunk driver had convinced the judge of the need to try the malpractice case first. The judge, to their delight, pushed for a record-setting pace of evidence discovery in the malpractice case to urge their case forward because of its potential impact on the case of the *State v. Tony Broderick*.

As they reviewed the hospital record, one thing seemed clear. The prosecution must have had personal testimony regarding Claire's failure to watch Sierra Jones's central venous line, as the hospital record did not incriminate her, except to record that she was observing Sierra when her death occurred. To be successful in winning a verdict against her, the prosecution would have to prove that Claire's actions deviated from standard medical practice, and that the deviation from normal care resulted in the harm that the patient experienced. Mr. Peters' first idea was that they could make the jury understand that the potential injury from the disconnection of the central venous line could not be proven to have made a difference in outcome. If need be, he explained, he could gently introduce the idea that Mr. Jones's refusal to allow his daughter to have an autopsy prevented them from being sure of the exact cause of death, and that it was unfair to hold Claire responsible for a death which was inevitable. He would find expert witnesses who would explain the rarity of death due to venous air embolism, and expert witnesses who would explain how easily a patient can die from massive liver injury. He would find an expert radiologist who could carefully go over the CT scan findings to illustrate how severely injured Sierra was, and cast doubt in the jury's mind that she could ever have survived. He would paint a picture of Claire McCall which revealed her to be a product of a superior medical education, an honor student picked because of her credentials to one of the most competitive training institutions in the country. He would offer testimony from her attendings about her competence and care.

The prosecution, Mr. Peters warned, would paint an entirely different picture of Claire. She would have to endure suggestions of her incompetence. She would likely be portrayed as a fresh intern without sufficient experience to handle the situation in front of her. They would call her dangerous, overconfident, and negligent, caring more about staying in the program than treating the ill. The whole process promised to be humiliating and agonizing.

Mr. Peters promised to be with her through it all. During the trial, if the case went that far, he would see to it that Claire could rest in the fact that there should be no surprises. She would be told how to walk, how to speak, what to wear, and where to look. Claire took comfort in knowing Mr. Peters had been in many legal skirmishes through the years, and he would put his experience to work to help her through.

They had six weeks to prepare for the first deposition. There, the opposing teams would have an opportunity to see each other's witnesses, and examine the expert testimony that the opposition had gathered. The depositions gave the prosecution and the defense a chance to see what they were up against, and gave ample opportunity for the case to be settled before it got to court.

When Claire ran into Brett in the hospital cafeteria, he acted toward her as he always did. There was no indication in his behavior to provide a clue to a significant change in their relationship. She sat opposite him at a small oval table and picked at the salad she'd selected.

It was time to put her fears to rest. She decided to broach the subject.

"Thanks for the wonderful dinner the other night." She looked down. "I'm afraid I didn't behave myself the way a proper hostess should."

He shook his head and smiled. "Ridiculous."

"I don't tolerate alcohol very well."

He raised his eyebrows. "Oh?"

"Stop being coy. You know what I'm talking about. I'm embarrassed by the way I acted. I want to apologize."

"You don't need to do that. I had a wonderful evening."

Claire tapped her fork. He wasn't offering any helpful information.

"Did you enjoy your time after we ate?" She studied his face for a reaction.

He was unflinching. "Of course." He leaned forward. "What's this all about, Claire? Are you upset about something?"

"I'm upset that I woke up in the morning and I don't have a clue how I got to bed. I went to sleep in your arms and . . ."

He smiled mischievously. "You don't remember what came next?" He laughed, then played hurt. "My ego is crushed. You don't remember?"

"Remember what?" She spoke with urgency, but quietly so the other lunchtime diners couldn't overhear.

He shrugged. "Don't worry, Claire, you were the best."

"Don't play games with me. I want to know what happened. I changed clothes somehow. Did you help me? Did you put me to bed?"

He chuckled. "You honestly don't remember?"

Claire could see that Brett was having entirely too much fun with this conversation. In fact, it made her very uncomfortable that he was having such fun at her expense. "I don't remember a thing. Brett," she pleaded, "tell me the truth."

He put his arms behind his head and stretched. "You told me I was wonderful, too." He paused, leaning forward. "The only problem is that you kept calling me John."

"I did not!"

He laughed heartily.

"This isn't funny, Brett. You're lying."

"You'll never know."

If her eyes had been scalpels, Brett would have been dissected. She pushed back her chair, still boring in on his face with her eyes. "Why, you—"

"Stay here, Claire. I was just joking."

She took a deep breath and tried to keep from raising her voice. "I thought it was sweet for you to treat me so nice, making dinner, giving me flowers. You acted like a perfect gentleman. But you're not being a gentleman now. I want to know what happened. And you're playing with me."

"Claire, I said I was joking."

He paused, and she studied his serious expression. She was seeing a side of Brett that she didn't like, a side that didn't seem to mind seeing her squirm.

Brett smiled and added, "I was joking. You never called me John."

"Brett!"

He appeared to soften, perhaps finally sensing Claire's rising temperature. "Okay, okay, I'll tell you the truth." His eyes were clear, and his voice low, wavering once or twice, thick with emotion. "You've got to know how I feel about you. I've wanted you since the moment I saw you that day at the beach. But try as I may, every time I make a move, you've turned me away. But not the other night. After dinner, you were the one making the moves. You made it abundantly clear what you wanted from me."

Claire blushed. Was he telling the truth?

Brett continued. "But I'm no fool, Claire. I'm at this university hospital for one reason, and one reason only. Because I want to be a surgeon. And sleeping with a woman who only wants me when she's drunk sounds like a problem to me." This time he stood up, his face still serious. "I'll be seeing you. I need to get back to the lab."

"Wait, Brett," she called to his back, but he kept walking and disappeared through the cafeteria exit.

Claire stared at her uneaten salad, amazed at what had just transpired. She'd gone from anxiety, to anger at Brett, to guilt for her behavior. Her self-accusations began. *You were angry because you thought he might have taken advantage of you, and you come to find out that you were the one playing the part of the aggressor.*

Wasn't that just like a McCall, acting deplorably under the influence of alcohol? For all these years she'd held up her righteous little war against drinking, and then she fell right into the same trap. Some Christian she was.

She was a lot more like her father than she'd ever admit.

She looked around, relieved that the crowd of people around her seemed too consumed with their own lunches to be observing her.

She stood and took her tray of uneaten food to a conveyor belt where it would be taken back to the kitchen. She wasn't hungry.

She was due in the OR to assist on a laparoscopic cholecystectomy. She was assigned to run the camera, which meant she needed to concentrate every moment to keep the video camera centered on the action. If the cameraperson drifted off, thinking of something else, everyone in the room immediately knew, as the video monitor would show a picture somewhere other than where the surgeon was working. Claire performed flawlessly, disliking only the way her chief resident elbowed her in the chest every time he changed his grasp of the gallbladder.

At five, she gathered with the oncology team for teaching rounds. When she arrived, she found Pepper entertaining the medical students with a rubber Foley catheter. Normally used as a flexible tube to drain the urinary bladder, Pepper had invented other unique uses for the device. He slid the open tip of the catheter beneath his scrub tops into his left armpit, trapping it against his body with his arm. He put the other end in his mouth and blew. The resultant raspberry noise was a brilliant imitation of forceful colon gas expulsion. The male medical students snickered. Claire rolled her eyes and snapped, "Grow up."

Pepper only grinned. "I can play 'The Star Spangled Banner' with a chest tube. Want to hear?"

The Foley catheter disappeared when Dr. Rogers arrived. During attending rounds, the interns and patients endured a litany of questions about cancers, the treatment, and the potential complications of surgical therapy. Pepper was on top of his game and couldn't be stumped. He even quoted a recent publication when answering a question about breast cancer. Claire was tired and distracted by hunger. She bobbled a question about how to handle metastatic colon cancer, but came through when asked about melanoma.

After rounds, they sat through a lecture by a visiting professor from Boston who talked about pheochromocytomas, something Claire would see on the board exams but would be lucky to treat once in a lifetime of private practice.

Claire drove home with her spirit showing a dramatic limp. She was scheduled to scrub on a pancreatic resection in the morning, and she knew it was important to read up on the procedure, especially since the chairman, Dr. Rogers, was the attending. Since the interns each only got one month on his service, it was of critical importance to shine when you had the chance. She wouldn't be doing the procedure as an intern, but all of the questions would be directed to the intern first, before the chief resident, who would actually be doing the case. Although a medical student would be present, the chairman would ignore him, considering his presence equivalent to a mechanical retractor. He spoke to a medical student only if he relaxed on the job.

But she felt like sleeping. Perhaps she could get up thirty minutes early to read about pancreatic cancer. Hopefully, skimming the high points would prevent her from making a fool of herself.

The mailbox contained a rare piece of personal snail mail, a letter from John Cerelli. Immediately, her heart quickened. News from home was like an oasis to a desert traveler. She collapsed on the couch and ripped open the letter.

My dearest Claire,

I am writing with a heavy heart. I've never been very good with spoken words, so I thought I'd put what I need to say on paper, in hopes that you will understand.

I have cried enough in the last twenty-four hours, tears I thought I was too much of a man to shed. I know all about Brett, and I am releasing you from our engagement. He certainly seems to respect you, at least enough to encourage me to talk this out with you in private, and avoid an ugly confrontation with all of us present.

I'm sure by now you know of my surprise visit to Lafayette, but I suppose the surprise was all mine. I never expected to find a man living at your place, and I never dreamed when I gave you a diamond that it would sit unworn on your desk.

I guess if the truth be known, I sensed your ambivalence from the moment you accepted it. I suppose I was just a dreamer to think I could hold such a prize as you from such a long distance and with the demands of surgery taxing you on a daily basis.

I'm thankful for the time we had together. Don't cry for me. I know God will continue to work out his plan for me.

If I have one regret, it is for the way I treated you. I was fooled into thinking that sex could be okay for our relationship, that our relationship was different, special, and that certainly God didn't demand a marriage license for us to enjoy what he'd created. Boy, was I wrong! I've opened a Pandora's box of temptation for myself and stolen a gift you can never regain. Can you ever forgive me?

I'd appreciate having the ring back. I hope that asking doesn't seem too tacky, but I know you're not wearing it when I'm not around anyway.

Sincerely,
John Cerelli

Claire's head began to swim. John Cerelli had been here? John talked to Brett? She didn't understand. What had Brett told him? Why didn't Brett tell her John was here?

She thought back to the evening she'd spent with Brett. Obviously John must have shown up before she came home and found Brett preparing dinner. She dropped her head into her hands. Unless John showed up after she passed out. If that was the case, what would he have seen? Her on the couch with Brett? Or worse? She remembered how Brett had described her behavior to him that night. The thought that John could have witnessed that kind of drunken behavior horrified her. *Oh God, how did I ever get this so messed up?*

She read the letter a second time. There was no mention of seeing her and he specifically stated, "I'm sure by now you know of my surprise visit to Lafayette." Certainly that meant he didn't see her, didn't it?

She ran her hand through her hair and sighed. What would John have seen if he showed up late, after Claire was in her own bed? Her bra on the floor? Evidence of a romantic candlelight dinner?

She felt sick. And guilty. She couldn't exactly call John and ask him what he saw. Maybe she could call Brett and ask him. But he wasn't any too happy with her either.

Oh well, it was the lesser of two evils. She picked up the phone and called Brett. After two rings, his answering machine picked up, and Claire pushed the "Off" button.

She took a deep breath and dialed John. She had to talk this out.

"Hello."

"John." She paused. "It's Claire."

He was silent for a moment. She heard the TV quieting down, as if he was walking out of the den. "Yeah." His voice was sober, definitely not enthusiastic.

She wasn't sure where to start. "I got your letter."

"Good."

Great. This is so like John. He clams up on the phone. This is serious, and he's going to give me one-word answers.

"John, I don't think you understand about Brett."

"I understand enough."

"John, it's not what it seems. I—"

"Claire, I saw what was going on. I saw the romantic dinner. I saw my ring. I even called back later in the night when I couldn't quite believe what I'd seen. And he answered the phone." He coughed nervously. "I understand plenty."

"John, I didn't sleep with him. We had dinner—"

"A candlelight dinner, Claire. With wine. Do we really have to go over this? I think my letter should be a gracious enough response to this situation."

"But you've got it wrong."

"Do I? Did you want him to stay?"

She sighed. "Yes, but—"

"Look, Claire, you don't really have to tell me about this. I'm not really in the mood to hear about this."

"When did you show up?"

"Right before dinner, I guess."

That relieved her a little. "And just what did Brett tell you?"

"Claire, I really don't feel like going over this."

"You assume you know what's going on. That's not fair, Cerelli. You don't trust me."

"Are you wearing my ring?"

Her right hand grasped her left ring finger. She still hadn't put the ring on since Brett had cleaned it for her in the lab. "I do wear it. I just—"

"Save it, Claire. Engagement is a commitment, just like marriage. It's to one person. And I'm not about to jump into marriage if you are acting this way now."

"Me? You don't trust me. And the last time I checked, trust is a pretty important component of a relationship's foundation."

"Trust? How can you twist this and blame me for this?"

"John, I'm not blaming you. I just want you to stop jumping to conclusions and hear me out."

She heard John breathing into the phone. "Okay," he snapped. "Tell me your side."

"He surprised me with the dinner. I didn't know he was going to do it. It wasn't my idea."

"Did you like it?"

"Sure, but women like that kind of treatment."

"But you're not supposed to get that treatment from anyone except me. That's the deal."

"So what was I to do? Tell him to pack up and get out? He was just doing me a nice favor. He's a surgery resident. He knows what internship is like."

"Why does he have a key?"

"He doesn't."

"He told me you gave him one. Otherwise, how could he have gotten in to surprise you? And just because he cooks you a meal doesn't mean he gets to have a sleepover."

"It's not what you think, John. Remember what I told you about the little girl who died in the CT scanner?"

He sighed again. "Yes, but what's that—"

"Let me finish. Her father is suing me for malpractice. And someone called my house the other night and called me a baby killer, and said he'd be watching."

"Who? The father?"

"I don't know. The caller wouldn't identify himself. But it's made me so scared that staying in my house alone frightens me."

"So I guess Brett is just being a good Samaritan and volunteering to stay overnight to protect you, huh? Give me a break! He has other intentions, Claire."

"We don't sleep together, John."

"Just what do you do after a romantic dinner with wine?"

"You know what happens when I drink wine. Remember that New Year's Eve party at Amy and Larry's? One glass of wine and I—"

"I remember, Claire. That's what scares me." He paused. "Okay, just what did you do?"

She bit her bottom lip and squeezed her eyes shut. "I don't remember exactly. I think I just passed out on the couch."

"Oh, that's rich. This Brett has eyes for you, and you get drunk, and he's got you right where he wants you."

"I told you I didn't sleep with him."

"And you also said you don't remember what you did. How do you know?"

"I asked Brett."

"You asked him? You were that unsure?" John's voice was booming.

Claire started to cry. "I'm sorry, John. I didn't want to hurt you."

John's breathing was heavy in the phone for a moment. This conversation wasn't going the way she wanted.

"I'm sorry, too," he responded. "I wouldn't have wanted it to be this way."

"Why don't you come back up? We can talk this out."

"It seems to me that you have all the support you need right there."

"John, don't do this. Don't push me away."

"I'm not pushing, Claire. I'm holding you with open arms. You're the one who chose to run away from Virginia. You're the one who chose to walk away from me—"

"I'm not walking away—"

"Having a candlelight dinner with your doctor friend is walking away." John's voice was strained, and his voice choked when he tried to speak again. "Send me the ring, Claire. I've still got enough self-respect to not allow myself to be mistreated."

"This is your decision, John."

"No, Claire, you made these choices. I'm just requesting that you stop playing games with my heart."

She hung her head. She was exhausted. John was hurt. And as much as she hated to admit it, even if she had been faithful not to actually sleep with Brett, she hadn't been faithful in her heart. "Okay."

The finality of the decision hung with sober silence until John spoke again. "Have a good year, Claire. I'll pray you find your dream."

With that, she heard a click, and the line went dead.

Claire stood blankly staring at the phone, as her own anger erupted. "God!" she cried as she smashed the phone to the counter. "I thought this dream was your calling. But just what will it cost?"

Her head sank to the countertop next to the sink and she began to weep.

Winter struck Lafayette in mid-November and continued dealing out fierce blows until even thick-blooded Northerners prayed for relief.

Back in Stoney Creek, Della formed an HD support group which met on the first Monday of each month. Margo finished the genetics testing program in January and received the news that she was negative on the coldest day the Apple Valley had seen in three years. Two weeks later, Kyle was back and Margo bought a new minivan. "Survivor guilt," a common response to testing negative to Huntington's disease, was not part of Margo's experience. She left a curt phone message on Claire's answering machine telling her that everything was wonderful and that Margo didn't need to think about the family curse being passed through her genes, at least.

Clay's life continued to disintegrate. He made it to work on most days, but one day in midwinter, he showed up at the cabinet shop visibly intoxicated. When his boss sent him home, he went instead to a local airstrip, where he demanded to go skydiving. A fight with a pilot ensued, and Clay spent the day in the county jail sobering up, and now faced charges of assault and battery, public drunkenness, and violation of his restricted driver's license. Clay continued to assume that his eventual manifestation of HD was inevitable, and refused all urgings by Della and even by Dr. Jenkins to get genetic testing. Why should he pay to find out something he already knew? And why shouldn't he drink? He was going to die young anyway.

Claire forged ahead through a month of orthopedic surgery, a second month of sitting hearts, and a month of plastics. In the dead of winter, she took the ABSITE (American Board Surgery Inservice Training Exam) and scored second among her intern group, having been edged out by Dr. Chris "Pepper" Bearss for the top spot and an opportunity to stand up in grand rounds for Dr. Rogers to see. For two weeks following the exam, Brett, who was taking the ABSITE for the second year in a row, seemed particularly bummed. Claire suspected he hadn't done well, but didn't want to upset him by bringing it up.

After she sent back John's ring, Claire spent some time with Brett, but she was careful to stay focused and cautious not to get too close. Brett seemed to accept his role as friendly confidant with limited happiness, and Claire could feel his desire to move to the next level. She made it clear she wanted some space before another romance. She wanted time to focus on climbing the pyramid. But she could sense his interest, and privately enjoyed the lustful way he gazed at her when he thought she was unaware. They still played, "If I were the program director," and Brett assured Claire that she would be chosen, but anguished over his own performance, and convinced himself that he was in spot number nine. He needed only one person in the top eight to fail. Or he needed to score big on a grant which would allow him to stay in Dr. Rogers' lab for one more year so he could compete with next year's intern group.

Claire wasn't convinced of her security in the residency. She easily counted eight other competent interns, and feared that her upcoming malpractice suit would forever cast her in a negative light with Dr. Rogers. The selections for second-year slots would be made in May, so those cut from the program would have a few months to scramble for jobs elsewhere. That meant that Claire had only two months until the first cut. Two months to find out if her dream would stay alive.

Communication with John was infrequent and strained. For Claire, it was painful and left her feeling hollow. It was worst during her nights at home. She wore his football jersey for two weeks after sending back his diamond. After that, she tossed it to the floor in the back of her closet and kicked it behind the remnants of a college genetics project on blood-typing.

Without John's urging for her to get an HD test, Claire put the issue of genetics testing on the back burner. For the most part, HD was her own private family secret, and she functioned around being at risk the way a driver tries to ignore a dirty windshield. The question was always there, but disregarded. She didn't have the time or the emotional energy to contemplate a positive test result. When Margo tested negative, Claire rejoiced, but quietly feared that at least one of Wally's children statistically should have HD, and if it wasn't Margo, her own chances seemed higher. And so Claire busied herself with her hospital work and desperately tried not to think about HD.

But when she stumbled, or dropped an object, or lost her train of thought, or did any of a myriad of the small imperfect things that characterize normal human life, she caught herself wondering, *Could I end up dancing like Daddy?* The thought terrified her, saddened her, and fanned a faint glow of anger toward God that threatened to become a fire of resentment.

The steps leading toward a malpractice trial were agonizingly slow, and to Claire's horror, it appeared the trial would be under way right about the time Dr. Rogers selected the second-year residents. Witnesses were deposed and examined by both the plaintiff's attorney and the defense. During the depositions, the attorneys had a chance to question the witnesses, and hopefully gain a better understanding of the case and avoid surprises at the trial. Present at each deposition, Sierra Jones's parents would huddle quietly with Ramsey Plank on one side, and Claire sat with her attorney, Franklin Peters, hospital attorney Peter Ondrachek, and Emmit Grabowski, CEO of Lafayette University Hospital, on the other.

In November, Ramsey Plank questioned the medical experts that the defense had gathered. In December, Franklin Peters deposed the experts that Ramsey Plank had garnered. In March, Ramsey had deposed Claire McCall, and agreed that Franklin could also question the plaintiffs, Roger and Celia Jones.

Part Four

Chapter Thirty-Five

March 2001

Claire hated depositions. She sat at the conference table with her attorney and yawned. "Ramsey should be here any moment. He's punctual to a fault."

"When it suits him, he is."

Claire wrinkled her nose. "I'm still not so sure I understand all this. Why does Ramsey want to talk to me? Why not depose someone like Beatrice Hayes? I'm sure she'd be glad to talk about me."

"You've told me yourself that you suspect Beatrice has already been giving information to Ramsey. It's clear someone did. Otherwise, I have my doubts as to whether we'd be here today. You only need to depose witnesses who won't talk to you otherwise. If Beatrice is feeding information to Ramsey already, there's no need for him to examine her in a deposition."

Claire nodded.

Franklin Peters smoothed the lapels of his gray suit and explained to Claire what she could expect of the deposition.

A few moments later, they looked up as the door opened and Ramsey Plank escorted in Mr. and Mrs. Jones. Claire stood and shook Ramsey's hand, but the Jones stood back. Celia looked at the carpet and clutched her husband's arm. When Claire briefly made eye contact with Roger, he quickly diverted his gaze to his wife. Claire studied Roger Jones for a moment, being careful not to stare or appear angry. But inside her plastic pleasant appearance, her stomach churned. *Have you been threatening me, Mr. Jones?*

Claire would go first. She quickly found out just how much Mr. Plank already knew. For the first ten minutes, all Claire had an opportunity to do was confirm the educational data that he had discovered. Claire relaxed. Mr. Plank was pleasant enough and he continuously apologized for asking probing questions.

"You are an intern, Dr. McCall?"

"Yes."

"And you were completing your first month of internship when Sierra Jones became your patient, is that right?"

"Yes."

"Dr. McCall, how many pediatric patients have you taken care of?"

Claire shrugged. "I don't know. I've cared for dozens of children while doing my medical school pediatrics rotation."

Ramsey smiled. "How many pediatric trauma cases have you managed?"

"A few. I don't know the exact number."

"Have you cared for any pediatric trauma cases outside Lafayette University Hospital?"

"Yes, a few during my surgery rotations at Brighton University."

"But you were a student then, were you not? And therefore you were not really responsible for the patient's care, is that right?"

"I learned from them, and helped take care of them, and I was a responsible medical student, but no, I was not solely responsible for their care."

"Dr. McCall, how many pediatric trauma patients did you care for during the month of July?"

"I'm not sure."

Ramsey pulled out a computer printout. "Let me refresh your memory. During the nights that you were on call during the month of July, the trauma team admitted twenty-two patients under the age of twenty-one, but only four patients under the age of twelve. And the other intern, Dr. Beatrice Hayes, who shared your night call, did the workups on the other three. That only leaves one patient under the age of twelve on whom you did the initial workup."

Claire shifted in her seat uncomfortably.

"And that one patient would be Sierra Jones. Only one. Could my information be correct?"

Her mouth went dry. "I suppose."

Ramsey seemed satisfied with that knowledge and opened his briefcase. He lifted a few papers. "Here is a copy of the health insurance application that you filled out when you became an intern at this university." He held it up to Claire. "Do you recognize this as your handwriting?"

"Yes."

"Dr. McCall, do you possess any health difficulty that could in any way hamper your ability to function as a physician?"

"No."

Franklin caught her eye and wrinkled his forehead as if to say, *Where's he going with this, Claire?*

Ramsey leaned forward. "Did you knowingly omit any information about your personal medical history from this insurance application?"

Claire shook her head. "Of course not."

"Is there any part of your past medical history, such as your family history, which you have intentionally kept hidden from the university because you felt it might damage your chances to continue in this program?"

Claire looked at Franklin. *How could Ramsey know about Huntington's disease?* She felt warm and longed to loosen the collar of her new navy dress.

Ramsey persisted. "Are there any illnesses that run in the McCall family?"

Franklin Peters shifted in his seat. "Ramsey, I object. This can't be relevant to this case."

Ramsey shook his head. "We agreed on the format for this deposition. There were to be no objections."

Franklin sighed. He tapped his pen against the table and looked at Claire. "Answer the question, Claire."

"There is a genetic illness that runs in the McCall family," she reported mechanically. "But I did not know of it when I started this internship and filled out the application you have in your hand."

"And it is?"

"Huntington's disease," Claire answered quietly.

The hospital attorney, Ondrachek, shuffled a stack of papers in front of him. Emmit Grabowski, the CEO, cleared his throat and glared at the hospital attorney.

Franklin stood up. "Could we have a recess?"

Ramsey smiled again. "Sure."

Franklin Peters shut the door to the small conference room where he had retreated with Claire. "What's Ramsey getting at? What is Huntington's disease?"

Claire paced the room. "A genetic illness which results in mental deterioration and loss of ability to control voluntary muscle movement. It usually has its onset in midlife. It has a dominant inheritance pattern, so that there is a fifty-fifty chance of children of affected parents inheriting the disease." She pulled up a chair and sat. "My father has it."

Mr. Peters frowned. "Do you have it, Claire?"

"I've never been tested. But I'm not showing any signs."

"This disease, it would prohibit you from practicing medicine?"

Claire nodded soberly. "Definitely. But there is no reason a person with Huntington's disease couldn't practice successfully until symptoms began showing." She leaned forward until she held her forehead in her hands. "But how does he know this? No one in Lafayette knows this." She paused. "Except one other resident." She shook her head. "And he wouldn't tell."

"Ramsey has his ways. He probably sent an investigator to your hometown or something. These guys have big money on the line here. Ramsey's cut on twenty million dollars could be huge."

"But this is irrelevant. What does this have to do with my performance on Sierra's case?"

"Nothing really, but Ramsey could use this in a few ways. First, he is setting you up in front of the jury to look as if deceit is part of your character. If he can convince them that you are less than honest in other areas of your life, he can make the jury suspicious of other things you say during trial. If Ramsey can convince them that you are a woman who would do anything to stay in the program, even deceive your own program director, he can make them question whether you might be hiding facts to make yourself look good in this trial as well." He took a deep breath. "Have you been keeping this a secret, Claire?"

She kept her head in her hands and focused on the tabletop. "Yes." She looked up. "I didn't know about the disease until I was already an intern. I have tried to keep this from Dr. Rogers, because I didn't want him to think I may practice only for a few years." She stood to pace again. "But I really don't think it's an issue here. I'm not showing symptoms. There's no way I could function at my present level if I had symptomatic HD."

Franklin scratched his chin. "People with this disease have intelligence problems?"

"A serious decline." She hesitated. "Mr. Peters, there is no way I'm showing symptoms—"

"But that's the second way Ramsey might try to use this to his advantage. If he can introduce the idea that you are already showing subtle signs of this disease, he can make them think that you knowingly put this child at risk by assuming her care. He can make them wonder whether you made a mistake because of this disease."

"That's ridiculous. I hadn't even diagnosed my father with HD at the time I cared for Sierra Jones. I would never knowingly put my patients at risk."

Franklin tilted his head suddenly and his eyes brightened. He held up a finger. Claire imagined seeing a lightbulb going on above his head. "What did you say? You diagnosed your father with HD?"

"Well, basically, yes."

Her attorney opened up a yellow legal pad and began scribbling notes. He looked at his watch. "Okay. I want you to tell me everything. There's got to be a way for us to turn the tables on Ramsey here." He tapped his pen against the table. "I'll probably want to ask you some more questions in front of Ramsey. That's a bit unusual for a deposition, since you're my client, but I think it might be beneficial in this case for Ramsey to see what he's getting into. It might discourage him from his present tactics." The corner of his mouth lifted slightly, showing the first hint of a smile. "And maybe, just maybe, it will help the Jones to understand you better too."

Emmit Grabowski was a hulk of a man, a suit-and-tie hospital administrator who'd bought a Harley during a midlife crisis and smoked Cuban cigars when his wife was sipping banana fruit smoothies at their private health spa. He tugged at his silk tie and grabbed Peter Ondrachek by the elbow, ushering him into his office during the recess. "Where's Ramsey going with this?"

"I haven't the foggiest. And I suspect Franklin is clueless as well, and he's probably giving that intern the once-over for keeping secrets."

"I don't like it." Emmit imitated Ramsey Plank's plastic grin. "Every time that weasel smiles, I just know he's up to something."

The hospital attorney nodded. "But don't be too quick to despair. Ramsey may have uncovered something worth listening to. If the intern really has deceived the university, it may give us a way to save face."

"What, use the girl as a scapegoat?"

Peter smiled. "It's too early to tell, but we need to listen carefully to what Ramsey says. We'll have to stand with our intern unless Ramsey makes the jury believe she's a real danger to patients."

"Then what?"

"Emmit, we have to think about the university. That's what I'm paid to do. It might be necessary, however unpleasant, to sacrifice the intern in order for the university to save face."

Emmit shook his head. "I won't enjoy letting her go." He rubbed his hand through his silver hair. "It doesn't help that she's so pretty."

"Really." The attorney lifted the corner of his mouth. "I'd like her to be my doctor."

"Not me," Emmit scowled. "Give me some ugly old man for a physician. Just let Dr. McCall check me for hernias, and I'd probably have a heart attack right then and there."

"You'd die happy and you know it."

The CEO chuckled. "Come on, Franklin," he spoke to no one in the room. "Let's finish this recess before I admit something I'll regret."

When they returned from the recess, Ramsey stood and looked intently at Claire. "Could you tell me if there is any test available for Huntington's disease?"

"Yes."

He chuckled. "Would you tell me?"

"There is a genetic test to determine who will develop the disease."

"Have you taken such a test?"

"No."

"Don't you think it would be prudent to be tested? Certainly you would want to protect your patients should your brain begin to deteriorate."

Claire risked a glance at Mr. Jones. His gaze was pure steel. With his jaw clenched, he sat forward with his eyes locked on Claire. She cleared her throat and answered the question. "Perhaps, but it is a personal choice I've made not to be tested for now. I am not showing any symptoms of the disease, and I am not a risk to my patients."

"How do you know? Have you been examined by a specialist to determine this?"

"No." Claire made no elaborations.

"So it is a personal choice?"

"Yes."

"But shouldn't you take a test which has the chance to put to rest our doubts about whether this disease could be affecting your performance even now?"

"No."

Ramsey tapped his fingers on the table. "A private choice? One you've chosen not to share with your superiors?"

"Yes. And one that has no bearing on my current performance," Claire added with her eyes glued to Ramsey's.

With that, the attorney declined to ask Claire any further questions. He seemed content to have raised the issues, and confirmed his suspicions that Claire's secret family life might work to his advantage.

"If you don't mind," Franklin said, "I would like to ask Dr. McCall a few questions of my own, for the record and for clarification." He looked at Ramsey, who nodded professionally.

"Dr. McCall, could you explain Huntington's disease to us?"

Claire nodded and gave a detailed answer.

"It's a rare disease?"

"Yes."

"And yet it was you who made the diagnosis of Huntington's disease in your own father, was it not? And you made this diagnosis of this rare disease during your internship as a relatively fresh young physician. I'd say that shows remarkable diagnostic skill for an intern."

"Thank you."

"And when did you become aware of this disease in your father?"

"After I began my internship."

"And therefore after you filled out those insurance forms that Mr. Plank showed you earlier today."

"Correct. I filled out all of the forms completely and honestly, with no intended deception."

"And you've made a personal choice not to be tested. Can you elaborate?"

"Huntington's is a horrible disease, and I'm not ready to accept knowing I would get a disease that has no known cure. I'd rather not know. It's a personal choice."

"Help us understand, Dr. McCall. The test would reveal only the presence or absence of a gene which could cause a disease in later life, is that right?"

Claire nodded.

"Answer verbally for the record."

"Yes."

"So, since the disease cannot be cured, the test, in effect, would have no ability to change destiny, is that right?"

"The test changes nothing. It only tells me whether I will later get the disease."

"So you've made a personal choice. But of course, if you had signs of the disease, you'd get tested to avoid any concerns about your ability to care for patients?"

"Of course."

"Dr. McCall, I know you are a humble woman, but would you please tell me about your recent board preparation exam which is given to residents in training to ready them for the American Board of Surgery exam?"

"Sure. I scored in the ninety-second percentile of all surgery residents in the country."

"All surgery residents? Certainly you mean among interns."

"I mean among all surgery residents, even chief residents in their last year of training." Claire smiled. She had been coached well. "Would you like to see a copy of my test scores?"

"That won't be necessary." He paused and looked at Mr. Plank and the plaintiffs, before gazing back at Claire. "Tell me, Dr. McCall, is there any way a person with Huntington's disease could pull off an exceptional score like that?"

"Absolutely not."

Franklin nodded and looked at Ramsey. "I have no further questions." He leaned over and whispered to Claire, "That should keep him from harping on your family history at trial."

Next, it was Franklin's turn to examine Celia and Roger Jones. When he suggested that he needed to ask a few questions, Mr. Jones shifted in his seat. "We aren't on trial here," Jones barked.

"But there are important issues that need some clarification," Mr. Peters responded, looking at Mr. Plank.

Mr. Jones huffed and shook his head. Ramsey leaned toward him and whispered. Claire could see Mr. Jones opening and shutting his fist as if he were ready to enter a boxing ring. Finally, she heard him respond, "Okay, okay, but make sure you realize I don't like this."

Mr. Peters was gentle and apologetic. He spoke to Celia first. "Mrs. Jones, I know this must be very painful for you to talk about, and I'm sorry to have to bring it up, but I need to ask you a few questions."

Celia looked down and nodded.

"Mrs. Jones, you have heard the previous testimony of the expert witnesses involved in defending Dr. McCall and Lafayette University Hospital. You understand that the extensive liver trauma suffered by your little girl is associated with a high chance of dying."

Mrs. Jones stared at the table.

"Mrs. Jones, you do understand that, do you not?"

"Yes," she said quietly.

"And you understand, again from expert testimony, that the complication of air being pulled into a central intravenous line is rarely a fatal event."

"But it can be fatal, you know that too, Mr. Peters."

He nodded quietly. "I know. But there is a critical question at stake here. In order to find my client guilty of malpractice, we have to prove that my client's actions deviated from the standard of care, and that if a deviation occurred, that deviation resulted in harm to her patient, your daughter, Sierra." He paused. "It is a horrible experience to lose a loved one. I can't imagine your sorrow. But it is also a horrible experience to be accused of causing such a horror. And there is a way to have determined for certain whether your daughter died from liver trauma directly, or whether the disconnection of the IV could have contributed. An autopsy could have been performed." He lifted his hand toward Claire. "And then we'd know for sure. But as it is, the question remains unanswered." He turned to Celia Jones. "Is it true that Dr. Overby approached you to request an autopsy examination of your daughter?"

"Yes."

"And is it true that you declined such an examination?"

"Yes."

"Can you tell us why?"

Celia pushed her fist to her mouth and steadied her voice. "Sierra had been through too much. The autopsy wouldn't bring back my baby," she sobbed.

"It was a personal choice, was it not?"

"Yes."

"And the outcome would have no power to change destiny. It wouldn't bring Sierra back."

Celia nodded. "I couldn't put her through it."

"I understand your feelings. But Dr. Overby explained that an autopsy could have answered the questions of exactly why Sierra died, did he not?"

"Yes."

"And you understood the reason the autopsy was requested?"

Celia nodded. "Of course. But I didn't want anyone carving on my baby girl."

"And yet, because an autopsy was denied, we will never know for sure why Sierra died, and the whole basis for this suit rests on the assumption that my client's actions were responsible for her death." With that statement hanging in the air, Franklin Peters sat down and opened his briefcase.

"I'd like to ask a few questions of Mr. Jones," Franklin added. "In the week following your daughter's death, you returned to the emergency room at Lafayette University Hospital to find Dr. McCall, is that right?"

Roger Jones clenched his teeth and looked at Ramsey Plank. Plank nodded. Roger spoke. "Yeah, I wanted to talk to her."

"I have witnesses who described the incident to me, and I want to see if I understand correctly. On that day, did you indeed claim that Dr. McCall had killed your baby?"

"I may have said that. I was angry. I just lost my daughter."

Franklin lifted a paper as if to read from it. "And you also were heard to make the statements, 'Someone's going to pay,' and 'I'll see to it that you go back to Virginia where you belong.' Is that accurate?"

Ramsey's eyes widened with alarm. Obviously he hadn't been told of the encounter. He stood up. "Come on, Franklin, my clients are not on trial here."

"You're exactly right, *Ramsey*," he responded, emphasizing his first name just as Ramsey had done. "But this deposition will help us to understand that perhaps the client's anger and desire for vengeance, and not my client's actions, are the real reasons for this suit."

"Ridiculous," Ramsey snorted.

"Please answer the question, Mr. Jones. Did you make the statements to Dr. McCall?"

"Yes. And I'm sorry," he added, looking toward Claire.

"And have you had any contact with my client since that time?"

Roger Jones shifted in his seat. "No."

"Mr. Jones, someone has been threatening my client, calling her on the telephone, saying she killed a baby."

"News gets around, I guess."

"Mr. Jones, have you made any phone calls to my client?"

"No."

Franklin paced a bit, then sat down and sorted his papers, clearing his voice once or twice. Claire figured he wanted to ask more questions and probably doubted Mr. Jones's word but didn't want to appear to be badgering him, even if they weren't in front of a jury.

Mr. Jones stood up and pointed a finger at Franklin's chest. "I know what you're trying to do. You're going to try to hide the truth. This doctor didn't have the training to be watching my baby, and her mistake cost Sierra her life!"

Ramsey scrambled to his feet to restrain Mr. Jones. But with Celia holding one elbow and Ramsey reaching for the other, Roger continued. "Go ahead with your fancy legal defense. God will see that the truth comes out!"

Claire sunk in her chair. *God?* Coming from Roger Jones, the reference to God stunned her. *I thought God was on* my *side.*

She felt the blood drain from her face. *You are on my side, aren't you, God?*

Franklin Peters didn't back down, but returned Jones's challenge with a voice steady and calm. "I certainly hope so, Mr. Jones. I certainly hope so."

Chapter Thirty-Six

laire stopped by Dr. Rogers' lab, hoping to see Brett before she headed home. She knocked gently at the door. "Hey, pal, how's the grant search?"

He shook his head. "I got an answer today." He held up a letter.

"Well?"

"Rejected again."

Claire frowned. "I'm sorry."

"Not half as sorry as I am. I might as well pack my bags. Rogers will never rank me in the elite eight."

"You'll probably get my spot," she groaned. "Not that I had one to give."

"Bad day?"

"I was deposed by Ramsey Plank. He made me feel like a fool. Somehow he got the data from the trauma registry or something. He told me Sierra Jones was the only pediatric trauma patient I took care of all year. I didn't even realize that until he pointed it out."

"Ouch."

"That's not the worst. Somehow, he found out about my father and Huntington's disease. He basically alluded to the idea that I might have the disease myself, and may not be suited to be an intern."

"How did your attorney handle that?"

"I think he was upset that I hadn't shared it with him, but honestly, I didn't think it was relevant." She sighed. "Now Rogers is going to find out for sure."

"There is a way out."

"What?"

"Get tested."

"Right. That will only help if I test negative. If I test positive, what are my chances of staying in the program?"

"Why would you want to? Why go through the torture?"

"You know why," she said, folding her slender frame onto Brett's desktop. "Because I love this stuff more than anything else." She smiled as her mind drifted momentarily. "I saw Dr. Keim do a rectus abdominus free flap to create a new breast for a cancer victim yesterday. It was incredible."

"So what are you going to do?"

"I don't know. The same thing I always do. Work hard and try not to think about HD or being sued."

"How was Mr. Jones?"

"Out of control. I just sat there watching him today, trying to understand what's inside his head. I'm sure he's the one who called me." She shook her head. "My attorney asked him about it, just to see his reaction. I thought he was going to come over the table for a second. He accused Franklin Peters of trying to hide the truth."

"I wish I could have seen that."

"It wasn't pretty." She sighed. "My attorney thinks we should settle the case before trial. I think he's worried that I'll collapse on the stand and say something that will ruin our case."

"What do you want?"

"I want this to be over."

He reached forward and tapped her leg with the side of his hand. "So are you off call?"

"Yep. Dr. Keim gave me the evening off because of the deposition."

Brett pushed back his chair from the counter. "So we've both had rough days. What say we go cry in our beers over at McPherson's Pub?"

She held up her hand. "Not me. No way. I seem to have bad memories of the way I acted the last time you talked me into a drink."

He smiled. "Why do you think I'm asking?"

She slipped from the desk and walked to the door, but she could feel his eyes following along.

"I guess that means no?"

She pointed at him from the doorway. "That means no."

She stopped in the hall and pivoted, before sticking her head back in Brett's small office.

"Change your mind?"

"No." She hesitated. "I need to know what you really think. What's Rogers going to do when he finds out about my HD risk?"

"He'll want you to be tested. If you're negative, you're okay. If you're positive, it's going to be very hard for him to keep you on." Brett sighed. "Even from a medicolegal standpoint, Rogers doesn't want to be responsible for training a surgeon who might get dangerous."

"That's discrimination. I could sue."

"Nobody sues for a spot in surgery and stays in very long. Even if you prove it, they find other reasons to kick you out. An African-American intern tried that a few years back. He claimed he was kicked out because of racial discrimination. He sued, and a judge forced Rogers to let him back in. But by then, every attending had it in for this guy. His life was pure misery. He couldn't be good enough for them. He never made the third-year cut."

Claire pushed a rebellious strand of blond hair behind her ear. "That's what I figured." She turned around again and mumbled to herself as she started down the hall, "The only problem is, I don't want to be tested."

I'm too afraid to know.

A few minutes later, Claire evaded the grasp of the hospital and stepped into the cool air. There was a breeze coming from the shore, filling her with a desire to escape the city. The opportunity to see Lafayette before sunset presented a rare dilemma. Deciding what to do with spare time created an unexpected challenge.

Claire mulled her options as she walked to her old Toyota. She desperately needed to clean house and shop for groceries, but that seemed a boring way to fill a free spring evening. She longed to head for the beach, but she needed to get home and change first, so she really didn't have time for that, and the idea of walking alone on the beach at night was too scary. Perhaps she should go to a movie, or treat herself to a meal at a downtown restaurant.

She thought about the upcoming trial and wondered whether she could stand up to Ramsey's questions in front of a jury. He made her feel so incompetent. She wondered whether she could possibly make the first pyramid cut when Ramsey finished convincing everyone that she was an overconfident, in-over-her-head, incompetent, first-month intern with a hidden past and a practice of deceiving her superiors.

She thought about John and her failed engagement.

And she thought about her family and her risk for Huntington's disease.

And suddenly, her desire to spend a happy hour of free time evaporated. The urge to go home and sleep, the idea that she could pull the covers over her head and forget her problems, tugged at her weary soul.

It was a common problem for the interns to remember exactly where they parked, so it wasn't too alarming that Claire looked through three rows of cars before coming to her small sedan. A siren screamed in the background and Claire shifted her focus to identify the ambulance which undoubtedly would deliver more business to her trauma colleagues. The noise pierced her, reminding her of sleepless nights spent baby-sitting broken patients in the CT scanner and a little girl who wanted a purple bicycle for her birthday. *I shouldn't be torturing myself. I should just go back to Brett and take him up on the offer to have a night out. A listening friend and one drink couldn't hurt.*

She threw her call bag in the back seat and planned to go back and find Brett, when she stopped to check her appearance in the reflection of the car's window. She wished for a better mirror so she could primp herself properly. As she flipped her hair behind her ear, she was struck with an odd familiarity. She'd seen her father make the same move a hundred times. He'd done it as long as she could remember, flipping his unruly hair behind his ear with nervous regularity. The thought that she was anything like her father chilled her and extinguished her plans to share a drink with Brett. *How often did Wally McCall say, "One drink couldn't hurt"?*

She groaned and opened the car door. She sat for a minute staring ahead without bringing anything into focus. Then she experienced a gentle nudge. It was an odd sort of feeling, indescribable. Vague, but recognizable. A subtle impression that she'd experienced before in the early hours of the night when she'd found herself suddenly awake for no apparent reason. Like a soft breeze, the sensation lingered, forming an idea. *You were made for something more. I love you.*

The hairs on her arm stood up. "God," she whispered, looking around the car. After a few seconds, she shivered, and the idea evaporated.

She drove south through the city, oblivious of the traffic around her. She pulled to a stop at a prominent intersection. On her right, her eyes were drawn to a sign in front of Lafayette Community Chapel. It was a large white sign with changeable black letters. She supposed she had passed it many times without noticing. There, in large block letters, the message read, "CHEER UP!" Claire squinted to read the words beneath. "You are worse than you think."

"Great," she mumbled sarcastically. "That's encouraging."

A car horn prompted her attention back to the green light ahead, but instead of going on, she veered right into the church parking lot. Another horn sounded, but Claire didn't care. She wanted to see the other side of the curious sign. She drove through the parking lot so she could read the next message.

"CHEER UP! God's grace is much greater than you can imagine." Claire looked at the large brick building and realized that cars were filling the parking lot. She looked at her watch and imagined a midweek service was about to begin. Maybe this was what she was supposed to do with her free evening. She had yet to attend church in Lafayette, and it wouldn't hurt to go to a meeting or two in hopes that God would smile on her, especially since she was facing a malpractice trial. She pulled into a parking space and checked her appearance in the rearview mirror. She was rarely this well dressed, but her attorney had insisted on it for the deposition. She freshened her lipstick quickly, aware that a car had pulled in beside her on her right. She looked over, preparing to offer a friendly smile.

Instead, her mouth dropped open as her eyes met the unmistakable steel gaze of Roger Jones. Her throat turned to cotton as she quickly looked away. A dread settled as the realization hit. *Has he been following me? Was he the one beeping?*

She fumbled with her door locks and grasped her keys. She risked one more glance at Mr. Jones, whose face was frozen in her direction. What did she see there? Anger? Surprise? She could hear the muffled tone of his voice. She couldn't understand the words, but the emotion of anger was unmistakable. She started the car and slammed it into reverse. With a squeal of rubber, she backed up, then lurched forward, turning out of the parking lot.

She stole a look in the rearview mirror. Roger Jones was pulling out too!

Claire focused on the busy traffic, weaving in and out with her accelerator to the floor. At the next light, she made a right, then an immediate left and up a tree-lined subdivision. At a stop sign, she made a left again and cut behind a convenience store and back out onto the main road leading back to the university. If Mr. Jones was going to follow her, he'd have to be quick. She glanced in the mirror and took a deep breath. Roger Jones was nowhere in sight.

The speedometer edged further to the right as she clipped through two yellow lights on her way downtown. At the hospital entrance, she used her magnetic ID to raise the bar preventing passage into the resident's lot, and slowed to a crawl.

After parking, she quickened her pace across the lot toward the research building. *I sure hope Brett hasn't left yet. I should have taken Brett up on his offer in the first place. Now I really need a shoulder to cry on.*

Brett walked Claire back to her car in the parking lot of the hospital. They'd taken his orange truck to McPherson's, where Claire spilled her story. She ate a chicken Caesar salad and a side of "Phierse Phries," the restaurant's version of fried potatoes, a spiced variety touted among the surgery residents as the food most likely to produce a gallbladder attack. Claire's gallbladder remained quietly submissive, and she cooled her thirst with two diet Cokes, purposefully avoiding stronger drink known to be a snare to the McCall family.

Claire rested her hand on the hood of her old Toyota. "Sometimes I wonder if it's worth it. When I left the hospital earlier this evening, it was hard to kill the urge just to go back to Stoney Creek."

"You spent your life trying to get out of there, remember?"

"I know," she sighed. "But on days like today, it wouldn't take much to push me over the edge."

He chuckled and looked away. "If you leave, can I have your second-year spot?"

She launched a playful jab to his spleen. "Don't you wish?"

She opened her car door.

Brett cleared his throat. "Will you be okay?"

She nodded. "As long as I don't see Mr. Jones, I'll be fine." She sat in the car and started the engine.

"You'll be okay," he said, leaning to her window. His voice didn't sound convinced. "Call me once you're home. I'll come if you need me."

She waved and headed for home.

As she drove, she checked the locks on the car and looked repeatedly in the rearview mirror. It was past dark, and she couldn't distinguish one vehicle from another by the headlights. Several times, she made extra turns, just to be sure she wasn't being followed. *This is crazy. All Roger Jones has to do is wait for me at my house.*

She tried to quiet her pounding heart. *I'm just being paranoid. He's suing me for more than I'm worth, so why would he want to torture me like this?*

She sighed and checked the locks again. *Is he so blind with anger over his daughter's death that he can't act rationally?*

She reasoned herself out of the obsession that Roger Jones was crazy enough to harm her. *The painted message on my door, the threatening phone call, and the way he acted in the church parking lot are just reflections of his inability to handle his grief appropriately. He's just acting out to scare me. He wouldn't really harm me.*

Claire turned into her driveway still trying to talk herself out of her fear. *I'm being irrational. Roger Jones is a depressed father, not a cold-blooded killer. He's harmless.* She unlocked her door and looked at the eerie shadows cast by the trees in front of the street lamp. "He's harmless," she verbalized to convince herself. *Isn't he?*

She gathered her call bag and stepped from the car. Her brownstone was dark, and she wished she had left on a porch light. Her grandma McCall claimed that if you whistled, your teeth couldn't chatter, and your fears would flee. It had made perfect sense when Claire was ten, but now she doubted the science behind Grandma's promise. But it couldn't hurt to distract her runaway fears, so she began to whistle. She started with a short scale, and then, satisfied that she could actually whistle without her lips quivering, she started in on the first thing that came to her mind, a whistled version of "Don't worry, be happy." She scurried across the grass and reached for her keys.

She kept whistling as she inserted the key, then looked up into the face of a man stepping out of the shadows beside the front door.

Claire screamed. The schnauzer next door barked.

And the man lifted his hands in the air.

Chapter Thirty-Seven

laire stumbled back off the porch as a second scream lodged in her throat. She rolled across the grass to get away from the man who continued to move forward.

Quickly, she was on her hands and knees, crawling, then standing to run.

"Claire!" The man's voice was familiar. "Claire, it's me!"

She squinted in the darkness. "Clay?" She breathed a sigh of relief and spat a blade of grass from her lips. "You scared me to death."

"I thought you saw me when you drove up. I waved."

"I–I didn't see you," she gasped. "What are you doing here?" She looked around. "How did you get here?"

"Long story," he mumbled. "Do you think we could go inside? I've been sitting on my suitcase for two hours."

She shook her head in amazement and began to brush off her skirt. "You owe me a pair of nylons." She unlocked the door. "How'd you know I'd be home?"

"I asked John."

"Cerelli?" *He keeps up with my schedule?*

Clay nodded.

"Why not just ask me?"

"I wasn't sure you'd invite me."

"Ridiculous. You're my twin."

"You haven't heard my story yet."

She stared at him, her eyes adjusting to the dim light. Clay appeared thinner than she'd remembered. His hair was uncombed, and the mischievous glint in his eye was noticeably absent. "Well?"

"Can we go inside?"

Claire nodded. "Of course."

They entered her front room. "Hungry?"

He nodded. Claire scrounged up a frozen pizza and opened a liter of diet soda while Clay freshened up. Then, in between bites, she listened to her brother's sad story. Clay's day in court hadn't been pretty. He was found guilty of public drunkenness, violation of his restricted driver's license, and assault and battery. But after listening to Clay's attorney explain his family's situation, and the turmoil Clay experienced from being at risk for HD, the judge softened and convened a conference among all the involved parties. The plaintiff's attorney agreed to a reduced sentence if Clay would behave. Judge Wilkins sentenced Clay to a thousand dollars to pay the pilot's dental bills, and took away his driver's license. He agreed with Clay's lawyer who argued to keep Clay out of prison, but made the judgment contingent on two conditions.

Clay looked up meekly from his pepperoni pizza.

"Just what conditions are you referring to?"

"I agreed to live with a responsible adult who will supervise my sobriety and will sign a log documenting my attendance at AA meetings three times a week." He shrugged. "And I have to find work within thirty days."

"Find work? What about the cabinet shop?"

"Got fired."

He turned back to his dinner. She studied him for a moment. She'd never seen him this low, this vulnerable. "Wait a minute. What responsible adult agreed to supervise your sobriety?"

He continued staring at the paper plate in front of him. "You did," he said quietly.

"I did?" She pushed back her chair. "Clay!"

"My attorney wrote the letter. He said I only needed to get you to sign it."

"So where's the letter?"

Clay held up his hand. "I knew you would sign it, if you had the time, so I, well, I—"

"You forged my signature!" She began to pace. "Clay, you could get in big trouble for this."

Clay looked up without speaking. In his eyes, Claire saw only dullness. He slumped forward and dropped his eyes to the table. "Judge Wilkins was pretty impressed by your letter. He said he was glad at least one McCall had made something of herself."

Claire sighed and sat across from her brother. "He's a jerk, Clay. You've made something of yourself. I've seen the furniture you've made. You're gifted."

"I have no job. No driver's license. No money. And everyone says I'm a chip off the old block 'cause I drink too much." He looked up, his eyes pleading. "And all I think about is ending up just like Dad." He pressed his hand to his mouth to cover a burp. "You should see him, Claire. It's awful." He paused, and she noticed his hands trembling. Evidently Clay noticed it too, as he quickly clasped his hands together. "I'd rather die than end up like that."

"Don't say that."

"You haven't seen him."

"Clay, just because Dad has Huntington's disease doesn't mean you'll get it. There is an equal chance that you won't."

"That's what Mom keeps telling me. But in my gut, I know I'm the one. If any of us end up like Dad, it'll be me."

"We all have the same risk, Clay. Why torture yourself without knowing? Have you thought of being tested like Margo?"

"I can't afford it. Besides, I think I already know the answer."

"I'm sure Grandma McCall would pay." She reached for his hand. "And you can't know the answer without a test. You have a right to be afraid, but you really can't be sure."

"Are you getting tested?"

"Not for now. I would like to know I'm not going to get HD, but I'm not ready to hear the opposite news."

"Really." Clay pushed back from the table and took his plate to the sink. When he was busy washing up the pizza pan, he asked, "So can I stay?"

Claire studied him for a moment. "How long?"

"I don't know."

She put her hands on her hips. *It is kind of nice not being alone in this house.* "You can stay until you find work and are established in a regular AA routine."

Clay cleared his throat and set his freshly washed plate on the counter with a clatter. "Oops." His hands trembled as he scooted the plate back from the edge.

Claire walked behind him into the front living room, observing him as he restlessly scratched first his right shoulder, then his stomach.

"I have a spare bedroom upstairs, but no bed." She pointed to the couch. "So this is the guest quarters for now."

Clay plopped down and immediately began tapping his foot.

He seems wired, nervous as a cat. What if he's getting alcohol withdrawal? "When's the last time you had a drink?"

"I haven't been drinking much, Claire. Really. I got it under control."

She eyed him as she walked to the front closet to retrieve a pillow and a blanket. She dropped them on the floor beside the couch and walked up to her bathroom. She inspected her gray suit, one she'd purchased specifically for the trial and depositions, and frowned at a grass stain on the left elbow. She slipped off the jacket as the phone began to ring. "Can you get that?" she called. She listened for a moment, and then, satisfied that Clay had picked it up, returned her attention to her clothing. Her nylons had a hole in the left knee. She pulled them off and wadded them into a ball. She dropped them into a plastic trash can beside the commode and then walked to the top of the stairs. She heard Clay hang up the phone.

"Who was that?" she called.

"I dunno," he mumbled. "No one said anything."

Roger Jones, I bet. With the experience she'd just had with Mr. Jones, she imagined him sitting at home seething, dreaming up ways to make her life miserable. She'd made a mistake, and he wasn't the type to let her forget it. At least not in this lifetime.

She heard Clay open the refrigerator. *Probably looking for beer. Oh well, I'd rather have my mooching brother visiting than sleep in an empty house.*

She changed out of her formal suit and looked at the clock. It was time to think about getting some sleep. Rounds at six-thirty would be painful if she stayed up too late talking to Clay.

I've never seen him so down.

She turned her head and listened to the sound of a starting car. *My neighbor's car sounds just as old as mine.*

She walked down the creaky steps. "I'm going to be leaving pretty early in the morning so just . . . Clay?" She skipped through the front room to the kitchen, where she closed an open cabinet door. "Clay?" She returned to the hall where she knocked on the bathroom door. "Clay?"

His suitcase was open on the living-room floor. She ran her hand across the desktop where she normally deposited her car keys. She pulled back the front curtain, her heart quickening. Her Toyota was gone.

She pounded her fist on the front door and vented. "Clay!"

Chapter Thirty-Eight

laire sighed and paced her living room wondering what to do. She could call the cops, have Clay arrested for driving without a license, or even car theft, but that didn't seem to be appropriate. *He's probably just making a beer run, or looking for a bar.* Too wired for sleep, she flipped on the news and stared at the TV screen. After thirty minutes, she decided to call her mom, who picked up after the first ring.

"Hello."

"Hi, Mom. Were you sitting on top of the phone?"

Her voice was edgy. "I was just expecting a call. How are you, dear?"

"I'm okay." She pulled back the curtain to look in the empty driveway. "Clay came for a visit."

A sigh escaped Della's lips. "Oh, God, thank you." Her voice became muffled. "Wally, Clay's at Claire's."

"Mom? Is everything okay? You're breathing hard."

"Yes, yes, everything's okay, at least better now that you've called. Clay is with you?"

"Well, not right now, but he's in Lafayette." Claire didn't understand.

"I'll have to tell the sheriff. I was so afraid he'd done something stupid," she said, her voice thick with emotion. She sniffed. "I was so sure he was dead. I thought he'd killed himself for sure."

"Mom, slow down. What are you talking about?"

"Didn't he tell you?"

"He told me about the trial, and how his lawyer sweet-talked him out of jail, and how I'm supposed to be supervising—"

"The trial?"

"Yes, he—"

"He didn't show up, Claire. Clay ran. His trial was to start this morning. But Clay never showed up." Della's voice became muffled again. "Wally. Our boy's alive!"

"But he told me that Judge Wilkins worked a deal with Clay's attorney so he could avoid jail time and—"

"Clay lied, honey. He was scared to death. His lawyer told him there was no way to avoid going to jail. But Clay's been so down lately. We thought for sure"—her voice cracked—"he was dead." She sniffed again. "Oh, this is such good news." Her voice dropped to just above a whisper. "I'm not sure Wally could have taken it if Clay had taken his life. Wally's been so concerned about him. I think he feels bad for the father he's been, and he keeps trying to reach out to Clay."

Claire shook her head, trying to imagine her father caring about anyone but himself. "Dad?"

"It's true, honey. Your father is a sick man. He knows his days are numbered. And since Dr. V started him on an antidepressant, his mood is so much better. Wally keeps telling me every day that he wants to make up for his drinking."

Claire didn't know what to say. If her father was changing, she'd have to see it to believe it.

Della continued. "Oh, Claire, you'll have to keep him there. Don't let Clay run off again."

"Well, er . . . he's not here right now. That's one reason I called. He left in my car about an hour ago. I think he must be out looking for a drink."

"Oh, dear. Your car? How'd he get there?"

Claire scratched her head. "I really don't know. I assumed he flew. But maybe he took a bus. He didn't have his truck here."

"Oh, Claire, he totaled his truck last week." Della blew out her breath into the phone. "That boy's life is falling apart. Now he's going to be in deeper trouble for skipping out on his trial."

"Don't worry, Mom. I'll talk to him. He can't run forever."

Della sniffed. "Tell him to come home."

"Okay, Mom. I'll call after I talk to Clay."

Claire hung up the phone and snapped off the TV, then collapsed on the couch to wait for Clay. By twelve-thirty, her fatigue overtook her anger, and she fell into a fitful sleep.

Thump, thump, thump. Claire rolled over and pried open her eyes. Was someone knocking?

Thump, thump, then the sound of the doorbell. *Clay!* Claire squinted at the digital readout on the front of the TV. *Two-thirty! I'm going to kill him. I don't care if he is my brother.*

Thump, thump.

"I'm coming. I'm coming."

She thought about jerking open the door and giving Clay an ultimatum. Instead, she took a deep breath and reminded herself of Clay's situation. She lifted the curtain from the front window and gasped. Police!

She opened the door and looked up into the face of a Lafayette policeman. He looked at the paper in his hand. "Ms. McCall?"

Her lip trembled. "Yes?"

The uniformed man stood head and shoulders above his partner. "I'm Officer Carl Stephens, Lafayette PD." He nodded toward his associate. "This is Officer Dean Blakemore. I'm afraid I have some bad news."

Her jaw slackened.

"There's been an accident. Are you Mrs. Clay McCall?"

"No. Clay's my brother."

She watched as the two officers exchanged glances.

"Accident? Is Clay okay?"

"He was taken to the university hospital."

"How did you find me?"

"The car he was driving was registered in your name."

"How's Clay?"

"We only heard that he made it to the hospital alive. Some surgery resident happened by the accident and saved him."

"Where was he?"

"Driving out the beach road toward the ocean. The car went off the road near the old Smithland Shoals Lighthouse."

Claire knew the road well. She'd driven it many times on her way to the beach. The road was curvy, the drop-offs on the ocean side steep and rocky.

"Was anyone else hurt?"

The officer shook his head. "No. It was a single-vehicle accident."

She slumped, supporting herself against the door frame. "I need to see him."

"Do you have another vehicle?"

She shook her head.

"We can take you."

"Give me a minute?"

He nodded. Claire grabbed her call bag, knowing she wouldn't be home for a few nights, and without a car for easy transportation. As she walked out the front door, she asked, "Was he drunk?"

"No alcohol was found in the vehicle, but I'm sure they'll test him at the hospital."

"Only one car was involved?"

The officer nodded and opened the car door for Claire.

As they pulled away, she felt her stomach tighten. *Single-car accident. Clay was depressed and on the run.*

Fear tightened around her heart. *Mom was right. Clay wanted to die.*

At the hospital, Claire quickly dodged an admission clerk wanting to ask insurance questions and headed to the emergency room. Clay wasn't there.

A nurse wearing bloody scrubs touched her arm. "He's been in surgery for hours." She pointed to a uniformed man in the hall. "The detective has been waiting for you."

Claire resisted the urge to run straight to the OR. To do so, she would have to bypass the Volkswagen of a man in her path. He nodded in her direction and held out his meaty palm. "Tom Beckler, detective, Lafayette PD. Are you Clay McCall's next of kin?"

Next of kin? Is Clay dead? Her chin quivered. "Claire McCall. I'm Clay's twin sister. Is he okay?"

"Don't know. I'm in charge of the investigation. Could I ask you some questions?"

"Just what happened?" Claire asked.

"He ran off the road just beyond the lighthouse, where the road is straight. He appears to have careened off just before the guardrail started, and plummeted to the rocks below."

Claire held her hand to her mouth. She knew the spot. But why there? Why lose control on a straight road? "But why? Was he drunk?"

"No. Blood alcohol and drug screen were negative." The detective shuffled his feet and hooked his thumb in his belt under the shadow of his belly. "Does your brother have any medical problems, a seizure disorder or something?"

Claire stepped back. "What?"

The officer held up his hand. "Just a question, Ms. McCall. I need to fill out an accident report. He was alone, not drinking, and he ran off a straight stretch of road."

She wanted to get to the OR. "My brother was healthy."

"Was your car having any problems? Brake problems? Steering difficulties?"

"No. It was old, but it handled well."

"He probably fell asleep at the wheel." He shrugged his rounded shoulders. "See it all the time in a university town. Students stay up late, then fall asleep driving home."

"It really wasn't late."

"We'll probably never know."

"My brother was depressed."

The officer raised his eyebrows. "I see."

"You don't suppose he did this on purpose, do you?"

The officer rocked back and forth on his brightly polished shoes. "Look, Miss McCall, things like that can't be proven. In my experience, it seems best not to torture yourself with ideas like that. I'd prefer to assume he fell asleep."

"Will you be investigating the vehicle?"

"Not unless there is a suspicion of foul play." He paused. "Did your brother have any enemies?"

She thought about Clay's recent scrapes with the law, and hiding out in Lafayette, far away from his own trial. She didn't want to bring it up. She shook her head. "Clay was friendly. No one would try to hurt him."

"Probably just fell asleep." The officer nodded, satisfied he could fill out his form.

"I'd really like to go see my brother."

"He's in surgery."

"I know. I'm a surgeon in training in this hospital. I want to see him."

"Do you know Dr. Daniels?"

She nodded. "Brett?"

"He was on his way home when he happened on the accident. He saved your brother's life."

"You're kidding! Brett?"

"He made the 911 call, helped stabilize him at the scene. He even rode in the squad with him."

Claire let the information sink in. *Brett Daniels!* "He lives just a few miles from there."

The officer nodded. "Good thing for your brother. Dr. Daniels is a heck of a surgeon. He stuck one of those breathing tubes right in his neck." He pointed at a crease in his chubby skin above his tie. "Slashed him right here. Never saw that before. He was something."

She'd heard enough. If Clay had been trached in the field, things had to be bleak. "Could you excuse me? I'd like to check on my brother."

Claire sidestepped around Officer Beckler and ran toward the operating rooms. Inside the double automatic doors, she came face-to-face with Janice Hilbert, the night charge nurse in the OR.

"Just where do you think you're going, Dr. McCall?"

"My brother's in surgery. I need to get scrubs."

Nurse Hilbert stepped into the doorway leading to the female changing room. "I can't let you go back there."

Claire stepped aside and began to reach for the door handle. "That's ridiculous. I'm a surgery resident in this hospital, and I'll go see my brother if I want to."

"No." Hilbert was firm, gripping Claire's arm.

"What can't I see? Is my brother dead?"

"No. But there's a lot of activity in that room right now. And it's against hospital policy to let patient's family members in the OR."

"Come on, Janice. I *work* here. You can't be serious."

"I wish I wasn't. Thc surgeons are hard at work in there, doing the best they can, and they don't need you distracting them. The surgeons will be out soon enough to talk to you."

Claire raised her voice and pointed her finger in the nurse's face. "Listen. That's my twin brother in there. I work in this OR every day. And I'm going in there to see—"

"Problem here?"

Claire looked up to see Dr. Tom Rogers.

"Uh, no, sir," mumbled Claire.

"Dr. McCall here seems to think she's above hospital policy," Nurse Hilbert said. "She wants in the OR to see her brother."

The chairman stroked his chin. "Janice is right. It's not a good idea to be playing doctor right now. Why don't you wait in the lounge, Claire?"

"I don't want to play doctor," she snapped. "He's my only brother. I want an update. What's going on in there?"

Dr. Rogers exchanged glances with the charge nurse. He wasn't used to hearing a resident talk back. He motioned for Claire to sit at the nurses' station. Claire silently obeyed.

"He's very sick, Claire. He has serious head, abdominal, and orthopedic injuries. Dr. Steiner did a craniotomy to evacuate a blood clot pressing on his brain—"

"Epidural or subdural?"

Rogers smiled. "I'm not used to talking to other surgeons. It was epidural."

She nodded. "What else?"

"Dr. McGrath did a splenectomy, and repaired a liver laceration." He paused. "And now, Dr. Suter is rodding his left femur." His eyes dropped to the floor. "He's lost a lot of blood. We've given him over twenty units to get him stabilized."

"Will he make it?"

He held up his hands. "I don't know, Claire. We'll do everything we can." He reached over and touched her shoulder. "If he makes it, you can credit Brett Daniels. He stopped at the scene and helped out. When the EMTs couldn't get an airway, Brett did an emergency cricothyroidotomy right at the roadside." He shook his head. "It takes a great resident to do what he did. He was quick on his feet and didn't lose his head in a situation few of us will ever face. What he did in stopping on the road to help says a whole lot about what kind of surgeon he'll be."

"That's Brett. Always lending a helping hand."

Dr. Rogers nodded.

He stood and smiled as Beatrice Hayes bounded through the swinging OR doors.

"Good morning, Dr. Rogers."

"Nice work with that central line, Dr. Hayes." His eyes shifted to Claire. "When your brother arrived, Beatrice could have been off sleeping in the orthopedic call room. Instead, she assisted the trauma service with his resuscitation." He looked at his watch. "I should come in at three A.M. more often. You really get to see who gets the work done around this place."

Claire studied Beatrice for a moment. The corner of her mouth turned up and she tilted her head forward as if to say, "What? Little ol' me?" *You put a central line in my brother?* "Have you been in with Clay?"

"Yes," Beatrice replied. "Dr. Suter is closing the skin. He should be in the SICU in thirty minutes. Can I ask you some questions about Clay's medical history? I need to do a history and physical write-up for the ortho service."

"Sure."

Dr. Rogers excused himself.

Beatrice didn't wait for him to get out of earshot when she began, "Tell me about the McCall family medical history. Any diseases in your mom or dad?"

Claire watched as Dr. Rogers seemed to hesitate at the door. Was he trying to overhear Claire's answer? She waited a moment and then locked eyes with Beatrice. *You must have heard about yesterday's grilling by Ramsey Plank. I should have known that news would spread like chicken pox in a day-care center.* Claire forced a smile. "No family history contributes to his present trauma."

"It's for the record, Claire. Anything at all? Alcoholism? Cancer? Genetic illness?"

You don't have to raise your voice. I suspect Dr. Rogers has already heard about the HD in my family, if that's what you're trying to accomplish. "The family history is noncontributory."

Beatrice didn't seem satisfied but moved on, as Dr. Rogers had slipped from sight. "Any reason to believe this was suicide?"

Claire stood up in disgust. Beatrice wasn't about to miss a chance to dig up some dirt on the McCalls. "Nobody knows, Beatrice. Now," she added quickly, "I need to notify my parents."

For the next hour, Claire shared the waiting room with a half-dozen other people anxiously pacing between rows of vinyl chairs. She'd never experienced being in their shoes before. And knowing more about what Clay was going through only magnified her fears.

She called her mom, who promised to come.

She bought a cup of coffee from the vending machine.

And she waited. And she stewed. *I can't believe I spoke so harshly to Dr. Rogers.* She flinched at the memory. *He told me not to "play doctor." Is that what he thinks I'm doing around here?*

And the way he talked about Brett, you'd think he could walk on water. And I thought he was going to slobber when he looked at Beatrice. "Nice work on that central line, Dr. Hayes."

Why does he call her doctor, when he calls me Claire?

And he tells me not to play doctor!

At three-thirty, Dr. McGrath came in. At four, she spoke to Dr. Steiner. At four-fifteen, she talked to Dr. Suter. Everyone had the same message. Clay was alive. He was on a ventilator. Prognosis was guarded. She knew the drill. Hang black crepe so the family won't be too disappointed.

But for how long?

At four-thirty, she held Clay's hand in the ICU and trembled. She didn't remember the last time she'd touched him.

She whispered words she didn't believe, "Everything's gonna be all right. Just you wait and see. Everything's gonna be all right."

When she finally collapsed onto a call-room mattress, she had time for only an hour's sleep before plastic surgery rounds. And as she closed her eyes in the darkness of the room, she was struck with the image of Brett Daniels helping her brother. Every time she was afraid, Brett was there for her. When a stranger called, Brett was there. And now, who was here to help the McCalls yet again?

Brett Daniels. What a man.

Are you trying to tell me something, God?

Chapter Thirty-Nine

After morning rounds, Claire attended a "lump and bump" clinic where the plastic surgery resident assisted her as she removed a variety of small skin cancers, moles, and other cutaneous lesions. For Claire, although the procedures were small, the morning couldn't have been better. The patients were happy, and she was holding a knife, not a retractor, for a change. After eight cases, she ran her scut list to be sure she had collected all of the important data for afternoon rounds.

Her attendings urged her to take off, but she refused, wanting to stay busy, to take her mind away from the horror of her brother's condition. She rushed through her progress notes, with her mind dancing between her work, her brother in ICU, and her desire to talk to Brett Daniels. Finally, by two P.M., with her upper-level residents still in the OR, she headed for Dr. Rogers' research lab in search of her friend.

She found him, as always, with his head buried in a book. She knocked on the open doorway. He looked up but didn't smile. "Hi," she said quietly. "Am I interrupting?"

"Yes."

"Too bad." She sat on his desk and pushed his book aside. "Tell me what happened."

He shifted in his seat and looked at the floor. "I was on my way home after our dinner out." He took a deep breath. "There was a car several hundred yards ahead of me, right on the beach road. I wasn't really paying attention, just vaguely aware of the taillights. And then, suddenly, the taillights were gone. I thought maybe the driver had just turned off the lights, but then I saw the car flipping through the air over the side of the road. I don't think he braked at all. He was just going down the road one second, and the next . . ." His voice trailed off. He shook his head and mumbled a curse. "Claire, I'm so sorry."

She reached for his hand. "What happened next? I want to hear this."

"I pulled over and ran to the guardrail to see. I didn't recognize your car. I saw a man lying beside the car. He had a pulse, but he needed an airway badly."

Brett's voice was monotone, mechanical, like he was reciting a textbook. "I pulled his chin forward, and that helped a little. He was able to take a few shallow breaths, but there was so much blood around his nose and mouth that I was sure he wouldn't last long without an endotracheal tube."

"So you slashed his neck?"

He looked up. "Yep. But not until after the EMS crew arrived and couldn't get the oral airway in. I thought he was a dead man. I knew it was his only chance, so I just went for it." He smiled. "To tell you the truth, I was pumped, major. I had no idea this was your brother, understand?"

"I understand. I would have been pumped, too." She paused. "Everyone's talking about it. You're a hero."

He looked away. "I'm no hero."

"You should hear what Dr. Rogers said about you."

"Well?"

"He told me you were a great resident. He even said that the fact that you stopped to help a stranger says a lot about what kind of surgeon you'll be."

"Rogers said that?"

She held her right hand up palm forward. "I wouldn't lie about something like this. It's a clear indication that he has plans for you in this program."

"You're serious?"

"Of course."

"Tom Rogers, our chairman?"

Claire rolled her eyes. "Thank you, Brett. You saved my brother's life."

"Why didn't you tell me last night that you had family in town?"

"He was waiting for me when I got home. I didn't know he was coming."

"Is he going to be okay?"

She sighed. "It's too early to tell."

He shook his head.

"Brett, it's okay to smile. You did something great."

"There is nothing great about this." Brett turned his face to the wall.

"Look, I know this is horrible, but this might be the break you needed for Rogers to recognize what a special guy you are." She placed her hand on his shoulder, nudging him to turn to her.

His expression remained flat, serious.

"Claire, I'm so sorry about all this. I—"

She put a finger on his lips. "Don't, Brett. I know you tried. You gave my brother a chance."

His eyes locked with hers. This time he didn't look away. Claire didn't flinch. In a moment, she was aware of her desire to fall into his arms, to find comfort and pleasure.

Her head began to swim, as her emotions collided in a collage of contrasts. She was hurting over her brother's accident, yet horrified that she could be capable of pushing that so quickly aside and feeling a desire for Brett. She was thankful, sad, and tempted, all at one time.

She closed her eyes. The darkness did little to settle her turmoil. She leaned forward and kissed Brett's forehead, resisting the urge to do more.

Brett, normally unrestrained in his responses, remained unmoving.

She let her fingers drift from his face and turned to the door. "I'd better go."

After rounds, Claire sat at Clay's bedside and watched his cardiac monitor. He was comatose, with his head shaved and a long staple line running in an arc from in front of his left ear to the top of his scalp. His lips were crusted with blood and his tongue protruded from a mouth no longer capable of containing the swollen meat. His eyes were taped for protection. The man in the bed looked nothing like her twin. His identity was lost, suspended in a spaghetti tangle of tubes exiting his scalp, nose, neck, and chest.

She looked over his bedside chart and asked the nurse to call her if he changed. Then she responded to her beeper and trudged to the emergency room.

There, she carefully repaired a lip laceration on a fourteen-year-old girl who'd fallen during a cheerleading stunt. The girl's mother had insisted that they call in someone from plastic surgery. The second-year surgery resident on trauma obliged the worried parent and called Claire, who had less experience than the second-year resident, but because she was on the plastic surgery team, the mother was happy.

The second-year resident was happy to be relieved of the job. And Claire was happy to get the experience.

Abby Sanderly, an ER nurse, interrupted as Claire was putting in the final stitch. "A man is looking for you."

Claire looked up. "Me?" Her mind flashed back to Roger Jones tracking her down in the same location.

Abby pointed across the chaos of the ER. "Over by the waiting room chairs. In the wheelchair with a gorgeous escort."

With suspicion and curiosity, Claire walked slowly toward the waiting area.

"Claire!" Della lunged forward from behind the Pepsi machine.

Claire gasped and hugged her mother. "You startled me." Her eyes immediately fell to the wheelchair beside her. Wally looked up with an intoxicated grin.

"Hi, Claire."

"D–Daddy!" She hadn't even considered the possibility that Della would bring him along. He sat in a wheelchair with the assistance of a large Velcro strap across his chest, which anchored his trunk but did little to stop the continuous movement of his arms, legs, and head. Claire froze for a moment as she studied him. The months since a diagnosis of HD had not been kind.

Claire glanced back toward the ER. Everyone was working, apparently oblivious to her new guests. She spoke in a quiet voice. "Have you seen Clay?"

Della put her hands on her hips. "The lady at the front desk said there were no visiting hours for the ICU patients."

"That's true, there aren't really visiting hours per se, but family members are allowed back in small numbers." She looked at the hallway leading past the ER. "Come on, I can take you." She took charge of her father's wheelchair and skirted up a side hallway to a lone elevator used for patient transport. On the second floor, they headed back toward ICU.

As they neared the entrance, Beatrice Hayes greeted Claire, who was trying to stare straight ahead and ignore anyone who might know her. "Here we are again, eh, Claire? Where's a medical student when you need one, huh?"

She thinks I'm transporting a patient! "Huh? Oh, right." She pushed her father on by and into the ICU. There, at the nurses' station, with his characteristic silver hair, sat Dr. Tom Rogers, his back to Claire and the entrance to the ICU. She pushed her father into Clay's cubicle and pulled the curtain. Clay's nurse was attending his vital signs. His body appeared lifeless, except for the rhythmic rise and fall of his chest and the eerie sound of the ventilator.

Immediately Della dissolved into tears, her hand clutching at the neck of her blouse.

Claire coaxed her forward. "It's okay to touch him, Mom." Claire leaned over Clay. "Clay, Mom and Dad are here." She looked at her mom, whose face was etched with anxiety. "He can't answer you now, but you can let him know you're here."

Wally stayed in the wheelchair, and Claire pushed him forward so he could reach his son. After two attempts, Wally clasped Clay's hand and cried, "Save him, God."

The scene was both pitiful and overwhelming. A distant father, racked with sobs over years lost to alcohol, begging for God to give him one last chance.

Della was a wet statue, crying, unmoving, her eyes frozen on the image of the one who bore little resemblance to her son.

Wally's hand was still for a few moments before jerking away. His chorea wouldn't let him rest. His head bobbed and his legs pulled against the restraints. Claire watched him from the corner of the room. How much had his Huntington's disease been responsible for his explosive temper, his need to find a respite in the bottle? She lowered her head. Embarrassment, anger, and pity filled her heart. Silently, she slipped from the room.

She wanted to talk to Dr. Rogers away from her family, hoping that if she talked to him at the center unit console, he wouldn't feel compelled to visit with her in Clay's room. She was sure he'd hear of her father's HD because of Ramsey Plank's investigation into her life, but hearing of HD and seeing her father were different items altogether. It was hard enough for Claire to see her family like this. She didn't want to color Dr. Rogers' opinion of her by letting him experience the McCall clan firsthand at their worst.

She approached Dr. Rogers quietly. He looked up from the chart he was examining. "Hi, Claire."

"Hi, Dr. Rogers."

"How's your brother?"

"He's stable for the moment. It'll take a few days before we know."

He nodded slowly. "Look, Claire, I know you've been under a lot of pressure, what with the upcoming trial, all your intern work, and now this. If you need some time away, I—"

"I'm fine, sir. There's no need to lighten my load. I can stop and see my brother during the day while I work. I'm not the type to want to sit around."

He seemed to be studying her face while he chewed the inside of his cheek. "You're not invincible, Claire. Surgeons have difficulty understanding that."

She watched as he returned to examining the chart in front of him. Claire didn't know how to respond. She'd thought that Dr. Rogers would be pleased with her ability to continue in the face of extraordinary adversity. Instead, she felt rebuked. She wanted to crawl away. "Of course," she mumbled.

Claire backed away and returned to Clay's cubicle. She pulled the curtain to see Wally's hand on Della's back as she leaned forward. "Oh, Clay," she cried. "You didn't need to do this, honey. I'm so sorry. I should have told you." She lowered her face to his and whispered something in his ear before turning back to face Claire. She pressed her hand to her mouth.

"Mom, it's—"

Della looked at Claire. "I have to know. Was he drinking?"

"He was sober, Mom. They tested his blood for alcohol. He was clean."

"Did the police think it was a suicide attempt?"

Claire shook her head. "They said it looked like Clay just fell asleep at the wheel."

"That's what he wanted it to look like." Her mother sniffed loudly. "He was so upset about his future. He shouldn't have done this. I could have stopped him." She dropped her eyes to the floor.

"Mom, you couldn't have—"

Della brushed past, crying into her hands. "I should have told him the truth."

Wally's glassy stare disappeared momentarily as he focused on his wife. "Della!"

Claire watched as her mother fled from the unit. She turned and tried to read her father, but his HD gripped his face again. His head weaved, and his face was an expressionless mask. If anything, Wally appeared as confused as Claire felt.

They waited a few moments together, father and daughter adrift in a haze of high-tech gadgetry. Claire's mind whirled between her conversation with Dr. Rogers, her shame of her family, and her confusion over her mother's remorse.

She touched her father's shoulder. "Would you like to stay longer?"

"No." He struggled with a Velcro strap. "Let me out of this chair. I want, I want, I want to find Della."

Claire grabbed the handles on the back of the wheelchair. "I'll push you, Dad. It will be faster that way."

She wheeled him away, dodging a steel cafeteria cart, and nearly colliding with a nurse pushing an EKG machine. She punched the wall switch to activate the automatic doors and dared not glance back to see if Dr. Rogers was watching.

Celia Jones plunged another greasy plate into the sudsy water. She really didn't mind doing the supper dishes by hand, although Roger had been promising to buy a dishwasher for more than two years. She tilted her head toward the den where ESPN blared. She walked to the entrance of the den, drying her hands on a paper towel, and frowned at the sight of Roger passed out on the couch with six empty beer cans stacked in a neat pyramid on the floor beside him.

She was just starting to think about nudging him when the phone rang. She muted the TV and picked up the receiver. "Hello."

"Celia! Ramsey Plank here." His voice was soothing. "I hope I'm not interrupting anything by calling you at home."

"Of course not."

"Listen, could I talk to Roger, or could you give a message to Roger for me?"

She looked over at the log on the couch. "I'll give him a message."

"Franklin Peters, Dr. McCall's attorney, called. It seems that Dr. McCall has notified him again today, making claims that she is being bothered by your husband."

"Roger wouldn't—"

"Just hear me out, Celia. She claims that he followed her in his car last night, that she had to race back to the hospital just to get away from him."

"That's ridiculous. We saw her in the church parking lot and—"

"Church, huh? Oh, well, spare me the details, would you? Mr. Peters is trying to focus the attention away from where it belongs, you understand? His client is a bad doctor, and he's trying anything he can to get the attention off the truth. And that's why he brought up all of that smoke about someone threatening his client during the deposition."

She looked at her husband as she listened to Ramsey. Roger had been awfully moody since Sierra's death. Sure he had blown off steam that day in the ER, but Roger wasn't the type that would try to get even. Or was he? "So you think Mr. Peters just made up that stuff about the phone calls?"

"Of course. He just wants you to feel sorry for his client and take the attention off of her mistake." He paused, and Celia could hear the chink of ice falling in a glass. "But listen, I don't want to hear about any contact between your husband and Dr. McCall. I can understand him being upset, but, just between us, if Roger threatens her, and Franklin can prove it, it will make us look pretty silly. So please watch him. We are very close to victory in this case. I think Franklin is running scared, and I don't want anything to mess up my—uh—our chances for a big win."

"I don't care about the money, Mr. Plank."

"I know you don't, Mrs. Jones. But you remember the concern you expressed on the first day you came to my office? You wanted to protect the public from this resident, to be sure others won't have to suffer at her hands." He cleared his throat. "Well, believe me, you won't have to worry about that when we're done. The university will rue the day they hired her." He chuckled, then his voice became serious again. "So tell Roger to lay low, you hear? I don't want anything getting in the way of our victory."

"But he's no threat to anyone. He just had a little too much to drink. He don't mean any harm."

"Keep a lid on him, Mrs. Jones. And remember why we need to do this. It's for the community. Legal action like this is a civic duty. It helps keep our hospitals safe for all of us."

She looked out the back door to an empty tire swing and sighed. "I remember, Mr. Plank. I remember."

Ramsey Plank set the phone in the cradle and smiled. This case could be a rainmaker. The university was going to pay big for improperly observing the resident staff.

The intercom clicked. "Mr. Plank? I have Franklin Peters on line two."

Ramsey's grin broadened. *He wants to settle before trial.* "Franklin. So nice to hear from you."

"Cut the pleasantries, Ramsey. I think after yesterday you should want to hear from me. I've spoken with the malpractice carrier for the hospital and Dr. McCall. We're ready to make a deal."

Ramsey nodded his head and said nothing. *I knew it.*

"We are ready to settle for 150,000 dollars." He let the offer hang without further explanation.

Ramsey snickered, chuckled, then didn't try to hold back a full belly laugh. "You've got to be kidding. What is the life of a six-year-old worth?" He paused. "That's a slap in the face to my clients."

"I know your clients have lost a great deal. But you've got to know that you're on shaky ground, Ramsey. There is no way to prove that my client's actions were responsible for the patient's outcome."

"The patient's outcome was death, Franklin. Think about that. You're insulting my client."

"My client may not have been watching the moment the little girl's IV became disconnected. We are ready to concede that. But her actions cannot be proven to have caused the death. You have to be reasonable."

"How do you think a jury will feel? What do you think they will do when they know that Claire McCall slithered away from the Apple Valley so that no one in faraway Lafayette would know about her family history? Your doctor is a walking time bomb, Franklin. I'm sure a jury will see her for what she is. And let her tremble just once in front of the jury, and I'll make sure they wonder if your doctor is already showing signs of her secret family illness."

"You're on thin ice, Ramsey."

"You're the one making the offer to settle." He tapped his fingers on the top of his mahogany desktop.

"You have to know that I'll push the autopsy issue."

"And I'll show the jury it's all an attempt to cover the truth."

"Come on, Ramsey. You're the one blowing smoke. Bringing up her family history was a low blow. It's irrelevant."

"I noticed she hadn't told you either, Franklin. That should tell you something about your client."

"Ridiculous. Dr. McCall is an outstanding young—"

"Save it for the jury, Franky. You'll need to come up with a lot more money to make me go away. I've got an obligation to protect the public from clients like yours." Ramsey could almost feel Franklin's anger through the phone. He imagined Franklin's cheeks reddening and smiled.

"We'll get back to you, Ramsey."

Ramsey leaned back in his leather chair and put his feet on the edge of his cluttered desk. "Just think about the image of a laughing little six-year-old on her birthday. Flash that in front of the jury and see if they think she's only worth 150K." He scoffed. "You're dreaming, Frank. You're dreaming." He set the phone down in the cradle without saying good-bye.

It wasn't time to be pleasant anymore. His opposition was on the run, and Ramsey was in the driver's seat right behind them.

Claire spent the night in restlessness, answering pages, assisting with an operation on a facial dog-bite patient, and checking on Clay.

Della and Wally declined Claire's offer to stay at her home, preferring to stay in the hospital guest house across the street. It was closer, and Claire didn't have a car anymore anyway.

Clay wasn't improving. At midnight, his blood pressure began to sag, and the trauma resident inserted a special pulmonary artery catheter to monitor his blood volume. Medications to support his pressure were infused through continuous drips, and although his pressure improved, his kidneys began to fail. His lungs began to fill with fluid, and more oxygen was administered to compensate.

By six A.M. trauma rounds, Clay's liver began showing signs of shock, and his clotting factors were depleted. More blood was transfused to keep up with ongoing losses from his operative sights.

By ten A.M. his brain swelling worsened. The family was summoned. The end could be anytime. Claire was released from her intern duties to sit with Clay. Della and Wally huddled together in the corner of Clay's room. Margo was kept abreast of the situation, but couldn't leave her girls at home alone. A chaplain prayed for Clay and prayed for the family.

Residents came in and explained all they could. Clotting factors were infused, but Clay's bleeding problems continued. The attending surgeons came in and talked to Claire, and began hanging crepe. "We've done all we can."

Claire watched it all in disbelief. How often had she been on the other side, looking in on families in despair?

Della sobbed.

Wally prayed for a miracle.

At two o'clock, the chief resident on the trauma service, Blaire Bickett, asked the family for permission to classify Clay as a "No Code." The end was inevitable, he explained. Why should they put Clay through chest compressions for no benefit?

Della agreed and buried her head in her hands.

Wally agreed and prayed louder.

Claire pulled the curtain to screen out the rest of the ICU and the world beyond.

At 2:37, Clay McCall's cardiac monitor registered a flat line. Dr. Bickett shut off the ventilator, leaving Claire, Della, and Wally alone.

Chapter Forty

Claire left the intensive care unit in a daze, walking numbly down the hospital corridor, not really attentive to her path. Down the stairwell, into the lobby, and past the gift shop she plodded. In an alcove just beyond the pay phones and before the rest rooms, a small chapel sat, sandwiched between them, labeled with a small sign. She'd not stopped there before, having passed it in her clinical duties hundreds of times without a thought, but now, in her moment of sorrow, it seemed to beckon.

The door was propped open, and, to her relief, the room was empty. The chapel was small, with eight short padded benches in two columns bordering a center aisle. A wooden cross hung on the far wall, and two stained-glass skylights cast a colorful mosaic around it.

The carpet was red, providing a sharp contrast to the white benches. Claire selected the last row and sat down. Her emotions flooded to the surface. Life was not going as expected. She was doing her part. She was trying to be faithful to her calling. So why was everything so hard?

She stared at the cross and cried. She cried for a twin who'd grown up and away, and who now would only be a memory. She cried for her family who seemed inept to deal with another tragedy. She cried because of her own hardships, for her struggle to fulfill her dream, and every roadblock that threatened to get in the way. And she cried because she felt so lonely. She yearned for Brett, and for the comfort she was sure he'd offer.

Then, for the second time in recent days, she felt a gentle wooing, the subtle sensation that she was missing out on something important. There was something just beyond her reach, a longing for love not yet experienced, the feeling that she'd forgotten something, but couldn't quite place what it was. God? She'd heard others talk of peace and intimacy with God. They spoke of him as a father, even a lover. She dropped her head. *Haven't I been working hard enough? Isn't this the work you've called me to perform? Then why do I feel so empty?*

A man in a dark suit stepped in and sat down across the aisle from Claire. She dried her cheeks, and supposing him to be a hospital chaplain, offered him a nod.

His eyes were blue, his hair gray. His smile seemed genuine enough, and the smell of peanuts was apparent when he spoke, even from across the aisle. "You seem disheartened. Have a loved one in the hospital?"

The thought of pouring out her problems to a stranger seemed unnatural to Claire, but his smile was so alluring that she began to drop her guard. "Yes." She sighed. "My brother."

"I'm sorry."

"He was in a bad accident. He just died this afternoon."

The man shook his head. "This must be so hard for you."

"He was so young. Do things like this ever make any sense?"

The gray-haired man shook his head. "Not very often."

It wasn't the answer she expected.

"Sometimes I can bring a little help in situations like this."

Claire studied him. He seemed sincere. "Help?" She hung her head. "Nothing can bring my brother back."

"Nothing can make up for the loss you've experienced. But my boss can help. There may be something that can ease your suffering and help to bring a little compensation. A small point of light in an otherwise bleak situation, you might say."

"Your boss?" She smiled. "I guess that's a code word for God."

He returned a chuckle, and the smell of roasted peanuts greeted her again. He shrugged. "God?"

"I appreciate a chaplain with a sense of humor."

The man leaned forward. "Chaplain?"

Claire locked eyes with the stranger. "I'm sitting in a chapel. You're offering me help from your boss. I thought you were speaking of God."

"My boss thinks he's God." He laughed again, this time louder. He handed her a business card. "Ramsey Plank, attorney-at-law."

Claire's jaw dropped. This man worked for Ramsey! He was the man she'd seen in the cafeteria! She wanted to scream, to tell him what she thought of his ambulance-chasing, conniving tactics. "Why, that—" The words stuck in her throat. Her face reddened and she counted to ten, looking from the floor to the wooden cross.

Then, suddenly another idea struck her, and she shifted in her seat and leaned toward the man across the aisle. "My brother's liver was injured. He had surgery and he seemed to do okay for a while, but then, he started bleeding again, and in spite of everything they tried, they couldn't help him. Maybe they made a mistake. Maybe he shouldn't have died."

"These are difficult questions, uh, Ms. . . ." He held out his hand.

"Elizabeth." She responded, noting the smooth texture of his palm. "I read in the paper recently about a little girl who died in this hospital after a liver injury. Isn't Mr. Plank helping her family?"

Peanut Breath grinned. "Yes. He's sure to win that one. The family will be able to live quite comfortably on what Mr. Plank is going to get for them."

"I didn't catch your name," she responded, touching his shoulder.

"William Davis," he said, grinning. "But you can call me Billy Ray. All my friends do."

"Would it be possible for me to speak to the family, Mr. Davis?"

"Billy Ray."

She nodded. "Uh, Billy Ray," she corrected. "Could I speak to the family? As a reference, I mean, to see if they are pleased with Mr. Plank's service. I wouldn't want to sign on with Ramsey Plank unless I was sure his customers were happy with him."

"I'm sure Mr. Plank wouldn't mind that a bit. I'd be glad to contact them and give them your name. I can have them call you directly if you like, then you can just—"

The squeaky wheel of Wally's chair interrupted his sentence. "Claire! We've been looking for you!"

Claire looked up to the familiar voice of her mother. Della hugged her daughter warmly, then turned her attention to the man. "Don't I know you?" She paused for a moment, tapping a sculptured fingernail against her temple. "Harvey Bridges! You're the insurance salesman!"

She turned to Wally, who sat beside her in the wheelchair. "You remember Mr. Bridges, don't you, Wally?"

Wally looked glassy-eyed toward the cross and said nothing.

Claire offered a thin smile to the man her mom called Bridges. "You've met my mother?"

"Uh, no, I don't believe we've—"

"There must be a mistake, Mom. This man works for Ramsey Plank, a local attorney. He's no insurance man."

The man seemed to relax a bit.

"I could have sworn . . ." Della's voice trailed off as she studied the man who was now looking the other way.

"Now, back to our conversation," Claire said, standing. "Please tell Ramsey's client that I want to talk. Tell her my brother just died, and I want to know if Ramsey did a good job for her." Claire couldn't keep from sneering just a little when she added, "Have her call E. Claire McCall. I'm in the phone book. But I think that Roger already has my number."

The man looked stunned. Finally, a lightbulb had gone on. "Dr. McCall? I–I had no idea who—"

Claire pointed her finger at his forehead. "By the way, Mr. Davis, obtaining my medical history under false pretenses is an ethical violation! I'm sure the judge will be very interested in how Ramsey Plank does his case research."

"You baited me. You're not dressed like a doctor. How would I know—"

"I'm not working as a doctor today. My brother's dead, and your boss can't help me!" With that, Claire pivoted and stormed from the little chapel.

As she left, she heard Della beginning a tirade in a volume unacceptable for both hospitals and chapels. "I never received the packet you promised! And that phone number was disconnected!"

That evening, Claire nestled against Brett's shoulder as they drove along the beach road in the orange Chevy pickup. "Thanks for letting me borrow your car. I should have known you'd come to my rescue again."

"You haven't driven it yet. You might want the truck."

He slowed down and pointed to a damaged guardrail. "That's the spot."

"Pull over, Brett. I want to see."

He shook his head. "I don't think it's a good idea."

"Come on. I want to see my car. They haven't moved it, have they?"

"I don't think so. I bet they have to get a crane to lift it out of the rocks."

She squinted at the road's edge. "You can't even see it from here."

Brett eased his foot back on the accelerator.

"Come on, Brett. Stop. I want to look around."

"Look, it's awful, okay? Blood. Death. A mangled car. I don't want to go down there again. It's eerie."

Claire could see he was serious. She sighed. "Maybe you're right."

"I know I am." He stared straight ahead silently until he pulled into the parking lot across from his town house. "I'm sorry about Clay. I wish I'd known him. If he's anything like you, I'm sure I'd have liked him." He planted a kiss on her nose.

She stroked his chin and kissed him back. "Aren't you going to invite me in?"

He looked away, toward the ocean.

"This has been one of the worst days of my life, Brett."

"Mine, too."

She kissed him again and laid her head on his chest. "Well?"

"Will you come in?"

"I can't."

"But you just asked me to invite you."

"No, I didn't. I just asked you if you were going to invite me."

Brett sighed.

"I just wanted to know if you were the kind of guy who would take advantage of a girl in mourning."

He smiled. "Maybe."

They exited the truck and walked over to a blue Mercedes.

He handed her the keys. "It's old, but it runs great."

She kissed him and left, wanting so badly to erase the pain of the day by resting in his arms, and knowing that was the very reason she needed to flee. She drove back the beach road toward Lafayette, pulling over on the straight stretch near Smithland Shoals Lighthouse. The shoulder was soft, so she left two wheels on the road edge, then jumped out to investigate. On the road, she saw skid marks leading up to the point of impact with the end of the guardrail.

That didn't make sense. If Clay was asleep, he wouldn't have braked. Unless he woke up just before running off the road?

And if this was a suicide, why would he try to slow down?

She shook her head. Things didn't line up, and an eerie dread began to claw at her stomach lining.

She stepped over the guardrail and took a few steps in the tall grass before she saw her car. It was upside down, a good fifteen feet below her, sandwiched between two rocks. Slowly, she climbed down the bank. She wouldn't have light much longer. She wasn't sure what she was looking for, but her own curiosity and a sense of anxiety pushed her forward. The back bumper was dented, the trunk smashed, and the left rear tire flat. Could a blowout have caused this? The car was old. She should have kept it up better. Maybe it was all her fault.

The driver's door was open, cocked at an unnatural angle, with the top of the window frame buried in sandy clay. Her heart quickened. The sand was deep red. Clay's blood.

She knelt on the ground and looked into the car through the driver's side door opening. The interior was in disarray. The windshield was smashed, and the roof crushed onto the seat back. She picked up a pair of twisted sunglasses, her own, and pulled her keys from the ignition. She was backing out of the wreckage when the glint of pink caught her eye.

Her cell phone! It was wedged between the dash and the shattered windshield. She carefully brushed away the broken glass and lifted the phone from its resting place. It was still on. That struck her as odd, as she always kept the phone off to save the battery, so it would be available to answer pages if she needed it. She pressed the redial feature and immediately the last call was displayed: 911.

Could Clay have been making a call?

He certainly couldn't have made it after the wreck. His head injury would have prevented that.

But maybe something prompted him to call before the accident.

The thought hung in her mind like a thick fog which refused to lift. Skid marks. A 911 call from her phone. Was Clay afraid?

She thought through the events of the evening of Clay's death. She'd been through the deposition, stopped at the church, fled the parking lot with Roger Jones in pursuit . . .

It was dark at the time of the accident. Maybe Roger Jones was waiting, watching her house, and when he saw her car leave, he started to follow.

She scrambled to her feet and stared at the twisted metal in front of her. There was a phone call to her house just before Clay left. Clay picked it up and told her no one was there. She touched her hand to her throat, aghast at her thoughts. *Someone thought I was in this car.*

She scrambled up the bank, clutching her car phone. She jogged the last few feet to the Mercedes, jumped in, and locked the door. She attempted to calm her racing thoughts. Her brother was dead. Roger Jones had been chasing her earlier in the day. Could he have been following Clay and scared him enough that Clay ran off the road? Or worse, could he have forced him off?

Claire started the Mercedes and pressed the accelerator, making a sharp U-turn on the beach road. She was too frightened to go home. Roger Jones must have snapped. There was no way she could stay at home with him watching. And the thought of spending another night in the hospital seemed crazy.

There was only one respite for Claire in this situation. She'd have to return to Brett's.

Chapter Forty-One

rett opened the screen door wearing only a pair of Nike running shorts and holding a can of beer. "Claire?"

"We need to talk." She pushed past him, pausing briefly to admire his build. "I think Clay was murdered."

"What?"

She picked up a shirt from the back of a kitchen chair and threw it at Brett. "Do you mind putting this on before we talk?"

He frowned.

"It's a compliment," she responded with a smile. "I'll get distracted."

"I think you've flipped. I told you Clay ran off the road."

"But it was dark. Is it possible that you didn't see everything?"

Claire explained her findings at the accident scene and recounted two possible scenarios. Either Clay was in more trouble with the law than she realized, and he'd fled Virginia for reasons other than just to avoid his trial, and someone really wanted him to be quiet, or someone mistook Clay for Claire, and was trying to harm her.

"Claire, be reasonable. None of this makes sense. Who would want to harm you?"

"Roger Jones. You should have seen him at the deposition. He left in a huff, swearing that the truth would come out. Then he followed me out of that church. He scares me, Brett." Her voice began to break.

Brett opened his arms. "Come here," he coaxed, and enveloped her in his arms.

He rocked her for a moment, moving together in the kitchen as a slow pendulum. She laid her head against his chest and looked out the window over the sink. Outside, the sky had changed into brilliant orange and purple hues. The night would arrive soon. It was a night Claire didn't want to face alone.

"Claire," he spoke softly. "I think you're reading too much into this."

"It's an intuition thing, Brett. Something doesn't feel right."

"I was there, Claire. I made the 911 call from your car phone."

"You made the call?" She lifted her head and pushed him to arm's length. She felt her cheeks flush.

He nodded.

"I feel so stupid."

"Give yourself a break, kid. You're under a lot of stress. It's easy to jump to conclusions." He pulled her close again and she slipped her hands around beneath his unbuttoned shirt.

"Duh!" she said, making fun of herself. "I could only think of Roger Jones trying to come after me again." She lowered her forehead to his chest.

She took a deep breath and allowed her fear to melt away again, feeling slightly humiliated at her hasty conclusions, but relieved nonetheless. She tugged at his chest hairs with her lips.

He responded by lowering his face to hers for a long kiss. Claire could detect his excitement.

"I'd better go," she gasped.

"Do you have to?"

She nodded. "I'm going to Stoney Creek tomorrow with my parents. Dr. Rogers has graciously granted me my last week of vacation to bury my brother."

"Nice guy." He paused and kissed her again. "I wish you'd stay. I'll fix dinner."

She felt her resolve weakening, but she knew she'd regret it if she stayed. "Brett, it's not that I don't want to, it's just, well, Clay . . ."

"It's not the right time."

She nodded. He understood. He pressed her against his bare chest one last time and reluctantly let her step away.

It was definitely going to be difficult to remain pure in a relationship with Brett. There seemed to be so much chemistry between them, and she hadn't really discussed her desire to wait until marriage for sex.

Whetting her appetite with John was definitely a bad idea. Falling the first time was tough. Falling this time would be so easy.

She stood on her tiptoes and kissed his cheek. "I'll call you." She smiled, feeling foolish again. "I think I'll be okay now. Maybe I just needed a hug."

He walked her to his Mercedes, where they said good-bye. Claire left, relieved of the anxiety which grew from her hasty conclusions, but aware that her soul was not completely at rest.

In a few minutes, she passed the accident site again. The road was definitely full of crisscrossing tire marks. A chill lifted the hairs on her neck. "Come on, girl," she whispered. "Don't start with that again."

Ramsey Plank reclined in his favorite chair attempting to dissolve the day's stress in his favorite Kentucky bourbon. Fourteen-hour days in the office had destroyed his marriage but provided a life filled with creature comforts he didn't have time to enjoy. So this routine, a drink or three, sitting in his plush office overlooking the night skyline above Lafayette, punctuated his lonely life and provided a brief oasis in a Sahara of legal sand.

His phone was ringing, an event he ignored after hours. His clients would have to call during daylight hours to expect him to pay prompt attention.

The ringing persisted. His answering machine should have kicked in by now, a fact which prompted his slow rise from his recliner. Sally must have forgotten to set the answering machine. Again. *If she wasn't so cute, I'd—*

His thoughts were cut short as he looked at the flashing light on his phone, indicating the call was coming in on his private line. *Who wants me now?*

He picked up the phone. "Ramsey."

"Ramsey. Franklin Peters here. Sorry to call you so late, but there are a couple of things that have come up. Things I think you should know."

"Listen, Frank, I'm not really in the mood to listen to your little offers for settlement. I think we both know the jury will think twenty million dollars from the university is a small price to pay for—"

"I didn't call to discuss a settlement. In fact, maybe a jury trial is exactly what my client would prefer."

"What?"

"We're on to your little Stoney Creek insurance scam, Ramsey. And the last time I checked, ethical violations like this are of great interest to the bar. And if I don't report you, I'll be considered a party to your little crime."

"What? You have no right to accuse me of ethical violations! There's no proof that—"

"Save it for the bar, Ramsey. Your employee, Billy Ray Davis, tried to solicit a case today. You might want to ask him about it."

"Franklin, I don't know what you're talking about."

"Shut up and listen, Ramsey. I'll explain it to you. Claire McCall's brother died this afternoon at Lafayette University Hospital. My client, Claire McCall, was approached by Billy Ray, who offered his condolences in the hospital chapel. He also offered your services. What your little business partner didn't anticipate was that he'd be recognized by Della McCall as the same man who tried to sell her a bogus health insurance policy."

"That's ridiculous."

"No judge will allow information you gather under false pretenses to be admissible."

"We can win this case without it."

"You might have a chance to try the case, if you still have a license after the bar processes my report of your unethical conduct."

"Easy, Franklin. We can work this out. You don't have to report this. I'm sure I can convince the Joneses to settle." He paused, weighing his words carefully. "Of course, it's difficult to place a monetary value on the life of a child."

"Are you suggesting that I not report this in return for an out-of-court settlement?"

"I'm not suggesting anything of the sort. I'm only saying that my clients may be willing to accept a reasonable offer if they are sure that their attorney is happy with the deal."

"Not reporting a known ethical violation is an ethical violation in and of itself."

"I've done nothing wrong, Franklin. If my associate obtained information under false pretenses, I knew nothing about his tactics. I'm innocent. There is no way to prove that I knew anything about his charade."

"But now you're suddenly willing to settle?"

"Perhaps. If you make a reasonable offer to relieve the Jones's suffering."

"Save it for the jury, Ramsey. I'll see you in court. If you haven't been disbarred by then."

"You—" Ramsey halted when he heard Franklin slam down the phone.

He cursed and dropped the phone on the desk before pouring himself another drink. It was time to fire Billy Ray. It wouldn't look good if he kept him on board after finding out about his conduct.

"How could you lie behind my back, Billy?" he whispered, slouching in his recliner again. He allowed himself to smile. "Sorry, Billy." He chuckled to himself and sipped his bourbon. "I'm not going down over your stupidity."

Claire slid her clothing along the closet hanging bar and stared at her sparse closet. She had one black party dress, but nothing suitable for a funeral. The thought of shopping for the occasion frustrated her and threatened to uncork the tears she had been holding in since Clay died.

No, she hadn't been that close to Clay for a long time, but he was her twin brother, a fact which had forged an unbreakable bond between them, one Clay had leaned on just before his accident by showing up on Claire's doorstep for a visit. She folded a pair of socks and placed them in the open suitcase on her bed. She turned again to her closet and selected her gray suit, the one she'd used for the depositions. It wasn't black, but it may have to do. She wasn't sure there'd be time to shop back in Virginia.

She knelt and chose a pair of navy shoes and paused to look at the poster leaning against the back of her closet. It was a family tree of sorts, an undergraduate project on blood-typing. She traced her finger from her father to her mother to Margo and then to herself. Clay was missing, too chicken to allow Claire to take his blood.

His absence on the family tree struck her as foreboding, a dark prediction of his later absence from their family. She shrugged off the moment as a bizarre coincidence and continued packing.

In fifteen minutes, she lugged the suitcase to the doorway and prepared for bed. It was there, in her protective cocoon of blankets, that she allowed herself to cry tears for a brother she'd never see again.

Why did he have to die that way?

Could he have taken his own life?

Were the marks on the highway evidence that Clay tried to stop? Then why did Brett think that Clay hadn't braked at all?

If it was suicide, why would he have braked so hard before going off the road?

And if it was an accident, why there? Why on a straight road?

If he fell asleep, did he wake up just before going off the road?

Claire's anxious thoughts mixed with her tears in a muddy conundrum, robbing her of sleep and gnawing at the lining of her stomach. Eventually, in the cool, still hours of the morning, she slept.

And dreamed of wings to fly away.

Chapter Forty-Two

ack in Stoney Creek, Claire found herself caught in a whirlwind of gossip over just what had happened to Clay McCall. It seemed everyone buzzed with their own theories about Clay's sudden death. The rumors, good and bad, had filtered their way back to Claire, making her stomach churn.

Ralph Knitter at the café offered his opinion to the mayor, who shared it with the mail carrier, who shared it with Kyle, Margo's husband. He told Margo and Claire the night before the funeral. "Everyone says it's the curse. Pure and simple. Suicide is sure proof."

Grandma McCall hushed the rumors but started others of her own. "The boy was in trouble. Someone wanted him dead."

The idea troubled Claire, but not because she believed her grandmother. Secretly, Claire couldn't expel the thought that she had been the target, and that Roger Jones was trying to get to her, and Clay had gotten in the way. The obsession stuck in her gut until the morning of the funeral when she slipped from the crowded living room at her grandmother Elizabeth's, where her family and close friends had gathered in preparation for the funeral that afternoon. She edged back the paneled hallway into her grandmother's bedroom, where she placed a long-distance call to Tom Beckler, a detective for the Lafayette PD. She spilled her theory, telling him about the tire marks, her cell phone, and being chased by Roger Jones earlier in the evening of her brother's death.

The detective seemed nonplused. "Thanks for sharing your concerns, Dr. McCall. I'll look into it."

"I want to know what you find out." She gave him her cell phone number and asked him to call.

"Look, we've already had a mechanic look at the car. We pulled it from the crash site early this morning. It seems to check out okay."

"So you think he committed suicide?"

"It's a possibility. But that's not a question I can answer."

"So you're not sure, are you?"

Her insistence seemed to irritate him. "You can leave the police work to us. I told you I'd look into it. I'll call you if I find out anything of value."

"Sir, I can't shake the feeling that something is amiss. This wasn't just an accident, and I don't believe Clay would have killed himself. Too many things don't add up."

"Dr. McCall," he sighed. "Are you suggesting someone was coming after you?"

"Maybe."

"Why would someone want to do you in?"

"I told you. Roger Jones is suing me over the way I handled his daughter's case. He wants revenge. You should see the way he looks at me."

Claire heard his voice, muffled, as if he had his hand over the phone. Then, more clearly, he stated, "I'll look into it."

Right. You're only saying what you think I want to hear. "Okay."

She put the phone down when she heard a click on the other end. Then, turning, she gasped as she saw a man's silhouette in the doorway. "Oh!"

Dr. Jimmy Jenkins nodded. "I didn't mean to startle you." He cleared his throat. "I don't mean to pry, but I overheard some of your conversation."

She lifted her eyes to examine the man who'd been a family friend as long as she could remember. "So?"

"Claire," he began. "I've known you all your life. You're a brilliant young woman." He paused. "And you're smart enough to know when you should leave something at rest. Nothing you do now can bring him back. Why torture yourself with the what-ifs? Just remember Clay for the fun-loving guy he was, and . . ." He coughed. "Go on."

"He didn't kill himself, Dr. Jenkins. Clay was depressed, but I don't believe he would kill himself."

The doctor nodded. "I know he was depressed, Claire. I gave him some of these last week, when he came in complaining of frequent headaches." He pulled a sample bottle of Zoloft from his pocket. "It's helpful when anxieties become overwhelming."

"He asked you for help?"

His voice was quiet. "Yes." He kept his voice low. "I haven't told your mother. I'd prefer to allow her to think that Clay just fell asleep at the wheel, if she can convince herself of it."

"Why tell me?"

"Because you are a doctor now. And you will be afraid for your own life if you read too much into this. Clay was depressed and ran off a cliff from a straight stretch of road. You told me so much yourself." He repeated an axiom he'd told her many times. "When you hear hoofbeats, think of horses, not zebras."

She studied him for a moment. It seemed so like him to keep the hurtful information to himself. He saw no reason to break a patient confidence and make a family worry even more. He turned and walked away.

"Thanks," she called to his back.

She turned to follow him up the hallway, as the irony of his last statement floated to the surface. *The last time I was accused of thinking of zebras when I heard hoofbeats was when I diagnosed my father with HD.*

That afternoon, on a spring day threatened by rain clouds, the Wally McCall family put their son in the ground. The graveside service was intimate, with family, a few friends of Clay's, a few coworkers, Dr. Jenkins and his wife, Ralph Knitter from Fisher's Retreat, and John Cerelli. He stood in the back and exchanged glances with Claire, who sat on a creaky folding chair beneath a tarp emblazoned with the gold lettering of Finch's Funeral Home.

Pastor Phil Carlson spoke in a loud voice in an attempt to be heard above the wind, and the mourners leaned forward to catch the words which seemed to dissipate into nothingness beyond the first few rows of folding chairs. "I know what many of you have been thinking. Many of you have spoken to me privately about your concerns. But let me speak publicly about this matter of Clay's state of mind and whether he could have brought this accident upon himself." He paused, and the little audience leaned even closer. "In the last few months, the McCall family has faced a new trial, that of learning of the genetic illness known as Huntington's disease. Clay confided in me of his risk of the disease, and of his fear of contracting it. But his response was to embrace life, not death, to pursue the activities which excited and thrilled him, so that even if his life was shortened by illness, he would not look back with regret that he had not accomplished the desires of his heart.

"Was Clay reckless?" He paused. "Perhaps. But in his recklessness, he embraced life with a fervency and fun that I envied. Clay did not fear death. If anything, he feared a life without passion, without gusto, and it was that longing which seemed to guide him.

"Clay was a craftsman, and his fine work will live on in many of our homes. It is a testimony to his love of art, and the creativity which reflects the nature of God himself. Clay made a commitment to God when he was a boy. It was a decision he took seriously. No, he wasn't a man without flaws. But as I had a chance to talk through things with Clay in recent months, he thought seriously about eternity, as those facing risk of serious illness are prone to do. He voiced openly his understanding that God had forgiven him, and loved him as he was. If there's one thing I appreciated most about Clay, it's that he was real, unpretentious, and not one to put on a face of self-righteousness when others, including me, were around. He seemed to understand the message of grace, and he wasn't caught up in striving to be accepted by God or others." The pastor nodded his head and gripped the leather Bible in his hand as he made eye contact with each one under the small tarp. "It's a message Clay would have wanted all of us to hear. Let us pray."

Claire bowed her head and strained to listen, but the pastor lowered his voice, and the wind prevented her hearing.

Wally wrestled against the Velcro straps in his wheelchair, Margo dabbed her eyes with a Kleenex, and Della sobbed. Claire watched as Dr. Jenkins gave her a hug and dropped a small white tablet into her palm.

Clay's casket was lowered into the ground, and Elizabeth held a hand up to accept the first drops of rain.

They retreated toward their cars to escape the storm, with Kyle pushing Wally's wheelchair and Claire following behind.

"Claire."

She turned to face John Cerelli. "Hi."

"I'm sorry about Clay."

She nodded in an awkward silence.

"Will you be around for a while?"

"A few days."

Rain began to fall around them, pelting them with large drops. "Can we talk?"

She nodded. "I'll be at my parents' place tonight and tomorrow. You can call." She looked ahead to her father's car. Della and Kyle were desperately trying to hustle Wally out of his chair, fold it up, and get it into the trunk of the car before getting soaked. "I should go. My family is eating dinner together at my grandmother's."

"Okay." He reached for her hand, shaking it formally, like a stranger. "I'll call."

She looked away, then back into the eyes she used to love. "Thanks."

He nodded.

"For Clay."

He understood.

And for me.

Claire opened her eyes the next morning with light spilling through the thin curtains onto her bed. With the disorientation that comes from waking up in unfamiliar surroundings, she noticed the sunlight and bolted from bed, knowing she was late for rounds.

Her feet hit the old floor as the cobwebs of slumber cleared away. Reality settled her soul and she collapsed in a thankful heap back onto the bed. For an intern, being late for rounds was a cardinal sin.

There, with the noises of her parents' morning preparations beginning in the room next door, she relished the rarity of the moment. She didn't have to be anywhere that day. There were no progress notes to write, no patients to examine, and no residents or attendings breathing down her back to check the adequacy of her work.

She took a deep breath. Here, in Stoney Creek, there were no threatening phone calls, no pyramid, no Ramsey Plank, and no Roger Jones in the rearview mirror. Here, there were no life-and-death decisions, there were no patients calling her "nurse," and no male surgeons appreciating the anatomy below her neck more than the brain behind her eyes.

Here, she was only Claire, Wally McCall's daughter, at fifty-percent risk for inheriting the Stoney Creek curse. If only she could have left that behind in Lafayette as well.

She sat up as other memories of home flooded her thoughts. She remembered times spent playing with a twin she'd never see again and felt her throat tighten with sorrow.

She listened as her mother assisted in dressing Wally, combed his hair, and brushed his teeth. She hadn't realized his own abilities had sunk this far. She lifted the curtain and looked out at the morning haze over the Blue Ridge mountains. And with the bump-bump, rustle, and clatter coming from her parent's room, her own anxiety floated to the surface again. It was a recurrent worry, a cloud that hovered overhead, the one she shoved aside with the business of Lafayette, but now, in the absence of her internship struggles, again loomed as a threat to her future aspirations. *Will I end up just like Daddy?* Claire rubbed her eyes and consciously tried to shift gears. She definitely didn't want to spend the day obsessing over that.

She fought the urge to pull out her daily planner and organize her day. With her spare hours, she could easily review a chapter or two in Sabiston, exercise, straighten the house, visit Grandma, maybe even visit the cabinet shop where Clay had worked to look at some of his most recent projects. She stood and began her own morning routine and picked up a brush from the suitcase beside her bed. Free time should be spent efficiently, in a way that would honor the Creator of time.

Be still.

The thought carried a familiarity, a uniqueness which pushed for recognition. She'd experienced similar vague feelings before, in rare moments when she dared to slow down and listen. She halted, laid the brush on the dresser, and pondered her own reflection in the mirror. Her face was thinner, her jawline sharply defined, evidence of her dedication to long hours at the Mecca without adequate calories. Her hands explored her ribs, more pronounced than she'd remembered. She'd given everything for God's calling on her life.

So why did she feel so empty and afraid when she was back in Stoney Creek without her work?

Be still. The same familiar words sharpened into focus. *God?*

She looked at her book bag, the one she'd packed as a carry-on for her flight down, the one she'd loaded with her Sabiston text and a half-dozen unread surgical periodicals, but no Bible. Her stomach tightened with guilt. *Okay, God, maybe I have been ignoring your Word. When I get back, maybe I can find a few Christians, start a resident Bible study, maybe go to church when I'm off and—*

Be still. The thought persisted, interrupting her plans to absolve her guilt.

The phrase was something she'd encountered before. Perhaps a verse fragment she'd read as a child, or an item from the pulpit she'd tucked away from her years in church in Brighton. Her right hand again caressed the skin which was taut over her ribs, as the realization of her own spiritual leanness dawned. If she'd had a Christian life at all, she'd pushed it aside, without necessary nourishment, and pounded it with doubts about God's love and trustworthiness.

She stood, unmoving except for her eyes which scanned her childhood room, aware of the longing in her heart for something more. She was caught in the moment, unsure how to proceed, but only wanting to obey the prompting to be still. Her eyes landed on an old camp craft project, a coarse cross whittled from a cedar branch and glued to a red felt background. It was at an evening campfire at Bear Creek camp that she'd first responded to the gospel, the sweet message of forgiveness by God's grace alone. Claire had been so enthusiastic then. So filled with the joy of a newfound relationship, the promise of intimacy with the Almighty.

But somehow in her rush of fulfilling God's call, she'd fallen short. Intimacy with God was forgotten, substituted by her relationships with men and her efforts at being the best. Grace, so sweet at its first taste, had been lost, substituted by good works which would never be enough.

Claire stood still, recapturing the memory of a heartfelt faith. *I was happy then. The future held only the promise of a walk hand-in-hand with my Father.*

Full of trust? Or was I naïve?

After a few moments, she sniffed away her tears, dressed, and walked to the kitchen where Della was fixing strong coffee.

"Morning, Mom." Claire studied her mother, whose face was more wrinkled than she'd remembered.

"Hi, Claire."

Della poured coffee, and they sat in silence until Della set her empty cup on the counter.

"John Cerelli called this morning, before you were up." She paused. "He wants to see you, Claire."

Claire sighed and looked at her mother's Bible sitting on the kitchen table. "Is the path up to Cedar Knob still open?"

Della nodded. "Are you listening?"

"I'm not ready to talk to him, Mom."

"He still has love in his heart for you."

"Mom, what makes—"

Della's uplifted hand interrupted Claire's question. "You'd have to be blind not to see it."

Should I tell her I've found someone else? That it seems that God is always putting Brett in my path, and desire for him in my heart?

Claire shifted in her seat and lifted the Bible.

"You need to at least talk to him, honey."

Claire shook her head. "I'm going up to Cedar Knob." She held up her mother's Bible. "Can I borrow this?"

"Sure."

Claire took a step away from the table. "John will just have to understand." She pressed the worn leather-covered book to her breast. "I've got another relationship that I have to straighten out first."

Chapter Forty-Three

 reunion between Claire and John didn't happen. She would have begged him to come to Lafayette right after their engagement hit the rocks, but now, the thought of a face-to-face encounter made her anxious. Things were different between them now. She'd gotten involved at an exciting new level with Brett, and facing John's questions would be a painful experience for them both. She settled for returning his phone call the following afternoon.

"John, it's Claire."

"Hi." He paused. "I was hoping you'd call."

She paced in the kitchen with a mobile phone. "I should have called you sooner, but things have been crazy since the funeral." It wasn't a lie. But things in Stoney Creek always seemed a little crazy to Claire.

"I'm sure. Can I come over to see you? When are you leaving?"

"Tomorrow. I want to get back to Lafayette a few days before I need to be back in the hospital."

"How about this evening? I could drive to Stoney Creek. We could—"

"John," she interrupted. "I'm not sure this should happen. I'm confused enough about my life and relationships. Maybe it's best if we just leave things like they are."

"There are still things to talk about. We've never really processed what went wrong between us."

She sighed. "It's complicated, John. It's more than one thing. And frankly, I don't have the energy right now to sort it all out."

"You have a new boyfriend?"

She hesitated. Is that what she called Brett? "Only since our engagement was broken."

She could hear his breathing. His frustration was almost palpable. She knew the answer hurt him, but lying would have been worse.

"Can I come to Lafayette to see you? After you've had some time to work through your feelings?"

"Maybe." She looked at the Bible on the kitchen table. "All I really know is that my life has been way out of balance, John. And it took losing my brother and getting away from Lafayette for me to quiet myself enough to hear."

"Claire, I still . . . well, I still have strong feelings for you."

The phrase brought a smile to her lips and a memory from her heart. It took John months of dating Claire exclusively before he said, "I love you." He danced all around it, saying he cared, he had strong feelings, or he loved being with Claire, but never, "I love you."

"I don't want to hurt you. But I know things were good between us before HD. But after, I felt so betrayed, so unloved. I couldn't see God's love, much less yours."

"Claire, you can't blame our relationship bombing on HD."

"But you'd have held me tighter if I hadn't discovered the family curse. I know that. I'll bet you were relieved not to have to deal with it anymore."

"My feelings for you didn't change because of HD."

It sounded nice, but Claire didn't buy it. How could the idea of a loved one suffering such a tragedy not change his feelings? And even if the misunderstanding about Brett had precipitated their breakup, certainly his response had to have been modified by her newly found at-risk status. "Look. We've been through some great times together, Cerelli. I'm going to focus on what we did right. I just don't have the energy now to figure out what we did wrong."

"So it's back to Lafayette tomorrow?"

She sensed his frustration with her schedule. "John, it's less than two months until the second-year residents are selected. Surgery has to be my focus right now. It's my dream."

"I think you should go for it. It's right for you."

"Really?"

He hesitated. "Sure." He thickened his voice into a Scottish accent. "It's when you feel God's pleasure."

She laughed. He'd remembered, *Chariots of Fire.* She paused for a moment. "I'm sure we'll talk again. I'll let you know about the selections."

They said good-bye, and Claire hung up the phone before listlessly gazing at the mountains through the kitchen window. She thought about the rigors of competition in the months ahead and tried to rivet the peaceful view of the Blue Ridge securely in her mind.

She knew she was going to need it.

Della saw Doc Jenkins at the grocery checkout and maneuvered her cart between his and the shelves of individual candies placed at eye level for the impulse buyers. She kept her voice low and leaned over her bulging cart. "Thanks for being around during the funeral. The family appreciated your support."

He nodded. "Sure." He began placing items on the black grocery conveyor.

"I felt a piece of me die when I put that boy in the ground." She sniffed. "Tell me, Jimmy. What did you feel?"

Jimmy shifted his eyes around the store. "Nothing. I felt sad, of course. But what do you mean? Something special, a part of me?" He shook his head. "No."

"That was your boy, Jimmy. You know it, don't you?"

He stiffened and returned her stare. "Don't do this, Della. Nobody knows that for sure. It was a long time ago, and now Clay's gone, and no one will ever know for sure."

Della sighed. "I guess not. But I just had such a curious feeling watching his casket being lowered in the ground." She broke eye contact and looked down. "I just wondered if I was alone."

"Clay was your son. Clay was Wally's boy. He always has been and he will always stay that way in the memory of those who loved him. We've never had proof of anything different." He paused and continued unloading his cart. "And now that Clay's gone, we'll never know anything different either." He leaned toward Della. "But what about Claire? How is she handling the Huntington's risk? You haven't talked to her about us, have you?"

"Of course not. But she's not so upset about it like Clay was."

"Claire is a woman of deep water, Della."

Della smiled. "Like her mother."

"There may be trouble brewing beneath the surface, and we'd never sense that something dark is lurking. She worries me."

"Claire is a smart girl. She can handle this."

"Can she keep a secret?"

"She doesn't need to. There's no reason for her to know."

Chapter Forty-Four

On Wednesday, Claire caught an afternoon flight back to Boston and drove Brett's Mercedes south to Lafayette. As she traveled, she back-burnered Clay's accident, letting her thoughts simmer in hopes of stumbling across some hidden clue. And as much as she wanted to leave the police work to Detective Beckler, she couldn't quite shake the feeling that they weren't doing enough to uncover the events behind Clay's crash.

The one item that seemed to concern her was the new information that Dr. Jenkins had shared. Clay had just been started on a medication for anxiety. Could Clay have overdosed and have lost control because he was abusing a medication?

She shared her newest thoughts with Brett, who had stopped over after work with a pizza.

She watched with fascination as Brett shook a heavy dousing of crushed red pepper over a slice of sausage and mushroom. "I'm frustrated by the PD's lack of enthusiasm. The detective I talked to promised to look into the accident, but I think he was just saying that to get me off his back. I think they just want to assume Clay fell asleep at the wheel."

"Why can't you let it rest? Clay probably did fall asleep at the wheel. I think we both know we'll never know for sure."

"But nothing about this thing feels right. And I get the feeling that the PD isn't doing anything. They don't smell a case."

"What detective did you talk to? Beckler?"

"That's the one. How did you know?"

"I saw him the night of the accident. But then last night he paid me a visit, asking me about my truck."

"What?"

"They found a chip of orange paint on the back bumper of your car. So ol' Beckler puts on his thinking cap and remembers that I was driving an orange truck on the night of the accident. So he wants to compare the paint. I told him not to bother. I knew it'd be a match. I bumped your car the other week when I pulled in behind you out front."

"Why didn't you tell me you bumped my car?"

"Claire, did you notice any paint on your bumper?"

"No."

"And that's why I didn't tell you. It was so minor, and your car, well, it wasn't exactly a new car or anything."

"Careful, Daniels. You're insulting my car. I loved that old bomb."

"What is it with this detective anyway? I stop to help, and he basically twisted it all around until I was the bad guy or something."

She gripped his hand. "Don't worry about it. The guy didn't strike me as being the brightest guy on the block."

His eyes glistened as he looked back at Claire. "That whole experience was horrible for me. And to have that jerk suggest that I was responsible, well . . ."

She leaned forward and put her finger on his lips. "Shh," she said, "I know the truth. You did your best to save Clay's life." She planted a kiss on his forehead. "I can't thank you enough."

She turned to the sink and began rinsing her plate in the sink. In a moment, Brett was behind her, with his lips against her neck. She chilled with the sensation of goose bumps on her arms.

He kissed her lightly at first, then more passionately, and slipped his hands beneath her blouse.

She stiffened and pulled away. "I'm not ready, Brett. Especially not for that."

He took a deep breath. "But you act ready."

"It's different for me." She paused. "I need time to sort out my feelings. I did a lot of soul-searching when I was at home."

"What do you want? In a relationship, what are you looking for?"

"I always dreamed of having a Christian family." She halted. "But finding out about Huntington's disease has changed all that. The thought of carrying an HD gene and passing it on complicates everything."

"It hasn't stopped me from wanting you." He pulled her face forward, and she accepted the gentle caress of his lips against hers.

"Brett," she whispered before clearing her throat. "I need a Christian man who understands my faith."

He released her and met her eyes. "I'm a Christian."

She didn't respond.

"Don't look so surprised. My parents took me to church."

"Going to church doesn't necessarily mean you're a Christian."

"And not going doesn't mean I'm not," he countered.

She sighed. "Then there's hope for me, too."

"Hey, I'm just like you. I'm a resident. I don't have time for church services. It's the life we've chosen."

She studied his blue eyes. They were misted, full of sincerity. *How can I make him understand?*

"I'll support your religion," he said. "I know it's important to you."

But it has to be important to you, Brett. "It's funny. I haven't always been very good at knowing what God wants for me. He put a passion in my life for medicine, and I've pursued it with everything I am." Her eyes met his. She hesitated to continue.

"What else is in your heart, Claire? What do you feel?" He reached for her hand and interlocked his fingers with hers. "Desire? Maybe God gave you that too."

"This year has been the worst and the best of my life. And every time I've been afraid, you've come to my rescue." She shook her head. "And even in Clay's accident, who was there to help?"

She paused, looking at the hand in hers. It was beautiful, smooth and strong, with long fingers possessing the gentleness needed for delicate surgery. She turned his hand over, palm up, their fingers still intertwined. She focused on their fingers together, side by side, before letting the image blur. In that way, she couldn't distinguish their fingers. They were together, woven in one, each one independent, but not clearly his or hers. After a moment, she wiggled her fingers, bringing them back into focus as her own.

"I don't know, Brett. It seems that over and over, you've been there when I was in trouble. Why did you stop at my house after Roger Jones threatened me? Why were you the one to help my brother? I can't seem to shake the feeling that maybe God keeps putting you in my path."

"These aren't coincidences, Claire."

The thought chilled her, bringing excited tingles to her shoulders again. God?

He coaxed her forward, kissing her again, caressing her lips, his mouth warm, seeking more.

"We need to go slow, Brett," she cautioned, her mind a whirlwind of confusion. Brett was right. He could sense her desire to give in. But she knew she needed space, an opportunity to regain balance in her life, balance that had been upset by her dedication to surgery, and the overhanging cloud of risk that HD had become.

She gently extended her arm, moving her hand against his chest. "If this is right . . . if we are right for each other, I'm sure God will keep bringing you in my path."

His eyes were searching. "I'm here now."

"Don't tempt me, Brett," she pleaded. "I don't want to be distracted from my goal. A romance with you is so appealing, but—"

"But what? How can you resist what's in your heart?"

She took a deep breath. A deep, cleansing breath. "HD is changing the way I look at my future. It complicates things, Brett. It complicates love, marriage, having kids, my life as a surgeon, and the way I look at the future. I may only have a few years left. I want to be sure I make the right choices."

"That's why you should only live for today. Embrace love today, Claire. We don't know what tomorrow holds."

She could see the hurt in his eyes. And knowing he yearned for her so badly made it agonizing to say no. She shook her head. "I need time, Brett. I want to be sure."

He looked away. Was he shielding his eyes, to hide his hurt? He walked to the entrance to the den before he turned around, his manly physique perfectly framed in the doorway. "Remember when we first met, how we walked on the beach?"

She nodded.

"Let's do it again, Claire. I'll make dinner Saturday night, a celebration of sorts, a toast to your commitment to making the right choices. We can stroll along the beach and dream about the future."

"The future," she muttered. A dream or a nightmare? "It scares me, Brett."

"Don't be afraid. I'll be there to hold your hand."

She nibbled her lower lip. She didn't want to cry.

"Seven o'clock?"

She wiped her eyes with the back of her hand. "It sounds wonderful."

Billy Ray Davis wasn't used to being discarded like junk mail. Sure, he'd opened his mouth when he shouldn't have, but he was doing it in an honest attempt to get Ramsey another case. If you could call anything that Billy Ray did "honest." How was he to know that the tearful young woman in the chapel was Claire McCall?

He huffed and yanked open a drawer of the metal filing cabinet in front of him. Ramsey couldn't say he didn't know what Billy was doing. In fact, over the years, Billy had honed the craft of squeezing his prey in just the right way to get the information he needed. And he'd done it under the tutelage of Ramsey Plank. So what gave Ramsey the right to blame everything on Billy Ray?

He shuffled through the files in front of him, investigations past, the secret lives of clients, the dirt he'd dug, enough manure to fertilize a large vegetable garden. There had to be something here he could use to his advantage.

Billy Ray paused and shoveled a handful of peanuts out of a glass container on his desk. He popped the nuts into his mouth, one by one, thinking of ways to even the score.

He thought about Claire McCall, and her mistake which would cost the university a fortune.

And he thought of Ramsey taking his third to the bank. Without Billy Ray.

He thought about his unfortunate encounter with Claire McCall after she'd lost her brother.

Hmmm. She asked me to talk to the Joneses and tell them about the doctor's brother. She wanted to know if they were pleased with Ramsey's services.

An idea began to formulate. He slowly chewed a mouthful of peanuts. Hard thinking like this definitely demanded more calories.

Ramsey seems to forget that I was the one who convinced Celia and Roger Jones to file this suit. I was the one who found them huddled in the hospital chapel after losing their little girl.

Maybe it is time I paid Celia Jones a little visit, just to have a little chat about Ramsey and poor young Dr. McCall.

The following day, Claire spent the morning nurturing her African violets and cleaning her neglected house. It wasn't exactly her favorite vacation activity, but things had deteriorated to a level of intolerance for her, and the minuteness of sweeping and dusting seemed to settle her soul.

At noon, she called Detective Beckler. She wanted an update, and he hadn't returned her call.

His voice was muffled, and she imagined him at his desk with a large deli sandwich. "I haven't had much in the way of luck, Dr. McCall. Everything seems to check out okay."

"What about the skid marks? A sleeping man doesn't brake."

"He does if startled awake just before running off the road."

Claire nodded. "Brett Daniels told me you talked to him about his truck."

"Another dead end," he groaned.

She heard a slurping noise. *Make that a large deli sandwich and a drink. You probably don't do diet soda, do you, sir?*

"What about Roger Jones? Did you ask him about chasing me?"

"He's got an alibi. His wife claims he was at church all evening." He paused, and Claire could hear the rattle of a foil bag.

Make that a large deli sandwich, drink, and a bag of chips.

"I'm no judge, Mr. Beckler, but Roger Jones doesn't seem the type to spend a midweek evening in church."

"His wife claims that she's been trying to get him to come for a long time. He hadn't gone since the funeral of his little—Oh, say, Dr. McCall, I'm sorry to bring that up." He cleared his throat before continuing. "Anyway, she says that her niece was being baptized, or something. He agreed to come and stood in front of the whole congregation for the ceremony. She said she'd give me a list of members if I wanted to question witnesses."

"Oh, I saw him at church. He chased me out of the parking lot."

"But that's not her story. She says seeing you there flipped him out, that he wasn't about to go in if you were there. So he stormed off. She says they weren't chasing you." He paused and slurped his drink. "Ms. Jones said she finally got him calmed down enough to return to the church."

"Do you believe her?"

"I'm not sure. They seem sincere. But something's bothering that woman big time. She feels guilty about something. I've got a few more leads to check. Maybe I will talk to someone in the church, just to make sure his alibi checks out." He paused. Claire heard more crunching before he continued. "But I've got to tell you, I have a feeling that all of this is going nowhere. I think your brother just ran off the road. Maybe a bee stung him or something. Maybe he was lost and was looking for a map in the glove box. There are a hundred reasons why he could have been momentarily distracted."

"I guess so."

"Try not to worry."

His voice became muffled again, before he came back. "Listen, I've got to run. I have your cell phone number. I'll call you if I get anywhere."

Claire hung up the phone and stretched. The detective's work hadn't solved the questions that she feared would remain unanswered forever. She drummed her fingers on the kitchen counter.

It was time to do a little snooping of her own.

The clerk in medical records pushed the patient record across the counter. "This can't leave the department. It hasn't been completely coded yet, and that means there's a lot of money outstanding."

"Sure." Claire smiled sweetly and carried the record to the physician dictating area.

She opened to the history and physical exam, reading the details of Clay's resuscitation and the frantic efforts to keep him alive. She saw a handwritten note by the paramedics which documented their failed efforts to secure an appropriate airway, and the emergency cricothyroidotomy performed by Dr. Daniels at the crash scene. Her skin bristled as she visualized the drama unfolding.

She turned to the next section, consultation notes, to read reports from the neurosurgeons and the orthopedic surgeons who assisted in Clay's care. She read through Beatrice Hayes' dictation, which detailed Clay's family history of Huntington's disease and alcoholism. Claire felt her blood begin to boil. Beatrice had asked her all those questions in front of Dr. Rogers, all the while knowing the answers! Claire hadn't given her any satisfaction, except to report that the family history was noncontributory, but Bea's report was full of the details that Claire had declined to give her. Bea just wanted to make sure Dr. Rogers found out about her father's HD.

She looked carefully at the lab data, noting the absence of any alcohol or drugs on the screening test. There went her theory about Clay overdosing on the medication Dr. Jenkins gave. Unless the Zoloft wouldn't be detected on the routine screen.

She turned the pages, flipping through the transfusion records, with a slip completed for each of the multiple units of packed red blood cells that Clay received. Each slip recorded signatures of the transfusionist, start and stop times, and his blood type. Everything was documented carefully to avoid a transfusion mismatch catastrophe. Wow. They must have gone through his entire blood volume three or four times.

She turned to look at his X-ray reports when the information she'd just read began to claw its way back into consciousness. Something didn't feel right. Her gut tightened. Her palms began to sweat. Dread had crept upon her, and she sensed a rising tide of panic.

Wait a minute! She flipped back to the transfusion slips. They had given Clay type-A blood.

Claire closed her eyes, attempting to remember. She was type O, the same as her mother. Wally was type B. She was almost certain. She'd done the blood-typing herself for a college project. No, it couldn't be. She needed to look at her genetics project again.

Clay couldn't be type A if Daddy was B and Mom was O. They gave Clay the wrong type of blood! That could have caused a problem with clotting, leading to the bleeding that he experienced and, in turn, his death.

She flipped the pages looking at each transfusion slip. Each one was the same. Type A. Clay was a victim of a fatal transfusion reaction.

Who was responsible?

She read through the progress notes documenting the nursing notes chronicling Clay's last hours. Yes, all of these things could have been the result of a blood-bank mistake.

Unless . . . A thought struck her head-on, derailing her initial assessment.

She stood, shoved the chart back across the counter at the records clerk, and stumbled from the room in a daze. It couldn't be.

She jogged across the parking lot to Brett's Mercedes and completed the trip to her rented brownstone, trying desperately to quell the terror rising within her. *I must have remembered wrong. Or could I have made a mistake when I typed Daddy's blood in my old genetics class?*

She jumped from the car and ran into her house and up the stairs to the bedroom closet where she dropped to her knees to pull out the old genetics project. Wally was type B. Della was type O.

Her hand went to her mouth as the realization struck.

Her mind raced with thoughts of betrayal, deception, lies, and cover-up.

Was someone trying to cover the truth?

Slowly she stood and went to the phone to dial her mother. After six rings, Claire was about to hang up.

After eight rings, she heard a voice. "Hello."

For a moment, she thought she'd dialed the wrong number. "Uh . . . hello."

"Claire!"

When he spoke her name, she recognized her father's voice. She hadn't known him to answer the phone in months. "Daddy?" She hesitated. "Is Mom there?"

"Sssheese at the ssstore."

Claire could hear a bump, bump, bump. Is he having trouble holding the phone still? Or striking it against his head?

"Could you have her call me? It's important."

"Sssure."

"As soon as she gets in." *Will you remember?*

"Okay."

She was about to say good-bye when she heard him begin to speak again. He spoke mechanically, and Claire could imagine his face twitching, refusing to obey, not allowing him to express his emotions through a normal smile or frown.

"Cllaaire," he started. "I llove yyyou."

The message caught her off guard. It had been years since she'd heard him say it.

"Daddy, I—"

It sounded like Wally was crying. His words were normally slurred, but his voice had thickened to the point where Claire had to concentrate to understand. But after a moment, she understood. He hadn't told Clay. Told him what?

He was upset about something.

Because he didn't have a chance to tell Clay he loved him.

The realization pierced her heart. He didn't want to make the same mistake again. Wally cried, and the sound began to break her heart.

"Don't cry, Daddy," she pleaded. "I understand. I do." She wiped away her own tears, weighing her reply. She didn't speak until she knew it was true. She searched her heart, and in amazement the perception grew. She'd forgiven him! Somehow in the hearing of those three little words, her heart had melted. The icy bitterness was gone.

"I love you too, Daddy. I love you too."

She said good-bye and laid down the phone.

As she walked to the bedroom, she felt her heart would burst. Her body retched with sobs, a release of emotion she could not and would not control. Oh, how she wondered at the impact of those three little words, the words she was certain her father would never speak again! She looked at the blood-typing poster on the floor. The message which had seemed so important a moment ago, now was almost forgotten, lost in the wake of the gift from Wally.

She studied the poster for a moment before gazing at her own reflection in the mirror. She lifted her index finger and traced the outline of her face upon the glass surface.

She'd gone to the hospital to see if she could discover the reason for Clay's crash. But in the process, she had uncovered something more disturbing than a reason for his death: she didn't know the reason for his life. His blood type revealed that Wally couldn't be his father. And if Wally hadn't fathered Clay, then who had fathered Clay's twin sister?

"Who am I?" she whispered to herself.

On the day her father had finally said "I love you," she'd discovered he may not be her father at all.

Chapter Forty-Five

Della arrived hugging an armload of groceries, to find Wally on the couch staring at the TV screen, with the phone on the floor beside him. His cheeks were moist. Perhaps something on the TV had upset him.

Della heaved the groceries onto the kitchen counter. "I'm home, Wally."

Wally didn't answer right away. Della didn't expect him to. Speech initiation was often a problem in HD.

Life had changed so much for them, since the mystery had been solved. Finally there was an explanation for his altered speech, his apathy, poor impulse control, his irritability, the emotional roller coaster that took him from high to low within a moment's time. Finally there was an explanation for his difficulty with making choices, even obvious ones like when to urinate or what to eat. Finally, there was a reason for the constant movements he couldn't control.

But Wally didn't often cry. This had been a recent development. Della had seen it when he watched Clay in the ICU, then later when he talked with Pastor Phil about Clay, eternity, and God's forgiveness.

Maybe it was a new stage, a loss of impulse control, just like his anger and frustration. She walked to his side and dried his face with a kitchen towel. "What's wrong, honey?"

He paused, his head in constant motion, unable to lock onto her face for more than a few seconds.

She'd learned to be patient. He would tell her if she waited.

"Cccla–Claire called."

Della sat beside him on the couch and waited as he jerked his story out. It seemed as though his breathing could not be coordinated with his mouth and lips. The message that he wanted to speak didn't arrive at his mouth and his lungs at the same time. But she waited, and eventually understood, through the jumble of starts and stops, and the slurred speech, what Wally had done.

Della understood. The tears were not an impulse problem. The tears were joy, and God's Spirit was the fountain from which they flowed.

She kissed his cheek, but not before their foreheads collided. Della knew that embracing a patient with HD carried this risk, but this opportunity was not to be neglected. Hazards to the wind. She needed to kiss her husband.

She stabilized his face in her hands and kissed him again. "Wally, you old softy." She tussled his hair into disarray and stood. "I'll fix you some lunch. I bought the Pringles you like so much."

After lunch, and cleaning up Wally, the floor, and the table, Della helped him into the bathroom, and then into his wheelchair before pushing him into the afternoon sun on the back porch facing the Blue Ridge. She sat on the porch swing and called Claire, nestling the phone against her shoulder and watching Wally.

Claire picked up after one ring. "Hello."

"Claire, it's Mom."

Della heard her sigh, a sure sign that Claire was worried. *What's up now, little girl? You're always stressed lately.* "How was your flight?"

"Mom, who is my father?"

The question blindsided her. *What? Where did that come from?* Della grabbed the phone and jumped off the swing. Then, with one glance at her husband, she slipped into the house. "Claire, what on earth—"

"Mom, I know. Don't play games with me."

Now Della was the one in need of a deep breath. But somehow, it wouldn't come. Her chest felt tight, constricted by a band of fear that wouldn't let her inhale. She stared at the phone. This was so like Claire. Direct. Straight to the bottom line. She'd never been the child to skirt around an important issue. "H–how?"

"I went over Clay's medical record. I saw his blood type, Mom. Clay is type A. He can't be Daddy's son."

Della stumbled into the bedroom and closed the door. The moment she'd feared for nearly three decades had come.

"I–I hardly know what to say."

"How about the truth?" Claire started to cry. "You deceived me, Mom."

"No, Claire. I was never sure myself." She halted, unsure how to proceed. *Oh, God, help me.* "Claire, honey, believe me. I only did what I thought was best. I made some bad choices a long time ago. And I never really thought it would make a difference if you knew."

"A difference? I don't even know—"

"Let me speak, Claire," she interrupted. "As a mother, I only wanted what was best for you and Clay. I didn't think it would be fair for you to grow up under the shadow of my sin. It was my cross, not yours." Della massaged her fingers against her forehead.

"Does Daddy know?"

She hesitated. "Yes. He knew of my affair. But he never seemed to question if our children were his. If he did, he never let on."

"But why keep it from us?"

"By the time you were old enough to understand, you and Wally were having a bad time communicating. I couldn't see throwing in another question that would threaten your relationship." She clutched the collar of her blouse. "Claire, I did the best I knew how. I'm so sorry."

"And what about now? Why not tell me so I wouldn't have spent months worrying about coming down with Huntington's disease?"

"Because I was never sure. I suspected, but I never really knew for a fact that Clay wasn't Wally's." She paused. Her breath was coming easier now. "So I guess you don't need to worry about HD. Margo's negative. It looks like HD will stop in the McCall family with Wally."

"Is this why you wanted me to talk Clay into being tested? You suspected he was negative all along?"

"I wanted him to stop all of his risk-taking."

"And you didn't worry about me? Didn't you want to relieve me too?"

"It seemed different with you. You were always stronger than Clay. I could see that you could handle it, but Clay . . . I was afraid he would . . . die." The words lodged in her throat, as she understood the irony. "Oh, Claire, do you think if I'd have told him the truth, that he'd be alive today? Did the threat of HD push Clay into the circumstances which killed him?"

"No, Mom. You can't allow yourself to think that way. You did the best you knew how. You didn't will for this to happen."

Della paced the little bedroom, not knowing what to say or what to think. A sin long buried was back in her face, tearing at her soul again.

"Mom? Momma?"

Della took a deep breath. "I'm here."

"I need to know something else." She was reluctant to continue.

"What is it Claire?"

"Could I be Wally's?"

"Claire, you're Clay's twin. You couldn't be."

"But we're fraternal. That means that we could have different fathers." She stopped. "If you were . . . with two different men . . . within a short time."

"A short time?" Jimmy made the house call a day before Wally returned from sea. She hesitated to confess. "I guess . . . it's possible."

"Then I could be Daddy's girl?"

"You're the doctor, Claire. I didn't know such things were possible."

There was silence on the phone for a moment. "Mom, I'm blood type O, just like you." More silence, and a tapping noise.

Della looked at her nails. Claire drummed her fingernails just like her.

"Wally is type B. I need to know the blood type of the other man."

More tapping noise.

"Who was he, Mom? Is he still alive?"

"He's alive."

"Mom, I need to know."

"I promised him I'd never tell another soul."

"This is different, Mom. It's my future."

Della closed her eyes tightly and let the name escape before she could retrieve it. "Jimmy Jenkins."

There was no audible response. She supposed Claire hadn't heard or was just being polite by not gasping.

After a moment, Della spoke. "Claire?"

"I heard you, Mom." She paused. "I'll need to ask him a few questions."

Della lifted the bedroom curtain and looked out at Wally. "Do what you have to do, honey," she spoke softly. "I'm so tired of keeping this secret."

Chapter Forty-Six

By the next evening, Claire was still brooding over the news of her mother's deception. She thought twice about canceling her date with Brett, then decided that having a friend to share the load might be just what she needed. Claire arrived at Brett's to find preparations in full swing for a romantic evening. He had set a table on his back deck, hors d'oeuvres were arranged on a clear plate shaped like a sea scallop, there were pink roses on the counter, and a bottle of wine was chilling.

She inspected the scene. "Brett!" she scolded, looking at the bottle of wine.

He pointed a finger in her face, gently tapping her nose. "You only get one glass. I know how you get when you drink."

"Where did you learn to do this?"

He shrugged. "My mother."

"I'd like to meet her. She must be a wonderful woman to put up with more than one surgeon in the house."

He poured the wine and handed her a glass.

She accepted with a twinge of hesitation. She took a small sip and set the glass on the counter. "Let's walk on the beach before dinner."

They crossed the road, hand in hand, and slipped off their shoes. The sand was cool between her toes. Brett dropped her hand and took long, leaping steps, making footprints in the sand. Claire followed, and tried to land in the impressions he made.

Brett frowned. "What's wrong? You are way too quiet."

"I talked to my mom last night."

They walked slowly, as Claire shared her new discovery about Clay's paternity, her mother's affair with the town doctor, and how Wally had said the words which broke her heart. "It's weird, Brett. Just hearing him say 'I love you' seemed to change something inside me."

His expression told her he didn't understand.

"Maybe it's just a father-daughter thing," she offered. "Maybe all these years that I've been running from home, trying to do great things, I was really trying to win his approval."

"You're sounding like a psychiatrist, Claire," he responded playfully. "I'm a surgeon. I don't usually get these things."

She punched his side. "You're a man. You'll never get these things." She paused. "Unless you have a daughter one day."

"If I do, I hope she looks like you."

Claire tried not to smile as she examined the man beside her. *You have fallen for me hard, haven't you, lifeguard boy?* She looked at the waves, conscious of the soothing effect the rhythm had upon her. Wally loved her. Brett was holding her hand. The air seemed to carry the expectation of brighter days.

"So what about Dr. Jenkins? Did you talk to him? Did you ask him about his blood type?"

She shook her head. "Not yet. I didn't know what to say. I started thinking about what his response would be, and I guess I chickened out."

"Claire, you need to know. This whole Huntington's disease cloud you've been walking under may all be imagined. You need to ask him about his blood type. Wally may not be your father after all."

Claire nudged closer to Brett and slowed her pace. The wind had picked up, and the spray of the surf felt cold on her neck. Brett responded and put his arm around her shoulders. "I know that, Brett. And believe me, I want to know about my risk for Huntington's, but . . . well, the fatherhood issue is different for me. It's not just a DNA issue."

"What is this, psychiatry revisited?"

"Don't joke, Brett. This is serious for me. I keep thinking about something my mother said to Grandma McCall about Daddy. I remember it so clearly because I sat there amazed that this woman, whom I'd written off as so shallow when I was leaving home, could come up with something so profound."

"Well?"

"She said that blood doesn't change fatherhood in the real world. Maybe yes at some biological level, but not in relationships where it counts."

She continued, looking out at the swells which crested near the shoreline. "For me, Wally is always going to be my father. That's what God intended for me. For years, I've hated the fact that my father was the town drunk. But I'm beginning to see him differently now. HD has changed everything."

"So what about Clay, his accident? Are you ready to move on?" He hesitated. "Let's make this evening a milestone, Claire. Let's move on. Together."

Claire leaned against Brett's strong frame, absorbing his strength, drawing from his encouragement to let the past go. She didn't want to cry. "Okay," she said.

They walked on toward the fishing pier which jutted sharply from the sand into the frigid ocean. The waves were large, crashing with a force which caused Claire to nestle even closer to Brett, and slow their stride to a meditative pace which they continued in silence.

They walked out onto the pier, an old wooden structure with thick pilings which held the walkway high above the water below. There was a small shack on the pier, a hundred feet back from the end, a bait supply which was empty now, left desolate by fishermen unwilling to endure the cold evening wind.

At the end, Claire looked down at the waves, frothing and grasping at the barnacled pilings some fifteen feet below.

"Here," Brett urged, "lean out into the wind." He guided her to stand upon the first crosspiece of the railing. "One more," he said. "I've got you."

She dared to obey, and with his strong arms around her waist, she leaned over into the wind. She could not look down, only forward. "I'm afraid."

"I won't let you fall. It's time to trust."

For Claire, it seemed a moment of epiphany. She had walked in her own strength for so long, priding herself in her own abilities, independent of her hometown, her family, her father, and her God.

She slowly raised her arms to her side. She was an eagle, ready for flight.

"Did you ever see *Titanic?*" he asked. "Here we are. I'm Jack Dawson."

"And I'm Rose," she responded. "I can almost hear the theme song."

The wind had picked up, and as she stepped down, they fell into a natural embrace. She lingered with her mouth on his, tasting the salt from the ocean spray on his lips.

She shivered and looked into his eyes. He seemed far away. Perhaps in a dream of his own, thinking of the future.

A chirping noise startled Claire to attention. *My cell phone. Who could be calling me now?* She lifted the phone from her pocket and unfolded it to answer.

"Hello." She shielded the phone from the wind but couldn't hear. She jogged to the bait shack and huddled against a wall which smelled of fish.

She glanced at Brett, who had stayed at the end of the pier. He was leaning over the water, with his hands in the air.

"Hello," she repeated, louder.

"Dr. McCall? Detective Beckler, Lafayette PD. Where are you?"

"I'm standing on the fishing pier, across from Smithland Shoals."

"I wanted to get your input on something. I think I may have gotten a break in my investigation into your brother's crash."

She leaned closer to the wall. "What?"

"I want you to listen to a 911 tape for me. I think we have a record of Clay's voice."

"Does he identify himself?"

"No, but the call was quick. It's pretty convincing."

"It can't be Clay. Brett Daniels was the one who made the call from my phone."

"Where did you find your phone? Was it in your car?"

"Sure. I told you that."

"Why would he put the phone back into a wrecked vehicle, Dr. McCall?"

Claire looked at Brett at the end of the pier, as an uneasiness drifted across her mind. "I don't know. Maybe he just threw it there during all the confusion."

"I don't think so. I don't think he's the man you think he is. Dr. Daniels was on the scene for a reason. He's the one who forced your brother off the road."

She coughed. "That's ridiculous. Brett's not like that. He tried to save my brother."

"Ask him about Lisa Dunn. My hunch is that this Dr. Daniels has a pretty sick way of chasing away the competition."

The idea struck Claire as absurd.

"Let me play you the tape. I think you'll understand."

You must be misinterpreting the facts. And here I thought I was grasping at straws. The wind whipped around the little bait shack. "I can hardly hear what you're saying."

"I need you to listen to the 911 tape. To see if you can identify Clay's voice." He spoke loudly. "Can I meet you somewhere?"

"I'm, well, I'm with Brett Daniels."

"Now?"

She looked up to see him approaching. "Yes. We're on the fishing pier, down from his place."

She heard the detective curse. "Pretend you're talking to your mother. Dr. Daniels is a sick man. He's not the friend you think he is. I'm on my way."

"Bye, Mom," she said, feeling a bit foolish for following his instruction. She looked at the phone as the line went dead. None of this made any sense. But the detective sounded so convinced. She folded her phone and slid it into her back pocket again.

Brett leaned forward, taking her in his arms. "Where were we?" he said, kissing her again. "Who called?"

Claire's mind whirled. Things were getting difficult to sort out. With Brett kissing her neck, the wind blowing through her hair, and the phone conversation clawing at her gut, she suddenly needed the world to stop. Facts floated by, but she couldn't seem to grasp the truth. Brett had been her savior, the one who'd been there over and over when she had been afraid. Wasn't that evidence enough of God's leading, bringing Brett into her life? *When I'd just come back to Lafayette, isn't that what Brett said?*

She replayed the memory of what she'd spoken. *"I can't seem to shake the feeling that maybe God keeps putting you in my path."*

What was it he said?

"These aren't coincidences, Claire."

"Claire?" He pushed his lips against her neck. "Who called?"

A knot rose in her stomach. She was a lousy liar. "My mom." The words were out of her mouth, without hopes of retrieval. *Please don't ask me what she wanted. My mind is blank.*

He rubbed her back, his hands searching, caressing. He slipped his hand into her hip pocket and edged her forward.

She withdrew and stepped away. "Stop."

He extracted his hand slowly from her pocket, knocking her cell phone out onto the pier. She leaned to pick it up, but he scooped it up quickly into his hand.

"Let me see this thing," he said, laughing. "I've never seen a pink one before."

Her throat was suddenly dry. "You've never seen it before?"

His expression was blank, clueless of her probing. "No. But don't get me wrong, pink is okay for you. It's just—"

She backed away, edging closer to the end of the pier. "Brett, you're scaring me."

"What's wrong?" He stepped forward, but she moved again. Away. Just out of reach.

"You said you used my phone to dial 911, remember?"

He looked like a deer in the road, frozen by car headlights. In a moment he turned his eyes away. "Oh, yeah. I guess I forgot in all the excitement."

Did you forget? Or? She took another step back and looked at the long row of boards leading to the shore. Behind Brett. "Brett, who was Lisa Dunn?"

He squinted and wiped the mist from his forehead. "An intern. She didn't make it."

"Did you scare her away?"

Brett laughed, a nervous laugh, a forced laugh.

He had been so slick, but now Claire was beginning to understand.

She stared at him, seeing him as if for the first time, as a horror began to dawn. And along with a nauseating dread, a fury rose within her, anger at her own blindness and at Brett.

"Why, Brett? Why?"

He stepped toward her, and again she maintained her distance by a step closer to the edge.

"It's not what you think, Claire. It was an accident. I swear—"

"You thought it was me, didn't you? You wanted me to die."

"No!" He hung his head. "I only wanted to frighten you."

"Was it you on the phone? Trying to scare me away?"

He held up his hands edging even closer. "Remember when I first tried to kiss you?"

She nodded. *Where's he going with this? I wonder if I can beat him to the beach?*

"Every time I wanted you, you slammed the door, Claire. I knew you'd never fall for a guy like me." His voice began to weaken. He was on an emotional precipice, about to tumble and cry.

She studied him as a rising horror seemed to threaten her breath.

"The first time you were scared, you turned to me. And suddenly, I was the one holding Claire." He wiped his nose with the back of his hand. The lifeguard boy that Claire had imagined . . . was gone.

"It was you! I would resist your advances, so you threatened me. And I turned to you."

"I was your hero."

"I told you about being chased by Mr. Jones. I ran back to you after that." She paused, incredulous. "So you thought you'd chase me? Scare me back into your arms?"

"Into my arms or out of the program." He held up his hands and stepped forward again. "Either way, I win."

"Didn't you think I'd recognize your truck?"

He shook his head. "Not at night. Not with my brights on. You'd never see the vehicle."

She stumbled backwards. "You killed my brother."

"It was an accident, Claire. I promise," he stuttered. "I only meant to scare you."

"Get away," she shouted. "Get away!"

"Claire," he begged, his voice on the edge of tears. He lunged forward with his arms open.

She sidestepped quickly to evade his grasp, but slipped on the boards which were slick from the ocean spray. She skidded forward beneath the wooden railing, her leg scraping the edge as she fell.

In a moment, she was airborne, in a free fall toward the frigid ocean. There was no time to brace for impact. She heard a scream, her own, and plunged into the sea.

Chapter Forty-Seven

Claire surfaced, coughing, tasting the ocean brine and feeling cold. A death-grip cold like she'd never felt before. She wrestled off her sweater and tried to swim toward the beach, but the current was strong, pulling hard away from shore. A wave slammed her forward into a wood piling, sending her chest and abdomen scraping against the barnacles.

Above her, she heard Brett scream, a muffled cry of distress which seemed far away, his voice dissipated by the howling wind. She grasped at the piling, pain searing through the lacerations on her chest. Her hands were quickly going numb, and she'd only been in the water a few moments.

I'm going to die. Just like Clay. Alone. I can't last long in water this cold.

There was more yelling above, and then a splash beside her, and Brett's voice, gurgling and screaming her name.

A hand gripped her ankle. He was dragging her under. *He's trying to kill me.*

I'm going to die.

For a moment, she was tempted to let the piling go. She tried to speak but her chin quivered, and the air escaped without sound. It would be so easy to slip beneath the water and surrender to the current.

She felt herself being torn away from the pier. Her hands were numb, refusing to obey. She kicked to be free of his grip, but he was too strong. Her hands broke free of the pier. She turned to lash out with her arms, choking on the water as she was pulled away. But as she struggled to reach him, her arm fell onto an open ring. She flailed for life, securing her grip around an orange rescue ring.

And then, the hand on her ankle was gone. Shivering violently, she managed to speak. "Br–Brett!"

There was noise above, and a man's voice yelling her name. But she could not speak again. She could only clutch in desperation to the ring in her arms.

The ring tugged forward, and for the first time, she realized it was attached to a rope. She was being pulled to safety.

The water made her heavy, too heavy to be lifted from the waves. But Claire hung on, unaware of time, aware only of the ring in her arms. She knew little else except for bone-chilling cold. Suddenly, she felt a heaviness beneath her. She could not feel her feet. But there was the sensation of pressure. *My feet are dragging on the sand.* She fought to stand, and a breaking wave crashed her forward. Then there were arms, strong arms, dragging her from the surf.

"Don't try to talk. I've got you now. You're safe."

She recognized Detective Beckler.

In the distance, she heard a siren. Help was on the way.

A few minutes later, inside a rescue vehicle, her clothes were stripped away and warm, dry blankets were placed against her skin. An IV was inserted, and an oxygen mask slipped over her mouth and nose.

She looked up to see the detective, leaning over her.

She caught his eye. "Brett Daniels did this. He was trying to drown me."

He shook his head. "I had thrown two life rings that were swept away before he jumped in with the last one. Brett Daniels saved your life."

"Where is he?"

He looked toward the surf and shook his head. "Out there."

The following afternoon, lying in her hospital bed, Claire listened as Detective Beckler played the 911 tapes.

The first voice was the emergency operator, a female.

"911 emergency."

"Someone's following me."

Claire leaned forward. The voice was strained, but it sounded like Clay's.

The female voice continued, "May I have your name and your location."

The sound of wind distorted Clay's answer.

The sound of screeching tires, and a gasp was followed by a dull thud.

The detective stopped the tape. "I think Clay braked and was struck from behind."

Claire looked up. "I guess that explains the orange paint."

"Exactly. My theory is that when Clay was struck, he dropped the phone."

He restarted the tape. The only sound was that of the wind and what sounded like a frustrated cry. "Ahhh!"

A few seconds later, the sound of tire rubber against the blacktop preceded the sickening crunch of metal against metal, brief silence, then breaking glass and a second deafening thud.

Claire put her hand to her lips. "Is that it?"

Beckler shook his head. "No. A second call came in moments after this call. Listen to this." He inserted a second tape.

"911 emergency."

"This is Brett Daniels. There's been a terrible accident on the beach road near the lighthouse. A girl's been hurt bad. My orange truck is parked off the road at the sight. I'm a doctor. I'll do what I can, but I need a paramedic crew now."

Beckler snapped off the tape. "That's all we have from Dr. Daniels. He ended his call before the operator could respond."

A knot rose in Claire's throat. "He told me he made the call from my phone! But he called from his own phone. Clay had made the call from my cell phone." She shook her head incredulously. "Brett told me that he didn't recognize my car, that he didn't know Clay was my brother." She halted. "But he told the operator it was a girl. He must have recognized my car. He thought it was me or he wouldn't have told them that a girl had been hurt."

The detective nodded soberly. "There's more." He put back in the first tape. "Clay never turned off his phone. We have a record of the first few moments of Brett's arrival as he climbed down to the scene. Listen to this."

The sounds were muffled, a voice cracking and anguished. "Claire! Claire!" Then softer. "Claire! I was just trying to scare you," the voice sobbed. The sound of crunching glass and a gasp. "Claire?" A curse followed, and the line went dead.

"I think what we are hearing is Brett looking in the car, not seeing your body, then seeing Clay outside the vehicle, and Brett realizing that it isn't you."

"Did Brett terminate the call from my phone?"

The officer shrugged. "I'm not sure. It's possible he found it and terminated the call, before throwing it against the dash in frustration."

Claire closed her eyes and looked away, her emotions threatening to overflow with tears. Again.

How could I have been so gullible?

The irony was not lost on Claire. *Oh, God,* she prayed. *Why was it so easy for me to trust Brett, but so hard for me to put my trust in you?*

Chapter Forty-Eight

A week later the twelve surgical interns gathered for an urgent meeting with Tom Rogers, the surgical department chairman and residency director. His mood was sober, and he addressed the interns with a nod of his head as he arrived.

The nervous chatter about the meeting ceased with his entry.

Claire watched as he stepped behind a podium and began.

"The life of a surgery resident has never been easy. We know that. It's a fact of life."

He sighed. "But there have been many voices within our department pushing for a change in organization. And Brett Daniels' death has given us reason to think again about the stress produced in this environment, the environment of a pyramid program.

"This program was designed to produce the best. And we are committed to continuing. But, as of the selection of our new incoming intern group in July, this program at Lafayette will no longer operate as a pyramid. It will be a block, with five interns slotted as categorical surgery interns. These five will be graduated through the program until they finish as chief residents. The other interns will be classified as preliminary interns, and it will be understood from the first day of training that they will have only a year or two here, and then they will transfer elsewhere to continue their training.

"In this way, we hope to foster less competition and more camaraderie in the trenches.

"But where does it leave you?" He let the question hang for a moment.

The interns glanced side to side, uncomfortable with the silence.

The chairman continued. "Next month, we will select five of you as categorical surgical residents to continue this program for the next five years. Three of the remaining group will be offered positions as preliminary surgical residents, but will understand that we can offer no assurances that they will finish the program.

"If any of you know that you are not continuing in the program, you must let me know this week, so I can make my selections."

Dr. Padgett raised his hand. "Dr. Rogers? I'll tell you right now. I've been offered a spot in ortho right here at Lafayette. I'm taking it. You can give my spot to someone else."

Beatrice Hayes whispered, just loud enough for the interns to hear, "As if you had a spot to give up."

"Okay," Dr. Rogers responded, holding up his hand. "Anyone else want to make my job easier?"

Dr. Griffin raised his hand. "I've got a urology spot in Georgia."

Pepper raised his eyebrows. "A little detergent should help with that urology spot, Griffin."

Beatrice rolled her eyes. "Dr. Bearss, must you continue?"

"Just trying to cope, Bea. Maybe you should try a little humor once in a while. Did you know it takes twice as many muscles to frown?"

Dr. Rogers ignored the banter. "Thanks, Dr. Griffin. Anyone else not coming back?"

The group was silent.

"Okay then. Selections will be made by next month. Each of you will get a letter informing you of my decision. I'm sorry it has to be such a large cut from the first year to the second, but if we're going to change this program from a pyramid to a block, the residents currently in the program are going to get squeezed.

"I know it hurts now, but in the long run, it will mean less pressure for the five of you selected to be chiefs."

The group groaned.

"Less pressure after the selection," Howard Button whispered just loud enough for the interns around him to hear.

Dr. Rogers made eye contact with each intern, as if assessing each one again. Then he pressed the lapels of his white coat with his hand and strode from the room.

There was a collective sigh from the group.

"I'm dead meat. I'll never get my research project off the ground by next month," Martin Holcroft, MD, PhD, whined.

"We're all in the same boat, Mart," Pepper said, slapping him on the back.

"There's always dermatology," Wayne Neal offered.

Pepper smiled. "Anyone know the four rules of dermatology? If it's wet, dry it. If it's dry, wet it. If you don't know what it is, don't touch it. If you know what it is, don't touch it."

The group was unanimous. "Shut up, Pepper."

Claire moaned. It was time to stand up again. The abrasions on her chest and abdomen were healing, but moving anywhere fast still presented a problem.

Beatrice leaned over and extended her hand. "Come on," she said helping Claire to her feet. Then, as the room cleared, she asked, "How are you doing?"

"A little sore. But okay. Thanks."

"What happened with Brett? He always seemed so . . . well, normal to me."

"I'm not sure, Bea. I think he wanted to be a surgeon so bad that everything else got mixed up. His priorities were screwed up. Right and wrong, relationships, everything else got pushed aside in the wake of his dream. A lot of us misjudged him." She looked down. "Especially me."

"We've all made compromises, Claire." It was a concession that Claire didn't expect from Beatrice Hayes.

Claire nodded, distracted by her own list of compromises. Her engagement, her relationship with God, and her family were all casualties of the battle known as surgical internship. She sighed and looked at Bea. "I'm tired, Bea. I'll be glad when the letters are written and this is behind us."

"Me too. I wish I'd have done better on my ABSITE."

"Honestly, I like your chances better than mine. I'm the only intern with an outstanding lawsuit. That's got to work in my favor," she added with a note of sarcasm.

They walked down the hall and stopped at a water cooler where several other interns had gathered. Beatrice held up her paper cup. "To the first-year cut."

Claire lifted her cup. "May the best men win."

The two women smiled.

The male interns grunted, "Hear, hear."

With that, they dispersed, each already focused on a few final weeks of competition.

During the next three weeks, the interns showed up early, worked late, and said "Yes, sir" to every request. Every request.

At the month's end, Claire rotated back onto the trauma service and applied her enthusiasm to nightly vigils in the ICU and the ER, and she did it with a smile. But this time, her focus was different. Now, on her alternate afternoons off, Claire bypassed Sabiston and spent time in solitude. This time, with her Bible open, she prayed for the intimacy with God that she'd lost in pursuit of her career. It was time to listen. And trust.

In spite of her desire to figure out whether Wally was indeed her biological father, she didn't look forward to a discussion with Dr. Jenkins, and so, with a new commitment to surrender her future into God's hand, she decided to wait. Finally, in the wake of Clay's death and her experience with Brett, she decided that being in the driver's seat in her own life was no longer the best option. Did it really matter if she was at risk for Huntington's disease? Could she use the mystery of the future, her at-risk status, as the genetics counselor had suggested, as a springboard to faith? It was decision time for Claire. Internship was drawing to a rapid end, and she would need to plan for the following year. But this time, she wanted God's advice. This time, a decision would be made on her knees.

After the first week of the month, the rumors were circulating. Dr. Rogers had made his selections. His secretary was putting the contracts in the mail.

It was midmorning and Claire was in the ER finishing up a history and physical on an intoxicated accident victim when she heard her name.

"Dr. McCall?"

Claire turned in the direction of the timid voice. She looked up, expecting to see a concerned family member, and her eyes met those of Celia Jones.

"Dr. McCall. Can I speak to you for a minute?" The woman clutched at the neck of a worn dress.

Claire looked at her second-year resident, who nodded his consent. "Go ahead. I've got things under control here."

"I was hoping I'd find you here. Roger told me this is where I'd find you."

Claire had yet to speak. "Uh, Ms. Jones," she started. "I'm not sure I'm supposed to talk to you. My attorney says that—"

"Don't worry about him. That's why I've come." She stepped toward the emergency exit. "Can we talk out here?"

The two women walked together through the automatic doors onto a concrete pad.

"I talked to Mr. Davis. He told me about your brother." She seemed to hesitate. "We're dropping the lawsuit, Dr. McCall."

Claire shook her head. "You don't have to feel sorry for me. You don't have to do this because of my brother."

Celia reached out and took Claire's hand. "We're not. But after listening to you in the deposition, and after finding out about how Mr. Plank got his information about you, I realized that I couldn't really trust him. He had convinced me that suing was the right thing to do. He told me it was an obligation I had to fulfill to protect others." She dropped Claire's hand and looked away. "But Mr. Davis told me about your education and your performance. As far as he could see, you were one of the top medical students in the country or you wouldn't be here."

"Ms. Jones, I—"

"Please, Doctor, I need to say this. I know you didn't mean to hurt my child. And we don't really know why she had to die. But God allowed it, and nothing I do can bring her back." Her voice began to break up, and she covered her mouth with her hand.

"Ms. Jones, I'm so sorry." Claire's eyes brimmed with tears.

Celia blew her nose and looked up at Claire. "Are you a Christian?"

Claire thought it an odd question. She nodded silently.

"I thought so. I suspected it when we saw you in the church parking lot that day. And I've been praying for you, knowing how hard this must be for you."

"Your husband . . . why was he so angry at me? Why did he chase me from the parking lot?"

Celia shook her head. "He wasn't chasing you. He was angry at me. I've been trying to get Roger to church for a long time. And I've also been trying to get him to talk about his feelings since Sierra died. He finally agreed to go for that evening service to watch a baptism, and then, who does he see in the parking lot but you. He thought I'd set up a surprise meeting for him so he could talk out his feelings peaceably."

"But he followed me from the parking lot."

"He wasn't following you. He just had to get out of there." She hung her head. "It took me a half hour to convince him to return. Roger isn't really a bad guy."

They stood in silence for a moment, two women brought together by tragic circumstance, both with losses, both with regret. Finally, Claire cleared her throat. "Can you ever forgive me?"

Celia's open arms provided the answer. She embraced Claire and whispered, "You didn't try to harm my baby. Forgive yourself."

The next day, Claire picked up her hospital mail after completing morning trauma rounds. The letter was there. She had the afternoon off, and she wanted to be in a private place to read Dr. Rogers' verdict. She tossed the letter onto the car seat beside her with an air of nonchalance she didn't feel.

By now, she was used to delayed gratification. So, instead of ripping it open, she took the letter home and placed it on her desk, undisturbed. What Dr. Rogers thought was important, but not that important. She'd placed her future into God's hands and made her decision, independent of Dr. Rogers.

She called her mother, who answered after the fifth ring. "Hello."

"Mom."

"Good morning, Claire."

"I've been praying about next year."

"Did you get the letter? Did you make the cut?"

"I got the letter."

"Well?"

"Mom, I want to come home. I want to help you with Daddy."

The silence on the other end revealed Della's shock.

"Mom, are you there?"

"I'm here. It's just . . . well . . . Claire . . . I don't know how to respond. I know you wanted to stay in surgery, but, well, maybe getting cut is the answer you needed."

"Mom, I didn't say I got cut. I just said I got the letter."

"Claire, I'm confused. You said—"

"I said, I want to come home. It makes sense, Mom. You need help with Daddy, right?"

"Well, sure, but—"

"And Margo's busy with her family. And without Clay, that just leaves me." She paused. "For the first time, I want to put someone else in front of me. I think that's what God wants me to do."

"But what about your calling? What about surgery?"

"There is still time for that. I'm young. Taking some time off training isn't going to derail my career forever."

Della started to cry. "Are you sure?"

"Mom, I need time away from surgery to sort out my life. My relationships need maintenance. I need time to regroup with you and Dad. I might not get this chance again. I need to take time to listen to God again. I let my calling get in front of the One who was doing the calling."

"I–I don't know what to say."

"Don't say anything, Mom. On July first, I'm coming home."

Claire said good-bye and hung up the phone. She looked back at the letter on the desktop and smiled. At one time, the chairman's decision held her future in captivity. Now, it didn't matter. Her future was God's and she was free.

She lifted the letter, weighing its contents in her mind and in her hand. "Maybe I'll open you tomorrow."

She slid open her desk drawer and retrieved a small picture, replacing it on the corner of her desk. It was from a happier time in her life, a picture of Claire with John Cerelli. She dropped the letter into the open drawer and spoke to it again. "Maybe tomorrow, I'll read what Dr. Rogers thinks of me. But just now, I want to talk to an old friend."

Epilogue

"One more push. You're going to have this baby," I say, gently pushing back against the infant's head.

The father, a nervous man with a video camera, is sitting on the floor with his head between his knees. Better there than fainting onto my sterile field.

The patient is great, strong and cooperative, thanks to an epidural catheter anesthesia put in three hours ago. Her forehead beads with sweat as she bears down with the next contraction.

The nurse on my left counts it off. "Now push! One, two, three, four. Good. Five, six, seven. You're almost done. Keep pushing."

The baby is born. I clamp and cut the cord and hand her to the nurse. Normally, I'd let the dad cut the cord, but this wimp is still sniffing an ammonia capsule.

The patient looks at her new baby girl and starts to cry. A nurse asks, "How many does this make for you, Dr. Jenkins?"

The other nurse, a veteran named Sarah, answers for me. "He can't count that high."

I tilt my head to see my episiotomy incision and curse my need for trifocals. I ignore Sarah's answer, but I know she is right. It seems like I've delivered every living person in Stoney Creek. Forever.

I finish my task and wash my hands.

"When's the replacement coming, Dr. J?"

"July," I sigh. "Not soon enough. My old buddy, Tom Rogers, is the chairman of surgery up at Lafayette University. He called and accused me of luring away his favorite resident. He said Dr. McCall's the best doctor he's worked with in years. He planned to give her a categorical surgery spot and finish her as chief resident someday."

"Your replacement is a surgeon?"

"She wants to be. But she's agreed to help out here until we can hire someone on a permanent basis. She wanted to come back home to Stoney Creek to help her father, so this job will be perfect."

"Back to Stoney Creek?" Sarah twists her expression. "You're talking about Claire?"

I drift, thinking about Stoney Creek's first female physician. Della has told me what Claire discovered about Clay. Leave it to Claire to figure things out. But she hasn't been brave enough, or bold enough, to confront me about my own blood type, to get a final answer.

She is quite a woman, that Claire McCall. If I'd had a daughter, I'd want her to be just like Claire. And all these years, as much as I was reluctant for the word to get out, I secretly hoped that she was mine. My blood type was AB positive. If Della was type O, and Wally was type B, and Claire was also type O, Claire had her answer. She couldn't be my daughter and be type O. As much as I hated to admit it, I fathered Clay, Claire's worthless twin. And Wally, the town drunk, fathered a wonderful woman named Claire.

Sarah touches my arm to bring me back to the present. "Dr. J., I asked you a question. You're talking about Claire McCall? Wally's girl?"

I nod. "Yep. She's Wally's girl."